For my Inner Circle Reader Group

You all keep me motivated, and connecting with you has been my favourite part of being an author. This one is for you — you asked for one more marriage of convenience novel, so here it is.

CONTENTS

CHAPTER 1

lena

I tip back my vodka mixer and order a second one, ignoring the bartender's attempts to flirt with me. Thank goodness for the horrendous pounding music that drowns him out. I'm in no mood to socialize tonight, as usual. I shouldn't have gone out at all, but I figured I should celebrate my 23rd birthday somehow.

The bartender hands me my drink, and I try to resist the urge to finish it in one gulp. I learned the hard way that liquor won't numb the emptiness and the worry I constantly feel. If it did, I would no doubt have become a raging alcoholic two years ago. It still gives me a pleasant buzz though, and tonight I'll settle for that.

I smile apologetically at the bartender who keeps glancing at me and turn away, my eyes roaming over the dance floor. It doesn't take me long to find the girls I came with. We all work at the same diner, and when they found out it was my birthday, they insisted that I join them tonight. I should've said no, like I always do. I feel like the odd one out, but I just can't get myself to care about who has a crush on who. I want to be as carefree as they are, just for one night, but I'm failing miserably.

I sip my drink as I navigate through the crowd of people and flashing lights, hating that I can barely even hear my own thoughts. Even worse, the bass is so loud that it's almost like I can feel it against my skin. I definitely won't feel my phone buzz if it rings, and the mere thought of that sends a jitter of anxiety running down my spine.

I breathe a sigh of relief when I make it to the rooftop. The warm air relaxes me and I inhale deeply as I weave through the throng of smokers and tables, toward my favorite hidden spot in the corner of the bar. Hardly anyone ever comes here, and on the odd occasion I try to act my age and go out, I end up finding myself here. The small hidden seating area is usually empty, but much to my dismay, tonight it isn't.

I grimace at the back of the guy who's sitting in my favorite seat. His broad shoulders and his obviously expensive tailored suit tell me he's probably a major douchebag. Exactly the type of guy I want to avoid tonight—or any night, really.

He tenses as though he feels me glaring at the back of his head. Then he turns around... and I'm certain my heart just stops.

"Alexander?" I say, his name leaving my lips before I realize it.

Our eyes meet, and my breath catches. To me, it feels like the world around us stills, but there's no recognition in his eyes.

Alexander looks at me in confusion at the sound of his name. He smiles politely, a questioning look on his face.

It's not surprising that he doesn't recognize me. After all, I've changed a lot since I was fifteen, in more ways than just physical. My entire life has changed. I'm far from his little brother's carefree friend.

A brief pang of hurt courses through me at the thought of

Lucian, my childhood friend and Alexander's younger brother. Luce is yet another person I lost when my father remarried, another part of a past life, a world I no longer belong in.

My eyes roam over Alexander, his sharp cheekbones, his thick dark brown hair, and those dark green eyes that have always captivated me. He's as handsome as ever, and he has no clue who I am.

It's better that way, anyway. I'm no longer merely an acquaintance. No... now he'll just see me as Matthew's younger sister. It won't matter to Alexander that I don't even speak to my brother anymore—I'll still be a reminder of the guy that stole his fiancée and severely damaged his company at the same time.

Alexander's eyes wander over my body, and I'm secretly thrilled to see the appreciation in them. Suddenly, I'm glad I let the girls pick my outfit for me. The emerald mini dress I'm wearing hugs my every curve and I feel amazing in it. The last time he saw me I was fifteen, grossly overweight, bangs covering half my face. The glasses and braces didn't help either. It's no wonder he doesn't recognize me.

Alexander smiles at me, and the look in his eyes can only be described as flirtatious. It's crazy how he can still turn my world upside down. He's always had that power over me, and he never realized it.

Before I can overthink it, I approach Alexander and take the seat next to him, my heart beating wildly.

"I don't think we've met. Surely, I would've remembered meeting a woman like you," he says, leaning back in his seat. The line is incredibly cheesy, but I still almost swoon. Alexander grins at me, and this relaxed, flirtatious side of him surprises me. The Alexander I knew was always stressed and overworked.

I neither confirm nor deny his statement. Instead, I smile at him and shake my head. "You've been in the news quite a lot over the last few years. It's almost impossible not to hear about *the* Alexander Kennedy, the heir to one of the world's biggest conglomerates. I'm pretty sure I saw a tabloid reporting that you went to the supermarket the other day. If I were you, I'd go around buying weird things such as a cucumber and some lube, just to throw the reporters for a loop."

Alexander looks perplexed, and then he laughs. It's the type of laugh that sends butterflies to my stomach. It's a deep, body shaking kind of laugh. I can't help but giggle too. He looks at me with interest and shakes his head.

I no longer belong in his world. Alexander isn't someone I ever expected to see again. This... this is all I'll ever have of him. Stolen moments. I'll take them, and I'll put them under lock and key, to be treasured, to brighten my darkest days. If this is all I'll have of him, I'm going to make it count.

CHAPTER 2

lexander

Her eyes... they have me captivated. The swirls of green amidst the light brown; they're beautiful, and vaguely familiar. The girl sitting next to me is stunning in a timeless way, and she's got me enthralled. I take in her ridiculously long lashes, her high cheekbones, and that luscious long hair. She's a classic beauty, unlike the plastic girls I'm usually surrounded with. None of that bullshit, the fake-everything, fake nails, fake lashes, fake hair, fake lips. I'm tired of it. This girl... she's real, and she might very well be the most beautiful woman I've ever seen.

She seems nervous as she sits down next to me, her fingers pulling on the hem of her dress, as though she's uncomfortable in that sexy dress that she's wearing. She has no reason to be. She's sexy as fuck without compromising on the classiness she oozes. She looks up, and when her eyes find mine, she's got me spellbound.

"You have me at a disadvantage. You know my name, yet, I don't know yours."

Her eyes widen ever so slightly, as though the question surprises her, and I'm intrigued. She seems so out of place here, yet her gaze is filled with an unspoken challenge.

"Diana," she murmurs, her voice wavering. She bites down on her lip, and my eyes follow her every move. I swallow hard as I wonder what those lips of hers will taste like. I have a feeling that stealing a kiss from Diana isn't going to be easy.

"Hmm, Goddess of the Hunt. What is it you're hunting tonight, Diana?" I ask, my tone teasing. She smiles, amused at the cheesy line.

"Honestly, just a bit of peace and quiet."

I raise my brows, my eyes roaming over her face. Yeah, I can see that. Every other woman I speak to is after *something*, but not Diana. If anything, she seems annoyed to find this seat occupied.

"So, you're on the run?"

Diana shrugs, but I catch a glimpse of sorrow in her eyes before she looks away. "Aren't you too? Otherwise, you wouldn't be in my seat."

I look down at my legs with a smile on my face, as if to verify that I am, in fact, in her seat. "Your seat, huh? Does that mean I'll find you here next time?"

Diana smiles and shakes her head. "No. I don't come here that often. But yes, when I do come to Inferno, I usually end up here."

I grin and nod at her. "Noted." I already know this is the first place I'll be going every single time I come here from now on, just in case I'll find her here.

"What is it *you're* running away from tonight?" she asks.

I sigh, my mind flashing back to the countless tasks waiting for me; my mother's endless demands, my grandfather's ridiculous requirement for *marriage* before he'll let me take over the company that I've worked myself to the bone for.

"Responsibility," I murmur.

Diana nods and looks away, as though she somehow under-stands, when there is no way she could. I see the cheap worn shoes, the rough unpolished nails. Diana is one of the lucky ones, the ones that think money solves everything when more often than not, they have the sort of happiness I can only dream of. A happy family, a fulfilling life, dreams of their own, a path of their own choosing.

"Since we're both on the run... let's run from negativity. Tell me three good things that happened to you today?" she asks, startling me out of my thoughts.

I stare at her, my eyes widening. That question... it sounds familiar, yet I can't place it. It feels nostalgic somehow, some-thing from my childhood, maybe? I smile at her and shake the thoughts away.

"Well, I finally closed a deal I've been working on for months. I took my mom out for our weekly lunch date today and we managed to have a good talk... and I met *you*."

Diana smiles, but her eyes tell a different story. A story of understanding tinged with longing. She looks down at her lap and nods.

"Hmm, sounds like a perfect day," she murmurs as I finish my champagne. A waiter appears seemingly out of nowhere to top up my glass, startling both of us. I hand Diana a glass of champagne, and she smiles at me.

"Being Alexander Kennedy certainly does have its perks," she says. "I've never had anyone come take my order here," she adds, nudging me with her shoulder.

I chuckle, I can't help it. She's not pretentious, like so many others. I've gotten so used to the entitlement that surrounds me that her relaxed attitude surprises me.

Diana and I stare at the Manhattan skyline, both of us perfectly comfortable. I can't even remember the last time I sat next to a woman that didn't chat my ear off, and I'm finding this oddly peaceful, despite the noise surrounding us.

"Hey, if you could have one wish, what would it be?" Diana asks, surprising me yet again.

I stare at her blankly. "I have to admit that no one has ever asked me that question before."

She laughs, her face tipped up, her eyes on the stars in the sky. She's beautiful, and she looks so incredibly sweet. Far too sweet for a man like me.

"That isn't an answer," she says. "You're not getting out of this one."

I laugh and take a big swig of my champagne, lost in thought for a moment. "I'd wish for genuine happiness, Diana," I tell her honestly. For a while, I thought I had the happiness I craved, but I was proven wrong. I shake my head, feeling lost for just a single moment. "What about you?" I ask, my voice soft.

She smiles, but her smile is bittersweet. "Health," she says. "Good health for everyone I love."

Health. Money can buy almost anything, but it can't buy good health. Even if she were to ask me for something like so many other women brazenly do, this isn't something I can give her.

I sigh and lean back in my seat, my eyes tracing over her. "Since we're both running from something, why don't we run together? At least for tonight."

I offer her my hand, and she takes it. I pull Diana to her feet, and she stumbles in her high heels. I catch her, my hands on her waist.

"Care for a dance, Diana?"

She laughs, and the sound courses through my body as she leans back in my arms. "Here?" she asks, looking around the tiny area we're hiding out in.

8

"Why not?"

I pull her closer until I've got her body flush against mine. She fits against me perfectly.

Diana and I sway to an old Ed Sheeran song, both of us humming along. I can't remember the last time I found myself smiling, doing something this silly. I can't remember the last time a woman actually made my heart race without being on her knees in front of me. Diana... she's something special.

"God, we both can't dance for shit," Diana says, laughing as I twirl her around again. She giggles when I pull her back to me, her arms moving to my neck.

"We? Speak for yourself, lady. *I'm* killing it," I say, swaying my hips badly out of tune. Diana bursts out laughing, and I drop my forehead to hers, enjoying this moment with her. When was the last time I laughed like this? I didn't even plan on coming here tonight, but damn, I'm glad I did.

My hands move to her waist, and I pull her closer until I've got every inch of her body flush against mine. She looks up at me, a sweet smile on her face. I look into her eyes, unable to shake the feeling that I've seen these eyes before, yet, they're perfectly unique.

"Are you sure we've never met before?" I ask her, my eyes falling to her lips.

She smiles and pushes away from me a little. "I thought you said you'd definitely remember me if we had?"

I take a step closer to her, bridging the distance she just created. Her hands move back to my neck while mine roam over her body, settling on her hips.

"Yeah, I definitely wouldn't forget you, Diana."

I lean in and brush my nose against hers before moving away again. "I'd like to ask you if you want to get out of here, but your phone has been ringing non-stop. It seems quite urgent," I say, tipping my head toward the table behind us.

Diana turns around to find her phone screen lit up, and the look in her eyes can only be described as dread.

I let go of her as she checks her missed calls, and my heart sinks when she smiles at me apologetically.

"I need to go," she says, her voice breaking.

"At least give me your number."

Diana shakes her head, flustered. "I don't think that's a good idea, Alec. But it was good to see you. I'm glad you're doing well."

I freeze and stare at her in disbelief. Less than a handful of people call me Alec, and never in public. She'd have to be close to my family to know my nickname. "What did you call me?" I ask, anger running through my veins.

"I'm sorry. I have to go," she says, her voice tinged with regret. She grabs her phone and purse before dashing past me.

I'm tempted to follow her and demand an explanation.

But I don't.

CHAPTER 3

lena

The nurse that usually takes care of my mother greets me warmly as I walk into her hospital room. "Happy birthday, sweetie. I wish we didn't have to call you tonight. You deserve to act your age every once in a while, but you know what Dr. Johnson is like."

"Thank you, June," I say, trying my best to smile at her as I sit down next to my mother.

Dr. Johnson doesn't believe in keeping my mother here when he could be using her bed for a patient that he might be able to save, but he can't turn me away either. Not while I'm still able to pay the bills.

Eight years. My mother has been in a coma for eight years now, and I'm the only one who still believes she'll wake up one day. I can't help but feel like it's a race against the clock. It's become a question of what will run out first, the money that keeps her alive, or my mother's remaining health.

The doctor walks into the room and nods at me. I don't

think I've ever seen the man smile. "Dr. Johnson," I say, nodding back.

"I have some difficult news to share with you," he says, a grave expression on his face. I close my eyes, not wishing to hear it. Whatever it is, it can't be good.

"Your mother has an infection. It's getting harder and harder to keep her state from deteriorating. There are many costs associated with the ongoing infections, too."

I nod, knowing what he's going to say. "I understand, doctor. But I'm not willing to give up on my mother. I still believe she's going to wake up. I'll pay whatever I need to keep her alive."

Dr. Johnson nods, and I hate the pity I see in his eyes. It's obvious he doesn't believe she'll ever wake up again, and I wish I could change my mother's doctor. I want her to be treated by someone who believes in her recovery as much as I do.

"Please sign here. I'll send you the bill. It's higher this month by a couple of thousand dollars," he says eventually.

I sign the forms, authorizing her treatment and the associated costs, my eyes falling closed in resignation the second I lift the pen off the paper.

I'm relieved when I hear Dr. Johnson close the door behind him. Five thousand dollars. A few years ago, I wouldn't have blinked twice at the amount. I used to own several handbags at least four times the price of that. Not anymore.

A year after my mother fell into a coma, my father managed to get her doctors to declare her brain-dead so he could get remarried. The day he married my stepmother was the day our insurance company informed me they'd stop paying for my mother's treatments. I didn't think much of it then, being a Rousseau, but I should've known. I should've seen the signs before it was too late.

I'd only been sixteen then, and within a few months I'd lost my mother, and my brother and I had been forced to live with our stepmom and her daughter. I hadn't coped well with the way my father abandoned my mother, but I would've found a way to deal with it. I even would've played nice if my stepmother hadn't asked my father to stop paying for Mom's medical bills.

I thought my brother and I would be able to save Mom. I thought he'd be on my side. I couldn't have been more wrong. My stepmother has her claws in him so deep, she's got him convinced that all I'm doing is wasting money on a lost cause. I barely recognize Matthew anymore. I left home as soon as I turned eighteen, but he stayed.

I'm lucky that my mother set up a trust fund for me that's allowed me to keep her alive. Until now. This time, I don't have the money. I literally don't have the money to keep my mother alive, and I can't help but burst into tears.

I regret buying myself those couple of drinks at the bar earlier, even though I know it wouldn't have made a difference. I've run through more than eight million dollars in hospital bills over the last six years, often paying roughly two-thousand dollars per day on days that she *doesn't* have complications. Eight million dollars is the exact amount of my trust fund, and I'm at my wits' end. The few belongings I had helped keep her alive a little longer, but I don't know how I'll be able to pay for next month's bill. I have no valuables left. I'm well and truly broke.

I hold my mother's hand, hoping she'll squeeze my hand back. Of course, she doesn't. Every single time my hopes are dashed, yet I never stop believing.

"Mom, please," I whisper, sounding as broken as I feel. "Please wake up. Don't do this to me. I really need you. I can't give up on you now, but I'm not sure how I'm going to get enough money this month. Please wake up, Mom. *Please,*" I beg, trying my hardest to suppress a sob.

No matter how much I plead, she never wakes up. Part of me believes that she'll wake up when she realizes I'm really in trouble this time, but realistically I know she won't. If only I could harden my heart. Would life be easier if I were more like Dr. Johnson and Matthew, and faced reality and the probability of my mother's recovery?

I rest my head on the edge of her bed, my hand desperately clutching hers. I cry my heart out, my lungs burning, and it's not until I feel someone patting my back that I realize I'm not alone in the room. I sit up and take the tissue nurse June hands me.

"I didn't realize you were struggling with the bills, honey."

She pats my shoulder, her eyes laced with concern. I try my best to smile at her, but I can't bring myself to. I can't bring myself to pretend that I'm okay.

"How long have you been struggling, sweetie? I had no idea that it's been hard on you financially."

I nod and wipe at my tears, my eyes on my mother. "It gets harder every year," I tell her honestly. "This time... this time I —" I can't even finish the words. I can't say what I know to be true. After years of fighting, I might... I might lose my mother. I sniff loudly, fresh tears in my eyes. Helplessness unlike anything I've experienced before overwhelms me and I inhale shakily, trying my best to remain positive, to keep my thoughts in check.

June takes a black business card out of her breast pocket and hands it to me, looking unsure.

"The sister of one of my other patients told me about this place," she says, hesitating. "When she struggled to pay her sister's bills, they helped her. I think it's a gentlemen's club or something like that. She... she told me they pay quite handsomely for innocent types."

June looks devastated, and it's obvious that she doesn't want to be telling me this.

"I hope you won't need to use this card. But if you do, know that there's no shame in doing what it takes to keep someone alive."

I nod and stare at the card. It just says *Vaughn's*, with an address. No phone number or other information. The card is thick and heavy, the letters gold. It looks incredibly luxurious.

I stare at it, praying I won't need to use it, and knowing I probably will.

CHAPTER 4

lexander

I pace in my bedroom, exhausted. I've been up all night, trying to figure out who Diana is. "Find her," I tell Vaughn, the owner of Inferno and almost every other nightlife establishment in this city. "She told me her name was Diana. Long brown hair, dazzling green-brown eyes... and that smile. I doubt she's a regular. She looked far too sweet to frequent your seedy places."

Vaughn laughs. "Since when are you into sweet girls?"

I bite down on my lip, unable to shake the thought of Diana. I can't even pinpoint what it was about her. I didn't even kiss her. All I know is that I want to see her again. I want to see her again and find out why she called me *Alec*. "She was different. I don't know."

Vaughn and I have been friends since we were children. He knows as well as I do that girls like Diana are far from my type. I usually go for alluring, sexy, and confident women. Not that Diana wasn't sexy... she was hot as fuck. But she didn't exude sexuality, almost like she didn't even realize how beautiful she is.

"I'll try, man. I'll have my bouncers keep an eye out for her, but damn. Long brown hair and unique green-brown eyes? You're not exactly giving me much here. I'll have my men go through the security footage."

I groan. "I can't believe I didn't get her number. She knew me, though. She called me Alec. It can't be that hard to find her if she's someone from our circle. There'll be someone that knows someone that knows her."

Vaughn clears his throat, falling silent. "Talking about the type of girls you usually go for," he says carefully. "There's something I've been meaning to tell you. I'd rather you hear it from me instead of the press."

My heart drops. There's only one topic he'd be this careful with. There's only one person he'd never mention to me under normal circumstances. My heart twists painfully at the mere thought of her, the feeling quickly replaced by rage.

"Jennifer got engaged," he says, sounding pained. "To Matthew Rousseau. They picked a wedding date already. They're doing a low-key secret wedding in the Bahamas next year... on June 20th."

June 20th. The day she was supposed to marry me. It can't be a coincidence. She clearly picked that day intentionally; another way to stab me in the heart and twist the knife like the vicious bitch she is.

Jennifer is the one I thought was different. The first girl that didn't seem to be after my money, that saw me for who I am, and not what my name is.

I was wrong.

Oh, so wrong.

I still don't know if anything we had was ever real, or if it was all a game to her. I know she's the one that stole corporate secrets, making me lose a multi-million-dollar deal that I'd been working on for years to *Matthew Rousseau*—but she's clever. Or so she thinks. She hid her tracks well, but not well enough. Over and over again, I'm tempted to turn her in, but I can't submit illegally obtained evidence. Even if I could, I wouldn't. I would never do that to her. Despite everything she's done, I don't want to see her behind bars.

"I'm sorry, man," Vaughn says. "I knew you'd find out one way or another. Pretty much everyone in our social circle knows already, so I knew the news would get to you eventually. Knowing her, there's probably going to be a media spectacle from the second they announce their engagement to the press, right up to the wedding day. She'll want every second of the limelight."

She would. Life is one big show for her. It always has been —I just didn't realize it until it was too late.

"Look, I gotta go," I tell Vaughn.

"Alexander—"

I hang up, my veins thrumming with barely restrained anger. I'd probably be able to get over everything she did to me. Hell, I might even have forgiven her. I couldn't care less about the money she lost me. I was ready to make her my damn *wife*.

But no. She just had to cheat on me with Matthew Rousseau. That asshole has been attacking my company for years now. Every decision I make, every project I pursue, he's always right behind me. This time it wasn't an acquisition he was after, though. No. This time, it was the love of my life, and she went willingly.

Would it have made a difference if she left me for someone else? I'm not sure. I don't think the pain would be any less, the betrayal wouldn't sting any less. I pick up the photo I keep on my nightstand. It's a photo of Jennifer and me, both of us smiling—a reminder of what happens when I allow myself to fall in love, when I allow myself to be weak. I keep this photo here for moments like these—moments where I temporarily find myself fascinated by someone, tempted by girls like Diana.

I put the photo frame back on my nightstand, my heart twisting painfully. What Jennifer and I had... was any of it even real?

I'll never know.

CHAPTER 5

lexander

I stare at the photos of my father in my inbox and tighten my grip on the phone in my hand. This time, he's in Tijuana with two blondes half his age.

"You know the deal," I say, my jaw clenching involuntarily. "Make sure these photos never see the light of the day."

"Of course," Elliot says, rattling on about the costs to make these photos disappear. "I don't care," I tell him. Elliot is one of my closest friends and he might well be the best hacker alive. Thanks to that, he has no qualms about extorting me in return for keeping shit like this off the internet. "Just make sure my mother never sees this. No one can ever see this."

I end the call, annoyed. My father is no longer even trying to be sly about his affairs. There are no excuses anymore, no more made-up business trips, no more lies. Now he just disappears for months on end, leaving my mother heartbroken, over and over again.

I have spent over twenty-thousand dollars trying to keep

his affairs hidden, but there's no way my mother doesn't know. I click the email away, revulsion settling in my stomach. Their supposedly happy marriage is all a sham. *Every marriage I know of is.* I can't even think of *one* happily married couple.

I check my watch and grimace when I realize that it's almost time for my weekly lunch date with my mother. It never gets easier to hide these things from her. It eats at me, like a slow-acting poison, a disaster in the making.

I sigh and grab my suit jacket, straightening my tie as I walk out. I drive home in my Aston Martin, the car I drive every single Wednesday—purely because it's a convertible, and my mother loves the way the wind blows through her hair as I drive her to lunch. It's the one time a week that I know I'll put a smile on her face.

She's already waiting for me when I pull up in front of our mansion. I get out of my car and walk around it to open the door for her, and she smiles at me.

"Hello, darling," she says.

I press a kiss to her cheek and smile. "Hey, Mom. Ready for lunch?"

She nods and sits down as I run back around my car. My mother grins when I lower the roof, and my heart warms. The happiness she's radiating right now... yeah, there's no way I'm taking that away from her.

I'm lost in thought the entire way to the restaurant, barely even present as we sit down. It isn't until my mother calls my name that I snap out of it.

"You're absentminded, sweetie," she says. "I guess you heard the news?"

I blink, realization dawning upon me. "Even you knew about Matthew and Jennifer?"

It looks like I was the last one to find out. Looks like

everyone has been tiptoeing around me, and I hate that. I hate being pitied.

"Alec," she says carefully. "Jennifer isn't like us. It was never going to work."

I smile wryly. "Not like us? What? Because she isn't rich?"

Mom nods, and annoyance crawls down my spine.

"Dad wasn't either," I snap. "Grandpa made Dad take your surname because he was a *nobody*. Everyone might act like they've forgotten, but that doesn't change the truth. If he was good enough for you, then why are you looking down on people just like him?"

Mom looks hurt, and I regret my words immediately. "Mom, I'm sorry," I say, shaking my head. "I shouldn't have said that. I apologize, truly."

She nods, a tight smile on her face. I can't help but wonder if she's so opposed to people outside of our social circle because of Dad. I worry she tries to excuse his behavior by telling herself that all their issues resulted from them being from different worlds, and I don't think that's what it is. I don't have one pleasant memory of my father. Not one.

I look at my mother with a heavy heart. Her hair is perfectly blonde, not a single strand out of place. I don't even see the tiniest wrinkle on her face. My mother maintains a perfect facade. The perfect wife, the matriarch of the Kennedy family. The mask she wears carefully crafted throughout the years. Each time my father walked out on us, another part of her facade was crafted. Sometimes I wonder what she sees when she looks in the mirror. Does she see the woman she once was, the one my father destroyed? Or has she started to believe her own lies?

Mom grabs a familiar manila folder from her bag, and I swallow down a groan. She opens it and starts to lay out photos on the table. "These girls and their families are all interested in forming an alliance with the Kennedy family. The Vanderbilts are my top pick. They're offering a merger if you marry their oldest daughter."

She smiles tightly, a pleading look in her eyes. "Just meet them, Alec. You never know whether you might fall for one of them."

Fall for one of them? Even after all these years, all the pain she's been through, all the times my father has abandoned her, *us*, she still believes in love. She refuses to see it for the curse it is.

"Besides, your grandfather's deadline is looming. Right now, the battle for his position of chairman is between you and Dylan. If you aren't married by the end of June, the position is automatically Dylan's, no matter how much more you deserve it. Do you really want the company falling into your cousin's hands? Dylan isn't half as smart as you are, and he hasn't worked as hard as you have, either."

I sigh, my eyes dropping to the photos. "Mom," I say, my voice soft. "Can't you talk to Grandpa? You're his only daughter —you know he has a sweet spot for you. Won't he reconsider? I've worked myself to the bone for our company, unlike Dylan. Dylan only ever puts in the bare minimum, and Grandpa knows it."

Mom shakes her head. "I've tried, honey. He won't budge. He still firmly believes in family virtues above everything else, and he won't bend the rules for you. Any member of our family that wants to take their seat on the board must be married. That included *me too*, sweetie. That has always been the rule, and it always will be. He might have made an exception for you if the position you were after wasn't *his*. His successor *must* be married, Alec. He won't change his mind."

My eyes fall to the photos, my entire body numb with resignation. There's no way I'll let the company fall into Dylan's hands. There's no way I'll let all my hard work go to waste. I've spent my entire life in anticipation of inheriting my grandfather's role, and I'm not about to give up on my goals now.

I sigh and nod at my mother. "As you wish, Mother," I murmur. "Go ahead and start arranging meetings with the girls you deem eligible. I'll choose one of them to marry."

CHAPTER 6

lena

I stare up at the grand mansion in front of me, the gates imposing. I inhale deeply before forcing my feet forward. I press my palm to the scanner, and a sigh of relief escapes my lips when the gates swing open. Part of me expected to be denied entry—I wouldn't put it past my stepmother to find a way to remove all my biometric data. She's tried to cut me off from my father and brother the moment she stepped into our lives, and she's succeeded. I wouldn't even be here if my mother's life didn't depend on it.

I'm nervous as I reach the door, my gaze dropping down to the old clothes I'm wearing and my torn-up shoes. A couple of years ago, I wouldn't have been caught dead in this outfit, and now I can't afford anything better. I hardly ever feel embarrassed for the way I live my life now, but standing here in front of my childhood home, knowing I'll be judged and found lacking... it hurts.

It kills me that I have to resort to coming here at all, that I'm incapable of caring for my mother on my own. I can't help but think back to every decision I've ever made, every bit of money I could have and should have saved.

I brace myself as I walk into the house, feeling out of place in this cold and foreign mansion, not a single trace of my childhood remaining. I stop by the dresser in the hallway, my fingers tracing over it. There have always been three photos here, one of my parents, one of Matthew and me, and one of the four of us. All three photos have been replaced to remove every trace of my mother and me. It's like my stepmother recreated every photo that used to be here, replacing only my mom and me. I grimace, a faint pang of hurt twisting my heart. This house used to be filled with love. This is the house my mother turned into a home. Now it's a place where I'm not even welcome.

"What are *you* doing here?"

I turn, a bittersweet smile on my face. I'd somewhat understand those words coming from Elise, my stepsister, or even from my stepmother, Jade. But no, it's my own brother.

"Hi, Matthew," I murmur, masking my aching heart behind a perfectly crafted smile.

He grimaces as he takes in my outfit, his disgust obvious. I tense, bracing myself against the pain I know he's about to inflict. My eyes drop to the woman next to him, and unease settles in the pit of my stomach.

"Is that your sister?" Jennifer asks. She and I have never met in person, but I've seen plenty of photos of her, most of them from when she used to date *Alexander*. A wave of possessiveness that I'm not even remotely entitled to washes over me as I think back to the way he always used to look at her, as though she rendered everyone else invisible to him. I don't understand how she could ever leave Alexander for an asshole like my brother, and I'm thankful I haven't been around to watch it happen.

Based on the rumors going around, I'm certain it would've eradicated the last shreds of respect I feel for my brother.

"No," Matthew says. "Can't you see she doesn't belong here?" he adds, turning up his nose.

I'm rendered speechless, tensing as I try my best not to take his words to heart. Back when Mom got into that car crash, Matthew and I fell apart too. He's convinced that I'm making Mom suffer by selfishly keeping her alive, and he's made sure I know it. Over and over again, Dad and Matthew have tried to convince me to let Mom go, until I could take no more. Yet here I am again, years later, at their mercy.

"I won't stay long," I say, my voice soft. "It's about Mom."

Matthew raises his brow and crosses his arm. "Did she die?" he asks, as though he couldn't care less about his own *mother*.

I grit my teeth as I shake my head.

"Then I don't need to know," he says, grabbing Jennifer's hand. She shoots me an apologetic look, but I don't miss the amusement in her eyes.

"What is all this commotion?"

I turn to find Dad standing in the hallway with Jade by his side. Hatred rolls over my skin, raising every hair on my arms. She looks irritated to see me, her eyes trailing over me in dismay.

"Dad," I murmur.

He sighs and shakes his head. "Look at you. What an embarrassment. Can't you at least dress normally, Elena?"

I bite down on my lip, desperation clawing up my throat. "I'm sorry, Dad," I say, wanting to take it back immediately.

Dad looks away. "Your mother left you a trust fund worth millions, but look at you. She'd be embarrassed to call you her daughter."

Jade tenses at the mention of my mother. It's subtle, but I see it. I see the hatred in her eyes, the defensive stance.

"Dad, could I speak to you, please?"

Jade raises her brows. "We don't have secrets in this family," she says. "Anything you say to your father, you can say to me."

Dad nods and wraps his arm around her waist. She leans her head against his shoulder, the two of them picture perfect. One year. It took Dad one year to have Mom declared brain dead and marry Jade. Did he ever even love Mom at all? Did he ever even love *me*? He's cast me aside with such ease that I can't help but wonder.

"It's about Mom."

Dad tenses, and for a second I could've sworn I saw a glimpse of worry for her in his eyes, but it's gone before I can even blink.

"I... Dad, I can't... I can't keep her alive any longer. I've run through my entire trust fund paying for her medical bills. I don't think I can pay the bills this month, and if I can't, they'll take her off life support. Please, Dad," I say, my voice breaking. "Please, help me. Help me save Mom, *please*."

Dad's eyes widen and he swallows hard, but then Jade tightens her grip on him and looks up at him. "Darling, that isn't a matter related to our family," she says. Then she looks at me and smiles. "And as far as I recall, *you* aren't part of this family either. You left all by yourself, swearing you'd never return, yet here you are, asking for money. It was my birthday last week, and you didn't even call. Yet now you expect us to give you money to waste on a lost cause?"

Dad tenses and nods. "Jade is right. Elena, it's time to let your mother go. What you're doing to her, it's unnatural, and I want no part of it. Besides, Jade was right to say you left this family yourself. You're no longer part of this family, and you cannot come back begging for money. I thought I raised you better than that."

An angry tear drops down my cheek and I swipe it away. It's

at the tip of my tongue to tell him that he *didn't* raise me—my mom did. But I can't say that.

"Please, Dad. I'll do anything. I'll come back to live here, and I'll work for you. Anything you want. Just help me save Mom, and I swear I'll be the perfect daughter."

Elise's shrill laughter sounds from behind me, and hopelessness overwhelms me. She walks up to Dad and her mother, and Jade wraps her arm around her.

"He already has the perfect daughter," Elise says, "and it isn't you."

Panic grips me and I drop to my knees as I try my best to remain in control of my breathing, but my desperation is suffocating me. I look up at Dad with tears in my eyes. "Dad, she'll die if you don't help me," I force myself to say, my voice labored. "I promise I won't ever ask anything of you again. Please, help me keep her alive. That's all I ask. I'm begging you."

Dad looks at me with fresh dismay. "You're making a fool of yourself, Elena. Get up, for God's sake. I've said it before, and I'll say it again. I won't spend another cent on your mother— she's been declared dead, and it's time you accept that and let her go."

Jade nods at him in satisfaction and pulls him away as I burst into tears on the floor. She looks back at me with a smile on her face and my eyes fall closed, my heart completely shattered.

I've exhausted every option to keep my mother alive. Every option but one. I think back to the card my mother's nurse gave me, my stomach recoiling at the thought even as I pick myself up off the floor.

I'd sell my soul to keep my mother alive—so if I have to, I can and *will* sell my body, too.

CHAPTER 7

lena

I look up at the beautiful building in front of me and double check the address on the card in my hand. This place is not quite what I expected. It doesn't look seedy at all. I was expecting an underground strip club or something similar. Instead, I take in the sprawling mansion with its perfectly manicured lawns, a huge gate separating me from what is sure to be the worst decision I will ever make.

I timidly walk up to the two security officers guarding the gate. Their rigid posture reminds me of soldiers guarding a palace, and the hostility on their faces does nothing to ease my nerves. Their cold eyes are on me as I approach, and for a second I wonder if they might pull out the guns strapped to their belts. I exhale in relief when they smile, or at least attempt to.

"Madam?" the guard on the right says, nodding at me. I fumble with the black business card in my hand, unsure of what to say. I can't tell them I'm here to sell myself to the highest bidder, can I? The guard's eyes fall to the card in my fingers, and he nods, pressing a button on the device in his hands. The gate swings open before I have a chance to say anything.

"Thanks," I mumble. There's no condemnation in their eyes, so I wonder if anyone with a card can walk in, and not just those intending to whore themselves out. Or maybe they're just used to this. I can't be the first woman who has found herself in this situation.

I walk toward the building, refusing to overthink why I'm doing this. I can't afford to have second thoughts. I focus on breathing in and out steadily, keeping my steps even.

The door to the mansion swings open before I reach it, and my heart drops. I freeze, and I'm pretty sure my heart actually stops beating for a second. I can't believe this is happening to me.

This is the last place I'd expect to run into my former childhood friend, Lucian. I blanch, and suddenly a wave of nausea hits me. Lucian walks toward me, and every step he takes sends bursts of pure panic through my veins.

At any other time, I would've been delighted to run into Lucian. I would've taken the time to apologize for walking out of his life like I did. I would've explained to him I had no choice, that they were going to forbid me from seeing my mother again. But not now. Now isn't the time.

Lucian pauses in front of me, and if he gets any closer, I'm sure he'll hear my heart pounding. I swallow and straighten, my spine rigid. "Lucian," I say, pleased to find that my voice comes out even, and not as shaky as I expected it to be.

"What are you doing here?" he asks, surprise written all over his face. I hesitate, unsure of what plausible reason I could possibly have to be here. I'm not sure what he's doing here either, but it's becoming clear that the building in front of me is *not* simply a brothel.

I don't have time to come up with an excuse, because a few seconds later Lucian's brother walks through the door, his brows lifting in surprise when he sees me. *Alexander.* Oh god.

He looks even more handsome in daylight than he did that night at Inferno. Sharp cheekbones, a perfectly chiseled face, and thick, dark hair. Alexander looked good six years ago, but he looks even better now. The way he fills out his suit is unreal, and I can only imagine what kind of perfect body he's hiding underneath it. For some reason, seeing him here, right now, really drives home what I'm about to do, and it makes me feel sick. Ashamed of myself. It makes me feel like I'm giving up a part of myself I'll never get back. I'm giving up on the girl I used to be back when Lucian and Alexander were a part of my life.

"Elena?" Lucian says.

Alexander freezes in his tracks when Lucian says my name, his eyes widening. I can see the exact moment the puzzle pieces fall into place.

I look at the door behind Alexander resolutely and walk toward it, keeping my mouth shut, ignoring the fury written all over Alexander's face. Nothing I do or say now is going to make him feel less betrayed. The one thing Alexander hates most is when people lie to him, and I did just that when I led him to believe we didn't know each other. When I stole a moment that otherwise never could have belonged to me.

My shoulder brushes against Alexander's arm, and suddenly I'm stopped in place, his hand on my wrist, his grip tight.

"Elena, is it? That's right. Elena *Diana* Rousseau. I guess you didn't lie, but you weren't honest either."

He doesn't bother hiding the anger in his voice, but it's too little, too late now anyway. I look down, unable to face him.

"This is no place for you. What are you doing here?" he asks, his voice sending a pang of nostalgia through me.

He sounds concerned, and that feeling, the feeling that someone might actually care about me, breaks my heart. I stare at his perfectly polished shoes, unable to face him. "I have an appointment," I whisper.

"I'll come with you. This isn't a place you should enter alone," he says, his voice brooking no argument. My eyes shoot up to his, and I know the panic reflected in them gave me away. Alexander tugs at my wrist and pulls me closer to him. "What are you up to?" he whispers.

I bite my lip as hard as I can in an effort to stay in control of my emotions, shaking my head as I yank my wrist loose. I walk past him, ignoring the stab in my heart. Why does it hurt just as much as walking away from the Kennedys six years ago?

I inhale deeply and make my way to the reception desk. I look around the huge room that mostly resembles a hotel lobby, wondering what I'm getting myself into and coming up empty.

"I'm here to see Mr. Vaughn," I tell the receptionist. She immediately nods, a look of understanding on her face.

"Miss Rousseau, isn't it?" she says, tapping away at her keyboard.

My eyes widen in surprise. Until an hour ago, I didn't even think I'd come at all, so why does she know who I am? I have a bad feeling about this, but it's too late to change my mind now. My mother's life depends on me seeing this through, so I nod.

"We've been told to expect you. Follow me, please."

CHAPTER 8

lexander

I can't believe I didn't recognize her. *Elena.* Those eyes of hers should've clued me in. She's the only girl I know whose eyes are an intriguing combination of light brown and green. I should've trusted my instincts when I thought she looked familiar.

The last time I remember seeing her, she was an awkward teenager with braces and glasses that were too big for her face. She was always quite pretty, but the girl I've come to know as *Diana*... She's downright stunning. The black dress she's wearing today hugs her figure, and it's quite obvious that Elena is far from a little girl now.

Why would she even hide her identity that night? Why would she deceive me?

I pause on the steps of Vaughn's club, unable to shake the feeling that something isn't quite right with her. I haven't stopped thinking about *Diana* since that night, but I can't shake the anger I'm feeling either. I feel like she toyed with me by hiding who she was, and it doesn't sit well with me. I grit my teeth at the thought of her brother, Matthew. She seemed so sweet, so innocent, but she's a Rousseau, after all. Looks like Matthew's little sister grew up to become quite the woman. Revulsion rolls through me at the thought of him.

I look back at the doors she disappeared through. What is Elena doing here at all? Vaughn's club is private, and it has been for years. It's a highly exclusive and prestigious *gentlemen*'s club. Member applications from women aren't even considered, let alone accepted. The only way a woman can walk in here is as a member of staff. What could bring Elena Rousseau here? Her family is too rich for her to need a job, and even if she wanted one, there's no reason for her to find one here. I think back to the clothes she was wearing when I saw her at Inferno... the Elena I used to know wouldn't even own clothes that cheap. I'm not a superstitious man, but I can't shake the feeling that something bad is about to happen.

"You know what that was all about?" I ask Lucian. The contemplative look on his face tells me he's as clueless as I am.

"I know things have been difficult for her with her mom being in a coma and her dad remarrying, but that's all I know. I haven't spoken to her in years. I follow her on social media, but she doesn't exactly post much, so I have no idea what's going on with her. Honestly, if I didn't follow her I wouldn't even have recognized her."

Though my baby brother would never admit it, I know the fact that he and Elena grew apart kills him. She was his only real friend in the superficial world that our family operates in. When Elena lost her mother, he lost *her*.

I frown and eye the doors Elena just walked through. She knew who I was and deceived me. Why? Was it a fun game for her to play? A way to mess with me? Maybe she picked up a thing or two from her brother—she's a Rousseau, after all. I shake my head and walk toward my car, but halfway there I pause at the same time Lucian does.

"Mom would kill us if we don't make sure that she's okay," he says. I agree with him, perhaps a bit too quickly. Together we turn back around and march toward the club. I grab my phone and text my head of security, Aiden, to request a background check on Elena. Something is definitely up with her, and I want to know what.

By the time Lucian and I reach the front doors, I've got my friend Vaughn on the phone. "Where is Elena Rousseau?" I ask, not bothering with pleasantries.

"Lovely to hear from you, buddy. I'm good, thanks, how are you?" he says, sounding amused.

I roll my eyes. "Cut the crap, Vaughn. Where is she? Elena *Diana* Rousseau. I saw her walk into your club a few minutes ago. What is she doing here?"

Vaughn pauses. "Fuck. It's *her*?" he asks.

"Yes."

"Alexander, someone called me to say Matthew's sister was going to show up. I thought I was doing you a favor, man. Fuck. I sent her to John. Conference Room eight. You're not going to like this."

CHAPTER 9

lena

I sip the tea one of the secretaries made me and nearly scald my tongue. I'm restless and nervous. It doesn't sit well with me that they knew me by name. This has Elise's name written all over it. I'm certain this is a trap of some sort, but I can't walk away either. Not when there's even the slightest chance that I can save my mother's life this way.

Maybe it was June who let them know I might drop by? It seems unlikely, but I'd rather have that than falling into another one of my stepsister's traps. The last time I walked into one of her schemes, I was almost charged with possession of drugs. Not just any drugs. One hundred grams of cocaine. Elise takes going hard or going home to a new level, and for some reason, she's always seen me as the bane of her existence. I'm not sure why, since I've never treated her unfairly. She's one of the reasons I couldn't wait to leave home. My heart sinks at the thought of my mother's nurse and Elise colluding. If that's the case, it means Elise and Jade have access to my mother. If they can get to June, they can get to *Mom*.

I look around the room, trying my best to battle my nerves. It looks more like a meeting room than anything else, with its long table and the cushioned chairs. This whole building is unlike what I expected. I thought I'd be walking into a nightclub, but instead, I found myself in what appears to be a downtown version of a very luxurious country club. I saw signs for countless facilities. If I'm not mistaken, I even saw one for a swimming pool and a golf area.

God, I hope I'm not in the wrong place. I shake my head. No, the receptionist knew who I was, so I'm definitely in the right place. I just hope they know *why* I'm here. I really hope I won't have to explain myself. If I do, I'm not sure I'll be able to go through with this.

Part of me wonders if running into Lucian and Alexander was a sign, a final chance to turn back around, before I lose any and all respect I have for myself. But then I think of my mother, and I know I'll always regret it if I walk away now. I'd never forgive myself if she died when I could've done something to save her. Even if she never wakes up again, I need to know that I tried everything in my power to give her the chance to. If our roles were reversed, I know my mother would do the same for me.

The door behind me opens, and it seals my fate. A tall blond man takes the seat opposite me, a lecherous smile on his face. A chill runs down my spine when he leans back in his seat.

"How's your tea, Elena?" he asks, his eyes on my chest. I frown. I'm not sure what's going on, but something doesn't seem right.

"I never gave anyone here my name."

He smiles, a hint of cruelty in his eyes. "You didn't need to.

There isn't much that we don't know about you. I'm John, by the way. You and I are about to get very intimately acquainted —as part of your job interview, of course."

I swallow hard, tremors running down my spine. I try to push down the fear I feel, but I can't. I start to tremble, my heart pounding, yet I smile. I knew what I'd be getting into... I knew what would be expected of me.

"So, tell me why you're doing this, Elena. Rich girl boredom? Daddy wouldn't buy you a new handbag?"

I'm at a loss for words. I wasn't really expecting that question. But then again, I wasn't expecting them to know who I am at all. I'd been intending to go by some alias. Something like Crystal or Candy. Or better yet, *Chastity*. So far, nothing is going the way I'd planned it.

"I need the money." It sounds stupid and obvious, but I'm not sure how else to explain why I'm here. I don't want to tell him about my family situation. I don't want him to know much about me at all.

"Well... this interview will certainly be fun for me. How about you stand and take off—"

Before he can finish his sentence, the door behind me opens and slams against the wall. I jump in shock and turn around to find Alexander walking in with Lucian right behind him.

Alexander's eyes are on John, his expression murderous. "You. Get out," he says, his voice deadly calm. John hesitates and Alexander looks at Lucian. "Get him out of here before I knock him out. Make sure you escort him to Vaughn's office."

Lucian nods and leads John out, a concerned look on his face. John looks back at Alexander, a vicious glint in his eyes. He grins at me and pauses at the door. "Not bad," he says. "Already have a high roller interested, huh? Can't even blame the guy. Not to worry. I don't mind having seconds."

My stomach lurches, and I breathe a sigh of relief when Lucian tightens his grip on John and pushes him out.

I blink in disbelief when the door slams closed, leaving Alexander and me alone. He clenches his jaw and walks toward the door slowly, the sound of the lock clicking closed making me tense further. He walks up to me and I take a step back, only to feel the table behind me. There is nowhere for me to go. I've never seen him look so angry before.

"Alexander..."

He pauses, his eyes raking over my body in disbelief. "Do you want to explain what you're doing here, Elena? Or do you go by Diana now?"

He takes a step closer to me and pinches my chin, forcing me to look at him. Disappointment and rage darken his eyes, and I inhale sharply. There's no doubt in my mind he knows exactly what I'm doing here. He just wants me to admit it.

"Alec," I whisper, shame coloring my cheeks crimson.

"Alexander," he corrects me. "We're not that close."

My heart breaks and I look away from his intense gaze, but I nod nonetheless. I've always been one of the few apart from his family that could call him Alec, and it kills me that I'm a stranger to him now.

"You're right, Alexander. We're not that close. There's no reason for me to explain to you what I'm doing here. Nor should you care." My voice is even, and I don't stumble over my words like I expected to. I stare into his eyes, praying my poker face is as good as I imagine it to be.

Alexander's grip on my chin tightens. His eyes travel down my body, taking in the skintight black dress I'm wearing. I chose it knowing it would highlight my body. Right now, the outfit makes me feel like a cheap whore. Quite appropriate, I guess.

"It just so happens that this club is owned by my friend,

Vaughn," he says. "I understand you're here to apply for a position. Vaughn, being the good friend he is, allowed me to conduct your interview on his behalf."

I look away in shame, unable to face him. Alexander's hands move to my waist, and he hoists me up onto the table behind me. Before I can react, he's nudged my legs apart so he can stand between them. I know he must've gotten a glimpse of my red lace underwear when his eyes darken. If I thought he was angry before, I clearly hadn't seen anything yet. His eyes are flashing with rage and his expression is tense.

"Elena, do you understand that men will be able to touch you whenever and wherever they want? Do with you whatever they please?"

I nod, swallowing hard. I'm not stupid. I knew what I was signing up for, and I'm not going to let Alexander intimidate me out of making this decision. Because that's exactly what he's doing. He's trying to intimidate me so that I'll run out of this room crying. Boy, is he in for a surprise.

"Yes. I'm aware. I understand that you're shocked, but I'm not going to change my mind." Someone like Alexander can't possibly understand what it's like to be in my situation. To have lost your home and to have no one around that you can rely on. Even worse, to have someone to provide for, and being unable to. The helplessness I feel tears me apart, and grants me steely determination at the same time.

A few years ago, I never would've been able to dream of finding myself in this situation, so I understand where Alexander is coming from. But I'm not doing this for the fun of it. My mother's life depends on me seeing this through.

"Very well," he says, his voice low.

Alexander moves one hand to my hair, and the other to my bare leg. "Is this what you want, Elena? You want men to touch

41

you whenever they feel like it? Spread your legs for anyone that throws some money your way?"

I shake my head, biting down on my lip. He strokes the inside of my thigh, his hand moving up slowly.

"This is what will be expected of you, and much more. I'm barely even touching you. Can you bear to drop down on your knees and suck my dick? What if I want to bend you over and fuck you?"

His eyes are on mine, and the way he's looking at me right now is how I always imagined he would in every single dream I've ever had of him. Like I'm someone he wants, and not just some kid that follows him around everywhere. Like I'm desirable. He caresses the inside of my thigh, slowly edging closer to my underwear. I hate myself for the burst of arousal I feel, but despite the situation, I can't help myself.

I stare at his collar, my heart racing. His fingers are at the edge of my underwear, moving slowly, teasing me, and I'm a jumbled mess of lust and panic. I know he's trying to shame me for my choices. I know this is meant to be a punishment, a way to change my mind. But all I can think is that I want more. More of what his fingers are doing to me.

Alexander gently tugs on my hair, making me lift my face. His rage hasn't abated at all, but there's something more in his eyes now. Lust. "Look at me. Tell me why you're doing this."

I look away, unable to face him. I want to explain, but all my words seem to be stuck in my throat. "If you can't even handle this, how are you going to fuck countless men?"

He caresses me with his index finger, right through my underwear, and I jump, a burst of arousal going straight to my core. Alexander's eyes darken when he realizes that I'm wet, and he seems even more pissed off. He shoves my underwear aside roughly and slides his finger along my slick folds. I'm so wet that his finger slides into me easily, eliciting a moan from me that surprises both of us. He tightens his hold on my hair when he realizes how turned on I am.

"You're fucking soaking wet."

He keeps his finger inside me and starts twirling his thumb around my clit, driving me insane.

"Tell me, does the idea of being used by men turn you on so much? Are you enjoying my finger inside you? You're so wet, I can probably slip my cock straight into you." His voice is husky, and he licks his lips. My eyes trace his tongue as it darts over his lips, making me wonder what those lips taste like.

Alexander finger-fucks me slowly, his eyes never leaving mine. "Tell me I'm wrong, Elena. Tell me you're not here to sell your body at Vaughn's club. Tell me that you didn't mean to deceive me that night."

When I don't answer, he increases his pace, his touch driving me insane. If this is what he thinks constitutes punishment, he's sorely mistaken.

"Alexander, please," I moan.

"Please what? Please stop? If you don't want me to treat you like a common whore, all you have to do is say stop. Say *no*. Push me away." He's panting as hard as I am, and the bulge in his pants tells me he's just as turned on too. He watches me as I drown in the feelings he arouses in me.

Alexander lets go of my hair and moves his other hand between my legs, using one hand to tease my clit while finger-fucking me with the other. The intensity is almost too much for me, and it takes all my willpower to not come right there and then.

I grab Alexander's shoulders and bite down on my lip to keep myself quiet. His fingers feel way better on me than my own ever have, and I know I can't hold on any longer, I'm about to come. Alexander watches me so intently that I can't help but close my eyes.

"Alexander, I'll... I can't... I'm going to—" I whisper, my voice sounding more like a moan than the protest I meant it to be. I'm about to come, and I know that if I do, Alexander will lose the tiny amount of respect he might still have for me.

Alexander groans and increases his pace as he pushes me over the edge. "Mm, oh fuck... *Please*," I moan, losing control. I come all over his fingers, and he watches me with a satisfied expression.

The moment between us breaks as the last tremor shakes my body, and Alexander pulls his fingers away suddenly, as though he scalded himself. I watch as he pulls his handkerchief out of his pocket and wipes his fingers, looking down at his hands in disbelief. It's like he can barely believe he touched me like that, and worse, that I enjoyed it. I look away in shame, reality suddenly catching up to me. I'm as disappointed in myself as Alexander is, if not more. I swallow back a sob as he turns his back to me, clearly unable to look at me.

Alexander sits down in one of the chairs in the conference room, his head in his hands. The silence between us is heavy and I don't know what to say. I clench my thighs closed, the wetness that's still there making me feel ashamed all over again. Alexander looks up at me and sighs, his eyes softening a little.

"I don't know what you're doing here, or what has caused you to be in these circumstances. What I do know is that you're coming home with me."

CHAPTER 10

lexander

I hold Elena's hand as I lead her back to the reception area where Lucian and Vaughn are waiting for us, her hand tiny compared to mine. Elena doesn't say a thing. She stares at the ground and lets me pull her along, her eyes red from the tears she's obviously holding back. I expected her to fight me when I told her she's coming home with me, but surprisingly, she followed me obediently.

Part of me is ashamed of how I treated her. How unreasonable I was, and how very much out of control I felt when I saw her sitting there, that defiant look on her face. She has no idea what she almost got herself into, no matter how much she may have tried to convince herself otherwise.

Part of me is still turned on though. The look on her face when I made her come has my cock hardening all over again. That expression of hers. The way her muscles tightened around my finger and the way she moaned. I clench my jaw and shake the thoughts away.

Lucian jumps up from his seat when he sees us approach and rushes toward Elena. She lets go of my hand and lifts her head, a reassuring smile on her face. I don't think she's smiled at me even once today, but then I haven't given her any reason to. I involuntarily clench my jaw when my brother pulls her into a tight hug, burying his face in her neck. She relaxes into him and he presses a kiss to her hair.

I glance at Vaughn, who is leaning against the wall, a concerned expression on his face. He shrinks back when he sees the rage on my face, and he looks at me apologetically. Fucking hell... I can't even be mad at him. He thought he was doing me a favor by screwing over a Rousseau. What almost happened to Elena... it's my fault.

"What were you thinking?" Lucian murmurs, his voice soft and worried. That is exactly how I should have reacted, but didn't. Instead, I condemned her for her choices before seeing the full picture. "Why didn't you ask me for help?" he asks her, his voice shaking. He looks at her red eyes and then at me, his eyes full of accusation.

One look at Vaughn tells me he must've told Lucian at least the basics, and for some reason, that doesn't sit well with me. I don't want anyone to know about what she nearly did today. Not even my own brother.

"Why didn't you?" I ask her. She pulls away from Lucian, and my body relaxes. I didn't even realize I'd tensed.

"I... we... we're not that c-close," she stammers, unable to meet my eyes. A faint blush darkens her face to a lovely shade of pink. I had a feeling the words I spit out in anger earlier today would come back to haunt me. I shake my head and grab her wrist, pulling her along.

Vaughn's eyes dart from me to her, and I can tell he's wondering what went down between us, but there's no way I'm telling him shit. He nods as we walk past him, and I just know

46

he's not going to let this go. Vaughn is a slut for drama and gossip, though no one would ever have guessed it. Part of me genuinely believes he runs his gentlemen's club purely to gather intel on the elite that frequent it.

"Where are we going?" Lucian asks.

"Home."

"We're taking Elena home? Good."

My driver opens the door of my limousine, and Elena hesitates before she gets in. Lucian jumps in after her, taking the seat next to her, leaving me to sit opposite her. I've always hated this pretentious car, even though I know it's necessary, since it's armored. Today though, with Elena's legs between mine, I hate it a little less.

I lean back and watch Lucian fuss over her. She shifts in her seat, and when she spreads her legs slightly, her short dress rides up. I can tell that her underwear still isn't back in place properly. It's still pushed to the side, the way I left it, exposing part of her delectable pussy. Suddenly I'm more than relieved that it's me sitting opposite her, and not Lucian.

"Sit properly," I tell her, my voice coming out harsher than I intended. Elena frowns at me, but crosses her legs nonetheless. I grin when she blushes, realizing *why* I told her to sit properly. She looks away from me, turning to face Lucian instead.

I take in her chestnut waist length hair that's draped over her chest and her perfect body. I can't deny that she's beautiful, but I've never let beauty distract me. So why is it that I just couldn't let her be? Just knowing that she's Matthew's sister should be enough to repulse me.

"Why didn't you come to me for help?" Lucian asks her again. "I know you wouldn't resort to this unless you were out of options," he adds.

I grab my tablet and go through the background check Adrian sent me. I read the file twice, certain that this information can't be right. I glance at Elena and the guilt I feel nearly wrecks me. I don't remember all that much about Alaric Rousseau, but I don't remember him being a monster. He always seemed to dote on Elena, even when the tension between him and his now ex-wife was running high. So how did Elena end up in the situation she's in? Surely, he keeps tabs on his only daughter? If my security team can find out about every single item she's had to sell in the last two months and every single bill she's paid for her mother, then there's no way Alaric is unaware. How did he ever let it get this far?

I listen absentmindedly as Elena hesitatingly tells Lucian that she needs money for her mother's medical bills, and that she left home years ago. That explains why she said that the one thing she wishes for most is good health for those she loves. She was talking about her mother that night at Inferno.

"I've already asked my father for help. If *he* can't even help me, how could I expect you to? We haven't even seen each other in years. Besides," she says, her voice faltering. "I've asked every single one of my friends, and no one could help."

My brother's face betrays his hurt. I've never seen him care much about anything, least of all a girl. If anyone other than Elena had come knocking on our door, he'd indeed have denied their request for help, no matter how severe the situation. Elena was always his weakness though. My selfish prick of a brother would always save her his last bites of pizza, watch chick flicks with her, and one time when they were little, I even caught him separating M&Ms by color, because Elena only likes the yellow and red ones.

"We were once close friends too, Elena. I'd have been there for you," Lucian says.

Elena nods and grabs his hand, entwining their fingers. She looks at him with such tenderness, and he looks at her the same way. They're already lost in their own little world, and it seems like they were never even apart.

"Even if I did come to you for help and you agreed, you'd help me maybe once or twice before I'd turn into a burden. I need a huge amount of money, Lucian. It's not right of me to rely on you like that."

I sigh. I can't fault her for wanting to stand on her own two feet and not trusting anyone else with her mother's life. She's right. How long can an outsider provide her with the type of financial assistance she needs?

Lucian clenches his jaw the way he does when he's trying to bite his words back, and I wonder what he wants to say. I've never seen my baby brother so animated before.

"I'd help you unconditionally," he says.

Elena shakes her head. "I need at least sixty-thousand dollars by the end of the month, and even more over time. That's not something I can just ask of you."

Lucian begins to reply, but I cut him off. "We'll discuss this at home," I say, my tone sharp. Lucian looks at me helplessly, and my heart softens. He's looking at me like he used to when we were still children. Like I'm his hero. He hasn't looked at me with such faith in years.

The driver parks in our driveway and Lucian jumps out, extending his hand to Elena. My eyes drop to her legs, reminding her to be careful when she steps out of the car, and she blushes, nodding at me. However, my brother must've interpreted her blush differently, because he blushes in return, his gaze firmly pasted on her face.

An uneasy feeling settles in my stomach as I watch them interact. I accompany them into the house, the two of them clearly already in their own bubble.

CHAPTER 11

lena

I follow Lucian and Alexander into their home, pausing at the doorstep as memories assail me. I spent a lot of my childhood in this mansion. I might know every nook and cranny as well as Lucian does. Other than some new furniture, nothing much has changed, and walking in here still feels like coming home —more so than my own childhood home does these days.

I didn't realize how much I've missed this. How much I've missed Lucian and the time we spent together. I've been so busy working and caring for my mother that I haven't really stopped to think about how lonely I've become. How isolated I've let myself become.

Growing up, Lucian was always the brother I wish Matthew was, and I suddenly feel bad for not trying harder to stay in touch. I should've contacted Lucian as soon as I left home, but by that time it'd been too late. We hadn't spoken in years, and we'd grown too far apart. I felt too guilty, even though I know I had no choice but to break off contact.

"Sarah?"

I look up at the mention of my mother's name. Lucian's mother jumps up from the sofa when she sees me and walks towards me, her eyes wide.

"No... *Elena*?"

She wraps me in a tight hug and I squeeze back just as hard, holding back tears yet again. I can't remember the last time someone hugged me like this, yet today two people have held me close.

"Sofia," I whisper, as though saying her name out loud will wake me up from this nostalgic dream. Sofia kisses the top of my head and tightens her hug.

Alexander clears his throat, and I reluctantly step back. He's looking at his mother with an expression I can't decipher. It's almost like he hasn't seen her in a long time, but I clearly remember him telling me he took her out for lunch recently.

"Elena is moving in with us," he says.

My eyes widen in shock. Alexander and I have never discussed anything of the sort, and I haven't actually told him that I've been struggling to pay my own bills, that I'm worried sick about both my own future and my mother's.

I glance at Lucian, who looks just as shocked as I do, but Sofia merely nods and hums in agreement. "All right," she says, no questions asked. "I'll get the staff to prepare a room for her."

I bite down on my lip in an effort to keep my tears at bay. Part of me wants to decline and retain my pride, to demand an explanation from Alexander, and ask him why he thinks he has the right to make decisions on my behalf. But then I remember what my alternative is and bite my tongue.

"A word please, Elena," Alexander says. He tips his head toward the grand staircase and I follow him obediently, still at a loss for words.

"The layout of this entire floor has changed," I murmur in surprise.

Alexander pauses and looks back at me. "Yeah. Two years ago, we renovated most of the house. Lucian, my parents, and I each have separate quarters now. They're all still in the same building, but they're essentially different apartments."

He leads me into his bedroom and I follow, barely able to contain my curiosity. It looks like he knocked down several walls to create a loft-like space, resulting in a large luxurious room, with its own seating area, a huge bed, and a freestanding tub right by the floor to ceiling windows. It's quite obvious that Alexander has created his own little sanctuary here, and I can't help but be impressed with how tasteful and luxurious it all looks.

Alexander leads me to his seating area and I sit down opposite him, rather than next to him, purposely creating some distance between us. With everything that's going on, I'm feeling overwhelmed. Overwhelmed and embarrassed. I can barely think straight. My mind keeps wandering back to Vaughn's, and the way he touched me. I hate myself for how much I enjoyed it. It's like my own body betrayed me, and I'm too scared to even imagine what Alexander might think of me now.

He stares me down in that way he used to when he was giving Lucian and me a chance to confess to whatever it was we'd been up to that day.

"Why don't you tell me exactly what's going on with you?"

I shake my head. "It seems like you already know more than I would've told you."

I'm not stupid. I know how the Kennedys operate. I know he'd have done a background check on me the moment he realized who I am, and I'm not comfortable with how much that would have revealed about me. About the way I've been living my life, and how far I've strayed from the girl he used to know.

Alexander's expression softens and he smiles at me pleadingly. "I'd still like to hear it from you," he says, his voice soft.

I hesitate. There's nothing I can say that he doesn't already know, and at least this way he'll hear my version of the story. So I tell him. I tell him about my father and stepmother, about their refusal to pay for my mom's bills, my stepsister's schemes, and my difficulties paying my own bills. Alexander just listens to me patiently, nodding every once in a while to encourage me to keep talking.

"I see," he says when I finish telling him my story. No questions, no judgement. Just simple understanding. It feels like a huge weight has been lifted off my shoulders. Other than telling Lucian about the basics in the car, I haven't told anyone the full story, and it feels nice to get it off my chest.

"What are you going to do now? Even if you did attempt to sell your body at Vaughn's club, you'd at most make 20k a month, and that's *at most*. That likely won't even be enough to cover your mother's bills on most months, let alone your own expenses on top of that."

I shake my head. "Honestly, I don't know. I have another week until my mother's current bill is due, or they'll take her off life support. I figured I'd go to Vaughn's and then take it from there. It's not like I have any other options. I've asked my dad for help countless times and he's always refused. I'm not in touch with any of my old friends either, not since I left home."

Just the thought of my mother being taken off life support sends shivers down my spine. I'm terrified, and I hate feeling this helpless. Alexander looks at me and then looks away.

"I can give you the money. Under one condition."

I sit up straight, filled with hope. "I'll do it. Whatever it is, I'll do it," I say, involuntarily revealing my desperation.

I notice the brief look of anger in Alexander's eyes and I know he's reminded of what I was about to do at Vaughn's, but I simply do not have the luxury of retaining my dignity right now.

"You don't even know what I'll ask of you, Elena. But then again, there's nothing you wouldn't do, is there?" he sneers. His hands move to his belt and his fingers twitch as he touches the clasp.

"If I ask you to get on your knees right now and suck my dick for 10k, would you do it?"

I bite down on my lip, unsure of what to say. I know this is exactly what I'd signed up for at Vaughn's, but when it's Alexander asking me, I suddenly feel ashamed of myself. Of my choices. I hadn't given much thought to what it'd be like to do stuff like this, but I thought I'd figure that out when it came to it.

"How about 20k? You know, I've been fantasizing about those lips of yours since that night at Inferno," he says.

He undoes his belt and zipper, and reaches into his suit pants. My heart is beating a mile a minute, and I can't tell if I'm terrified or excited.

CHAPTER 12

lexander

"Come here," I say, my voice harsh.

Elena obeys. She gets up and slowly walks toward me until she's standing between my spread legs. She's got that infuriating defiant look on her face, and I almost failed to notice the way her hands tremble slightly.

I pull on her hand, and she falls to her knees on my hard marble floor, her face precariously close to my dick. Her mere proximity has me rock hard.

"You were willing to do this for John at Vaughn's, weren't you? Had I not entered the room when I did, would you have dropped to your knees for him?" I raise my hand to her face, my thumb tracing over her lip. "Would you have opened your pretty little mouth for him?"

Her eyes flash with disgust at the scenario I'm confronting her with. The real thing would be far worse—she has no idea how much worse. "Men from your father's circle frequent

Vaughn's. Do you know how many men that you *know* you'd have to fuck? Do you understand that they'd humiliate you? Any anger that they might have toward your father, they'd take out on you."

Fear melts away her previously confident expression and she looks away. She and I both know that men in our circle don't get where we are without getting our hands dirty. It's clear she hasn't actually considered anything beyond her mother.

She doesn't even realize that she walked right into a trap. Vaughn told me someone called to say that Matthew Rousseau's sister was going to drop by. He was going to allow her to offer her body to avenge me for all the shit Matthew has put me through, and Elena has no idea. She has no idea how bad things would have gotten for her.

She looks up at me, frustration bringing tears to her eyes. "What is it you're offering me, Alexander?" she asks. "You want me to suck you off? I will. If it helps save my mother's life, there's *nothing* I won't do. If our roles were reversed and it was your mother's life on the line, can you honestly tell me you wouldn't go to hell and back to save her?"

She places her hand over the hand I'm palming my erection with and squeezes. She's looking up at me through her lashes, her expression a jumbled mess of desire, desperation, and shaky confidence.

I push her hand away and re-adjust myself before taking my time zipping up my trousers and fastening my belt. I run a hand through my hair and look out the window. How do things escalate every single time I'm alone with her? When I came up here with her, this wasn't what I intended to do at all.

"Get up," I snap, more angry at myself than I am at her.

She rises and sits down next to me. I lean back in my seat and stare at the ceiling, sighing.

"This isn't going the way I intended it to, at all," I say, sounding just as defeated as I feel. "I honestly barely recognize you, Elena."

She looks away, but the way she draws herself up like a wounded animal tells me she's hurt by my words. I sigh and stare out the window, at a loss for words. "Why didn't you tell me who you were that night?" I ask eventually.

She struggles to hold my gaze and looks away in guilt. I wonder what she'd say if she found out that I'd been planning to go back to Inferno every weekend until I ran into her again.

"It was the way you looked at me," she tells me. "I recognized you straight away, but I knew that as soon as you found out who I am, you'd change. You were flirting with me and you were being playful. I saw a side of you I've never seen before, and I selfishly wanted more of that. I wanted more of the Alexander who actually saw me as a woman, and not the awkward teen that followed him around everywhere. I wanted to be more than the little sister of the man you hate."

I'm not sure what I was expecting her to say, but this isn't really it. I thought she was playing games with me, or making a fool out of me for not recognizing her. I didn't think she did it because she was actually interested in me. She's right though, she *is* Matthew's sister.

I grab her hand and entwine our fingers, staring at our joined hands silently before clearing my throat. I look at her and brush her hair behind her ear with my free hand. She looks startled, a small blush coloring her cheeks rosy.

"Like I said, I'll give you the money, Elena. You might not have been part of our lives for the last few years, but that doesn't mean my mother ever forgot about you. She was devastated when she was informed that only immediate family is allowed to see your mother, and then you and Lucian stopped being friends, and she lost you, too... I could tell by the warmth she portrayed just now when she hugged you. Seeing her with you was like seeing the woman she was when I was a child."

I sigh, struggling with words for probably the first time in my life.

"You're from a good family, Elena. You're well connected and Ivy League educated—with a full scholarship, no less. I know you won't accept charity, and had I been in your situation, I wouldn't either. I wouldn't trust anyone with my mother's life, and I wouldn't be able to live with not knowing when someone's goodwill runs out."

She nods, but she looks confused, and I can't blame her.

"Elena, I want you to marry me."

She stares at me in disbelief, her eyes wide.

"You... *what*?"

"Marry me, Elena."

She blinks, her lips moving but unable to form a reply. I tighten my grip on her hand and smile at her gently.

"You're aware that the heirs to our conglomerate must be married before taking their seat on the board?"

She nods, her cheeks reddening. She's no doubt remembering the way our mothers used to joke about their children getting married. I always wondered who they imagined her getting married to, me or Lucian. I guess the decision is out of their hands now.

I clear my throat and look away. "My mother has been arranging dates with socialites and acquaintances. I don't have time for this shit, and I'm not looking to get married. However, I don't have a choice. I know my mother wants to try and change the rules for me, but my grandfather won't let her. I worked too hard to lose everything now."

Elena nods and bites down on her lip as she mulls my words over. "Why me?" she asks.

"You need a place to stay and money for your mother's hospital costs. I'm pretty sure you don't want to be a charity case and leech off whoever is willing to help you. I need a wife who won't get in my way and won't expect me to put any effort into making our marriage work. If I have to marry, I'd rather marry someone who owes me. Your family background is good enough, and you're bound to inherit your mother's shares, so you'll be able to increase the Kennedy family's wealth and influence. Besides, my mother has always loved you, so I know you'll fit well into our family."

Elena rises to her feet, and I follow. She starts to pace in my bedroom, and I walk up to her. She takes a step back for every step I take toward her, and before she realizes it, I've got her backed up against the wall.

"That... is that the truth?"

I nod.

"Is it the whole truth?"

I smile and cage her in, my forearms on either side of her head, our bodies almost flush.

"Clever girl," I whisper. "No," I tell her honestly. "The whole truth is that in addition to everything I just told you, I'm really looking forward to parading you around Matthew, to have him know I'm fucking his sister, that you're *mine*."

Elena laughs, the sound tinged with desperation. "You're a fool if you think he'll care," she says, her eyes on mine. "But you're even more of a fool if you think you can buy me like I'm yet another one of your countless assets. There's nothing I won't do for my mother, Alexander—but know that even if you own my body, you'll never own *me*."

I smile at her and brush her hair out of her face gently, giddiness filling me at the thought of the look on Matthew's face. "Oh, he'll care," I whisper, "and you *will* belong to me. It's not just your body that will be mine, Elena. It's your every thought, your every dream. Your entire future is mine."

I can see the tiny cogs in her brain turning, her eyes betraying her helplessness. She wants to fight me and deny my words, but she doesn't have the power to. I see the way she's holding herself back and I can't help but smile. I wonder which words she's swallowing down right now. What would she be yelling at me if I didn't hold her mother's life in my hands?

"What will this entail? Is it a paper marriage?" she asks, her tone resigned. Surprisingly, I don't like seeing the fight leave her eyes. I don't enjoy getting my way, watching her give in. That's a first.

I shake my head. "Not exactly. Kennedys don't divorce, *ever*. You're well aware of that. It'll be a legitimate marriage. I'll give you access to all my funds, and I'll support you the way is expected of me as your husband. I won't ask much of you. All I ask is that you behave like a good daughter-in-law to my mother, and that you act like a doting wife whenever required in public."

She nods slowly and looks up at me thoughtfully.

"What about in private?"

"I won't interfere with your private life as long as you don't interfere with mine."

"Does that mean you intend to have... lovers?"

I tense. "No," I snap. "Neither you nor I will have any *lovers*. Don't even fucking dream of cheating, Elena. Don't even fucking look at another man, you hear me?"

Her eyes widen in surprise and I hate the way she's looking at me—as though she's trying to read me. I relax slightly when she nods. I don't know what I'll do if I ever catch her straying, but I do know any man that touches her is going to be six foot under before he realizes what's happening to him. I'll be damned if I let her treat me the way Jennifer did—the way my father continuously treats my mother. "I won't be made a fool of, Elena."

Elena nods, her chest rising and falling rapidly, her eyes on mine. The way she looks at me... I fucking hate seeing the sympathy in her eyes. Elena stands to lose everything, yet it's me she pities. All thanks to Jennifer. She made a national fucking laughingstock, to the point that a girl that's lost everything feels bad for me.

"What about divorce? What if one of us falls in love with someone else?" she asks. The mere thought of her leaving me infuriates me, and she isn't even mine yet.

I shake my head. "It's not an option. I won't ever sign the papers. If we were to divorce, my grandfather would disown me without a second thought. I won't do it. If you agree to this, you'll agree to a life without love. Think it over carefully."

She nods and sits in silence. I'm oddly nervous as I watch her face for clues as to how she might be feeling.

"I don't really have a choice, do I?"

I shake my head. "You do, Elena. If you asked my mother to foot your mother's bills, she'd likely do it, no questions asked. Probably for as long as you want her to."

She looks torn.

"Why don't you take some time to think it over?"

Elena shakes her head. "No. I'd rather spend money that legally belongs to me as your wife than become a charity case and be at your family's mercy. I need a place to stay, and I want to be 100% sure my mother receives the best care. If I rely on your mother, I'll only be able to pay for her current level of care for the time being. If I marry you, I can get world renowned doctors to examine my mother, and I could move her into a private facility. So long as you guarantee you won't ever restrict my access to her or limit the amount of money I get to spend on my mother's care, I'll marry you, Alexander. Use me as a pawn in whatever stupid rich-people-game you're playing. I don't care. If you help me save my mother's life, I'll be whatever you want me to be."

I smile at her. "I promise, Elena. As my wife, money will always be the least of your worries."

CHAPTER 13

lena

I follow Alexander back down in a daze, my heart pounding. I can barely believe I just agreed to marry *Alexander Kennedy*.

"Elena."

Sofia's voice snaps me out of my daze and I pull my hand out of Alexander's, unaware of when I even grabbed it.

"Lucian filled me in a little on what's been going on with you. I've already called the hospital and paid any outstanding fees. Don't worry about a thing, my dear."

I pause and blink back the tears that are gathering in my eyes. She hasn't seen my mother or me in years, yet she still goes out of her way to help us.

Alexander clears his throat and sends me an inquiring look. I nod at him. Even now that my mother's hospital fees have been taken care of, I'll still agree to marry him. He's right. I wouldn't feel right letting them spend a fortune in fees without repaying them somehow. Without worrying that their generosity might run out. Marrying Alexander is an easy solution for both of us.

Alexander and I take a seat, and he grabs my hand. "Elena and I decided to get married," he says simply. He leans back into his seat, as though he didn't just announce some shocking news.

Sofia doesn't say anything. She just looks at the two of us, a thoughtful expression on her face. Lucian is the first to respond.

"Fuck, no. Why the hell would you two get married? *Elena*?"

I look at him, but I'm not sure how to explain myself. Everything made sense when I discussed it with Alexander, but now I suddenly struggle to express myself.

"Did you agree to marry Alec, sweetie?" Sofia asks me. Her voice is soft and kind, but she fails to hide the concern reflected in her eyes. Part of me worries she might think I'm not good enough for her son, that he can do better. She'd be right. I'm no longer the rich, well-connected heiress I used to be.

"You two have my blessing if you choose to get married." She glances at Alexander, staring at him thoughtfully for a couple of seconds before nodding. "I'd have added her to the file had I thought of her, so I do approve."

Sofia glances at me, and the motherly concern I saw earlier is gone. She looks at me as though she's appraising me, yet I can't read her well enough to figure out how she assessed me. "However, please think it over some more, Elena. Marriage is for life."

Alexander looks annoyed at his mother's words, but Lucian looks positively enraged. "Surely, you're not seriously entertaining this ludicrous idea, Mom?" he asks, his voice raised. He pulls me to my feet and puts his hands on my shoulders, clenching tightly.

"Elena, if you want to marry into this family, *I'll* marry you,"

Lucian says, his eyes blazing with sincerity. My heart feels so full it might actually burst. I smile at him but shake my head. The mere idea of marriage to Lucian is so absurd, it never even occurred to me.

"Over my dead body," Alexander snaps, moving closer to me. He puts his arm around my waist and pulls me to him, moving me out of Lucian's reach.

Lucian steps up to him, getting into his face. He jabs Alexander in the chest, and I'm so shocked I don't even have time to get between them. Lucian has never been even remotely violent. I'm the one that always had to defend him against bullies.

"Why the hell would you marry her? You're thirty. She's twenty-three, you pedophile. It makes more sense for her to be with *me*. We grew up together. We're the same age. We're childhood friends. I actually *know* her."

Lucian pushes Alexander, but he doesn't even stumble. He merely looks at his little brother with a carefully guarded expression, keeping me behind him.

"Lucian!" Sofia snaps. "What is wrong with you? How dare you speak to your brother like that. Apologize!"

Lucian glares at his brother and then shakes his head. He walks off, slamming the front door closed behind him. Alexander looks at me, his brows raised in question, but I just shake my head. I have no idea what just happened either. Sofia rushes after Lucian, leaving Alexander and me standing here.

"What was that just now?" he asks.

I shake my head. "I don't know," I whisper.

"What's going on between you and my brother?"

He sounds suspicious, and for a second I wonder if he's jealous, but I dismiss the thought just as quickly.

"Nothing," I answer truthfully.

He frowns. "Nothing? That didn't sound like nothing. I'll

ask you again. What's going on between you two? If it were *nothing*, my brother wouldn't have reacted the way he did."

I look up at him, my entire body tense with anger. "What exactly is it you're accusing me of?"

He takes a step closer to me and grabs my chin, forcing me to look at him. "I don't fucking share, Elena. I don't like people touching what's mine."

I smile at him through my outrage and place my palm on his chest, feeling his muscles tense underneath my touch. "I'm not yours yet, Alexander."

He grits his teeth, clearly disliking my answer. "But you will be. Soon, you will be, Elena." He smiles as he traces his index finger over my lips. "Resist all you want, fight me, deny it... but in the end, it'll be my name on your lips when I make you come —*again*."

He takes a step away, his body still radiating with anger. "I'll warn you now. I won't tolerate rumors about you. You'd better stay the fuck away from my brother. Betray me, Elena, and it'll be your mother's life you're risking."

I look at him with barely contained resentment. He's just like every other man in my life—revelling in my helplessness. I hate that I've been reduced to this, yet I have no other choice. If I want to save my mother's life and provide her with the care she needs, I'll have to be whatever Alexander asks me to be.

My shoulders sag and he smiles at me, no doubt enjoying his silent victory. Everything is a game to men like him.

"We'll get married tomorrow," he says, his eyes dark.

"What? *Tomorrow?*"

"No point in delaying. Let's get the paperwork out of the way, so I can formally start providing for both you and your mother. I want you out of that waitressing job you're doing, and I definitely want you out of the sketchy apartment you live in. If you're going to be my wife, we need to start fixing your image immediately."

I look away, resentment and embarrassment melting together, adding to my indignation. It seems like his background check was quite thorough. He even knows I was unable to find a corporate job.

"A guest room has been prepared for you, but I expect you to move your stuff into my bedroom tomorrow."

He looks at me, his eyes dropping to my lips. "Tonight is all you have to change your mind, Elena. Tomorrow afternoon, I'm making you my wife. Instead of selling your body at Vaughn's, you'll be selling it to me. Think it through carefully, because from tomorrow onward, you'll be mine."

His gaze lingers on my lips, and for a second I think he's going to bridge the distance between us to kiss me, but then his expression hardens and he takes a step away.

He walks towards the stairs, pausing midway. "Oh, and Elena?" he says, turning back to look at me. "I'm taking you bare. Get on the pill if you don't want children yet. The first time I fuck you, I want to feel all of you."

He smiles and walks away, leaving me standing here in shock.

I can't believe I'm marrying him... *tomorrow.*

CHAPTER 14

lena

The whole ceremony was a blur. Alexander took me to City Hall, and we walked out a few minutes later with our marriage certificate in hand. He's nothing if not efficient. The entire process was mechanical and impersonal. I don't know what I was expecting, but this isn't really it.

I look down at my outfit. I didn't have time or money to buy anything special, and I don't even own a white dress. Instead, I'm wearing black formal pants and a white blouse—my job interview outfit. It's the nicest thing I own. Besides, I guess it's only fitting that I wore black to start this soulless marriage with. Alexander doesn't say a word to me as he walks back to his limousine, he's lost in thought as much as I am.

"I'm going to be busy for at least the next couple of days. Keep to our agreement: don't interfere with my private life unnecessarily, and I won't interfere with yours."

I nod and swallow down the lump in my throat. This feels so wrong. What have I done? What was I thinking?

I shake away my thoughts as Alexander opens the door for me. I sit down and nod at the driver, surprised to find that there's a woman I don't recognize sitting next to him. Alexander joins me, ignoring both of them. He reaches for the bag in the seat opposite me. It wasn't there when we left the car earlier.

The woman turns to look at us and nods at me. "Good afternoon, Mrs. Kennedy. Congratulations. My name is Alice Porter. I'm Alexander's secretary."

I'm startled, and it takes me a good ten seconds to realize that it's me she's talking to. *I'm* Mrs. Kennedy now, and the sound of it sends a thrill down my spine. I nod at her and paste my most polite smile onto my face.

"Nice to meet you, Ms. Porter."

She shakes her head and smiles at me. "Please, call me Alice." Alice is a beautiful, sophisticated lady. Short, perfectly straight blonde hair falls just above her shoulder, and her makeup is flawless. I think she's probably around Alexander's age, maybe a little older. I listen as she walks Alexander through his schedule for the upcoming week. When he said he'll be busy, that was clearly an understatement.

He opens the bag in his lap while she talks and takes out a new mobile phone. He unboxes it and starts playing around with it. I watch as he uses the phone to ring himself with, and then hangs up. He hands it to me and grabs his own.

He starts typing on his phone, and a few seconds later the phone in my hand vibrates. I see an incoming message from *Husband*. Why didn't he just program himself in as Alexander?

Husband: *This is your new phone. It's fully encrypted using our company's latest technology. You'll find a new laptop and tablet in the bag too. They're similarly encrypted. It's important that you use only technology provided by me. Corporate espionage is a serious issue that we've been battling, and you'll become a target soon.*

I type a reply and hit send.

Elena Kennedy: *I got it. Don't worry.*

I blink twice as I notice the name that he's set up in my message settings. Yep, still there. Not just Elena. Elena Kennedy. I wonder what my name is in his phone for this new number. Probably just Elena. Maybe 'Old Ball N Chains.' I scroll through my contacts and find that he's programmed in everyone I might need to reach, including his security officer, Aiden, and Alice.

Husband: *Remember your identity from now on. You're my wife now. Act appropriately in front of others.*

I frown at his text, feeling oddly offended. What does he think I'd do?

Elena Kennedy: *I'll try to refrain from falling to my knees to suck off the highest bidder.*

I regret the text the moment I send it and keep staring at my phone instead of looking up to face him. My words were uncalled for, but I still feel bitter about the way he humiliated me when he offered me 20k to suck him off. I'm not sure what bothers me the most. That he offered it at all, or that I would've done it if he hadn't stopped me. I know I should be grateful to him for offering me a solution instead of feeling bitter, but I can't help myself.

Husband: *I just gave you half my net worth by marrying you. Matter of fact, there's a duplicate of my credit card in the bag too. Remember, Elena: I'll always be the highest bidder. Shall I put up the privacy shield or do you think you can be a good girl and 'refrain'?*

I see him reach for the button that puts a privacy screen up between the front seats and us, and I jump up to stop him, pretty much tumbling in his arms. "No need," I say, panicked, but I'm too late. The screen rises, and Alexander chuckles.

He pulls me onto his lap and puts his lips against my ear. "Things between us might have started unconventional, but

70

that doesn't change the fact that you *are* my wife, Elena. You *are* Mrs. Kennedy now. You're mine."

His words against my ear tickle, and my eyes shutter closed. I squirm in his arms, clenching my legs tightly. Just the memory of how he touched me has me wet again, and I'm embarrassed. I hate how he makes me feel, yet I can't fight it.

"I thought we agreed on this, Alexander. It's just my body you purchased, nothing more."

Alexander wraps his hands around my waist. His fingers almost touch each other around my waist, and it makes me feel small. He pulls me closer and smiles as he threads his hand through my hair.

"Just your body, huh? Very well. That's all I want from you, Elena. You'd better remember that *your body* is mine now." His index finger brushes over my lips and he smirks, his gaze heated. "These lips are mine now, you hear me?"

I nod, and satisfaction flashes through his eyes.

"Good girl," he whispers, leaning in closer, his lips brushing against mine. "There's a crucial part of the wedding ceremony we missed out on," he murmurs.

"What's that?" I whisper back, my heart racing, my lips brushing against his with every word.

"The part where I kiss the bride," he answers, before lowering his lips to mine fully.

A soft moan escapes my lips when he kisses me, and Alexander groans, deepening our kiss. I lose myself in him, in us. Not in a million years did I think I'd find myself kissing Alexander Kennedy.

He pulls away and drops his forehead to mine. "You're my wife now, Elena. I'll take care of you. I'll provide you with anything you could possibly need," he says, pulling away further. "But you won't ever get love from me. You know that, right?"

I nod, the situation suddenly seeming so much more real. I've felt like everything was a blur in the last few hours, a dream. Only to wake up to find that all my biggest problems have been solved. I wonder what my mother would think of me if she knew I had to rely on a man to get out of a sticky situation. Would she be disappointed with my lack of independence, or would she be proud of me for doing the only thing I could?

Alexander smiles at me and seems to hesitate before he continues. "I like you, Elena. You're a nice girl, and you're a good fit for my family. I'm glad you know not to expect much from me. If you want sex, I can give you that. But flirting, love, and romance? You won't get it from me. I won't woo you."

I nod at him in understanding. "I don't need love from you, Alexander," I say, my voice soft. "I just need you to help me save my mother's life."

I knew what I was getting into when I agreed to marry him. Despite that, part of me was hoping I'd see more of the Alexander I met at Inferno, but he's back to being the Alexander I knew growing up. I wonder if this is all I'll ever have of him. I dreamt of marrying Alexander when I was younger, and now that it has actually happened, it's a bit... disappointing. I guess my marriage is an accurate reflection of my life so far, but I'm not dumb enough to take what I have for granted.

"All of your mother's current medical bills are already paid. Before we left, I authorized her move to a secure private facility that my family uses exclusively. Aiden, my security officer, should be making that happen as we speak. He's also looking into the experts that might be able to help her, and they'll create a new treatment plan for her. You'll be able to visit her again tomorrow."

I can barely breathe as I listen to his words. These are all the things I wished I'd been able to do for my mother, but the maximum amount I was allowed to take out of my trust fund per month wasn't enough to cover it. In hindsight, that's a good thing. I'd have run out of money far sooner, and I don't even want to think about what that might have meant for my mother.

"You'll also get your own security team and driver. They'll answer to you, not to me. For the time being, you can use Alice as your personal assistant for any matters you require, and my mother's personal stylist has been assigned to you as well. You can hire your own staff if that arrangement doesn't suit you. All I ask in return is that you accept the boundaries I've set."

"I understand, Alexander. I won't bother you needlessly. I'm grateful for what you're offering me. I'll play the role of doting wife and daughter-in-law in public, and I'll respect your boundaries. I promise you."

He nods and looks at me, his gaze searching, as though he's trying to make sure I mean what I say, that I won't bother him with useless expectations. What he sees in my eyes seems to please him, because he nods in satisfaction.

He pauses and stares at me for a few seconds. "It's quite likely that my mother is already aware that we decided to proceed with our marriage, and she'll have taken your image in her own hands. You're a Kennedy now, and you'll need to look like one. We won't announce our marriage for the time being. Instead, we're going to stage an entire relationship. We'll go on high profile dates, I'll publicly propose to you, and we'll have a grand wedding ceremony on the 20th of June."

I frown, and Alexander sighs. "The media are tough on us," he says. "They've followed me everywhere, and they've seen me on plenty of dates, some of them fairly recent. They know we can't be married. I don't want our marriage to start with rumors about me two-timing you while we were dating, so we'll need that to die down first. We'll stage a perfect relationship for the press and my grandfather."

I look into his eyes, feeling oddly hurt. "Just tell me the truth, Alexander. June 20th? It's my brother's wedding day. You want to use me to overshadow the news of their engagement and wedding."

He places his index finger underneath my chin and lifts my face. All I find when I look into his eyes is ruthlessness. "Clever girl," he says. "Yes. We're going to do just that."

My heart breaks even as I force a smile onto my face. I was terrified that all he'd be able to think about when he sees me is Matthew.

But it's worse.

When he looks at me, it's Jennifer he sees.

All I am is a tool to get to her, to rattle her, to hurt her. Even now, when it's me that bears his last name, it's her he thinks of. It will always be her.

CHAPTER 15

lena

I walk through Alexander's bedroom, feeling restless. He helped me pack my belongings and dropped me off before going back to work, so I've got at least a few hours to myself. I'm nervous as I glance at my luggage in the corner. Sharing a room with Alexander... just thinking about tonight has my heart racing.

This entire space is amazing, and from now on, this'll be home to me. It feels like a luxurious suite in a six-star hotel. He must've hired an interior designer to remodel everything. It's been years since I've been surrounded with such sheer luxury.

I pause beside his bed, my heart sinking when I notice Alexander has a photo of Jennifer and him on his nightstand. I pick it up carefully and sit down on his bed, my hands trembling. It's been over a year since they broke up, yet he still has a photo of the two of them. Is this what he looks at before he goes to bed, is she still the first thing he sees when he wakes up?

My heart constricts painfully as I put the photo back. He's made it clear that he won't ever love me, but I still remember the way he loved Jennifer. It was clear for everyone to see that she was his entire world. I'm not much of a dreamer; every single hope and dream I had came crashing down on me when I lost my entire family, each of them in a different way. But part of me... part of me hoped I'd someday have a family of my own. A husband that loves me, a home filled with laughter and happiness. I won't have any of that now that I've sealed my own fate.

I can't have romantic notions. I can't have hope. Alexander has been clear from the very start, and I can't delude myself into thinking he'll love me one day. I can't set myself up for heartache.

I glance back at the photo and bite down on my lip. I may be his wife now, but there's no guarantee that he won't come to regret marrying me. If my father and brother can turn their backs on me, then so can Alexander. I need to remember that.

I try my best to clear my mind as I walk into Alexander's walk-in closet, pausing in surprise when I find a whole wall full of women's clothes, shoes, and bags. For a second my heart drops, but then I notice that everything still has the tags on. My eyes flutter closed as relief courses through me.

Looks like the family stylist works quickly. I shouldn't be surprised they've got my size. Alexander's background check must've been quite comprehensive.

Everything in here is the kind of stuff I'd expect Alexander's wife to wear. Semi-formal, classy, and crazy expensive. It's the kind of stuff I used to wear, before I was forced to sell everything I own to pay my mother's bills.

"Do you like it?" a soft voice behind me says. I turn around in surprise, finding Sofia leaning against the door frame, a small smile on her face.

"I do, this is amazing."

"I got a call as soon as you registered your marriage. I get informed about a lot of things my sons do, though they don't realize it."

I chuckle, not surprised at all. Even when we were younger, she always knew what everyone was up to. She took having eyes in the back of her head to a whole new level.

"I guess congratulations are in order, but I do hope you know what you got yourself into, Elena. Alec... he's not looking for love. I'm glad that the one he married is you, but at the same time I wanted more for you. This isn't what your mother would want for you, either. Alec has been through a lot, and I'm not sure he'll even be able to give you a chance. I hope he does, Elena. I really hope he does. If anyone can mend his heart, I think it'll be you."

I nod, my heart sinking. "I understand, Sofia. I'm ready to deal with the consequences of my choices."

Sofia sighs and grabs my hand. "Call me Mom, sweetie. You're my daughter-in-law now."

I force a smile onto my face and nod at her.

"I'm selfishly glad that it's you. You have no idea how much your mother and I wanted you two to end up together when you were little. If things were different, if we weren't who we are, if the Kennedy name didn't destroy every hint of love, then maybe you and Alec would've been perfect together."

Her words surprise me. She's always been a hopeless romantic, so when did she become so jaded? I haven't seen Alexander's father around, and I wonder if that might be the cause of it.

I look up at her with a heavy heart. "You two wanted Alexander and me to end up together?" I ask, disregarding her other words. "Not me and Lucian?"

She smiles. "Of course not. Lucian and you are incredibly incompatible, for numerous reasons."

She looks at me as though she wants to say something, but doesn't. "I'll leave you to settle in," she says, smiling at me. I nod and stare after her as she walks out, shutting the bedroom door softly.

I sigh as I walk into Alexander's bathroom. His bedroom and bathroom are mostly open plan, and there is no door, just a whole lot of stone and glass. His huge tub is freestanding, and rather than in the bathroom, it's in front of his windows like a statement piece. The view is astounding, and I can only imagine what it'll look like as the sun sets.

I walk through his bathroom and play around with all the buttons. He's got controls for everything. There's a radio, a TV screen in his shower, and different types of lighting. I push one of the buttons, and a water curtain appears at the shower's entrance, like a waterfall, obscuring the inside of the huge stone shower. I press the button a few times and smile. I shouldn't be surprised that Alexander's room is so tech-intensive.

I eye the tub in the corner longingly and check the time. Five pm. Probably enough time to take a bath and be down for dinner at six. Alexander said he had to work late, so I doubt he'll be back soon.

I undress and let my clothes drop to the floor as the tub fills up. My lace bra and panties follow, and I'm suddenly reminded of the way Alexander touched me. It feels like a lifetime ago, but it was only yesterday.

I step into the tub and press one of the little buttons in it. A small amount of soap drops into the water. It smells like lavender, my favorite. Looks like Alexander has good taste. I press the button a few more times for good measure and then turn on the jets.

"Oh God," I moan. The jets are hitting me from every angle, massaging my entire body. I didn't even realize I was this tired until I laid down in here. Combined with the stunning view, this feels like such a luxury. I lean back and close my eyes, letting the jets massage me. I haven't felt this relaxed in as long as I can remember. It's been years since I've felt so at ease. Taking a long bath used to be one of my favorite things to do, but I haven't been able to take one in years. Not since I moved out of my father's house.

I move my hands over my breasts and down my stomach, enjoying the smooth feel of being underwater. I've never been a very sensual person. Sure, I've touched myself a few times, and after a few tries, I can usually make myself come. But sex has never appealed to me much. In part because I simply never had time to date, and casual sex isn't my thing. I never had the chance to get close enough to someone to *want* them. The one time I had sex wasn't very memorable at all.

Yesterday, though... that was the first time I wondered what I might be missing out on. I've never come as hard by myself as I did with Alexander.

I lightly brush over my clit with my fingers, teasing myself. I drag one finger over my skin, remembering the way Alexander touched me. The way he looked at me with eyes filled with desire, despite his anger. I move my fingers in the exact same way he had, replaying the scene in my head. I push one finger inside while I circle around my clit with the other, mimicking his movements. I'm breathing hard and moaning, losing control over my body and my desire quickly. In my mind, I'm touching Alexander's body as he touches and kisses me. I know I'm seconds away, but I'm enjoying it so much, I don't want it to end.

"Elena?"

I yank my fingers away and sit up in alarm, forgetting to

cover my breasts, exposing them above the water. Alexander is standing in front of the tub, his crotch at eye level. I can clearly see the outline of his erection, and I freeze.

CHAPTER 16

lexander

I walk into my bedroom and pause, closing the door behind me softly. Are those my tub's jets I hear? The closer I get, the clearer the sound gets. I walk up to the tub and see Elena's head sticking out, her long dark hair hanging over the edge, her head tipped back. She looks so seductive.

I'm about to call out her name when she moans and moves her shoulders slightly. Is she touching herself in my tub? I walk closer to her and watch her face as she pleasures herself, her eyes closed.

She probably didn't hear me walk in over the sound of the jets, and I take that moment to just watch her. She looks fucking gorgeous, her body swaying a little, as though she's riding her own hand. I wish the fucking bubbles weren't in the way so I could see her body. Just the sound of her has me rock hard, and I can't help but wonder what it'll be like when I finally get to have my little wife. Her body is all I've been able to think about since I've had my fingers inside her, and I need more. More of *her*.

"Elena?" I say, my mouth moving of its own volition.

She shoots up in alarm; her breasts rising above the bubbles. *Fuck.* She's beautiful. Perfect teardrop tits, probably more than I can fit into my hands. She sits up in the tub, clearly not realizing how much of herself she's exposing. Her eyes are on my pants, and I belatedly realize my erection is right in front of her face.

"What are you doing?" I ask her, and I marvel at my ability to keep my tone light, when all I really want to do is lift her out of that tub and finish what she started.

Her cheeks turn bright crimson, the color extending to her chest. She looks so embarrassed, her barriers down, eradicated by the shame she's clearly experiencing. She looks stunning, and oh so fucking innocent.

I tear my eyes away from her and grab a towel.

"Come here."

Elena's eyes widen, and I grin at her. "Come here, *wife*," I repeat.

She's breathing hard, and when her gaze meets mine, I recognize the lust in those gorgeous eyes of hers. Lust, but also annoyance. Elena doesn't like taking orders, and I love giving them, even if it's just to see her eyes flash like that.

"Need I remind you that you sold your body to me?"

Elena rises slowly, the water gliding over her skin, and she takes my damn breath away. I clench my jaw in an attempt to stay in control, to keep myself from lifting my wife into my arms and taking her to bed.

She stands before me, naked, her eyes glistening with an unspoken challenge, and I smile at her. "Beautiful," I murmur, my hand gliding up her arm and around the back of her neck, my thumb on her throat. Her pulse is racing and she's

82

breathing hard. I wonder if she even realizes that her body betrays her.

I lean in, and her eyes flutter closed as my lips drop to hers. I bridge the distance between us, and this time I kiss her slowly, taking my time enjoying those delicious lips of hers. Elena whimpers, as though she wants more, and I smile against her lips. She pretends to resist me, but the second I touch her, her body betrays her.

My hands roam over her body, her skin slick and wet against my fingers. Elena shivers just slightly, and I pull away from her. I grab the discarded towel and wrap it around her.

She looks disappointed, and I smile as I cup her cheek, my thumb caressing her lips. "Baby, we've got all night, and it's my bed I want you in."

Her eyes drop to my now wet shirt and she traces the damp spots with her fingers. Her touch sets me ablaze in a way I haven't experienced in years, if ever at all. I grab her hand to keep it in place, and Elena presses her palm against my chest. The way she's looking at me drives me crazy.

"This... this is how you looked at me at Inferno," I murmur. "That look in your eyes, it's been haunting my dreams ever since that night."

Elena blushes, and I smile. "Tell me what you're thinking. Do you want me, Elena? The way you're looking at me makes me think that you're wondering what's underneath this shirt."

Elena smiles, but she looks slightly nervous. "I... well," she whispers. "Yes," she says. "Yes, I'm wondering exactly that, and I intend to find out, Alexander."

CHAPTER 17

lexander

Elena looks into my eyes, both her palms pressed to my chest, a blush coloring her beautiful face crimson.

"Open them," I say, placing her fingers over the buttons on my shirt. Elena bites down on her lip, a provocative look in her eyes. For a second I think she'll disobey me, but then she does what I told her to.

I watch her as more and more of my chest comes into view. Her breathing quickens and her hands move over my body eagerly, giving away the lust she feels. She hates how much she wants me, and I'm loving every second of it.

My shirt falls open, and Elena gulps. I can't help but grin. Everything about her is so genuine, her every reaction, every emotion displayed in her gaze.

I lift her into my arms and she gasps, her arms finding their way around my neck. I carry her to my bed and place her down carefully.

She looks up at me and grabs the sheets, covering herself

up as best as she can. Her actions betray the nervousness behind her bravado, and I bite back a smile. I'm tempted to pull the sheets away so I can watch her lying in my bed, her pale skin in contrast with my dark sheets. But I let her be... for now.

Elena's eyes are glued to my hands and I take my time shrugging out of my dress shirt. It falls to the floor, and she bites down on her lip. Her gaze roams over my chest and she takes her time admiring my abs, no longer even attempting to hide her desire.

I smirk when her eyes follow my hands down to my pants. I play with the button, enjoying the impatience in her eyes.

"Come here," I tell her.

She hesitates for a split second before obeying. Elena rises to her knees, the sheets falling away. Her beauty takes my breath away—her body is utter perfection, and this woman, this beautiful woman, she's mine.

I take her hands and place them on my fly, enjoying the way her eyes widen when she feels how hard I am.

"You know what to do."

Elena looks into my eyes as she unzips my pants. She smiles when she places her hands on my hips, tugging on my pants carefully, dragging my boxers along too. I grin at her impatience and bury my hand in her hair, pulling her closer just as my clothes drop to the floor.

Elena's eyes fall closed when my lips meet hers and I tighten my grip on her hair, kissing her harder, deeper. She moans against my lips and I lean into her. She falls back onto my bed, her hair spread all over, her body on display for me.

I smirk as I lean over her. Elena lifts her hand to my face, her fingers grazing over my cheek. The way she looks at me... It's lust and contempt, all mixed together. Those eyes of hers... they make me feel things I shouldn't.

I lower my body on top of hers and hold myself up on my forearms, taking a moment to just look at my *wife*.

"From this day forward, Elena. From this day forward, you're mine."

She tenses, her hand weaving its way through my hair. Even now, with her body pressed against mine, she's fighting her desire.

"Say it."

Elena tightens her grip on my hair, her gaze unwavering, a smirk on her lips "My *body* is yours, Alexander Kennedy. All yours."

I drop my forehead to hers and smile. "That'll do for now," I whisper, my lips dropping down to her neck. I kiss her softly, eliciting a moan from her. I'll have all of her sooner or later.

I work my way down, leaving a trail of kisses on her skin. Elena tenses when I lean in to take her dark, hard nipple into my mouth. The way she moves her body underneath mine drives me insane. She's so eager, so sensitive.

Elena hooks her leg around my hip when I move down, and I smile before pressing a kiss to her stomach.

"Alexander," she moans, her hands tangled into my hair, her gaze heated.

"Tell me what you want, Elena."

"You. Just you," she whispers.

I move back up, lying down beside her, holding myself up on my elbow so I can look at her. She looks into my eyes as my hand trails over her body, teasing her. I stroke her thigh, and she squirms. I know what she wants, but I'm enjoying her little gasps too much. I love the way she's begging for more with those eyes of hers.

I trace my index finger over her wet folds, and Elena moans, the sound music to my ears. "So fucking wet, baby. You want me that badly, huh?"

Elena looks up at me through her lashes, her desire on display for me.

I slip a finger into her, another moan escaping her lips, her eyes falling closed. "No," I tell her. "None of that. Look at me, Elena."

Her eyes flutter open and she looks at me, her lips slightly parted, her cheeks flushed. She's fucking beautiful.

"Good girl," I murmur. "You look at me when you're in bed with me, you hear me?"

I swipe my thumb over her clit just as I stimulate her G-spot, and Elena's head tips back in ecstasy. "Yes," she moans.

I keep her right at the edge, enjoying the pleading look in her eyes. The way she looks at me... fucking hell.

"Do you want to come for me, Elena?"

She nods and tightens her grip on my hair. "Please, Alexander."

I smile and give her what she wants, pushing her over the edge, her eyes on mine and my name on her lips. Possessiveness unlike anything I've ever felt before overwhelms me and I roll on top of her, parting her legs further with my knee.

"I told you, Elena. From now on, my name is the *only* name you'll ever have on your lips."

She nods and grabs my hair, pulling me closer as I push into her slightly, her pussy like a fucking vice. "Fuck," I groan. I look into her eyes as I sink all the way into her. Elena whimpers underneath me, struggling to adjust to my size. She pulls me in for a kiss, her arms around me.

"Alexander," she whispers, and my lips find hers. I kiss her slowly, taking my time with her. She moans against my lips and relaxes underneath me, and I pull back, almost all the way out of her.

"This pussy is mine, you hear me?"

"Yes," she says, and I slam back into her, a loud moan

escaping her lips. She pulls on my hair with one hand, her other hand leaving scratch marks on my back. She pants my name, her eyes on mine. The way she sounds... *fuck*.

I hold myself up on my forearms and lower my lips to hers. Her nails scrape over my scalp as she pulls me closer, bridging the distance, eager for a kiss.

"You feel amazing, baby. So fucking wet, so fucking tight."

I pull back almost all the way and thrust into her hard. She takes me eagerly, and the way she moans my name has me close.

She pulls me back in for a kiss, her movements frantic. She catches my bottom lip between her teeth before kissing me, her tongue tangling with mine. The way she kisses me is as sexy as she is. She's got me breathless by the time I pull back to look at her.

The way she moves with me has me close already. I don't even remember the last time I felt this desperate, this passionate.

"More," Elena moans, and I give her what she asks for, increasing the pace.

"Oh God," she pants, and I lower my lips to hers, swallowing all her moans. I fuck my wife hard and rough, and she takes it all eagerly.

Elena contracts around me suddenly, an unexpected orgasm washing over her, and I lose control. I drop my forehead to hers and smile as I wait for Elena to catch her breath.

"That was amazing," she whispers.

I chuckle. "Baby, we're only just getting started."

CHAPTER 18

lena

I walk into my mother's new hospital room, if you can even call it that. I'm in shock as I look around. The room she's in is huge and luxurious, resembling a hotel room instead of a hospital room, yet it has every bit of medical equipment my mother could need.

I knew Alexander would take good care of her, but this is beyond my wildest expectations.

"Hi, Mom," I whisper, sitting down next to her. I glance around, my heart filling to the brim with gratefulness, happiness. She's still here, she's still alive. All thanks to my husband. It feels strange to even think of him that way, but that's what he is now. My husband. I grab my mother's hand and press a kiss to it. "I've missed you."

Part of me still expects her to one day smile and tell me she missed me too. It's getting harder for me to remember the sound of her voice, the sound of her laughter.

"There's something that I've got to tell you," I say carefully.

Throughout the years I've always spoken to her the way I would if she were awake, because part of me genuinely believes that she can hear me, that our conversations help.

"I... I got married," I say. "I married Alexander Kennedy, remember him? He's Sofia's son. Do you remember your friend Sofia? I'll bring her to see you soon. Alexander... he's managed to move you to the Kennedy's private facility, so you can have guests now. There's no rule here about only immediate family coming to see you. I think it might be nice for you to see Sofia again, don't you think?"

I smile at her, feeling anxious somehow. I don't want her to find out I married Alexander because of her. She'd be heartbroken if she knew I did that for her. "I know it sounds a little sudden, but it wasn't. He's very good to me. It'd been a few years when Alexander and I ran into each other again, and he didn't even recognize me, you know? But there were sparks, Mom. Things moved a bit quickly between us, I know... but I'm happy, Mom. He's changed a lot since you last saw him, and I wonder what you'll think of him."

The door opens behind me, and I look up in surprise. "I thought I'd find you here," Lucian says. I rise to my feet when he walks up to me, his eyes on my mother.

"Hi, Sarah," he says, blowing my mother a kiss. I smile, my heart warming at the gesture. I love that he didn't just ignore her.

"What are you doing here?"

His smile drops, and he sighs. "I need to talk to you," he says.

I glance at my mother and nod, leading him out of her room, the door falling closed behind us.

"I know what my brother is like, Elena," he says, "and I know what you're like. He probably guilt-tripped you into marrying him, and you probably felt like you owe him and agreed."

Lucian looks pained and hesitates before he continues. "You don't owe us anything. Do you really think my mother wouldn't help one of her oldest friends? No matter how many years have passed, or how much we might have grown apart, your mother and mine were childhood friends, just like we were. We'll be there for you unconditionally."

Though his words ring true, I can't help but feel guilty nonetheless. Lucian runs a hand through his hair and sighs. "I know what you're like. I know you'll feel indebted to us, and you'll want to repay us somehow. I'm sure my brother convinced you that marriage is the best way to do that, but I assure you, it's not. Divorce is not an option in our family. You would literally be exchanging your life for money that we won't even miss. It's not a fair exchange."

I smile at him, grateful for his thoughtfulness. "I know you're worried about me, and I love you for it. But I know what I'm doing, Luce," I say, his old nickname escaping my lips without a second thought. "Though the amount of money we're talking about might not mean much to you, it's literally the difference between life and death for my mother, and the difference between being homeless or not for me. All Alexander asked for in return is that I marry him."

Lucian shakes his head ruefully. "You don't understand, princess. My brother... he isn't who he used to be. You won't be happy being married to him. I know what your heart is like, and my brother will destroy it. If you think you need to marry into the family to repay us, then marry me instead."

"Luce, like you said, divorce isn't an option in your family. You and I could never be together. You know it would never work. Do you really want to trap both of us in such a marriage?

We'd just end up resenting each other. Besides... it's too late now. Alexander and I... we signed the papers."

The look in Lucian's eyes breaks my heart. He looks so torn, and I know he wishes things were different between us.

"Why? Why would you shackle yourself to him? I'd give you freedom, Elena. I'd support you one hundred percent with whatever you do. I'd take care of you and your mom, and I'd give you the freedom to love whoever you choose."

I shake my head. "Do you hear what you're saying, Luce? We'd just be unhappy together. If not that, we'd at most be somewhat content. It would destroy what's left of our friendship. What do you think it'll do to your mother? And what about children and intimacy? Can you even see yourself sleeping with me?"

Lucian looks away and we both fall silent. "I can't believe you went through with the marriage without taking the time to think it through, princess. I know you don't view it as a sustainable solution, but I'd have been more than happy to give you an interest-free loan."

I sigh and shake my head. "Luce..." I say, my voice soft. "It's done now. There's no point in regretting this. I've made my choice, and I'll live with it."

Lucian's words have me second guessing myself, though. Did I rush into it when I chose to marry Alexander? Should I have taken more time to consider what the ramifications of my choice would really be? Perhaps I should have just taken a loan from Lucian. I'm honest enough with myself to admit that part of me agreeing to marry Alexander stems from the torch I've always carried for him. But will my childish infatuation lead me to waste away my life in a loveless marriage?

CHAPTER 19

lena

I lie in bed by myself, unable to fall asleep. I don't even know what time Alexander will be home tonight.

Outside of the bedroom we don't talk—there are no texts, no phone calls. I have no idea what his days even look like.

Even now that I'm married, I fall asleep alone almost every night. My heart aches as I think of everything I wanted out of life. A happy family of my own that would be nothing like my own family. Children that would be loved beyond compare. A husband that adores me.

I saved my mother's life, but I gave up my own in return. I have no regrets. If given the choice, I'd do it all over again—but that doesn't mean that I don't mourn the dreams I'm giving up on. It doesn't mean I don't wonder what I might be missing out on.

I turn around in bed, my eyes falling to Alexander's pillow. How is it possible to experience heartbreak over something I've never had?

The door opens and I sit up in surprise, the sheets falling to my waist. Alexander doesn't even notice me as he walks in, his eyes on his phone.

I slip out of bed and walk toward him. He glances up and pauses, his eyes roaming over my body.

"Alexander, you're home."

He nods and takes a step closer to me, bridging the remaining distance between us. He brushes my hair behind my ear, an unreadable expression on his face. "You're still awake."

I nod. "Couldn't sleep."

We've been married for a week now, but we've barely spent any time together. Alexander comes home after I fall asleep, and he's up before I am.

"How was your day?" I ask.

He frowns. "Long."

I nod. "You look tired."

He runs a hand through his hair and sighs. "I am. My cousin, Dylan, is fucking useless. I'm always doing twice as much work as I should be doing. I'm sick and tired of cleaning up his messes."

He pulls his tie off and inhales deeply.

"Hmm," I say, trying to think of a way to lighten his mood. He and I will be stuck together for the rest of our lives, and we had a rocky start, to say the least. I won't hurt to be nice, to be civil. "Tell me three good things that happened to you today?"

Alexander looks at me, his expression making me freeze.

"Elena, what is this?"

I blink, surprised. "I... what do you mean?"

"What's with the small talk?"

I bite down on my lip, suddenly annoyed. "Just trying to cheer you up. You seem stressed."

He shakes his head. "Didn't we agree you wouldn't interfere with my private life? This isn't a real marriage, Elena."

My heart twists painfully even as my anger rises. "You had no issue with me asking that question at Inferno."

He takes a step closer to me and buries his hand in my hair, his face close to mine. "I didn't know who you were at Inferno. Back then you were just a pretty girl that caught my eye. I didn't know that you're *Matthew's* sister," he says, his voice low. "Now? Now I own you. I told you the day before you married me that you'd be selling yourself to me the way you would at Vaughn's, didn't I?"

I nod, my heart racing, nervous jitters running down my spine. I know what I signed up for, yet I foolishly hoped Alexander and I would be able to enjoy each other's company the way we did at Inferno.

"It's not your mind you were selling at Vaughn's, Elena. It was your body. That's all I want from you."

He traces the straps of my nightgown with his fingers, and my heart starts to race.

"You want to cheer me up?"

I glare at him, but all that does is make him smile. Alexander pushes the straps off my shoulders and leans in as my nightgown falls to the floor, his lips brushing against mine once, twice, before he finally takes my lips. His hand wraps around my waist and he pulls me flush against him. He kisses me, taking his time, until I finally melt against him. A soft moan involuntarily escapes my lips and I rise to my tiptoes, deepening the kiss.

By the time he pulls away, we're both breathing hard. He grabs my hands and places them against his chest, his eyes on mine.

I obey his silent order and unbutton his shirt, my arousal increasing with every button I undo. His shirt falls open and I trace his abs with my fingers, enjoying the way he tenses underneath my touch. He thinks he's got so much power over me, but he craves my touch just as much as I do his.

Alexander smiles and lifts me into his arms, carrying me back to bed as if I weigh nothing. He places me down gently, his eyes on mine as he finishes undressing. He's watching me, enjoying the desire I don't bother to hide.

He leans in, his fingers hooking around my panties. "Up," he orders, and I raise my hips for him as he tugs them off. Alexander grins at me as he raises the lace fabric to his face, inhaling deeply.

"Fucking delicious, Elena."

He lets my panties drop to the floor and joins me in bed, holding himself up above me. He lowers his lips to mine and I thread my hand through his hair, pulling him closer. He smiles as he lowers himself on top of me, his body flush against mine.

A small moan escapes my lips when he kisses me, and I pull on his hair, wanting more. Alexander chuckles and moves his lips to my neck, kissing me in places I didn't even realize were sensitive.

He strokes my inner thigh, teasing me, and I moan when he finally touches me where I want him. "So wet and slippery," he says, pulling his fingers back. He grins at me as he brings them to his lips, tasting me. "I knew you'd be as delicious as you smell."

I wrap my leg around his hip, wanting more, wanting him closer, and he smiles. "So hungry for my cock, baby. If anyone saw you right now, they'd think I starve you."

He lines himself up and pushes in just a little, making me whimper. "Alexander," I whisper. I push my hips up, trying to get him in deeper, and he smiles.

He pushes into me slowly, inch by inch, taking his time. I moan in delight when he's finally deep inside me, and he drops his forehead to mine.

He fucks me slowly, the long deep strokes driving me half insane, and he knows it. I pull on his hair and he chuckles as he grabs my hands, pinning them above my head.

"Has no one ever told you that patience is a virtue, baby?"

He pulls back almost all the way and slams into me, pinning my wrists down with his weight as he does so. "Patience is overrated," I tell him, and he smiles.

"Looks like I'll need to teach you a lesson."

He slows the pace down even further, teasing me with every stroke. "Can you come for me just like this, baby? Let's find out."

He pushes into me slowly, stimulating something deep inside me every time he does so. I feel the pressure building inside me, and I'm impatient for more.

"Please, stop teasing me," I moan, my voice husky.

He looks into my eyes and smiles as he continues to tease me. "You're a little slut for my cock, aren't you? Look at you. Look how desperate you are to come on my dick."

I swallow hard, trying my hardest to hold on, but I can feel my control slipping.

"Come for me, Elena."

He pulls out almost all the way and pushes into me hard, taking me right over the edge. "Oh God," I moan, pleasure washing over me, wave after wave. My muscles contract around him over and over again, and his forehead drops to mine.

"Good girl," he whispers. He increases the pace, thrusting into me hard and fast, his eyes on mine when he comes.

He collapses on top of me and turns us over so I'm lying in his arms, both of us panting. He wraps his arms around me, holding me tightly.

I listen to his heartbeat as mine slowly returns to normal. My eyes start to feel heavy and my breathing evens out. Right before I fall asleep, I hear him speak, his voice barely above a whisper.

"A new acquisition, the sun streaming in from my office window, and having you in my bed."

CHAPTER 20

lena

"Let me see?" Sofia says.

I hold my hand up excitedly, admiring my own nails.

"They did a great job," she says, and I nod. I can't even remember the last time I was this pampered. Sofia arranged an entire spa day for the two of us. We got massages together, followed by hair and nail appointments. It's been incredibly nice, but more than that, I've missed this feeling—the feeling of spending an entire day with a mother figure. There's nothing like it.

"Thank you," I tell her.

She smiles at me and shakes her head, her hand in mine. "Darling, you're my daughter-in-law now. It's my job to spoil you."

She brushes my hair behind my ear, a huge grin on her face. I've noticed that more often than not, she's lost in thought at home, a sad expression on her face. But not today. She's enjoyed today as much as I have.

"Alec explained that you two will be staging your relationship for my father and the press? You know that won't be easy, right?"

I nod nervously. "I know," I murmur. "But we don't really have another choice. He and I... we got together too suddenly. Alexander is worried his grandfather won't buy it."

Sofia nods. "He wouldn't be wrong. I love my father, but he's a sly fox. Best to tread carefully. If he so much as suspects that you two aren't in love with each other, he'll give his position as chairman to Alec's cousin. Alec has worked far too hard for that to happen."

I nod thoughtfully. "Don't worry," I tell her. "We'll be fine."

Sofia smiles at me, her eyes twinkling. "Yes, I think you will be."

Our bodyguard opens the door to the restaurant for us, and Sofia sighs as we walk in. "I hate these charity lunches," she tells me. "I'd much rather just donate some money and leave. But unfortunately, we need to show our faces. I do believe it's a good opportunity for you to get reacquainted with some of the people you lost touch with. Connections are a Kennedy's most valuable asset, and you'll need to start making some of your own."

I nod at her nervously. Sofia smiles at me reassuringly and grabs my hand, squeezing tightly. "I'm here," she tells me. "You're no longer alone, Elena."

I sit down next to Sofia, feeling out of place. There's a blonde sitting next to me that I've never seen before, and I smile at her, trying my best to portray confidence and failing badly.

She grins and sticks her hand out. The gesture is so different from the air kisses I'm used to that I'm startled, in the best way.

"Emilia," she says, her smile genuine and friendly, unlike the ones I'm used to in these circles.

I shake her hand and nod politely. "Elena."

Sofia smiles and leans in. "Emilia is Carter Clarke's wife. They don't live here, but when Emilia is in town, she usually joins us for lunch. Emilia and Carter have founded many charitable organizations, and Emilia is always trying to make a difference. I think you'll really like her."

Emilia winks at me. "Carter is the Fintech guy," she says, referring to her husband.

I look at her with wide eyes. "Oh! His company recently branched out into medical research, and the findings have been astounding. I looked into it for my mother, but I..."

My heart sinks. There was no way I could even get in touch with Carter Clarke, much less gain access to some of his technology.

Emilia looks into my eyes, her gaze searching, and then she smiles. She reaches into her purse and slides a card my way. "This is my husband's direct line. Call him and tell him I told you to get in touch with him. Whatever you need, he'll get to you."

I stare at the card, hope filling my heart. Alexander is already trying to fly in some of the best doctors in the world, but this might help too. This might help my mother. I clutch the card tightly, my heart racing.

The room suddenly falls silent and I look up in surprise to find Jennifer walking in. She frowns when she sees me sitting here and walks over, tensing when she realizes Sofia is seated next to me. Everyone all at once starts to congratulate Jennifer on her engagement, and she blushes. "Oh," she says. "We were trying to keep that a secret."

I just about keep from rolling my eyes. From what I understand, she's been telling anyone that would listen.

I sit back as she answers questions about her upcoming wedding, and about what married life might be like. She glances at Sofia and grins.

"No one knows more about happy marriages than Sofia Kennedy," she says, nodding at my mother-in-law. "Tell us, how do you stay happy throughout so many years? It's been what? Over thirty years?"

Sofia tenses, and Jennifer doesn't give her a chance to reply.

"That reminds me, where is Mr. Kennedy, anyway? Another business trip?"

The room falls silent, and my heart aches for Sofia. I long suspected it, but having been away from everyone for so long, I couldn't be sure. It looks like Mr. Kennedy straying is an open secret, though.

"Forget marriage," I say. "I want to hear more about the engagement. You know, my brother never even told me how you two met. Tell us all about it. When did you fall for my brother?" I say, knowing full well that she cheated on Alexander, and everyone else knows it too.

Jennifer blushes, her eyes flashing angrily. She starts to reply, but I turn away from her, not interested in her story.

Sofia grabs my hand underneath the table and squeezes in gratitude. When I look at her, the same lost expression I've gotten used to is back on her face, and it breaks my heart.

She wears that same sad smile throughout the rest of lunch, and by the time we walk out, she's absentminded and resigned. We walk in silence, our bodyguard trailing behind us.

"You're my daughter-in-law now, Elena," she says. "So it's only fair that you know—everyone else does. It's only my two sons that think I'm unaware. They try to protect me from the truth as best as they can, but there's no escaping this."

She sits down on one of the benches by the road, and I sit down next to her.

"I married for love, much like your mother did," she tells me. "But Anthony was different. My father didn't approve, not initially. You see, Anthony was from a very poor family, and his parents were divorced. Two things my father frowns upon."

She sighs and runs a hand through her hair, ruining her ever perfect hair-do.

"But I was in love, so all of my father's arguments fell on deaf ears. Eventually, I wore him down. It took me close to a year, but my father allowed me to marry Anthony—provided that he take the Kennedy name, and that our children do, too."

She inhales shakily, and I grab her hand.

"When I think back to it, I can't remember us ever being happy once we got married. Anthony felt emasculated and indebted, and he resented me for it. Our marriage went downhill very quickly. The money, the pressure, the glitz and glamour. Anthony reveled in it, but our marriage suffered for it."

I take her hand, my heart breaking for her. "So why do you stay?"

The look in her eyes tears me apart. "Kennedys don't divorce," she tells me. "Asking for one means getting disowned. But sometimes... sometimes I wonder if it might be better. I see the damage that witnessing my marriage did to Alec. He tries so hard to protect me, but in doing so, he's hurting himself. His father's affairs combined with what Jennifer did to him... it's made him lose faith in love. He doesn't think it can last. He's come to view it as a weakness, and that's largely my fault."

A tear runs down her cheek and she catches it with her thumb, inhaling shakily, trying her hardest to pull herself together.

She looks at me, smiling through her tears. "Elena, my son's heart is broken, and it has been for a very long time. Maybe it's damaged beyond repair, but maybe, just maybe, it takes the right touch."

CHAPTER 21

lexander

Elena walks into the bar I asked her to meet me at and I sit back, watching her from afar. She's wearing a red dress that at once looks fucking sexy on her, yet perfectly appropriate. Her eyes find mine, and she smiles, drawing attention to her red lips.

I told Elena to meet me here so we can start getting the rumor mill going about us. I'm certain someone will attempt to take a photo of us, so I told her to dress up. I didn't expect her to look this beautiful, though.

We've been married for two weeks now, and we've gotten into a routine of sorts. I was worried that she'd be needy, that she'd promise me one thing and demand another, but that hasn't been the case. She's kept out of my way without me having to remind her of her promises, and she's been keeping my mother company when I can't be around. She's been the perfect daughter-in-law, and she's been an even more perfect wife, spreading those beautiful long legs for me without complaint, without any drama. She agreed to give me her body, and she's done just that, without demanding my time outside of bed.

Elena walks up to me, and I'm not the only one that notices her. I watch as at least a handful of men follow her with their eyes, but she doesn't even notice it. Most women I know revel in the attention, but not Elena. She's looking at me.

I rise from my seat as she reaches our table, my arm wrapping around her as soon as she's within reach. I pull her into me, my lips finding hers. Elena is startled and freezes, but then she melts against me, her arms finding their way around my neck. I don't pull away until she's breathless, her lipstick smeared.

She looks into my eyes, our arms still wrapped around each other, and I smirk. I love that flustered expression of hers. Making her blush has become one of my favorite activities.

"Hi," she says, sounding a little breathless.

"Hi."

Elena's lips tip up in a smile and she brings her thumb to my lips, wiping away the lipstick she doubtlessly left. "Red looks good on you."

I smile at her teasing tone. "It does. You should try leaving it on the rest of my body too."

Her cheeks redden, and I chuckle as I pull away from her. Elena takes a seat, tensing when she realizes all eyes are on us.

"This is the best place to create some rumors about us. It's the place to see and be seen. That kiss was the perfect start." She nods, her cheeks tinged red as I pull my chair closer to her. "It won't take long for people to start gossiping."

Elena orders a cosmopolitan and I lean back with a whiskey in hand. "You look nervous."

She looks up at me and shakes her head. "No... I... maybe a little? It's been a long time since I moved in these circles."

I lean in and trap her chin between my thumb and index finger. "You'll need to act natural. You're playing the role of my girlfriend right now, and soon, you'll be known as my wife. I need confidence, borderline arrogance. Right now, you aren't merely my *possession*, Elena. During these little acts of ours, you're my equal, the only person who has any rights to me." My words only make her more nervous, and I smile as I lean in closer. "Kiss me," I order.

Elena hesitates, and then she threads her hand through my hair, pulling me closer. Her lips find mine and her hand cups the side of my face. She kisses me softly, deeply, her tongue making me wonder what her lips will feel like wrapped around my cock. By the time she's done with me, I'm rock hard.

Elena smiles knowingly when she pulls away, and I shake my head. I grab her hand and place it over my bulge, enjoying the way her eyes widen. "I told you to kiss me—not to fuck my mouth with yours. Don't make me drag you into the restrooms. I'll have you on your knees and I *will* fuck your mouth. I'll watch you leave red lipstick rings on my cock. I'll show you just how good red looks on me."

Elena licks her lips, and I almost give into temptation right here and now. "That was meant to be a threat, baby. Don't look so excited."

She laughs and sits back, pulling away from me with a satisfied look in her eyes. Elena Rousseau... she's an enigma.

I lean back, my eyes roaming over the room, settling on a girl that looks vaguely familiar. Isn't she one of Jennifer's friends? I look away and take a sip of my drink, hiding my smile behind my glass.

"Hey, I wanted to thank you," Elena says, her voice soft.

I look at her with raised brows.

"I know we have a mutually beneficial agreement, but even so, I... I'd have lost my mother if not for you." She swallows hard, an anguished expression on her face. Elena blinks and forces her lips into a smile. "You saved her life, and you saved mine."

I push her hair behind her ear and shake my head. "I did no such thing. *You* saved your mother's life. As for yours... your life I *bought*."

I expected my words to wound her, to remind her that I'm not doing her any favors, that she's paying a hefty price for her mother's life. But Elena merely smiles, her expression serene.

"Yes," she says. "But I'd rather belong to you than be at Vaughn's."

The thought of her there infuriates me. Had I come in just a few minutes later, who knows what might have happened to her? John would have had her naked, his hands over her body. Who fucking knows how he might have touched her, what he'd have made her do.

I cup the back of her neck, my thumb on her throat. I almost walked away from her. When I saw her standing there, when I realized that she'd deceived me, *fuck*. I almost left her there, and Vaughn would have let his members use every part of her body. Because of me. Because he thought he'd be avenging me.

"You're mine now, Elena. No one is touching you but me."

I lean in and kiss her, her full bottom lip caught between mine. A soft sigh escapes her lips when I pull away, her throat moving against my thumb as she swallows.

"No one touches what's mine, Elena. No one will even dare think of you, dream of you. You belong to *me* now, and I don't share."

CHAPTER 22

lexander

I groan as I turn off my computer. This work day has taken far too long—it's nearly 10pm. My phone buzzes just as I'm finally on my way home, and I unlock it with a sigh, assuming it's more work waiting for me. Instead, I find a text message from the last person I expected to hear from.

Jen: *I think I made a mistake, Alec. I miss you so much. Please, can we talk?*

I stare at my phone in disbelief, my heart twisting painfully. How dare she text me after all this time? She's engaged to fucking Matthew Rousseau. She's marrying him on the day she was supposed to marry *me*. What the fuck does she mean *she misses me*? I guess rumors about Elena and me reached her ears. I know what Jennifer is like—even if she doesn't want me, she won't want anyone else to have me either.

I clench my phone in my hand, sorrow filling my heart. She fucking broke me, and now she has the gall to text me? The worst thing is that my first instinct is to text her back. To ask her if she's okay. If something happened. If she needs me.

But I'm no longer the person who fulfils that role. I'm not the person she chose.

I'm absentminded and angry as I walk into my bedroom. Elena sits up in my bed, and I freeze, feeling guilty as hell all of a sudden. When Jen texted me, for just a couple of seconds, I forgot I even got married.

Elena smiles at me, and my heart wrenches. She looks so fucking beautiful sitting in my bed like that, the sheets at her waist and her sexy silk nightgown on display. "Hey, you're home," she says.

I nod and force a smile onto my face. Elena Rousseau... I married Matthew's sister for a reason, so why haven't I made use of her yet? Why haven't I thrown her in Matthew and Jennifer's face yet? Part of me wants to keep her hidden, keep her here in my home, where she's safe from the press, the rumors, the pressures she'll face as my wife. But I can't. I didn't marry her to protect her. I married her so I could use her. So I could use her as a weapon against Matthew, as a shield against my grandfather's terms.

My eyes roam over her face. She's so damn beautiful, and she looks so fucking innocent. But then again, she knew what she was getting into by marrying me. I've never made her false promises.

I start to unbutton my shirt and pause when I feel her gaze on me. I look up to find Elena staring at me, a sweet smile on her face. There's not even a hint of ruthlessness in her eyes, only innocence. She might have known what she was getting into, but she didn't have much of a choice, and I bet she underestimated how hard life would be as a Kennedy—as my wife.

I sigh and walk out of view to undress before walking into the shower. I press the water curtain button, obscuring myself. Water pours down on top of me, and I lean back against the wall.

If I hadn't married Elena, what would I have done? Would I be going running to Jen right now? And if I did, would it matter? I've spent months missing her and hating her, wanting her. Now that she's finally reached out, I'm in no position to even reply.

I close my eyes as memories assail me. I fucking loved Jennifer with all my heart. I never used to believe in marriage, considering what my parents' marriage looks like. I don't even know a single happily married couple, and I wanted no part of that. But then there was Jen. She was merely one of my employees when we met, but she became everything to me. She was different. She saw life through different eyes, and she taught me to enjoy the little things in life in a way I'd never done before. I still don't know if it was all a sham, if any of it was ever real.

My mood is ruined as I get out of the shower. I can barely even face Elena. My conscience is weighing heavily on me tonight. I've got Elena in my bed, but it's Jennifer that's on my mind. It should be my wife that I'm focused on, but all I can think about is whether Jen is okay.

The way Elena looks at me as I walk towards the bed wearing nothing more than boxers would usually have me rock hard already, but today all it does is increase the guilt I feel. The thought of using her makes me feel filthy. I lie down in bed and grab my tablet, using it to close the curtains and turn off the main lights.

"That's impressive."

I smile tightly and turn onto my side to look at her, propping my head up on my elbow.

"How was your day?" she asks, her voice soft.

I turn to look at her. That smile of hers, no matter what happens, no matter what I say... it rarely wavers. I didn't think she'd dare make small talk after the way I reprimanded her the first time, but she acts like my viciousness doesn't affect her, like it amuses her.

"Tiring. Yours?"

Her smile widens, and my heart wrenches. "I went to see my mom this afternoon. I haven't had a chance to say this to you, but her new room is perfect, the new facility is amazing."

I nod. "I'm glad to hear it. I'm flying in a few renowned physicians that might be able to help her. Apparently, Carter Clarke's wife convinced him to loan us one of the doctors his company employs. I don't want to get your hopes up yet, but I want you to know I'll do whatever I can to assist your mother's recovery."

The way she smiles at me, the trust and hope in her eyes, it guts me. When she married me, she had no choice. She's not in this for selfish reasons, she married me to save her mother's life. Can I really use someone with motivations that pure?

"Thank you," she says, her eyes filled with genuine gratitude.

I nod at her. "Elena, we'll need to stage our first few proper dates within the next few weeks. We'll be portraying a whirlwind relationship and a lavish engagement and wedding. Are you ready?"

She nods, her expression turning serious. "Of course, Alexander."

"I'll take you to see my grandfather soon. By now he should've heard some rumors about us, and he'll have heard that you've been seen with my mother in various places, so he'll know I'm serious about you. There isn't much that escapes him. He doesn't like hearing about things relating to us through the press, so I'm going to introduce you to him as my girlfriend before photos of us reach the tabloids. He adored you when you were little, so there's a good chance he'll be happy for us."

Elena nods, her expression serious. I hate how mechanical this all feels, but our marriage is a sham, and it always will be. It's best that Elena gets used to it now.

CHAPTER 23

lexander

"Are you ready?" I ask, glancing over Elena's outfit. She's wearing a formal classy dress today, looking like an executive of some sort—like a Kennedy. "You look perfect."

Elena smiles at me, but the way she keeps touching her dress betrays her nerves. She follows me to my Aston Martin, her brows rising.

"Didn't you say we were going to your grandpa's?" she asks, looking around. "I thought all Kennedys live on the same estate."

I smile and open the door for her. "We do, but the Kennedy estate is massive. This is just my mother's mansion," I say, tipping my head towards our house. It's imposing all on its own.

"My grandfather had his estate built so that each of his siblings and all of their kids would have their own space. It's essentially an entire private neighborhood, so while this is all still private property, it takes about eight minutes to drive to my grandfather's house. There's no way we're walking that far."

She looks around in awe and shakes her head. I forget that the only mansion she's ever been to is ours.

"If we ever have children, we'd probably move to a mansion of our own. Traditionally we'd move into a new property on the estate when we get married, but I don't like the idea of leaving my mother by herself. Lucian isn't home often, and when he is, he prefers to stay in his room. My mother doesn't do very well when she's alone for long stretches of time." I sigh and run a hand through my hair. "She's fallen into depression a few times now, and it worries me. It doesn't matter how much staff we have, how many people surround her—it doesn't stave off the loneliness that she pretends not to feel."

Elena nods, her expression pained. "I understand," she says. "Besides, it does feel like we have our own apartment within her mansion, which I guess, we technically do. Your mother doesn't ever even drop by when you're home, so I don't think moving out would make much of a difference. I actually enjoy having dinner with her whenever you have to work late. I think I'd miss that a lot."

I breathe a sigh of relief. Jen always insisted on us moving out. She wanted an entire mansion of our own—just having one floor in my mother's residence was never enough for her.

I glance at Elena, my heart stirring. She's such an amazing woman, and here I am, driving to my grandfather in an effort to use her. I tighten my grip on my steering wheel, feeling conflicted.

My grandfather looks up when Elena and I walk in, and I frown at him. He's on his knees on the floor, a large plant pot in front of him, his hands covered with soil.

"Come help me with this, Alec," he barks out.

Elena and I walk over, and I sigh. My grandfather is always

up to something. Why can't the old man just rest every once in a while?

"Grandpa," I say. "This is Elena Rousseau, my girlfriend. You've met her before, when she was much younger. Do you remember her?"

My grandfather barely glances up at Elena, and I tense. Jennifer always hated being rebuffed, but Elena merely smiles and drops to her knees. She sticks her hands into the soil and helps my grandfather repot his orchids.

"The leaves are too dark," she says, a finger tracing the edge of the stem. "When they're this dark, it means they aren't getting enough sunlight. Orchids are a little moody," she adds, laughing.

My grandfather pauses and looks up at her in surprise. He glances at her soil-stained hands and clothes, a smile tugging at the edge of his lips. I bet he expected that she wouldn't get her hands dirty, that she'd be too worried about her clothes.

Elena doesn't even realize she's being tested. Damn this old man. I bet he's been expecting us since the very second we stepped into the car.

"You know about orchids?"

Elena nods. "They're my mother's favorite. We used to have so many in our house."

She touches the edge of the white flowers, a sad smile on her face. The longing in her eyes breaks my heart.

"Orchids are a little peculiar," she says. "They love the morning sun, but they want to be in the shade for the rest of the day. Moody little plants, I tell you."

She glances around and points out a corner of the room. "That should be the perfect spot," she tells my grandfather. "That angle should give them the morning sun they so love, but once the sun moves, they should be covered in shadows."

Elena and I help my grandfather move the pot to the corner she pointed out, and my grandfather smiles.

"Come on," he tells her. "I'll show you my greenhouse."

I groan inwardly, but Elena actually looks excited as she follows him.

"Oh my God," Elena says, walking over to the vines on the wall. "Melons?"

She glances at my grandfather and shakes her head. "You sure do like a challenge, don't you, Mr. Kennedy? These are so hard to grow!"

He smiles at her and tips his head toward the rest of his crops. "You can call me Grandpa," he says, and my eyes widen. Elena has no idea what he's just offered her, and she smiles cluelessly. Everyone is always trying to gain access to my grandfather, and he notoriously keeps everyone at a distance. *Grandpa* is reserved for his own grandchildren only, not their spouses, not any distant cousins.

He wraps his arm around Elena, showing her every single one of his vegetables, and my heart nearly stops when he starts to create a basket for Elena to take home. The only one that's ever walked out of this greenhouse with any of his babies is my mother. Not even my uncles have managed it, neither have I, and I've tried many times.

"Oh, this is amazing," Elena says, her eyes twinkling with delight. "I can just imagine how good this is going to taste. How about I make lunch for you soon, Grandpa?"

I frown. My grandfather doesn't eat anything that isn't made by his own cook. He doesn't even go to restaurants. The only person whose food he'll eat, other than his cook, is my mother's.

"I'd love to," he says, and I stare at him with raised brows—not that he notices, all his attention is on Elena.

I've brought Jennifer over a handful of times, and each time he acted like she didn't exist. I wonder if it's because she wasn't the type of person he wanted for me, but then again, he let my mother marry my father.

I grab my phone and pull up Jen's text messages. She's been contacting me more and more frequently since rumors about Elena and me started to spread. I can't figure her out. Does she want me now that she thinks she's truly lost me? Or did she realize that being with Matthew isn't all she thought it would be? I don't know, and each day, I'm more tempted to text her back. I want answers.

"Tell me your favorite dishes," Elena says, and I look up at her. She and my grandfather are lost in conversation. I stand back as the two of them talk, discussing recipes and ingredients. I can't help but think about Jennifer. Would she ever even consider offering to cook for my grandfather? I don't even recall her ever offering to cook for *me*. I shake my head and snap out of it.

"I look forward to it," my grandfather says, his smile genuine.

Elena glances at her soil-stained hands and brushes them against each other, trying to get them clean. Grandpa points out the sink at the back of the greenhouse, and she walks off with a smile, promising to return soon.

I cross my arms and glance at my grandfather. I expected him to drop the sweet-old-man act the second she walked away, but instead, he's still smiling, his eyes twinkling.

"She's a nice girl, Alec. Very kind. I'm old, son. I'm old enough to know, to see how genuine she is. She's the type of person I want raising my great-grandchildren. You've chosen well. Now don't fuck it up. You let her slip away, and you'll regret it for the rest of your life."

I nod, my gaze trailing towards Elena. "Yes," I tell him. "I know."

CHAPTER 24

lena

I wake up with my head on Alexander's bare chest and snuggle closer. He's got one arm wrapped around me, and I bury my nose against his neck.

I smile at the memory of last night. He came to bed late last night, waking me up with countless kisses on my skin. The way touched me... he's both rough and tender with me at the same time.

Most days he's gone by the time I wake up, but every once in a while, I wake up in his arms. I love those moments right before he wakes up, those moments when he'll hold me close, when he makes me feel cherished. Those moments make our marriage more bearable—they help me forget that what we have isn't real.

"Your hair tickles."

I freeze in his arms, my entire body tense. I push away from him, but he won't let me go. Instead, he pulls me closer. I blink, turning my head just a little. He's got his phone in his hand, scrolling through his emails leisurely, his other hand on my waist.

"Let's go on a dinner date tonight. I think it's time we start making front page news."

I nod, slightly nervous at the thought. Alexander and I don't see each other much outside of our bed, and we barely talk during the day. Going on a date with him, no matter how well orchestrated, makes me nervous.

"You need a ring too. Meet me at the Kennedy Mall later. It's where our family jeweler is located, and we can go try the new Michelin starred restaurant on the top floor too. Perfect location to stage a date."

I blink, feeling somewhat out of place. The Kennedy Mall houses some of the world's most expensive brands, and I haven't even set foot in there for years now. It's silly, but I feel somewhat intimidated. I feel like a fraud. Like everything might come crashing down on me soon.

"All right," I say, pushing away my doubts. I lift my face, my lips brushing against his throat. "You also need a ring."

He tightens his grip on me when I kiss his neck. "Then you'd better bring that black card I gave you."

I pause, remembering the black card that Alexander gave me along with a new phone and other electronics. I recognized it straight away. Only ten are issued globally, and I distinctly remember my father applying for it every year throughout my childhood, and every year his application was rejected. I haven't dared to use the card. I've barely even dared to look at it.

Part of me finds it exhilarating to have access to something so exclusive, but a bigger part of me resents that I'm unable to provide for myself and my loved ones the way I used to. I never wanted to be the type of woman that depends on a man, and look at me now. Not only do I depend on Alexander, but my mother's life is in his hands too.

Alexander lets go of me and slips out of bed, getting ready for his day. It's rare for us to spend any time together in the mornings, and I shamelessly watch him get dressed. He smirks at me knowingly as he walks out, and I'm still smiling as I get ready myself.

My smile is wiped off my face the second I look in the mirror and see the kiss mark Alexander must have left on my neck last night. I blush scarlet, my mind drifting back to the way he held me, the way he touched me.

I grab a scarf that could easily pay for at least a day's worth of hospital bills and sigh as I cover up the mark on my neck, transforming myself into the prim and proper wife Alexander asked for. I stare at my reflection, surprised at what I'm seeing. For the first time in years, I don't look overworked and stressed out. I don't look exhausted and *sad*. I look a lot more like I used to.

I grab the bag my mother got me shortly before her accident and frown at it. The edges are worn, and it's discolored from the lack of maintenance, but it's the last thing she ever gave me, and I never had the heart to sell it. Not that I'd get much for it—my mother had my name embossed inside it, so I doubt I'd ever be able to sell it anyway. Now that I can finally afford it, I'll need to get it restored. I should be able to do that after visiting my mother.

My day flies by, and I check my watch as I walk into the Kennedy Mall. I ended up spending more time with my mother than I planned to, but I still ended up getting here early, with enough time to enquire about my bag. I hesitate just slightly in front of the store, feeling entirely out of place. I no longer feel like I belong here. After struggling with bills for so many years, spending an outrageous amount of money on material things doesn't make any sense anymore. I glance down at my bag, and my heart wrenches. I still remember the smile on my mother's face when she gave it to me. Usually there's a waiting list of several years for this particular bag, but not for my mother. No, she had this one custom made for my birthday, and I'd been so ecstatic.

I inhale deeply before walking into the store. The store assistants smile at me, and I nod politely, feeling oddly nervous. "Hi," I murmur, placing my bag on the counter awkwardly. "I'd like to enquire about getting this bag serviced. Do you think that'd be possible?"

Sharp laughter rings out behind me, and I tense, recognizing my stepsister before I even turn around. "How embarrassing. You can't even afford to just buy a new bag?" Elise says.

I turn to look at her, a forced smile on my face. I should've known there'd be a chance she'd be here. This is her favorite brand, and this is their flagship store. It's the only place to get their newest products, and Elise has been buying at least one thing from this brand weekly for as long as I can remember.

"Elise."

She looks me over and then bursts out laughing. "Look at you. The last time I saw you, you looked like a beggar. Now you're wearing clothes you can't possibly afford. Is this fake?" she asks as she pulls on my scarf, unraveling it.

I clutch it, panicked, but it's too late. She gasps when she sees the kiss mark on my skin, and then she bursts out laughing.

"I see. A sugar daddy, huh? I guess you had no other choice after Dad cut you off. Where'd you go, a gentlemen's club?"

I turn away from her and fix my scarf, my cheeks burning with shame. Her words grate on me, and it hurts to have her confirm my suspicions—she's the one that sent me to Vaughn's. It's my biggest fear come true. If she could get nurse June to hand me that card, then there's much worse she can do, much more she has access to.

Even the sales assistants look embarrassed on my behalf, and I wish I could just sink straight through the floor. "So, the bag," I say, trying my best to remain unaffected. "Can it be fixed?"

Elise laughs. "I can't believe your sugar daddy can't even buy you a new bag. But then again, these are so expensive they're the equivalent of a couple of hospital bills, aren't they? Man, you must be sucking some old wrinkly dick to be able to pay all that."

The sales assistant looks as flustered as I feel and shakes her head. "Damage like this we just can't undo," she says, sounding apologetic. "It's the leather that's damaged beyond repair," she adds, trailing a gloved finger over the tears.

"I see," I murmur. "I... would it be possible to get an identical bag?"

Elise laughs again, the sound grating. "Are you stupid?" she says. "You could never afford a new one. Stop wasting everyone's time."

I turn back towards her, annoyed. "Why are you so concerned about me, anyway? Mind your own damn business."

Elise grins. "Oh, I'm just bored waiting for the staff to bring out the new bags Dad ordered for me. Besides, how could I not be concerned after the way you came to our house the other day, begging for money?"

My heart twists painfully. It's not even the humiliation or everything I've lost—what hurts the most is that my father clearly has the money to buy a bag Elise doesn't need, but he wouldn't spend that same money to save my mother's life.

I'm shaking so hard, and even though I want to come up with a retort, I can't. My throat is closing up, and words escape me.

I'm close to bursting into tears when a strong arm wraps around me. "I'm late, Buttercup, but I'm here now."

CHAPTER 25

lexander

I stand at the entrance of the store, silencing the sales assistant with my finger. I recognize my wife straight away, but unfortunately, I also recognize the woman standing next to her. I stand back, out of view, my focus entirely on Elena.

I listen as Elise accuses her of having a sugar daddy, as she throws Elena's mother's hospital bills in her face. It doesn't escape my notice that she purposely makes it clear that the bags Alaric Rousseau bought for her are of the same value as the hospital bills.

I keep waiting for Elena to stand up for herself, but she doesn't. None of the confidence she has when she resists me is present. She's feistier when she's reminding me that all I own is her body, than she is right now.

She starts to shake, and I walk toward her. Elise's eyes widen when she sees me, but I keep my attention on Elena. "I'm late, Buttercup," I say, wrapping my arm around her. "But I'm here now."

Elena relaxes in my arms and looks up at me in relief. The trust in her eyes... it does funny things to my heart. I tear my eyes away from her and turn toward the sales assistant with raised brows. "Didn't you hear my girl? She asked if you can make her an identical bag."

The sales assistant's eyes widen and she mumbles an apology before rushing off to the computer to process Elena's order. I'm going to need to educate my wife on the treatment she should demand. She's a Kennedy, damn it.

I sigh and grab my phone. "Baby," I tell her. "You don't ever have to talk to mere staff. Especially not in a mall we *own*. You just call the CEO of this brand's company, you hear me? I'd love to see him deny any of your requests. He'll have his stores booted from every Kennedy Mall faster than he can blink."

Elena nods, her eyes moving from me to Elise. I can see Elise posing from the corner of my eyes, and it disgusts me. She's crazy if she thinks she could ever catch my eye.

I turn away to find Elena fidgeting with her scarf. I frown at it and look at her through narrowed eyes. "Trying to hide the damage I did?" I ask. "Who for?"

I pull on the scarf, unraveling it to admire my work. Elena blushes when I put her scarf in my pocket. "Alexander," she murmurs, her cheeks bright red, and I can't help but smile. I love making her blush. She looks so sweet when she does, so disarmed. I lean in and press a lingering kiss to her lips.

"You can't be serious," Elise says. "This... this was all a rumor, wasn't it? You two... you can't..."

Elise's eyes roam over Elena's neck, and I see the annoyance in her eyes. Considering that she just admitted to being the reason my wife ended up at Vaughn's, her days are numbered.

"Who are you even?" I ask Elise, knowing full well who she is.

She looks at me in disbelief. "Elise Rousseau. I'm Elena's sister."

I glance at my wife, anger flashing through her eyes. "You have sisters, babe?"

Elena shakes her head, and I nod. "I didn't think so," I say, before turning back to Elise. "What has the world come to for a mistress's daughter to liken herself to my girl? You must've lost your mind."

The sales assistant returns with a quote, and I shake my head. "Don't bother looking at it," I tell Elena. "Just put your card down, Buttercup. This bag clearly means something to you. It's worth any price." She's a Kennedy now—prices are irrelevant.

Elise smiles. "Oh, Alexander. You do know Dad disowned Elena, right? She's broke." Her words are meant to hurt Elena, and I smile to myself as Elena takes out her wallet. It's as worn as her bag is, and I'll need to make sure we select her a new one before we leave this store.

Elena looks into my eyes, and I wink at her. She bites down on her lip as she takes out her black card, and Elise blanches.

Elena settles the bill, and Elise glares at her the entire time. "If you had that card, why did you come ask Dad for money?"

Elena freezes, and I see the nerves and shame in her eyes. I pull her closer and press a kiss on top of her head. "Because my girl is stubborn," I tell Elise. "Because for whatever reason, she thought her father has a heart, because she wanted to give him one final chance. For the longest time, she flat-out refused my help."

I nod at the security guard by the door, and he rushes up to me. "Get her out of here. I'm done entertaining her. I don't ever want to see her in any of my malls again."

I can tell she wants to make a fuss, but she knows she'd only embarrass herself.

"Good riddance," I say, sighing. "Where the hell is your security team, Buttercup? Little fruit flies like her shouldn't be able to get anywhere near you. Enough of this bullshit."

She rises to her tiptoes and wraps her arms around me before pressing a kiss to my cheek, startling me. "Thank you," she whispers. "For everything. I know you only really entertained her so I could have a bit of payback. It's petty, but I needed that. I... thank you, Alexander."

I bury my hand in her hair and shake my head. "Elena, you're my wife. Any insults thrown your way, I'll take personally. Besides, I don't like it when people mess with my possessions."

Despite my words, Elena smiles at me, as though she can see straight through me.

CHAPTER 26

lexander

The waitress leads us to a secluded spot by the window, but Elena doesn't even notice the view. She's absent minded. Even ring shopping didn't seem to excite her. I offered to buy her additional jewelry, but she wasn't interested.

I move my chair closer to her, so I'm sitting next to her rather than opposite her, and she looks at me, a sad smile on her face.

"My father hasn't checked up on me since I turned eighteen, but he takes such good care of Elise," she says, her voice breaking. "He doesn't even seem to care whether I'm dead or alive."

I see the tears pooling in her eyes and grab her hand. Seeing tears in her eyes, fuck. I can't stand it. "I know it isn't the same, but you have me now, Buttercup," I say involuntarily.

She looks at me and nods. "I do. I do have you," she says, her eyes never leaving mine. "There are a few things I want to do, Alexander... but I can't do them by myself. Will you help me?"

I raise my brows, and she tightens her grip on my hand. "I... I want to hire a private investigator. I'd like to look into my mother's car accident. I know it's been years, but I just need to know. Besides, Elise clearly had access to my mother's former nurse somehow. It doesn't sit well with me."

I smile at her and lift her hand to my lips. "Elena, you don't even need to ask me for something like that. You have a whole security team at your disposal, most of them ex-FBI. Give Aiden a call and tell him what you want done. I've already told you that cost isn't a concern."

She looks at me as though I've just given her the world, and it kills me. Every single thing she's ever asked me for has been for her mother. She's not once asked me for anything for herself—not even my time. Every woman I've ever dated has selfishly asked me for anything that came to mind, but not Elena.

"There's more," she says, her voice soft, insecure.

I drag my chair closer and wrap my arm around the back of her chair. "Tell me."

She bites down on her lip, and I hate seeing her so breakable, so vulnerable. She's my wife, easily amongst one of the most powerful women in this damn country, yet here she sits in front of me, uncertain and hurt.

"When I left home, my brother and father got me to sign some documents. At the time, my father told me that if I was going to leave, I'd better be serious about it. He told me he'd cut me off, and I agreed. So, I signed."

She hesitates, her eyes dropping to her lap. I place my index finger underneath her chin and raise her face.

"What is it you want, wife? If it's within my power, I will give it to you."

128

She nods and inhales deeply. "I want the shares I signed away back. I want everything that's my mother's. I don't care about my father's stuff, he can keep that. But I want every single thing my mother has worked for. I don't want Jade getting her hands on any of it."

I nod and smile when I see the flash of determination in her eyes. "All right, Mrs. Kennedy. Then let's make that happen. What about Matthew's shares?"

She hesitates and stares at me as though she's trying to guess what I'm thinking. "I want those too," she says eventually. "I know you hate him, and though I don't know all the details, I know there's bad blood between you two. Take whatever you want from him. I don't care. He was happy to let Mom die, so I don't see why he should have anything she left him."

I nod. "With pleasure," I tell her. "This is hardly a request. More of a present to me, really. Another way to screw over your brother? I'll do it happily."

Elena laughs, but I see the heartache she's trying to hide. She still loves her brother, but she's lost faith in him, she's given up on him. Matthew is a fucking idiot.

"Tell me about your childhood," I say. "You've told me about the last few years, but you never told me how you ended up becoming estranged from everyone you love, how you ended up deciding to leave home."

Elena sighs, her expression heartbreaking. "It was all very gradual," she says. "My mom got into that car accident, and she fell into a coma. For months, my father, brother, and I were a team, we were united, we were hoping for her recovery. My grandparents passed away years ago, so all we had was each other. I didn't even notice Dad slipping away. I was completely blindsided when he introduced me to Jade, and I was a wreck when he told me he wanted to marry her. I expected Matthew to side with me, but he didn't. He welcomed Jade and Elise with open arms, and they returned the love he showed them."

Elena inhales shakily. "I couldn't do it, and it caused a lot of friction, a lot of arguments, and endless accusations about my refusal to accept Jade into our family. Over and over again I'd be told that I was ungrateful for not wishing for my father's happiness, for wanting him to live in the past. And it wasn't that at all, you know? I was just sad about my mother, and all of a sudden, I was asked to pretend my mother doesn't even exist. At that point, I didn't even know my dad was trying to get the doctors to declare her brain dead."

A tear drops down her cheek, and I catch it with my thumb. Elena smiles shakily, and she looks so damn broken, so hurt. It makes me want to tear the world apart for her. She was never supposed to mean anything to me. She wasn't supposed to be someone I'd care about. All I wanted her to be was my trophy wife, someone to keep my bed warm, someone that'd keep my mother happy and entertained, and my grandfather off my back. I shouldn't care about her tears, but I do.

"I found out about that the day my father married Jade. That's when the insurance company called me to say they'd stop paying for her care. I was foolish, because I laughed it off. I was Elena Rousseau, after all. I knew we had the money. What I didn't expect was how hard Jade was going to work at erasing every trace of my mother. It started with things around the house, and then it moved to the relationships we had. The Kennedys, and your mother in particular, are close friends of my mother's, so Jade stopped me from hanging out with Lucian, probably because she didn't want the reminder. If I refused to listen, she'd make sure that I couldn't go see my mother at the hospital for weeks, so I obeyed, and slowly but surely, I ended up losing all my friends. I'd been so focused on my mother, and I'd been so young... I just didn't realize what she was doing, not until it was too late. When she convinced my dad to stop paying for my mother's care, I was all alone. I had no connections left, no one to reach out to. All I had was my trust fund, and I just prayed it was enough. Maybe I shouldn't have left home, but at that point it had all just become too much."

I try my best to suppress the rage I feel, the need to punch Alaric Rousseau in the face. I can't believe everything she's been through. Despite all that, she never lost hope, she never stopped fighting for her mother. Why is it that there's so much about my wife that I'm only just finding out about? I guess it's because I never bothered to get to know her, to talk to her.

"Do you know what happened to the shares you had in your father's company? Everyone knows he wouldn't have come as far as he has without your mother—she famously provided him with the start-up money in return for half his company's shares. I've heard the story at least a dozen times."

Elena nods and bites down on her lip. "Yes, she did do that. Matthew and I inherited those shares. Dad wasn't able to take my shares from me directly, but he did manage to sign them over to Matthew instead, before I turned eighteen. So long as the shares go to either my brother or me, he can get away with that. I haven't fought him on it. I care more about everything my mother built. I'm not really interested in my father's company."

I grit my teeth and shake my head. "Every single thing you've lost, we'll get back. Everything."

She looks at me with a small sparkle of hope in her eyes, but I see the fire douse almost as soon as it's lit. She doesn't dare put her faith in me, and I can't blame her. Not after everything she's been through. I'm essentially telling her I'll give her everything the entire Rousseau family owns, and I get that it's hard to believe. But it isn't impossible. For her, I'll make it happen.

When I asked her to marry me, I was after a simple girl, someone that would feel so indebted to me that she'd stay out of my way. Someone that wouldn't dare bother me with useless expectations and notions of love.

Elena is everything I thought I wanted, but now I find myself wanting to give her everything that she's refusing to ask for. I want her to rely on me more. I want her to ask me for help. I want her to use every single connection I've got to regain everything she's lost.

And that's where the danger lies... Elena makes me want to give her the world.

CHAPTER 27

lena

My phone buzzes just as I've made myself a cup of coffee, and I frown, surprised to find my brother calling me. I hesitate before picking up.

"Elena? What the hell do you think you're doing? Why the hell am I looking at photos of you with Alexander Kennedy?"

Took him long enough. Alexander and I have been going on dates in the most public places we can think of for weeks now. It was only a matter of time before it came to Matthew's attention.

I sigh and run a hand through my hair. "Hi," I say. "I'm good, thank you. So is Mom, by the way."

"I'm not in the mood for your bullshit," he says. "Why were you with Alexander? You know full well the guy and I don't get along. That he can't stand Jen choosing me over him. You need to stop playing games."

I shake my head and take a sip of my coffee. "I love how you're making this all about yourself, as usual."

Matthew laughs, the sound sending a chill down my spine. "You're still as stupid as you've always been. Do you really think he'd even look at you twice if you weren't my sister? It's me he's after. Me and Jen."

He's not wrong. It hurts to admit it, but Matthew is right. Would Alexander even have married me if I didn't provide him with an opportunity to take revenge?

"We're dating," I say, shaking away my thoughts. "And I'm very happy."

Matthew groans. "You stupid fucking bitch," he mutters. "Don't fucking come running back home when he leaves you. Men like Alexander Kennedy don't date girls like you. They just fuck 'em and leave 'em. You're being used, and you can't even see it. Dumb fucking whore."

He hangs up before I can even retort, and I'm left feeling shaken. When did my relationship with my brother deteriorate to this extent? I see the way he treats Elise, and he's never once treated me that way. Not even before Mom's car accident. I see all the photos on social media, of Matthew and Elise going out for lunch together, of them hanging out with mutual friends. Matthew has never done any of that with me. He cares about Elise the way a brother should, but me, his actual sister... he can't even get himself to speak to me politely. What have I ever done for him to treat me this way?

I think of Alexander, my heart sinking. He, too, has always made it clear that he won't treat me the way he'd treat someone he'd actually want to be with. Alexander and I... we knew what we were getting into. He's been clear about what to expect, and more importantly, what not to expect. Yet despite all that, Matthew has me questioning myself. I wonder if Alexander will end up leaving me. If Jennifer ever wants him back, would he leave me? And if he did, what would that mean for my mother? Would my mother's life be at risk all over again?

"What's wrong?" Lucian asks, and I blink, disoriented.

I shake my head and force a smile on my face. "It's nothing," I murmur.

"Are you sure?" he asks, worried.

I smile at him and shake my head, trying my best to reassure him. "Just my brother being a dick," I say as I grab my bag. "I'm having lunch with Alexander."

"Ooh, a date," he says, teasing me, and I force a smile onto my face.

"No," I say, shaking my head. "It's just part of our agreement. We said we'd go on a couple of high-profile dates, and then we'll stage a proposal so we can convince your grandfather that we're in love. Alexander is going on a business trip tomorrow. He'll be gone all week, so today is a good day to stage a date."

Luce wriggles his brows, and I can't help but smile. I shake my head and move to walk past him, but he stops me. "Hey," he says, and I turn to look at him. "I'm so happy that you're back in our lives. I've missed you, Elena. I know things aren't back to what they used to be, but I'd really like it if we could work on that. You're the only real friend I ever had. The only person I ever confided in, the only one I've ever really trusted."

My heart warms, and I hug Lucian tightly, squeezing him. "I've missed you, too," I whisper, feeling vulnerable all of a sudden. For years, Lucian was my closest friend, and having him back in my life just when life couldn't get any harder has felt like a blessing. "And yes, let's work on that."

Lucian presses a kiss to my forehead and tips his head toward the door. "Come on, I'll go with you. I was planning on dropping by the office anyway."

I frown and Lucian blushes just slightly. "I met someone," he says, looking down. "It's complicated... one of my brother's employees."

My eyes widen, and I grin. "My gosh, Luce, that's amazing! You'll have to tell me all about it."

He nods, but I see the nervousness in his eyes. "Let's go out for lunch soon, and I'll tell you everything."

I smile and we walk out together, surprised to find the limousine waiting for us. Lucian frowns and raises his brows before grinning.

"Well, damn, you've won over my brother, huh? He sent the limo to pick you up?"

I'm about to deny his words, but then the door opens, and Alexander steps out. My heart skips a beat when our eyes meet.

He smiles at me, but his expression drops when he notices Lucian. "Why are you here?" he asks, annoyed. His eyes move between Lucian and me, his gaze tinged with distrust.

Lucian elbows me and leans in to whisper into my ear, annoying Alexander even further. "Wow, he came to pick you up himself? He never does that."

Alexander is frowning at Lucian, and I see the suspicion in his eyes. He walks up to me and threads his hand through my hair, his body tense. He leans in and lowers his lips to mine, putting on a show of possessiveness, telling Lucian that I belong to him without uttering a word.

He pulls away to look at me, his gaze heated. When he looks at me this way, it gets hard to remember that it's only my body he wants. That all we have is an agreement, that none of it is real.

Lucian shakes his head and pushes past us, making me pull away from Alexander. I'm flustered, embarrassed, and he leans in, his lips brushing against my ear. "I told you, Elena. I'm going to make sure it's evident to every man that you're mine—Lucian included. It's *me* you married. Remember that."

I look into his eyes as he pulls away. "Was that really necessary? I'm just another of your belongings, aren't I? Lucian already knows that. You don't need to stake your claim, Alexander. There's no one around to put on a show for."

Alexander blinks, and I push past him, getting into the car. My heart is aching today. I'm tired of being reminded that I don't mean anything to anyone, that I'm just a thing to be owned, used, and discarded. I know I have no rights to Alexander, but I'm sick of feeling like I'm a mere object.

He sits down next to me and buckles me in, taking his time, his touch lingering. His eyes are on me, his gaze searching. He frowns as he sits back, his hand on my knee and his phone in his other hand. I'm tempted to push his hand away, wanting a bit of space, but I resist.

I resist, because Lucian is staring at the two of us, his eyes twinkling. I look at him through narrowed eyes, trying to convey that he needs to knock it off, but he continues to smirk at us. I know he's seeing things that aren't there—Luce is like that. He's a hopeless romantic, and he's falling for his brother's theatrics.

"Buttercup," Alexander says, sighing. "I need to head back to the office. Something came up."

I nod, and he gently pushes my hair out of my face. "Come with me," he says. "Come to the office with me. I don't know how long this'll take, but we can grab some food after? Or if you're hungry now, I can just order you some food to my office?"

I look at him with raised brows. If we aren't putting on a show, why do we need to spend any time together?

The mildly impressed look on Lucian's face tells me that Alexander taking me to his office instead of just cancelling our date is unusual, and I hate that it gets my hopes up just slightly... I hate that it makes me wonder if maybe, just maybe, he wants to spend time with me as much as I want to spend time with him.

CHAPTER 28

Elena

All eyes are on us as we walk into the office. I'm nervous and try to pull my hand out of Alexander's, but he holds me tighter instead. He leans into me, his lips brushing over my ear. "Back straight, chin up. You're Mrs. Kennedy," he whispers.

I look up at him, and he grabs my chin, pinching gently as he leans in for a kiss, right in the middle of the lobby. He smirks as he pulls away, and I'm certain my cheeks are scarlet. Lately he'll kiss me in public as often as he can, ensuring we end up in tabloids every week. He seems to revel in making me blush, seeing me flustered. I guess it's yet another game for him.

I look away and catch Luce rolling his eyes despite the smile on his face. Alexander throws his arm around me as we walk towards the elevator. "Remind me why you're here?" he asks Lucian.

I see the flash of panic in Lucian's eyes, but he gets it under control within seconds and smiles at his brother. "I'm meeting a friend," he says, getting off at a lower floor than us.

I wink at him as he walks away. "Have fun," I tell him, and his cheeks redden just slightly as he rushes off.

Alexander frowns, but thankfully, he doesn't ask any questions. He holds my hand as we walk toward his office, and Alice seems surprised to see me. Her eyes drop to our joined hands in confusion, and it takes her a couple of seconds to smile at me.

"I need to attend the Willis meeting," Alexander says, leading me into his office. Alice follows us in and he nods at her as he pulls out his desk chair for me. "Make sure my wife is well taken care of. Get her some takeout menus too."

Alice nods, but her expression displays disbelief. "I... you're leaving her in your office? Alone?" she asks, clearly trying to be somewhat discreet, and failing.

Alexander straightens his tie, nodding. "You were there the day I married her, weren't you? She's *my wife*. What is she going to steal from me? She owns everything already."

I tense. Alexander has never mentioned it, but Lucian told me that Jennifer stole corporate secrets and handed them to my brother, losing Alexander a deal he'd been working on for years. I bet attempting to explain a data breach like that, on top of the lost expected revenue, can't have been easy. I can't even imagine how his grandfather and their shareholders must have responded, how hard he's had to work to make up for it.

It surprises me that he's willing to leave me alone in his office. In his eyes, I'm a Rousseau, after all. But then again, he's right. He owns me.

Alexander turns to walk away, but then he pauses and turns back. He pulls me up and out of his chair, his hands around my waist. He kisses me roughly, quickly, and then he pulls away, leaving me standing there in a daze, startled. He brushes my hair behind my ear. "I'll be back soon, Buttercup," he says. He leans in for one more kiss and then walks away, leaving me staring after him. Why is he behaving this way? There's no need to put on a show for his secretary, is there?

I'm not the only one that's dazed—Alice is staring at the door too, and it makes me feel uncomfortable. It visibly takes her a minute to pull herself together, and when she looks at me, she struggles to meet my eyes. I sit back down in Alexander's chair and glance at his desk. It's as tidy as our bedroom always is.

"Can I offer you a drink?" Alice asks, and I nod, asking for a coffee.

She walks away, smiling tightly, and I stare after her. Alexander made it clear from the start that we'd be exclusive, but I can't help but worry nonetheless. I can't shake the feeling that I'm not good enough for him. That I never will be. When I was younger, I was bound to inherit my mother's company, but that's now under my father's control. I can't help but wonder about my mother's company's performance. Is it doing well under my father's control? I bite down on my lip and click on the keyboard in front of me. I'm not surprised to find it locked. I hesitate and then decide to text Alexander.

Elena Kennedy: *Could I use your computer?*

He texts me back almost immediately, startling me.

Husband: *Use the fingerprint scanner on the keyboard.*

I frown at it and carefully place my index finger on it. Much to my surprise, his computer unlocks.

Elena Kennedy: *How is that possible?*

Husband: *All our security is tied to biometrics. One of my friends, Elliot Everson, implemented it for me. The guy is a whiz. I'll introduce you at some point.*

I sit up when his email inbox appears on the screen, filled with dozens of emails with my father's company as the subject line. I frown and click on one of the emails curiously. I blink in disbelief as I read through it. He appears to be purchasing company shares from all shareholders that are willing to part with theirs, and he's paying quite handsomely for them.

Why?

Why would he do that?

I read through the entire thread, shocked at the amount of money he's spending to acquire my father's shares.

I'm still reading through the correspondence when Alexander walks back into the office, looking stressed out. He runs a hand through his hair but pauses when he sees my expression. I look up at him, unsure of how to even ask the endless questions I've got.

"What happened?" he asks, his brows raised.

"I... you got an email."

He glances at the screen and runs a hand through his hair. Alexander pulls me out of his seat and sits down, pulling me back onto his lap.

"I'm buying as many shares as I can. It might take some time, but every single thing your father took from you, I'll return to you. Everything, Elena."

He kisses my neck and my eyes shutter closed. "A hostile takeover?" I ask, my voice tinged with disbelief.

He nods. "You're a Kennedy now, Elena. More importantly, you're *mine* now. Your father is a fool for messing with us. Shit like buying his stepdaughter bullshit bags instead of helping you save your mother's life? Fuck that. The mere thought of what you almost resorted to because of that asshole has me seeing red. I'll take every single thing from him, the way he took it all from you until he's begging for mercy at your feet. And once you've got him there, I want you to walk away from him the way he walked away from your mother and you."

I turn in his arms to look at him. "You don't have to do that for me," I say, my voice trembling. I've already asked so much of him. I don't want to be indebted to him even further. "I only really care about my mother's company. I don't need my father's financial empire. We can't mess with him, Alexander. We're just asking for trouble if we do. Besides, this isn't part of our agreement. I don't want to inconvenience or bother you."

He turns me in his lap, so I'm forced to look at him. He cups my cheek and looks into my eyes, his expression serious. "Elena, who am I?" he asks.

"You're Alexander Kennedy."

"Indeed. And who are you?"

"I... I'm your wife."

He nods. "I've said it before and I'll say it again. Anyone that messes with you—messes with *me*. And I? I'm not someone to be trifled with."

He pulls away and looks into my eyes. "That company wouldn't exist without your mother funding it. It's rightfully yours, and I'm going to make sure it ends up in your hands. Besides, I can't wait to see the look on Matthew's face when I take everything from him."

There it is. There's the real motivation. I never asked him for my father's shares. I only ever wanted my mother's. He's going after them because of Matthew.

Just like Matthew said, Alexander is using me. This time, he's using me as an excuse. I'm tired of being used, but I'm even more tired of being helpless.

For years I was powerless, but not anymore, not with Alexander by my side.

I wrap my arms around his neck and lean in to kiss him, startling him. The only thing he's ever asked of me in return is my body, so I'll give it to him, and I'll do it with a smile on my face. Alexander grins against my lips and kisses me back. Before I know it, he's got me lifted on top of his desk, my legs spread wide so he can stand between them.

"I can't get enough of your lips. I'm not sure I can live

without them for an entire week," he whispers against my lips. "Come with me on my business trip."

I look into his eyes and shake my head. "I can't leave my mom. What if she needs me? You promised me you'd never restrict my access to her."

Alexander sighs in resignation and buries his hand in my hair. He leans in and kisses me, eliciting a moan from me. His hands run over my body and I squirm when his fingers trail over my thigh. He pulls away, and the passion swirling through his eyes makes me want him even more.

I bite down on my lip and place my hands on his chest, the tips of my fingers tracing over the buttons. His muscles feel so hard underneath my palms, and I love the feel of him.

He watches me, as though he's wondering what I'll do, and I yank on his tie, pulling him back toward me. He's grinning when his lips come crashing back down on mine, and I close my legs around him.

Alexander moans and pushes up against me, sending a thrill through my body. I unbutton his shirt, a desperation I've never felt before making me frantic. He shrugs out of his shirt and pushes my dress up until it's bunched around my waist.

"Elena," he whispers, sounding just as needy as I'm feeling. He groans when I unzip his suit pants, but it isn't enough. I want more of him.

His fingers brush against my wetness just as I wrap my hand around him, and my eyes flutter closed in delight. "I need you," I moan. "Now. Please."

He pushes my underwear aside roughly and slips a finger into me, the way he did at Vaughn's. The way he plays my body is insane.

"So needy," he whispers. "You're so wet for me, baby."

I yank on his clothes and pull him closer, making him smirk. "Always so hungry for my cock," he groans, lining himself up against me. His eyes are on me as he pushes into me, and I whimper impatiently. He's taking his sweet time filling me up, loving how he's driving me crazy.

"Good girl," he murmurs. "Taking my cock like that."

He pulls back almost all the way and then slams into me, finally giving me what I want. I moan in delight and Alexander buries his hand in my hair, pulling me closer. He kisses me roughly, and I lose myself in him.

"Tell me how you want it, baby. I want you to come for me," he says, his lips lingering on mine.

"Just like this," I tell him. "More."

He grins and grabs my thighs, slamming into me harder, the pressure building higher and higher. The way he looks at me almost pushes me over the edge.

I grab his hair and kiss him harder as my muscles start to contract, a powerful orgasm rocking my body. Alexander's lips smother my moans and his grip on my hair tightens, his own release not far away. "Elena," he groans, increasing the pace. The way he moans when he comes undoes me. It's the sexiest thing, seeing him like this.

He exhales and drops his forehead to mine. "You have me hooked on your pussy," he tells me, and I smile at him. "I'm going to hate being away from you next week. I understand you can't leave your mother, but damn, baby. How am I supposed to survive without feeling you come all over my cock?"

Alexander leans in and kisses me, slow and deep, before pulling away. He looks at me like I'm all he can see.

When he looks at me this way, I'm convinced that what we've got is more than he's willing to admit to himself. He gives me hope, and that's the one thing I cannot afford to have.

CHAPTER 29

lena

I've been restless all week. I'm used to not hearing from Alexander during the day, but I always know he comes home to me. Even when we don't talk for days, I know it's me he falls asleep with. Now that he's on a business trip, there's been no contact between us at all. I'm tempted to call or text him, but he told me not to bother him unnecessarily, and I don't want to overstep. I didn't think I'd miss him... but I do.

"Earth to Elena," Luce says.

"Sorry, I zoned out again."

He shakes his head at me, annoyed. He's been updating me on his love life, and all it's done to me is make me worry about my own. I sip my tea and lean back into my regular chair at our local coffee shop.

"Your mind is as absent as my brother is."

"Have you spoken to him this week?" I ask, unable to help myself.

Lucian shakes his head. "Nah, but I know he speaks to Mom every day. Hasn't he called you?"

I shake my head. "Do you think he's just ignoring me?"

Lucian shrugs. "I dunno. Maybe he finally figured out you have a huge crush on him and it freaks him out."

I slap his arm lightly. "Shut up."

"Don't worry, baby sis. When it comes to emotions, my brother is a bit slow."

I roll my eyes. "We're the same age, moron."

He shrugs. "I'm like, three months older."

"Whatever."

It hurts just a little that Alexander does seem to have time for phone calls, yet he hasn't even texted me. I wish I'd told him I'd come with him when he first mentioned the trip, but I'm too scared. I'm too scared my mom might need me, and I'd be too far away.

"Elena, you remember our pact, right?" Lucian says, snapping me out of my thoughts. "It's childish, I know, but still…"

I nod, my expression turning serious. Lucian always knew about my crush on Alexander growing up. We used to fantasize about becoming siblings when I'd marry his brother, and we'd made each other countless promises just in case it ever actually happened. Even though most of our promises were childish, there's one I know Lucian will want me to keep.

"I will always keep your secrets, and I will try to never be caught between your brother and you," I promise him.

He grabs my hand and presses a kiss to the back of my hand. "I knew I could count on you, princess. I wish you hadn't done it, because I don't want to see your beautiful heart break. And honestly, my brother wouldn't recognize love if it hit him in the face. But since you went ahead and married him, we'd better come up with a way for you to win my brother's heart.

The next time he goes on a business trip, he'll be so in love with you that he'll be calling you every second he's got."

I groan, this has disaster spelled all over it.

"You know the way to a man's heart?" he asks.

I nod. "Through the stomach," I answer.

Lucian shakes his head. "Nope. It's through his dick."

I blush and look around me, but luckily no one is sitting near us. "God, Luce."

Lucian crosses his arms and nods at me. "Tell me, what is your sex life like? Don't you dare leave any of the juicy details out."

I blush. "Really, Luce? I can't." I say, shaking my head furiously.

Lucian grins. "So he has at least fingered you then?"

I slap my fingers over his lips. "Shh! Are you nuts?"

"Have you seen *his nuts* yet?" he mumbles through my lips.

I kick him, and he groans, putting his hands up in defeat. I let him go and look around warily, terrified of being overheard. "Yes, and yes," I admit, begrudgingly.

He grins like a maniac. "Tell me everything," he says, chuckling.

"There's not much to tell," I say. "We, uh, we sleep together a few times a week. Other than that, he... he touched me at Vaughn's."

"Holy shit. Come to think of it, I've never seen him so mad before. Tell me exactly what he did."

I groan, he's never going to let this go unless I tell him the whole story. So I do. I tell him about Vaughn's, and I end up telling him about the time Alexander forced me to my knees between his legs right before he proposed, and the time he caught me in the tub. By the end of it, Luce is equal parts amused and equal parts amazed.

"Well, damn. He caught you in the tub? I had no idea my robot of a brother could be that passionate."

I blush and nod.

"Damn, so why the hell isn't he trying to sext you, or you know, have full-blown phone sex? Do you think he's avoiding you because despite everything he says, he doesn't want to use you? Maybe he grew a conscience over there."

I smile, I can't help it. Luce always wants to believe in the good in people, and though he's the first to admit that his brother isn't perfect, Alexander is still the person he looks up to the most. "That makes no sense. He was very clear on the terms when we got married. He's a bit nicer now, but he still doesn't hesitate to remind me that he owns me."

Lucian shakes his head. "Alec isn't as ruthless as he thinks he is. I bet you've shaken him already. No one has ever triggered his protective instinct like you always have, even when we were younger. He could have easily waited a couple of weeks or months to formally marry you, but he locked you in the second he could. It's not like you'd have ran off with his money and refused to meet the terms on your end, yet he refused to wait. Alec is *never* impulsive, but he wanted you. I doubt he even realizes it himself."

I look up at Lucian in surprise, scared to even believe his words. "He told me he needed to marry anyway, that your grandfather requires it before letting him take his seat on the board. He told me not to expect much, and not to expect romance. That he only married me for convenience."

Lucian nods. "That's true, I'm sure part of it was convenience for him. But do you really think my brother would marry anyone just for that reason? He wouldn't have married you if there was no way to make things work between you two, but he probably doesn't want to acknowledge to himself that he feels that way. Besides, he has a few more months until my grandfather retires. He didn't really need to rush into marrying you. He could've waited until your wedding ceremony, but he didn't."

I frown, lost in thought. "He was fulfilling his end of the bargain by taking care of my mother's bills, by taking me in. It does make sense that he'd want me to fulfil my promises too. I think signing the marriage papers was really just another contract to him."

Lucian thinks over my words, neither of us able to figure out Alexander's behavior. "You know what you need?" he asks. I shake my head, too scared of what kind of nonsense might come out of his mouth this time.

"Something sexy."

I roll my eyes. "That's your plan? Your mother's stylist already took care of all that. Every single one of my nighties is sexier than anything I've ever worn."

Luce ponders my words and shakes his head. "No. You need something sexier than that. I'm dead serious when I tell you that the way to his heart is through his dick. Come on, we're going shopping."

Luce grabs my hand and drags me to the closest lingerie store, and I know I'm in a whole world of trouble.

CHAPTER 30

lexander

I watch Elena interact with my brother over dinner, both of them giggling and making inside jokes. One week. I was gone for one week, and I come back to my wife and brother being two peas in a pod.

I haven't forgotten that Lucian wanted to marry her in my stead. It's obvious he loves her. Maybe I was selfish when I told her to marry me. I rushed into it when I realized that my usual jokester of a brother wanted her. The guy who was never serious about anything was willing to spend the rest of his life with her. I took her away before he even had a chance.

I watch her giggle at something he said, and my whole body just screams *Mine*. The need to claim her as my own is unreal, and something I've never experienced before, not even with my ex-girlfriends. Not even with Jennifer. I don't understand where it comes from. Maybe it's just because Elena is my wife, and as my *wife*, she's supposed to be mine. Maybe it's simply because I own her, and I've never liked sharing my things. Whatever it is, I don't like it.

I take her in, and the way my heartbeat quickens irritates me. She's wearing a tight white dress today and her beautiful eyes are glowing. She's curled her hair, and it falls in big loose waves around her face. She looks like a beautiful mermaid or something, a siren. All I can think about is how those curls are going to look on my pillows tonight. No, there's no way I could let her go.

My phone buzzes and my mood drops even further when I realize that it's another text message from Jennifer.

Jen: *Please, Alec. I just want to talk. The way we left things... neither one of us got closure.*

Closure? Yeah, I do have countless questions. But getting answers to those won't undo the pain she inflicted. It won't take away that she cheated on me. I lock my phone and slip it into my pocket, feeling torn. Part of me wants to take her up on her offer to *talk*. I want to know why she did what she did, but another part of me takes great pleasure in ignoring her. Jennifer *hates* being ignored, and it must be driving her insane.

My brother grins at me, and I realize he must've said something. I hate that his face annoys me these days. I love my brother to bits, but I hate having him around my wife. Elena seems to bask in his attention. If I were to stay away longer, would she stray like Jennifer did? Would she leave me for my own brother?

"What?" I snap.

Lucian groans, annoyed that he's got to repeat himself. "I

said, don't you think Elena looks beautiful today? I picked her entire outfit. Top to bottom."

I give her a once over, and her cheeks redden slightly. "Entire outfit? Isn't it just a dress? It's beautiful, by the way."

Elena's smile drops, and I realize I complimented her dress, but not her. Rookie mistake. "You're gorgeous, Buttercup. As always." Some of the frost in her eyes melts, and she smiles at me, making my heart beat just a little quicker.

"Yes, her entire outfit. What, did you think she was naked underneath?" Lucian says, and my mother coughs, sending him a warning look at the same time that Elena hits his arm, her entire body tensing. I'm tempted to pull my brother over the table and demand clarification on his statement.

"Are you trying to tell me you picked out Elena's lingerie?" I ask him, staring him down. My voice sounds harsher than I intended it to, and I watch his eyes widen slightly. I can tell he didn't expect me to react as strongly as I did, and he doesn't answer my question. I look at my wife instead. "Elena?" I ask. She doesn't reply either and looks down at her plate. It's like I'm back in the past, the two of them putting up a united front against me. Except this time, Elena should have been on my side.

I drop my cutlery and let it clatter onto my plate loudly. I sit back, folding my arms over my chest. I see Elena and Lucian glance at each other, both looking panicked, and I have my answer.

"Why exactly are you picking out my wife's lingerie?" I ask Lucian, pinning him down with a stare.

"I... he... Luce is just joking, Alexander."

I glare at Elena, annoyed that she's calling me Alexander instead of Alec, yet she calls Lucian *Luce*.

She's my wife, yet it's my brother she has a nickname for. The worst thing is that it's my own fault. I'm the one that took away her rights to my nickname in a childish fit, telling her we weren't close enough for her to call me Alec.

I stare at Elena, and I wait for her telltale sign. There it is. She blinks twice. She's done that whenever she lies ever since she was five, and I doubt she even realizes it.

I feel my anger rise. I'm usually well in control of my emotions. I'm known for my poker face and leaving emotions out of my decisions. I couldn't have helped my grandfather grow the family business into what it is today without that. But as soon as it involves Elena, all my famed rationality goes out the window.

"Elena, a word please," I say, tipping my head toward the stairs. "Excuse us, Mother."

She nods at me, a smile on her face, and I get up. I head toward the stairs without checking if Elena is following. I walk slowly, trying my very best to regain control over my emotions, Elena's heels clicking behind me.

I close the door behind her and lead her straight past the sitting room, into the bedroom. She's fidgety, something that hasn't changed either. She always used to fidget whenever she knew she did something wrong. "Sit," I tell her, pointing to the bed. She sits down at the edge, and I kneel on the floor in front of her.

"Explain. I told you to get the thought of being with anyone else out of your mind. That I won't tolerate rumors about you. So why the fuck is my *brother* insinuating that he picked out your underwear? Did you forget who you belong to in the week I was gone? Do I need to fucking remind you?"

I push her legs apart slowly and watch her dress ride up to her thighs. Her eyes widen, but she doesn't stop me. As her legs part, the tiniest scrap of white lace I've ever seen comes into view.

"What the fuck?"

CHAPTER 31

lexander

There's a gap between the two sides of her underwear, exposing the middle of her perfectly smooth pussy. The thought that my little brother picked out this sexy little thing for her sickens me, and the thought that she's wearing this for *him* sends pure uncontrollable rage through my veins. I pull her to her feet and turn her around, unzipping her dress and letting it fall to the floor.

"Alexander! What are you doing?"

My eyes are drawn to her perfectly full ass that's pretty much exposed except for the tiny piece of white string that disappears between her deliciously full ass cheeks. Her hair falls almost to her ass, only just about exposing the dimples on her lower back. I turn her around and push her back onto the bed. She sits down in the same place she was before, covering her breasts with her arms and clenching her legs tightly together.

I grab her thighs and part them, lowering myself so I can kneel between them, and she lets me.

"I said *explain*."

I grab her wrists and pull her arms away from her chest, my breath hitching when I see what she's hiding. My eyes are on her barely covered breasts. The sheer white lace covering them does nothing to hide them. If anything, it highlights her dark, hard, nipples. I can barely keep myself from putting them in my mouth, and I know I'll need a taste before the night is over. I glance down at her exposed pussy and lick my lips.

"Alexander, I..."

I bury a hand in her hair and place my lips on her breast, flicking my tongue over her nipple through the lace fabric. She gasps, and I watch her squirm.

"Alec. From now on, you'll call me Alec at all times."

"Alec," she moans my name as I softly bite down, enjoying her response. I lean back to look at her flushed face.

"Lucian knows you're mine, and he still had the guts to go shopping with you for *this*?" I say, waving over her body to indicate her lingerie. She bites down on her lip and looks down.

"You can't tell me he picked this out for you without wondering what you'd look like in it."

I trail a finger from her chest down to her stomach and keep going down the middle of her pussy until I reach her slit.

"He wouldn't," she whispers. It takes me a moment to remember what she's talking about.

"Oh, no? Why wouldn't he? Did you model it for him?"

I see the panic in her eyes and my heart drops. *Fuck*, she'd better not have. I push her shoulder softly, and she falls back on the bed before she has a chance to answer.

I lean in, and before she can react, I trail my tongue down the middle of her pussy, shutting her up. "Mm," I moan at the same time as Elena. I lick circles around her clit and fuck her with my tongue, taking my time to drive her insane.

"Ah... Mm, I can't. Please. *Oh, God.*"

She buries her hands into my hair, as though she wants to pull my head away but can't get herself to. I get her close several times, only to stop and start all over again. I make sure to frustrate the hell out of her, refusing to let her come. She lifts her legs and wraps them around my shoulders, using her leg muscles to bring my face in closer. I smile against her clit and bite her softly.

"Oh, God. *Please.*"

"You wanna come for me, wifey?" I ask her.

"Mm, yes."

I smile and flick her clit with my tongue. "This pussy is mine, Elena. You're mine. Say it."

"I'm yours, Alexander," she says, panting. She lifts her hips and pushes her cunt into my face.

"Alec," I correct her. "Tell me you're sorry, Elena."

Elena moans, her body trashing underneath me. "I'm sorry, Alec. So sorry," she groans.

Deciding I've punished her enough, I push my middle finger into her tight, hot pussy and stimulate her G-spot while I swirl my tongue around her clit. Elena moans loudly.

"Oh, Alec. Mmm, yes, like that. Fuck... *yes.*" She sounds frantic, and I doubt she realizes how seductive the sounds and pleas coming from her lips are.

I increase my pace and feel her walls tighten around my finger. I suck on her clit hard, and my wife comes on my tongue, my name on her lips. I give her a minute to recover, and then start licking her softly again, staying away from her sensitive clit for the next few minutes. I stroke her G-spot and add an extra finger, barely able to fit it in. Her pussy is so tight, there's no way I can fit my cock in there. "Oh, God, Alec. I can't take it.

Please, I can't..." She begs, but I don't relent. I push against her G-spot harder, moving my fingers in and out quicker, and within a minute she comes again.

She's panting and her face is flushed. She looks at me through her lashes and she's the sexiest thing I've ever seen. I pull away from her and undo the buttons of my shirt. "I warned you, Elena. I won't say it again. You're *mine*, and this behavior isn't acceptable."

I shrug out of my shirt and undo my pants button, taking my time. Elena's eyes are on my skin, her gaze heated.

"I... yes, I know," she whispers.

Her eyes widen when my boxers slip past my hips, and I can't help but smirk at the look in her eyes. "Like what you see?"

Her cheeks are crimson, and she gasps when I get into bed with her. "I gotta admit, this shit is pretty nice," I tell her, my fingers grazing over the white lace. Elena is breathing hard, and she bites down on her lip when I rip her bra apart, the lace so fine that it tears easily. I pull it away from her and lean in, taking her nipple in my mouth briefly, teasing her as I swirl my tongue around her. She writhes against me, and I smile against her skin. I pull back and lower my lips to her neck. I suck down on her skin, marking her over and over again, leaving little kiss marks in every spot I can reach, slowly making my way down.

"I told you you're mine, but you don't listen," I whisper, right before sucking down on her breast, marking that too. "You're mine, and you'd better remember it. I'll make sure I'm all you can think of when you look in the damn mirror, you hear me?"

She moans when I suck down on her inner thigh. "The next time you see Lucian, all *he'll* be able to see will be the kiss marks I left on your skin. You belong to me, Elena, and it's time he realizes it too."

I move up and settle on top of her, my dick right between her legs. She arches her back up, and I doubt she even realizes she's doing it.

"I'm sorry, Alec," she says, wrapping her arms around me. I look into her eyes, and I hate how much she fucking captivates me. I hate that I love those eyes of hers.

"Elena, I'm going to fuck you so hard. You'll be so sore tomorrow that every time you move, you'll think of me. I'm going to leave my mark on you. I'm going to make sure you'll never again forget who you belong to."

She nods and wraps her arms around my neck. "Yes, Alec," she whispers, and I push into her slightly, stretching her out.

"Fuck, you're so fucking tight."

Elena's eyes fall closed and I freeze in place. "Look at me," I order, and she does. "Look at me when I fuck you."

I pull out of her slightly and thrust back into her, watching her as she moans, her eyes on mine. I've gotten too lax with her. It's about time I remind her who owns her.

CHAPTER 32

lena

I'm nervous as I walk into the rooftop bar Alexander asked me to meet him at. I'm so tense that I can't even enjoy the stunning view from here—or the beautiful, luxurious interior. He's been withdrawn lately, his anger palpable.

My eyes fall to the clusters of round sofas, each of them a separate booth facing a glass barrier, resulting in an unparalleled view of both the skyline and the bar. I spot Aiden in the corner and he nods at me, stepping aside as I walk up to him. Alexander is leaning back on the sofa, his eyes on the skyline in front of us.

He looks up when I sit down next to him, his gaze sending a thrill down my spine. He hasn't been himself lately. Ever since he got back from his business trip, he's been cold and distant.

I've tried over and over again to explain to him that nothing is going on between Lucian and me, but he won't listen to reason. I can't even blame him. I messed up. I never should have entertained Lucian's ideas. I should've known how Alexander would respond to that.

He raises his fingers to my mouth, his thumb tracing over my lips. "Red lips? Perfect."

My heart races when he smiles at me, his eyes dark, anger still flashing through them. His gaze roams over my body, taking in the tight black dress I'm wearing.

He looks into my eyes and then pats his legs. "Come here."

I blink, my cheeks heating rapidly. He wants me to sit in his lap? I glance around the packed bar, my heart racing. I might not know everyone, but I recognize many faces.

"I won't repeat myself."

I swallow hard and rise to my feet. He smiles in satisfaction and grabs my hand, pulling on it so I fall into his arms. His hands wrap around my waist and he positions me squarely in his lap, my back toward the crowd.

"Alexander..."

He looks at me with raised brows, his hands roaming over my body. "I told you to call me Alec."

I stare at him, unable to figure him out. He told me at the very start that he and I aren't close enough for me to use that name, and I know that's true. I can count the people that call him Alec on one hand. It's just his parents, Lucian, his grandfather... and Jennifer. Not me. Never me.

"Embarrassed?" He asks as his hand glides over my skin, until he's cupping the back of my neck, his thumb on my throat. "You're mine, yet you seem to have trouble remembering it. You leave me no choice, baby. I'll have to make sure everyone knows it."

I can feel him hardening underneath me and my heart starts to race. I shift in his lap and he grins. "Like what you feel?" he asks, his hands moving to my waist. He holds me right below my breasts, his thumbs caressing my nipples. They harden for him like the traitorous little bitches they are, and he smirks.

"Tell me what you're wearing underneath this dress."

My eyes widen and my cheeks heat even further. "I... um... just underwear."

Alexander chuckles. "Color?"

I swallow hard. "It's black."

"Is it lace?"

I nod.

"Did my brother pick that out for you too?"

I look into his eyes, my heart twisting painfully. "No, of course not. It's not what you think. It was bad judgement on my part, I admit, but there's nothing going on between Luce and I."

Alexander grits his teeth, tightening my grip on me. "Luce? Hmm... I don't like how familiar you are with another man. It's *Lucian* from now on."

I shake my head and look at him through narrowed eyes. "Like hell it is. He's my childhood friend, and you're being unreasonable."

He chuckles, but there's no humor in his eyes. "Hmm... disobeying me, are you? I was away for one week, and you're all over Lucian. You're forgetting who owns you, Elena. You're mine, and you'll do as I say."

I look down, hurt by his constant reminders. I hate that he keeps reminding me I'm just another possession of his. That he and I aren't in a relationship—that we never will be. He leans into me, his nose brushing against my neck. Alexander kisses me softly, where he knows I'm sensitive, and a thrill runs down my spine. His tongue grazes over my neck, and then he bites me softly before sucking down on my skin, marking me as his.

A soft gasp escapes my lips and he pulls away, a smile on his face. His hand slips down my chest, over my hips and underneath my dress, his finger trailing over my thighs. I inhale sharply, willing my body not to respond to him for once, but as always when it comes to Alexander, it disobeys me.

He pushes my underwear aside and smirks. "Wet. Of course you are. You're a little slut for me, aren't you? Always eager for my touch. I bet I can make you come right here, in my lap, with hundreds of people surrounding us."

I gulp and shake my head. "Alec, they'll notice. You can't!"

He grins and brushes his thumb over my clit, making me jump. "Stay still, baby. Don't move, and no one will know. Your back is toward the crowd and we're caged in," he says, his head tipping toward the privacy barriers between the sofas. "Now, let's see if you can come quietly or not."

My lips fall open when he slips a finger into me, while simultaneously twirling his thumb over my clit. He laughs huskily, his eyes on mine. "Struggling?"

He increases the pace and I grab his shoulders, holding on tightly. "Alec," I whisper, my voice coming out as a moan.

"Yes. Moan my name, Elena, just like that. Remember who owns this body, baby. Come for me."

I'm panting and I know I won't be able to hold on for long. My fingers thread through his hair and I pull him closer, my lips crashing against his. He swallows all of my moans and I kiss him the way I know drives him insane. He pushes me over the edge just like that, his lips on mine.

I'm lightheaded by the time I pull away, my forehead dropping to his. He smiles at me, a possessive glint in his eyes. "Good girl," he tells me. "So obedient, after all."

Alexander's smile drops as he looks over my shoulder, and I turn to follow his gaze, but he grabs my chin, keeping my eyes on him.

"Your brother just walked in with Jennifer on his arm."

He tenses as he pulls his fingers away, and so do I.

"Damn it. That asshole is headed this way, and I wasn't done with you yet."

"Elena. What are you doing here?" I hear my brother say. My cheeks are still flushed, and I pray he won't realize what we were just up to.

I try to get off Alexander's lap, but he won't let me go. He tightens his grip on me, so I turn in his arms instead.

Matthew's jaw is ticking, and that on its own would have made my evening. Better still, though, is the jealous look in Jennifer's eyes. She looks at Alexander, but for once, he isn't looking back at her. He rests his chin on my shoulder, leisurely pressing a kiss to my neck, as though Matthew and Jennifer aren't even there.

"Matthew. Good to see you," I say.

Matthew clenches his jaw, and I wonder if he'll reveal the asshole within. He reaches for me, but Aiden grabs his arm, his grip tight. Aiden doesn't say a word, he just pushes Matthew's arm away roughly.

"You're a fucking embarrassment, Elena. What the fuck do you think you're doing, sitting in someone's lap like a fucking prostitute? You'd better get up right now, or so help me God," Matthew hisses, his voice low.

His words wound me, but after years of him hurling abuses at me, the impact is dampened. It doesn't sting the way it used to. Now it's just a dull ache, the type of pain you experience when you know you're holding onto something that you should've let go long ago. I look at him, and I barely recognize him. In the years since Mom fell into a coma, he's strayed further and further from the brother I grew up with. We were never close, but he was never cruel either, the way he is now.

Alexander chuckles at Matthew's words and presses a kiss to my shoulder, ignoring him.

"You stupid little girl. He's using you. You think it's you he wants? It's not. You're just a fucking pawn."

Alexander looks up at Matthew. "So what? So what if I'm using your sister?" he asks, his voice low. My heart twists painfully at those words. I know I don't mean a thing to him. I know he's just using me. But half the time he makes it so easy to forget that. He makes it too easy to fool myself into believing that what we have could be real one day. It's things like asking me to call him Alec, when that's only reserved for those closest to him. It's him acting jealous constantly and publicly claiming me as his that gives me the wrong idea. It gives me hope, and hope is the most cruel emotion of all. I glance at Matthew, a bittersweet smile on my face. If given a choice, I'd pick his cruel words over Alexander's sugar-coated lies any day.

Matthew grinds his jaws. "You need to stay the fuck away from my sister, Alexander."

Alexander chuckles, the sound sending a chill down my spine. "The way you stayed away from my fiancée?"

Matthew smiles and looks at me. His smug expression just adds to the pain Alexander's words inflicted. I know it's Jennifer he loves, but being confronted with it like this hurts. I glance at her, and the satisfied glint in her eyes kills me. She knows that even though it's me in his arms, he's not over her.

"I told you, Elena. There it is. That's all you are to him."

Matthew shakes his head and takes a step back, his anger waning, until all that's left is annoyance.

"You want her, Alexander? You can have her. You think I care about her? Nah. You're embarrassing me, I'll give you that, but I'll survive the reputational damage my slut of a sister is doing. But this? This won't hurt me." He laughs, the sound chilling. "You picked the wrong sister. This one I don't give a fuck about."

Matthew smiles and wraps his arm around Jennifer. He

looks at Jennifer and pulls her toward him, kissing her, putting on a show for Alexander. He tightens his grip on me, and my heart shatters. He's holding me while pining after someone else.

Matthew smiles and grabs Jennifer's hand. I watch them walk away, Matthew's words reverberate through my mind. My eyes fall shut and I inhale shakily.

"You got what you wanted," I say, my voice breaking. "You've thrown me in Matthew and Jennifer's face. He was right, you know? You've treated me like some sort of call girl tonight—and I let you. Because you're right, Alexander. You own me. Is this enough now? Have you embarrassed me enough?"

He tightens his grip on me, his arms wrapped around me tightly. "Elena, there's nothing shameful about sitting in my lap. No one knows anything more than that happened. That was just between you and I. If I wanted to treat you like a call girl, I'd have had you on your knees, sucking my dick for everyone to see. Instead, it's your pleasure I was after. You're letting your brother get into your head."

I inhale deeply, trying my best to believe his words. "Was he wrong, though? You're using me. I don't mean a thing to you. You're no different to my brother, Alexander. I'm just a tool to you."

His lips graze against my ear, his voice soft yet harsh. "And you're no different to Jennifer," he whispers. "You're disloyal. At least Jen never would've had *my brother* pick her fucking underwear, Elena. She's a cheating bitch, but even she never would've stooped that low."

I let my eyes flutter closed, helplessness overwhelming me. Alexander and I... we're on a collision course. The way we're headed... there's no saving us. And this time, I'm to blame. He's never going to forgive me for Lucian's antics.

CHAPTER 33

*E*lena

"Don't worry. She'll wake up. Your mother and I have been friends since we were kids. She's one of the strongest women I know. Don't give up hope, sweetie."

Sofia holds my hand tightly as we sit next to my mom's hospital bed. She's been accompanying me to see my mother once a week for a while now. She'll sit here for hours and just talk to my mother about their childhood memories, about Lucian, Alexander and me. I like to think that my mother can hear her, and that the happy memories will help her want to wake up.

Today Sofia has been far more quiet than usual, and I know she's worried about Alexander and me. He and I have barely spoken recently, and I can tell that it's affecting her. Usually, we'd have dinner with her every other night or so, and the way Alexander would joke with her, the affection he'd display toward me, it's always made her happy. Now he doesn't even bother putting on an act for his mother anymore. He mostly ignores me, and it's worrying Sofia.

My mother's new doctor walks in, his face buried in his notes. The doctor looks surprised when he realizes my mother isn't alone. "Ah, Ms. Kennedy?" he asks.

"Yes," my mother-in-law and I both say. I look at her, flustered.

The doctor looks confused and stares from me to her. "Ms. *Elena* Kennedy?" he clarifies. I nod and stand up to shake his hand.

He blushes as he limply shakes my hand. "I—you—you're so young," he blurts out. I stare at him wide eyed and he shakes his head apologetically. "I didn't mean it that way. God, I'm so sorry. It's just, because you're the guardian—"

I laugh and shake my head. "It's quite all right. Please call me Elena. You're Dr. Taylor, I assume?" He doesn't look old enough to be a doctor, but Alexander assured me he's a prodigy and an expert in his field. It took Alexander weeks to convince him to come work for us.

He nods and proceeds to tell me about my mother's condition. "I flew in a few days ago and wasn't told anything about who I'd be treating or what the patient's condition was. The Kennedys have been really hush-hush about everything, so I didn't really know what to expect. I'll be your mother's permanent physician from now on. She'll be my only patient, and I'll provide her with round-the-clock care. For now, we're keeping her on the same drugs the previous hospital had her on so as to not shock her system, but I noticed some anomalies in her chart and well... it doesn't seem right. It looks like her brain activity is really high for a patient who's been in a coma for so long, and she certainly isn't brain dead. I'll be performing several tests throughout the next couple of weeks, so I'll know more soon. Having said that, I actually believe there's a chance she might wake up someday, Elena."

I stare at him in disbelief, my eyes filling with tears. She might actually wake up again one day? A relieved sob tears through my throat, and I bury my face in my hands. His words are like a lifeline to me, after years of disappointment. I sniff, trying my best to keep my emotions under control, and Sofia wraps her arm around me.

"That's wonderful news, sweetheart. I knew it. Your mom has always been a fighter."

I nod, smiling through my tears. I drop my head against her shoulder and inhale shakily. "Yes, she is, isn't she?"

The door opens behind us and I straighten, surprised to find Alexander walking in. His eyes find mine and he frowns when he realizes that I'm holding back tears. He walks up to us and places his hand on my shoulder, a hint of concern visible through his cold demeanor.

"What happened?" he asks, his voice soft.

"The doctor said she might wake up," I whisper, trying my best to blink away my tears.

Alexander's eyes widen, and he smiles, a real smile—the first I've seen in days, if not weeks. He brushes my hair behind my ear gently. "That's wonderful news, Buttercup."

I sniff, a shaky smile on my face. "It's all thanks to you. If not for you, she wouldn't be in this facility, and she wouldn't be receiving such good care."

He looks into my eyes and shakes his head. "It wasn't me," he tells me. "It was you. The faith you have, the sacrifices you've made."

Sofia nods in agreement and tightens her grip on me, hugging me tightly, a wide smile on her face.

"Mother," Alexander says, pressing a kiss to her cheek. She

smiles at him, her eyes moving between the two of us. I guess this is the most we've spoken in a while.

Alexander walks over to my mother and grabs her hand carefully. He presses a delicate kiss to the back of her hand and the sweet gesture sends tears to my eyes all over again.

He then turns towards my mother's doctor, who looks at him nervously. "I assume the research facilities are to your liking?" he asks.

Dr. Taylor nods. "Certainly, Mr. Kennedy. I'm beyond grateful for your funding of my study."

Sofia grabs my hand and smiles. "Alec and I have a standing lunch date every Tuesday. He said he wanted to check in with your mother's new doctor, so I asked him to pick me up here," she says.

I glance at her and shake my head. So she orchestrated this. She's trying to push Alexander and me together.

"I won't intrude," I say, knowing Alexander won't want me around. He's been going out of his way to avoid me recently. "You guys go ahead. I'll sit here with my mom a bit longer, and then I'll head back home. I have an appointment at three."

Alexander stares at his mother for a couple of seconds and sighs. "Come on," he says. "There's plenty of time. I'll drop you at home later."

I frown at him, but Sofia nods happily. Alexander holds my coat out for me, but it's his mother that he's looking at. I helplessly put my arms through the sleeves and then step away. Before I have a chance to do the buttons up, he wraps his hands over mine and smiles at me. He looks into my eyes, and I can't help the way my heart skips a beat. It feels like I haven't seen him in forever. I'm pretty sure he's been waiting to come to bed until he's certain I'm fast asleep. I've been trying to stay up and wait for him, but he never shows... yet every morning his side of the bed is messy.

Alexander steps closer to me and slowly does my buttons up, taking his time. I see Sofia beaming from my peripheral vision, a relieved look in her eyes. She doesn't even realize that it's all an act, and part of me wishes she would. I don't want to do this anymore. I don't want to pretend to be happy together when he won't even look at me in private.

Alexander grabs my hand and entwines our fingers before wrapping his other arm around his mother. He leads us to his car, and I'm surprised he didn't arrive here in his limousine. He opens the passenger door of his sports car for me and smiles apologetically.

"I'm sorry, Buttercup. You'll have to squeeze into the backseat. If I'd known you'd be here, I'd have come in a bigger car."

I smile and shake my head to indicate I don't mind. The backseat of his Aston Martin really is tiny, but thankfully I manage to fit just fine.

The restaurant we're going to isn't very far, and Sofia thoroughly enjoys the ride. Alexander lowers the roof for her so she can feel the wind blowing through her hair. He watches her with an indulgent smile every time she shakes her hair out, a huge grin on her face.

He takes such good care of her, and I can't help but lose a little bit of my heart to this version of him.

CHAPTER 34

lexander

We've only just made it to the restaurant when Elena's phone buzzes. She glances down at it, her eyes widening.

She looks up at me, a shimmer of panic in her eyes, and then she looks back down, hiding her phone away in a rush. Unease settles in my gut when she smiles tightly without meeting my eyes.

"I... I need to go. Something came up," she says.

She smiles at my mother and then turns to walk away before I can even stop her.

"Elena," I call, rushing after her. "Where are you going?"

She looks into my eyes and the guilt I see in them wrecks me. She's hiding something from me. "Oh, it's nothing. I just need to head back to the hospital real quick," she says.

And then she blinks twice, her telltale sign. She's lying.

She grabs my hand and smiles at me. "Go ahead and have lunch with your mother. I'll see you later."

She squeezes my hand, and then she walks away, flagging down a taxi as she goes. I stare after her, my heart uneasy.

I grab my phone and call my security team the second she steps in the taxi. "Tell me exactly who just texted my wife, and what the contents of that text were," I order as soon as Aiden, my security officer, picks up.

"Yes, sir," he says.

I pace on the pavement as I wait for him to retrieve the data. "Everything okay?" my mother asks. "Where did Elena go?"

I shake my head. "It's nothing, Mom. Something came up, though. Can we reschedule?"

She frowns at me and nods, but I can tell she's concerned. She's been worried about us for a while now, and I've let my anger at Elena overwhelm my mother's needs, her happiness. "Of course, Alec. I'll have the driver pick me up."

I smile at her and press a kiss to her cheek as she grabs her phone to call our driver.

"Mr. Kennedy," Aiden says on the phone. "It appears the text message came from your brother. The contents were as follows: *I need you, Elena. Now. Please meet me at this address,*" he says. I wait for him to give me the address, a thousand thoughts whirling through my mind. What the fuck are they up to? An affair? After she swore to me that nothing was going on between them? I should have known better. I should have known the second I found out about the fucking lingerie bullshit.

Pure rage fills my every vein when I realize the address is a room in one of our hotels. My hands are shaking as I get behind the wheel. Each scenario that comes to mind is more painful than the last. It feels like Jennifer all over again. Finding her in the apartment I bought for her, Matthew on top of her. I was stupid to put my faith in Elena. To think that money could buy her loyalty.

I'm seeing white as I walk into the hotel lobby. The receptionist is visibly nervous to find me here in person without any prior notice, and she stares at me with wide eyes. "Give me a duplicate key card to the Presidential suite," I tell her.

She blinks and hesitates, but thankfully for her, her manager steps up and hands me the key before I can fire her for her incompetence.

I take it and wrap my hand around it so tightly that it cuts into me. Dread fills me as I take the lift up, scared of what I'll find. I stand in front of the door, my heart aching in a way it never has before. Elena... I should've remembered whose little sister she is. Whose daughter she is. She's had me fooled.

I slide the keycard through quietly and open the door as soundlessly as I can, catching it before it slams closed.

I lean back against the wall, listening for moans, but instead all I hear are pained sobs. I freeze, straightening.

"He broke my heart. Tore it to shreds."

I frown, confused. I take a step closer until Elena and Lucian come into view. My heart drops when I find my half naked brother in my wife's arms. It appears all he's wearing is boxers, but Elena is still fully dressed.

I struggle to make sense of what I'm seeing, what I'm hearing.

This... this isn't an affair.

"I really thought Marcus was different," Lucian says. "I fell so hard, Elena. I thought he was the one. I was going to tell my family about him. He already works with my brother, so I thought it might be easier to accept for them. He's Alec's CFO, and I know Alec quite likes him, so I was really hopeful." He inhales shakily, his eyes falling closed. "But Marcus was just after the money. Today was the first time we slept together, and it was magical to me, so magical, Elena. But he... he filmed it and he's blackmailing me."

Elena hugs him tighter, her expression anguished. "We'll figure something out, Luce. Everything will be okay. We need to tell Alexander. He'll know what to do."

Lucian pushes her away harshly, pure panic transforming his face. "No!" he shouts. "My brother can't find out," he says, his voice high, panicked. "He'll never see me the same way. He'll lose all respect for me. He'll find me despicable. A gay brother? He'll never accept it. To have gotten blackmailed, too? He'll just think I'm weak. You can't tell him, Elena. You promised. You *swore* you'd never tell."

Elena wraps her arms around herself, looking as panicked as Lucian does. The anguish on her face... fuck.

I walk into the bedroom, startling them both. Lucian's expression transforms into one of betrayal, and then hatred. He looks at Elena in disbelief and I shake my head.

"She was acting suspicious," I tell him. "So I followed her."

I walk toward the bed and pick up his discarded clothes, my eyes roaming over the messy room. I throw Lucian's clothes at him and shake my head. "Get dressed," I tell him.

Elena rises to her feet, looking worried, and I sigh. I don't even know what to say to her. To think I suspected her of cheating with my own brother, when I couldn't be more wrong. I've somehow managed to push my brother so far away that he trusts my wife more with his secrets than he does me. And my wife... I've accused her of disloyalty over and over again, when I couldn't be more wrong. It's her *loyalty* that kept her from telling me the truth, when that would have resolved all our issues. She kept the promises she made to Lucian, even as I made her suffer for it.

Tears stream down Lucian's face as he gets dressed, and he's choking back sobs, unable to look me in the eye. It breaks my fucking heart to see him like that. I can't remember the last time I even saw him cry—not in *years*. I should've been the first person he turned to in this situation, yet I'm the last person he wanted finding out.

I grab my phone and call Elliot, one of my closest friends, and a total computer genius. He picks up almost immediately.

"What's up?" he says. "How do I get to extort you today?"

I bite back a smile and shake my head. "I need camera footage removed," I say, glancing at Lucian.

"How were you filmed, Lucian?" I ask, my voice soft. "With what device?"

He swallows hard and lifts his head slowly, fresh tears in his eyes. "I... Alec..."

I smile at him and shake my head. "Just tell me what device it was."

He nods, big fat tears rolling down his cheeks. "It was his phone. I don't remember what model it was."

I sigh and nod at him. "Elliot, I need you to fry every single device owned by Marcus Smith. He's one of my employees. I'll write you a blank cheque."

I hear Elliot typing furiously through the phone before he replies. "It's for Lucian?" he asks, his voice soft.

"Yeah," I murmur. "His boyfriend betrayed him."

Elliot falls silent. "I see. So, he's... uh, he's gay?"

"Yeah, so?" I snap, furious. "Is there a problem?"

"No, *no*," Elliot says. "I just—I just always thought he was really cute."

I blink in surprise, completely thrown. I don't even know what to say to that. I clear my throat awkwardly. "Well, I'm sure you know how to get your hands on his contact details, though now probably isn't a good time."

Elliot laughs nervously. "Okay, well, consider it done. No charge, since it's for Lucian."

I laugh, I can't help it. How am I only just finding out that two people I've known forever aren't straight? Am I really that clueless?

"Thank you," I say. "I need you to uncover every bit of dirt on him and have it go viral. I need enough to be able to fire him without having a lawsuit on my hands. I don't want him ever being able to find another job."

"Come on," I tell Elena and Lucian. "We're leaving."

CHAPTER 35

lexander

"Where are we going?" Elena asks as I lead them to my car. Lucian has barely even looked at me, and I don't know what to say to him either. I've failed him as an older brother, and I didn't even realize it.

"What's going to make you feel better?" I ask Lucian, at a loss myself.

He looks up, his eyes red. "Honestly, Alec... I'd give anything to just egg the hell out of his house, however juvenile that might be."

I bark out a laugh and nod. Very well. I'm planning on doing much worse than that, but it's not a bad start.

"Convenience store first, then."

Elena and Lucian are both quiet as they follow along, and it isn't until I park in front of Marcus's house that Lucian panics.

"Alec," he says, sounding anxious as he steps out of the car. "Maybe this isn't a good idea after all."

I smile at him, eggs in hand. "This guy is about to find out what happens when you mess with a Kennedy. Besides, you'll feel better after this."

I hand him an egg and he stares at it. "You aren't mad?" he asks. "You're not disappointed?"

I frown at him and wrap my arm around his shoulder, involuntarily sending a burst of fresh tears to his eyes. "Lucian, you've done nothing to be ashamed of. You'd never disappoint me. If anything, I'm the one that has disappointed you."

He bursts into tears and my heart breaks when he swipes at his tears angrily, clearly hating that he can't stay in control of his emotions today. As if I'd suddenly look down on him for being emotional after everything he's been through today, when he's usually so stoic.

"I know everything that's going on is a lot, and I'd be just as upset. Hell, I'd be crying too."

He nods and hugs me, and I hold him tightly. Elena looks at me with such relief in her eyes and I shake my head, sighing. How long has she been keeping his secret? How hard must it have been for her to keep quiet every time I questioned her about her relationship with my brother?

"Come on," I murmur. Lucian nods and pulls himself together, straightening his clothes. He gasps when I reach back and throw one of the eggs with as much force as I can, and a burst of laughter escapes his lips when it cracks against Marcus's window.

I hand him a couple of eggs of his own and lean back against my car as he throws them, his mood improving with every egg that smashes against the house, until at last, he's laughing.

I glance at Elena, overwhelmed with guilt. The things I said to her... I've hurt her, and I did it knowingly. I've been ignoring her, avoiding her, and all the while, she's been taking care of my family better than I have. I feel sick when I think back to the pain I saw in her eyes when I compared her to Jennifer, when I told her that even Jennifer was more loyal than she is. I sat there and watched her brother insult her, and I didn't stand up for her. I let it happen because of my misguided anger.

I walk up to her, hesitating. Elena looks at me in a way that has my heart working overtime. There's no anger in her eyes, no judgment, no vindication. Instead, she smiles at me reassuringly, knowingly. I raise my arm to wrap it around her and exhale in relief when she walks into my embrace. She has every right to be mad at me for being as harsh with her as I have been, when she so clearly didn't do anything wrong. Instead, all I see in her eyes is relief. Her focus isn't on being right, it's on Lucian and his well-being. I lean in and press a kiss to her cheek, startling her.

"Thank you," I whisper. "For taking care of him in my stead."

She smiles at me, a look of understanding in her eyes. I'm so lost in my wife's eyes that I don't notice Marcus storming out of his house until Lucian tenses beside me.

I straighten and intercept him before he can reach either my wife or brother. The victorious look in his eyes irritates me, and I draw back my arm before punching him in the jaw as hard as I can. He stumbles backward and falls onto the floor, ass first. I shake my head and dust off my fist, irritated that I had to get it dirty in the first place.

Marcus bursts out laughing, the sound hysterical, and holds his phone up. "I'd be careful if I were you. Your brother has secrets. Secrets I can reveal with the touch of a button."

I smile at him and nod. "Go ahead," I tell him.

Marcus's smile wavers, but then he grins widely. "Don't think I won't."

I cross my arms over each other as he picks himself up off the floor. "How about you show me what you've got on him?"

Lucian walks up to me and places his hand on my arm. I can feel him trembling, and it sends fresh rage through my body. By the time I'm done with Marcus, no one will recognize him.

Marcus clicks on his phone, his smug smile slowly transforming into disbelief.

"It doesn't work? Your phone is fried, huh? What a coincidence," I say, my tone threatening.

Marcus laughs, the sound hysterical, crazy. "I have backups. I'm not stupid," he says, just as three black cars pull up at the curb.

"Yeah. So do I," I tell him.

Aiden and the rest of my security team step out of the cars, guns strapped to their waists. Standing there in their black suits, even I have to admit they look intimidating as hell.

"Boss," Aiden says, and I tip my head towards Marcus's front door.

"He says he's got backups of something I want destroyed, so I guess we have no choice. Destroy every single thing in that house and bring me every single piece of electronics he owns— but smash it to pieces first."

Marcus charges me, but my men have him restrained within seconds. I glance at Lucian and sigh. "That's who you fell for? Seriously?"

He looks distraught, and I regret teasing him immediately. I wrap my arm around him and sigh. "Everything will be okay, kiddo," I tell him. "But we need to work on your taste in men. Elena seems to have good taste. She can give you some pointers."

Lucian laughs, and I breathe a sigh of relief.

"You have no idea what I've done to your brother," Marcus yells. "I've had him suck my dick. I've stretched out his little ass. Had him yelling my name."

Lucian wraps his arms around himself, his head down. His cheeks are red, and he looks humiliated beyond belief. I grab one of the remaining eggs and hand it to one of my men.

"Gag this asshole. I'm done hearing from him. Matter of fact, it seems like it might be best to never hear from him again." I turn to my little brother and raise my brow. "Do you want me to make him disappear?"

Before Lucian can even answer me, police sirens sound from a distance. I glance at Marcus. He looks fucking stupid standing there with an egg in his mouth, but the victorious glint in his eyes is what pisses me off.

"This motherfucker managed to call the police before Elliot fried his shit."

I sigh and pull out my phone, hating that I now have to ask for a favor. I manage to get the Director General of the Police on the line just as the police car parks in front of us. Two agents step out of the car, their guns drawn, their eyes on the men that are restraining Marcus.

"Afternoon, officers," I say, nodding.

They point their guns at me, and I sigh. "Terrible idea," I mutter. "Could you please tell me your name, rank, and station?"

Both of them blink, startled for just a second. They know as well as I do that they have to provide me with the information I asked for, and they do it grudgingly.

"Got all that?" I ask the Director General.

"Got it," he repeats. "But you owe me, Alexander."

I grit my teeth. "I know," I say, ending the call.

I glance at Marcus with renewed hatred before turning back to the police officers in front of me.

"Now, I'm going to need you to let this man go," one of them says, his voice calm, his gun aimed directly at me. I have to admire his temperament. We've got them outnumbered at least five to one, but it doesn't faze him.

"I'm afraid I'll be doing no such thing," I tell him, feeling somewhat bad for him.

Lucian is clutching my sleeve while Elena's hand trembles in mine. I hate that I put them in this situation. This isn't something either of them should have to experience, and this is entirely on me. I'm the one that brought them here. I should've known to come alone.

"I regret to inform you," I tell the officer, glancing at my watch, "that in less than a minute your receiver will inform you to stand back."

He glances at the device strapped to his waist and laughs. When he looks back at me, it's clear that he thinks he's dealing with a psycho of some sort. He wouldn't be entirely wrong.

He grabs his receiver and raises it to his lips to ask for backup, and I can't even blame the guy. Unfortunately for him, his device crackles just as he's about to speak. "Stand down. Leave the premises at once," I can just about make out, recognizing the Director General's voice. Both the officers look shocked and take a step back to request more information, their voices low, but eventually I see their shoulders sag.

They look at me, and the annoyance in their eyes is justified. I bet they became police officers because they wanted to make the world a better and safer place, only to come to the realization that none of it matters—this world is ruled by money. It always has been.

"Very well, Mr. Kennedy," one of them says. He glances back at Marcus and then sighs. He shakes his head as he walks back to his car, his colleague in tow.

"How?" Lucian asks, his eyes filled with admiration I haven't seen in years. I smile at him and ruffle his hair.

"Connections, Luce," I murmur. He doesn't need to know just how dirty I get my hands for our family.

Elena drops her head on my shoulder and I wrap my arm around her.

"Let's go home," I say.

Elena and Lucian both nod. They look exhausted, and I'm not surprised.

"Take care of him," I tell my men. "Make sure he doesn't talk."

Lucian looks back at Marcus one more time, his eyes red. Then he turns resolutely, renewed confidence in his eyes. He looks up at me gratefully, and I smile at him as I open the door for him.

Marcus is going to regret messing with my brother.

CHAPTER 36

lexander

Lucian stops me as I'm about to walk to my bedroom, his hand on my sleeve. Elena glances at the two of us and slips away, a sweet smile on her face.

Lucian looks nervous and stares down at his feet. "I... I just wanted to say sorry," he says. "I caused so much trouble today, but you didn't hesitate to help me. Not just that... I know Elena and you have been arguing. I know I came between you two, and I could've fixed everything if I'd just spoken up, if I told you the truth... but I didn't."

I place my hand on his shoulder and smile. "You're my little brother, Lucian. I will always have your back. Always. I'm sorry I wasn't someone you could confide in."

He swallows hard and nods. "You—you're okay with it? You're not ashamed of me?"

I frown at him. "What? No. Why would I be? Nothing has even changed. You're still my baby brother, Luce."

He looks at me in confusion. "But, Alec... I'm *gay*. This isn't a phase. I've tried all my life, but I'll *never* be attracted to a woman. At some point, the world will find out."

I smile at him. "Well, when you're ready to tell the world, I'll be right there with you, if that's where you want me. I'm not very good at this, Luce. I'm just not. I don't know what the right thing to say is. I don't know what you need to hear. All I know is that you're my brother, and I'll always love you the same. I don't care who you sleep with." I narrow my eyes at him. "So long as it isn't my wife."

Lucian's eyes are filled with tears, but he bursts out laughing. "You were worried about that, huh? Elena has always only ever had eyes for you. Always, Alec. I'm sorry I didn't speak up sooner. She has a heart of gold, and she would *never* betray you."

I've been married to Elena long enough to know that, yet I let my past blind me. I smile at Lucian and nod in acknowledgment.

"Does Mom know?" I ask carefully.

Lucian blanches and shakes his head, his expression anguished. "No."

"Do you want to tell her?" Lucian looks at me, and the longing in his eyes is clear as day. "Do you want to tell her together?" I add.

He nods, and I ruffle his hair. It's been so long since my little brother looked this cute. "Just say the word. Whenever you're ready, I'll be with you."

Lucian nods. He hesitates before taking a step closer, throwing his arms around me suddenly. I stand there, frozen for a couple of seconds, before I hug my brother back.

He pulls away, visibly emotional. "I'm sorry," he says. "Thank you. For today. For being there. I'm grateful to have you as my brother."

He smiles tightly and turns to walk away, looking a little

flustered. It seems like today's events really took a toll on him. His usual confidence is completely absent, and I hate seeing him look so vulnerable.

I watch him walk down the stairs, and I can't help but worry that Marcus scarred him. Even worse, I don't know how to make it better.

I'm still worried about Lucian when I walk into my bedroom, stopping in my tracks at the sound of the shower. Elena... fuck. I've gone out of my way to make her feel like she's nothing to me, like she is indeed a mere tool to me. I fucked up. Badly.

I undress quietly and hesitate before walking through the water curtain. Elena looks up at me in surprise, and I pause to look at her. She looks so fucking beautiful standing there, water running down her body. I've missed her. I've missed her body against mine, her smile.

I walk up to her and pause in front of her. She leans back against the wall and looks into my eyes. There's no condemnation in her eyes, no pettiness, no *I told you so*'s. There are never any games with her, no keeping score. I should've known better. I should've known she wouldn't betray me.

I move closer to her and bury my hand in her wet hair. Elena places her palms against my chest, sliding them up, until her arms are wrapped around my neck.

"Are you okay?" she asks. She should be gloating right now, showing off how much of a fucking idiot I am for not seeing the truth, for not believing her. She should be punishing me for the way I've treated her, my mistrust, the things I've said to her. But there's none of that. All I see in those beautiful eyes of hers is concern. Concern for *me*.

I nod and take a step closer, until our bodies are flush against each other, the water pouring down on us.

"I'm sorry," I whisper. "I've been so fucking horrible to you, baby. I've ignored you, hurt you... I was punishing you for a crime you didn't commit. This afternoon, when I followed you... Elena, I expected the worst."

She nods knowingly and rises to her tiptoes. "I know. The look in your eyes when you saw me hugging Lucian on that hotel bed; it broke my heart. I saw the puzzle pieces fall together, but before it all clicked, I saw the pain in your eyes. Alec, I would never do that to you. I know you don't believe in forever, but that's what I promised you the day I agreed to marry you. I'm your wife, *forever*. You will always be the only one for me."

I lean in, my lips brushing against hers, once, twice, before I kiss her, savoring her. The way she makes my heart race terrifies and thrills me all at once. I never expected to feel this strongly about her.

Elena rises and deepens our kiss, a moan escaping her lips. She runs her hands over my body; her touch eager, desperate. She pushes me against the wall, and I grin against her lips, turning us around instead.

I lift her into my arms and push her against the wall. Elena wraps her legs around me, her hands finding their way to my hair.

"Tell me you forgive me."

Elena smiles and tightens her grip on my hair. "Then ask me for forgiveness, Alexander. Don't command it."

I drop my forehead to hers, my eyes falling closed. "Elena, will you forgive me for my stupidity? For the way I've treated you and hurt you? I have no excuse. All I can say is that I can't stand the idea of any part of you belonging to someone else."

She cups my cheek and raises my face to hers, her lips finding mine. She kisses me slowly, setting my heart ablaze. I exhale shakily when she pulls away. "I forgive you. I'm sorry for not telling you the truth. It wasn't my story to tell."

I nod and hold her tighter, pushing her against the wall harder. Her lips find mine, and the way she kisses me... *fuck*. She's driving me insane and she knows it. I'm panting by the time I pull away.

"It's time for the next act of our press performance," I tell her.

Elena groans when I push up against her. The way she tilts her hips up in a silent bid for more makes me smile. "What act?" she asks, breathless.

She writhes against me, until she's got the angle just right, and I slip into her. I groan and drop my forehead to hers. I'll never get used to the feel of her. It's been so fucking long. I've missed her. All this time that I stayed away, I was punishing myself more than her.

"The proposal," I tell her. "A public proposal for the press. I can't wait any longer, Elena. I want my ring on your finger."

She smiles at me and tightens her grip on my hair. "I want nothing more, Alec."

A thrill runs down my spine when she calls me Alec. It sounds so good coming from her lips. I grab her hips and pull back before slamming into her hard, the way she likes it. Her moans are like music to my ears.

"Forever, huh?"

Elena nods, a gasp escaping her lips when I thrust into her. I pull back again and look into her eyes.

"You'll moan like this for me forever?"

Elena nods, and I push into her, giving her what she wants.

"Tell me, Elena. Will you always look at me this way? Will you always want me this way?"

She tightens her grip on my hair and nods. "Forever, Alec."

I keep her on the edge, needing her with a desperation I've never felt before. I want all of her. I told her love would never be an option for us, but I want to be the one her heart belongs to, the only one she can see.

I lean in to kiss her, losing myself in her. The way she feels, the way she whispers my name. She's perfect, in every way.

Elena's breathing accelerates, and the way she pants and moans has me ready to come. "You're so fucking beautiful," I whisper against her lips.

"Alec," she whispers. "I can't..."

Her muscles contract around me, and the sounds she makes push me over the edge. I come deep inside her, her name on my lips.

I drop my forehead to hers, my eyes falling closed. Forever, huh? The thought both terrifies and excites me.

CHAPTER 37

lena

I pick up the photo on Alexander's nightstand, my heart twisting at the sight of it. We've been married for months now, and even though I'm the one he falls asleep with, it feels like Jennifer is still the one he thinks of when he closes his eyes. I think back to the way he used me to make her jealous, the way he held me in his lap on that rooftop bar. It was all a show... for *her*.

The bedroom door opens suddenly, and I jump, startled. The photo frame slips out of my hands and falls to the floor, the glass shattering into hundreds of pieces. I gasp and bend down to pick up the frame, cutting myself with one of the shards as I do so. I hiss in pain, a drop of blood appearing at the tip of my finger.

"Fuck, Elena," Alexander says, rushing over.

I look up at him, panic engulfing me. "I'm sorry," I tell him, my voice shaky. "I shouldn't have touched it. I'm so sorry. I'll replace the frame, Alec. The photo... the photo can be saved."

His gaze drops to the broken frame, and his eyes widen. He sighs and shakes his head, and my heart drops. I feel both ashamed to have gotten caught touching something that's obviously precious to him, and incredibly hurt that the person in the photo with him isn't me.

He bends down and lifts me into his arms in one fell swoop, one hand behind my back, and one underneath my knees. I gasp and throw my arm around him. "What are you doing?" I whisper.

Alexander shakes his head. "Clumsy, wifey. You need to be more careful. What if you cut yourself really badly? What if the cuts leave scars?"

He puts me down on his bed and kneels down in front of me, assessing my hands. He brings my finger to his lips, sucking down on it. I've never seen him so concerned, so worried.

"I'm fine, Alec. But the photo..."

He smiles at me, his eyes flashing with satisfaction. "Such a good girl, calling me Alec. Feel free to smash everything in our bedroom if it'll finally make you call me Alec outside of bed."

He looks at me and I pull my hand to my chest, cradling it, suddenly feeling vulnerable. "Fuck the photo," he says. "It has no place in our bedroom. I should have removed it the day I married you. I'm sorry, Elena."

I look at him with wide eyes. This is the first time he's ever called his bedroom *ours*, and to get rid of that photo... I doubt he knows how much that means to me. He cups my cheek gently, his eyes blazing with sincerity.

"I'm sorry, Elena," he repeats.

I shake my head, flustered. "There's nothing to be sorry about," I tell him, feeling conflicted. I don't feel like I even have the right to be angry about the photo. He's promised me many things, but never love. It's always been clear to me that that's been reserved for Jennifer.

"Stay here," he tells me as he grabs his phone and walks out of the room.

A minute later the housekeepers walk in with cleaning supplies, Alexander right behind them. He oversees their work with a frown on his face. "I don't want a single shard remaining," he tells them. "If my wife cuts herself on even the tiniest piece, I'm firing all of you," he threatens.

I look up at him in surprise. He's changed since the incident with Marcus and Lucian. When he looks at me now, his eyes are filled with remorse. He's treating me better, and while I'm enjoying this softer version of him, I wish it wasn't born out of guilt.

He looks back at the shards on the floor and then walks over, pausing in front of me. "How do you feel?" he asks. "Are you in any pain?"

Alexander glances over and grabs my hands, checking for cuts, and I shake my head. I've never seen this side of him. "I'm fine," I tell him, but he continues to check my arms, before kneeling down in front of me to check my feet.

My eyes widen in shock when Dr. Taylor comes rushing into the bedroom. "Mr. Kennedy," he says, walking over to us.

"Alec," I whisper. "Please tell me you did *not* call Dr. Taylor over because of some tiny cuts."

He purses his lips and ignores me, turning to the doctor instead. "My wife cut herself," he says, still on his knees in front of me.

My cheeks are bright red, and I hang my head in shame before gathering the courage to look at Dr. Taylor. "Um, they're essentially just paper cuts," I tell him, my voice small.

Alexander shakes his head and holds my finger up for the doctor, who somehow manages to keep his expression perfectly blank. "They're not just paper cuts," he says. "She could get infected. There are cuts on her feet too."

Dr. Taylor nods and kneels down in front of me, a medical kit on the floor beside him. "I see, Mr. Kennedy," he says, nodding, as though Alexander is right, and my injuries are actually grave.

I look at Alexander wide-eyed. "You can't just call a doctor over because of some tiny little cuts, Alec!" I whisper-shout.

Dr. Taylor tries his hardest to suppress his smile, but he fails, while Alexander just ignores my reprimands.

Alexander staring at the doctor so hard that even I am nervous. All he's doing is touching my hand and feet, but the way Alexander is looking at him is so threatening that I feel bad for him.

Dr. Taylor and I both breathe a sigh of relief when he's done, and Alexander finally relaxes when he packs up his stuff.

He greets us politely before walking out, and Alexander stares at the closed bedroom door. "I don't like him," he says. "I don't like the way he looked at you, the way he touched your feet. He's too young to be a doctor anyway. I'm requesting another background check on him."

I bite down on my lip to keep from bursting out laughing. "You don't like the way he touched my *feet*?"

He looks at me, dead serious, and nods.

"I mean, yeah, he's quite handsome, isn't he?" I say, my tone teasing.

He frowns and grits his teeth. He grabs my chin and turns my face toward his. "You're mine, Elena. Your body is mine, but make no mistake, your every thought is mine too. Don't you dare even *dream* about anyone else."

I smile at him provocatively. "Oh, yeah? And what will you do if I don't listen? The way you touched me after you found out I went shopping with Lucian was amazing..."

He looks at me through narrowed eyes and lifts me into his arms, repositioning me on the bed before leaning over me.

"Elena, don't tempt me. Your injuries won't stop me."

I laugh, I can't help it. "Injuries, huh?" I whisper, my fingers tracing over his face. I pull him closer and kiss him, startling him.

He grins and lowers himself on top of me, kissing me gently, carefully. I whimper underneath him, eager for more. "You do realize that I'm not actually injured, right?"

He holds himself up on his elbows and looks into my eyes. "But you are," he says. "I don't want to see you hurting in any way, Elena. I don't want any harm coming to you—not even something so small as a paper cut."

I smile at him, my heart twisting painfully. He's hurting me every single day by withholding the one thing I want from him most. Things have gotten much better between us lately, and he's never treated me this well before, but it's not love.

CHAPTER 38

lexander

I stare at the engagement ring and rotate it to see how the light catches. "Magnificent job," I tell Francesco, the owner of the jewelry store my family has frequented for years. I can't wait to see the look on Elena's face.

The ring in my hand is the one she couldn't stop looking at when I brought her here to pick her ring. It's the one she so clearly wanted, yet didn't dare ask for. I smile to myself, imagining what it'll look like on her hand.

"Six carats, emerald cut," Francesco tells me. "Perfect for Mrs. Kennedy."

I nod at him. "Perfect, indeed." The carat weight is perfect for someone of Elena's stature—for my wife. Yet the band itself is simple. It suits her.

"Alec."

I freeze with the ring in hand, chills running down my spine. I'd recognize her voice anywhere, and it makes my heart ache. I don't turn. Instead, I keep my eyes on Elena's engagement ring.

"That... what is that?" Jennifer says.

Francesco nods at her, his poker face in place. I've brought Jennifer to this store countless times. She owns many of Francesco's priceless pieces, and it's here, at my family's jeweler, that I came looking for a ring for Jennifer.

"Pack it up for me," I tell Francesco, and he nods politely.

"Alec," Jen repeats, her voice soft.

I turn to face her, bracing myself. She smiles at me, and my heart twists painfully. Her long blonde hair is perfectly straight, and she looks at me as though she never stabbed me in the heart, and then twisted the knife.

"It's Alexander," I correct her.

She looks stricken and glances at Francesco. "That... was that an engagement ring?"

I cross my arms over my chest. "Speaking of engagements," I say, "I hear congratulations are in order. It slipped my mind the last time I saw you. I can't think straight when I have Elena in my arms."

Her cheeks redden, and she twists her engagement ring around her finger. My heart twists just a little at the sight of her ring, and I take a sick type of delight in knowing Elena's ring is bigger.

"That's cute," I tell her, nodding at her ring.

She hides her ring behind her other hand and grins up at me. That smile I used to love, it no longer looks the way it used to. It doesn't look innocent and sweet. Now, it looks fake and calculative. Was it always that way, or am I only just realizing it?

"Don't take this joke too far. I'm not sure what you're trying to accomplish, but being with a girl like that isn't going to make me jealous. Did you know she came running to her father's house not too long ago, begging for money? She looked so pathetic, tears and snot running down her face, crying on the floor. She was even wearing disgusting torn clothes. You could never be with someone like that."

Anger courses through me. My Buttercup was in such a bad state? "Not too long ago, you were the one wearing cheap clothes," I say, giving her a once over. "But look at you now." I shake my head and smirk. "Elena was born with class running through her very veins, no matter what she wears. You might marry one of us, Jennifer, but you'll never *be* one of us. Not truly."

She looks at me as though I've slapped her and grits her teeth. "She's using you. You know that, right? She needs money for her mother's hospital bills or something like that. Is she the reason you've been ignoring all of my text messages?"

The lack of empathy astounds me. I always thought Jennifer had a heart of gold, but now I'm wondering if that was all an act too. Or maybe she never even put on an act, and I was just too smitten to see her true colors.

"What Elena needs is none of your concern," I tell her. "It's mine. *She's* mine."

Jennifer looks at me through narrowed eyes. "If I wasn't good enough for you, there's no way someone as pathetic as Elena would be. Your mother would never allow it."

I frown at her. "What are you talking about?"

Jennifer laughs, but there's a hint of pain in her gaze. "Your mother. The second our relationship got serious, she started to show me how ill-suited we are. She'd take me to all these events where she knew I'd be out of my depth, and she'd never give me any warnings or advice. I could take that, you know." Jennifer brushes her hair out of the way the way she does when she's flustered. "But then we spoke about marriage, you and I, and your mother gave me an incredibly restrictive pre-nup."

I raise my brows. This is all new information to me. Neither my mother nor Jennifer has ever mentioned anything of the sort. As far as I'm aware, Mom is doing the same thing with Elena. Not to show her we're ill-suited, but to ease her back into society, to help her make new connections. It's likely that that's what she was attempting to do with Jennifer, too. My heart sinks as I think of my mother. Is she unknowingly the reason Jennifer walked away?

"I couldn't do it," she says. "Constantly being made to feel like I'm not good enough for you, like I don't deserve you. I couldn't live the rest of my life like that, no matter how much I loved you, no matter how much I *still* do."

"So you cheated?" I ask, my voice deadly calm.

Jennifer's eyes widen, and she shakes her head. "It wasn't like that. Matthew was just a friend at the start, but he was just always there. You were always working, and you'd cut me off the second I said anything negative about your mother. He was just there when I needed someone."

I smile at her and nod. "I see... so it was *my fault* you cheated on me?"

Jennifer shakes her head, flustered, and I laugh. "My mother was right about you all along," I tell her. "A pre-nup shouldn't have mattered to you if you didn't think we'd ever get divorced. I know my mother, and any pre-nup she'd have asked you to sign would have still provided you with enough money to live off. All she would have done was safeguard Kennedy assets."

Jennifer's eyes flash with guilt and dismay, and I know I'm right. The money she was offered was likely quite a sizable amount.

"Either way," Jennifer says. "I was so devoted to you, and I still wasn't good enough for you according to your mother. If I wasn't, then I don't see how Elena will be."

I stare at her, the difference between Elena and her greater than I initially thought it was. Jen looks fake in every way—her hair, her lips, her tits, but also her smile and her kindness. None of it looks or feels real. She isn't worth the hatred, the mental real estate she's been occupying.

I glance at Francesco, who rushes toward me, a ring box in hand. I smile at him as I take the box from him and place it in my suit pocket.

I glance back at Jennifer, seeing her in a different light. "It was good to see you, Jennifer," I say. "I wish you and Matthew the best. You deserve each other."

I walk away, and this time, I don't look back.

CHAPTER 39

lena

My hands are trembling as I hold my phone up, a photo of Alexander and Jennifer staring back at me. She's smiling at him, and he's looking at her; the two of them standing in the jewelry store he took me to pick our rings. Based on the suit he's wearing in the photo, this must have been just a few days ago.

Has he been seeing her all along? I can't make sense of this. The way he reacted when I broke that photo frame made me think that maybe, just maybe, he was actually moving on from her. But the way he looks at her in this photo... it's the same way he's always looked at her.

I don't understand why he's even with her at all. Why wouldn't he have told me about it? He's been acting so possessive lately that I was under the impression that I'm the only woman in his life. Was I wrong? Was his behavior really just him projecting his own unfaithfulness?

"What's wrong?" Lucian asks, startling me.

I lock my phone and look up at him, shaking my head. He's been so incredibly depressed after everything that happened with Marcus. He's barely leaving his bedroom, he sleeps most of his days away, and he's too scared to leave the house, scared that someone found out his secret, somehow. There's nothing I can do or say to convince him that everything is fine, that his secrets are safe.

"It's nothing," I tell him, pasting a smile on my face. I don't need him to worry about something so trivial. This is between Alexander and me, after all.

My phone buzzes and I frown when I realize that it's the private investigator I hired. "Ma'am," he says. "There have been some developments in the case. I have some evidence to show you. Would today be a good time?"

I swallow hard and try my best to keep it together, even though my heart is sinking. I was hoping I was wrong, that my suspicions were just that—suspicions. "Yes," I say, my voice shaky. My mind is buzzing as I give the PI my address, my heart racing.

I don't even realize when Lucian helps me to the sofa. "Elena, you're worrying me," he says.

I turn to look at him and blink, absentmindedly, before forcing a smile onto my face. "It's nothing, Luce. I'm sorry."

He sits down next to me, searching my face. My phone rings again, and this time it's Alexander. I watch it ring until it finally stops. Before I saw that photo, he'd have been the first person I'd want to speak to after hearing that there's a new development in my mother's case. But now? Now I need some distance.

He calls me again, and this time I click the incoming call away. Lucian frowns at me and wraps his arm around me. "Okay," he says. "Something is definitely wrong."

I shake my head and put my phone down as Aiden walks in, the PI in tow.

"Mr. Starling," I say, nodding at him. He and I have never met in person. In fact, it was Aiden that found him for me.

"Please call me Lucas," he says, smiling. Lucas looks around in wonder, and I belatedly realize that the Kennedy residence isn't a place people usually get to see from the inside. I wonder if I should have met him elsewhere, instead.

He pulls a manila folder out of his bag and places it in front of me. "You were right to be suspicious," he tells me, his expression serious. "We found evidence that there was foul play in your mother's car accident."

My heart twists painfully, and I rub my chest as though that'll alleviate the pain. Lucas lays out some photos for me and my heart sinks. "These... these are parts of my mother's car?"

He nods, his expression grim. "It looks like nothing was wrong with it, and honestly, it took me weeks just to find some of the scraps. Someone went through great lengths to make this car disappear."

I nod, a shudder running down my spine. "So, what happened?"

Lucas points at one of the photos. "This console, it's connected to the car. Somehow, someone managed to manipulate it, to make your mother lose control of her car. I've brought the part here for you. All my technical team could tell me is that it was tampered with, but I was unable to find out more."

He opens his bag and takes out an almost unrecognizable piece of technology. I take the plastic wrapped object with trembling hands and examine it before turning to Lucian.

"Luce," I murmur. "Could you call Elliot for me?"

Lucian blinks, a blush creeping up his cheeks, and the edges of my lips tip up slightly. The only positive words to have come out of his mouth since Marcus have all been about Elliot.

"I... yeah, I guess," he says, fiddling with his phone.

I sit up in surprise when the doors open and Alexander

walks in, a worried expression on his face. His eyes find mine and he storms into the living room, his eyes blazing.

"You're ignoring my calls and texts," he tells me, his voice rough.

I frown at him, annoyed, and cross my arms over my chest. His eyes roam over the room, settling on Lucas.

"Who the fuck are you?"

Lucas rises to his feet, his eyes bouncing between Alexander and me.

"Lucas," I say. "Meet Alexander Kennedy."

Lucas nods but struggles to hide his surprise. I turn to Alexander and sigh. "Lucas Starling is the PI Aiden hired. He's found some evidence that there was foul play in my mother's accident."

Alexander nods and walks up to me, taking a seat next to me as Lucas runs him through the case. He places his hand on my knee, his thumb stroking my skin. I'm tempted to push his hand off, but I don't want to be childish or petty.

"Elliot can figure this out," Alexander says, nodding at me. "I'll call him."

I shake my head. "No need. Lucian is on it. We have this under control."

Alexander looks into my eyes, his gaze searching, and then he sighs. "You're mad at me."

I turn away from him and rise to my feet as Lucas packs his belongings. "I'm sorry that this is all I was able to find, ma'am," he says. "I'll keep looking into this case."

I shake his hand and smile. "I'm grateful for the work you've done," I tell him honestly. "This is more than I dared hoped for. Without you, I'd still be living with fear and suspicion. Now I have something to go on."

He nods, his smile as sad as mine must be. "I'll get to the

bottom of this," he promises, and I smile at him gratefully as the housekeeper walks up to him to lead him out.

Alexander leans back in his seat, his eyes on Aiden. The second the doors close behind Lucas, Alexander glares at him. "Where did you find that guy?" he asks, his tone sharp. "He looks younger than I am. There's no way he's an experienced PI."

Aiden smirks and shakes his head. "I assure you, he's one of the best. He comes from a long line of law enforcement and private investigators."

"Thank you," I tell both Aiden and Lucian, and then I rise to my feet and walk away, making my way to the bedroom.

As expected, Alexander follows me.

CHAPTER 40

lexander

Our bedroom door closes behind me and Elena turns to look at me, her arms crossed in a defensive position.

"Are you okay?" I ask, concerned about everything the PI just told us. "I promise, Buttercup, we'll get to the bottom of this."

Elena smiles, but her smile is forced. "Yes, I hope so. Thank you for providing me with the resources I need. If not for you, if not for this marriage, I'd still be living in ignorance."

She's overly polite, her tone clipped. The way she looks at me unsettles me.

"You saw the photos."

She grits her teeth and nods. "Explain yourself, Alexander," she snaps, her voice raised.

She looks furious, but goddamn it, she looks beautiful. She'd murder me if I told her just how stunning I find her right now. I can just imagine the fire in her eyes if I dared tell her how hot she looks. I suppress a smile, but I clearly don't do a well enough job, because Elena's anger rises.

"Do you think this is funny? Did you have fun making a fool of me? You keep talking about portraying the perfect relationship for the press and your grandfather, yet here you are, embarrassing me for everyone to see. After everything you put me through with Lucian, this is how you behave?"

"Baby," I say, "it's not like that at all. I just ran into her, that's all."

Her eyes flash with anger as she points her index finger at me. "Don't you call me baby. I'm not your baby," she yells, and she's got me enthralled. Why the fuck does she need to be so beautiful when she's mad?

"Okay, Buttercup."

She groans and puts her hands in her hair. "Don't you dare call me Buttercup, either. Don't call me anything!"

She glares at me and then tries to storm past me, but I grab her and pull her against me. Elena pushes against me, but there's no way I'm letting her walk out in anger.

I push her up against the wall, trapping her in with my arms. I smirk at her, which only makes her angrier.

"I swear, Elena. I ran into her when I went to pick something up at Francesco's. I congratulated her on her engagement and then I came home. To you."

She looks at me through narrowed eyes, and though she's radiating anger, I see the insecurity underneath it. "Elena," I murmur. "You're my wife. You. No one else. You will always be the only one for me."

Her anger drains away, leaving only sadness in its wake. "But will I?" she asks, her voice barely above a whisper. "You say that, but it'll never be me that owns your heart. It's still her. It's always been her. If I hadn't dropped the photo you kept on your nightstand, she'd still be in our bedroom. I saw the way you looked at her in that photo, Alec. And you know what? You've never once looked at me that way."

I see the pain in her eyes, and it kills me. I drop my forehead to hers and inhale deeply. "Elena," I whisper. "When I proposed, I told you I wasn't after a love marriage."

She inhales shakily and tightens her grip on me. "I know," she murmurs. "I know."

I pull away a little to look at her. "I'm not going to lie to you, Elena. I never want to do that. I don't know if I'll ever love you. I don't know if that's even what I want. I certainly don't want you to expect it, or to wait for it. Love... even if you and I find it together, it won't last. My marriage with you is forever, Elena. And love? Love doesn't last forever. I much prefer what we have right now. A partnership. Mutual trust. Amazing sex."

Elena looks so sad, so hurt, that all I want to do is promise her the world. But I can't. I can't give her false promises.

"What I *can* promise you, Elena, is this. I don't love Jennifer. There are no lingering feelings there—whatever I thought was there is gone. I didn't feel a thing when I saw her. All I could think about was you and wanting to come home to you."

She looks into my eyes as though she wants to believe me, but can't. Elena cups my cheek, looking lost. "It's okay," she says. "I knew what I was getting into when I married you. You've been very clear on what not to expect, and I'm fine with that, I am. It's just that when I saw those photos... Alec, it hurts. It hurts to know you gave her everything that you don't even *want* with me."

I hold her closer and drop my forehead to her shoulder. If anyone deserves to be loved, it's Elena. I hate that I can't give her what she needs, and part of me worries that one day she'll go looking elsewhere for it.

"I'm giving you all I can, Elena. All I am. All that's left of me."

I carry her to our bed and lay her down gently before joining her in bed. She looks up at me, looking so damn vulnerable, and I hate that I put that look in her eyes.

"I hate myself for being so upset about that photo when I just received such devastating news about my mother's car accident, but I can't help myself, Alec. Both events feel equally painful to me. I'm trying so hard not to be affected, but I can't. I can't do it. I can't pretend not to care."

I press a kiss to her forehead and sigh. "You don't have to pretend, Elena. I'm your husband, and I'm not always the best communicator, so I need you to tell me these things. I need you to tell me when I hurt you, when I do something stupid. I will always listen, Elena, and I will always work on the things that are within my power. That goes for the photo you saw today, *and* for the news you received today."

She looks at me in question, and I lean in, kissing the tip of her nose. "I'll be sure to keep my distance from her, okay? If you don't want to see me with her, then I'll make sure I stay away from her."

I see hope bloom in her eyes, and it kills me. It kills me that this is all I can give her. That I can't promise her the one thing she wants most. It kills me that she wants it at all. Love won't last. When it all fades, we'll still be tied together. I don't want her to resent me in the end, and if we ever fall for each other, she will.

"As for your mother, I'll use every connection at my disposal to help you unravel what really happened. Elliot is probably already on it, if it's Lucian that asked him for a favor," I say, a smile on my face.

Elena nods and threads her hand through my hair. "Thank you," she whispers, and I lean in to press a chaste kiss on her lips.

"If it's your father that did this, I'll take him down. I'm

already working on putting a hostile takeover in place, but it's taking some time. Not everyone wants to sell their shares, and I need to do this slowly, undetected. I can't hit him until I have enough shares."

She nods, looking far more relaxed than she did earlier.

"This... this is enough, Alec. I'll take every bit you'll give me, and if this is all I'll ever have of you, it's enough. You are enough."

I fucking hope so, because I can't even imagine my life without Elena anymore.

CHAPTER 41

lexander

I'm oddly impatient as I wait for Elena by the entrance of the restaurant. I told her I'd take her to the opening of our latest restaurant, and she told me she'd meet me here. I smile to myself when my limousine pulls up to the curb. I walk up to the passenger door and open it, my breath catching when I see her.

She's wearing a stunning black dress that hugs her figure beautifully, but it's her eyes that get to me. It's the way she looks at me like she and I are the only ones that are in on a secret.

"You look beautiful," I tell her as I help her out of the car. Elena smiles at me, and my heart skips a damn beat.

"You don't look so bad yourself," she says, her eyes roaming over my body. "Though I think you'll look even better on top of me tonight."

My eyes widen in shock and Elena smirks in satisfaction. She's getting more and more brazen with the things she says to me lately. She loves provoking me, shocking me. I grin at her and pull her closer, kissing her right in front of the restaurant.

The flash of dozens of cameras go off at once, and I hold her a little closer.

When I pull away, Elena has a torn expression on her face. I lean in and brush my lips over her ear. "That wasn't for show," I whisper. "This is."

I kiss her again, slowly, until she melts against me. My heart is racing by the time I pull away again and I shake my head. "I'd better stop," I murmur. "Or I'll be giving them a real show."

Elena laughs and I offer her my arm. I don't remember the last time I felt this way. I'm excited for a date... with my own wife.

Elena freezes when we walk into the restaurant, and I follow her gaze. I spot her father and the rest of her family at one of the tables. Matthew has his arm wrapped around Jennifer, and she looks up at me, our eyes meeting across the room. I expected to feel something, but instead there's just... nothing. I've held onto her for so long, letting her go feels freeing. In hindsight I don't even understand what I saw in her. Part of me feels like it isn't her I was so upset about, but rather, the betrayal itself. I spent years convincing myself that I wouldn't end up like my mother, but I did. I smile to myself and Elena tenses next to me. She attempts to pull away from me, and I hold her even closer.

Matthew stares at me, and he looks annoyed at my lack of reaction to seeing him with Jennifer. Even the last time I saw them together I was more concerned with irritating Matthew than I cared about hurting Jennifer. It's only now that I realize that. I grin and press a kiss to Elena's temple, enjoying the way his hand fists into a ball.

"Elena, Alexander Kennedy," Alaric Rousseau says, nodding politely. He calls a waiter over and asks for two more seats, and Elena tenses. "You must join us," he says. I look at Elena, but her expression doesn't give anything away.

"Father," she says, nodding at him. She doesn't acknowledge the rest, and a small smile tugs at my lips.

"Come, come join us," he says. "How have you been?"

She freezes, and I can tell that she's caught between the love she has for her father, and the hurt she's still trying to heal from.

"I'm good, father. We're on a date, so we cannot join you today. Perhaps some other time."

"Nonsense. You must join us." I see the calculative glint in his eyes, and it makes me more determined to take everything from him. Elena wasn't worth a dime to him until news about us reached his ears. I'll be damned if he uses her in any way, ever again.

"No," she snaps. "I was trying to be polite," she says, looking around at the countless faces turned toward us. "But since you can't take a hint, let me remind you of the words you spoke when I left home, and then again when I begged you to help me save my mother's life: I'm no longer part of your family. And quite frankly, I'd rather eat shit than sit with people that'd happily let my mother die."

I try my best to bite back a smile, but I can't. Eat shit? A low chuckle escapes my lips and I nod at Alaric. "The lady has spoken," I say, leading Elena away without a second thought.

The waiter leads us to a table by the window, and even I have to admit that the view is stunning. I pull Elena's seat out for her and she glares at me. "Are you sure you don't want this seat?" she asks, her jaws clenched. "You'll have a better view of Jennifer from here."

I raise my brows and bite down on my lip to keep from smiling. It's crazy, because usually jealousy irritates me, but on Elena it merely amuses me.

"Are you going to sit down or do you need me to kiss the

hell out of you until your knees give in?" I ask her, hoping she'll challenge me further.

Elena huffs and sits down, her gaze trailing back toward her father. She looks so incredibly hurt, and I don't know how to make it better. I brought her a small present, but I'm not sure if even that will cheer her up.

The waiter brings us champagne, but Elena doesn't even notice him. She's lost in her thoughts, a pained look in her eyes.

"I know it isn't the same, but my family is yours now, Buttercup."

She looks into my eyes and nods. "Hey, why do you even call me Buttercup?" she asks, clearly not wanting to talk about what just happened. Very well.

"You really don't remember? I've called you that since you were about six and you were obsessed with The Powerpuff Girls."

Her cheeks turn bright red. "You're kidding me, right? You named me after the most violent one of the three? I don't have a violent bone in my body. I'm clearly Bubbles."

I smile at her outrage. "Buttercup is also the bravest and the most headstrong, baby," I say, pacifying her.

She glares at me, and I can't help but laugh. I lean in to kiss her shoulder, and she narrows her eyes at me as though she just thought of something, her gaze suspicious.

"Hey, what's my name in your phone programmed as?"

She grabs my phone, but it's password protected. She lifts her brow in expectation.

"Don't tell him, but it's Lucian's birthday backwards."

Her eyes widen when she successfully unlocks my phone.

"No way. Lucian would love this. You know you're his hero, right?" she tells me.

I shake my head in denial. "Maybe once upon a time I was, but these days we aren't that close anymore."

Elena smiles at me and shakes her head. "The way you protected him when all that stuff with Marcus went down? I'm not sure what was going on when I wasn't part of your lives, but right now you're his hero."

I smile at the thought of that. Elena has managed to bring me closer to my own family. It's something I never asked of her, but she did it nonetheless. That's just who she is.

Elena uses the search function to find her phone number, and I see her outrage when she finds out she's programmed in as Buttercup Kennedy. I chuckle as she changes it into Wife.

"That reminds me. I don't think we've taken a single selfie together since getting married."

She opens my camera app and poses, gesturing to me to join her. I wrap my arm around her and smile at the camera, watching in amusement as she pulls a few funny poses.

"God, you're so cute," I murmur, kissing her cheek. She manages to capture the exact moment and saves the photo as my screensaver before handing my phone back to me.

Elena takes a big sip of her champagne and I take the envelope I prepared for her out of my pocket. I slide it toward her with a smile on my face. "It isn't much, but this is for you."

Elena opens it curiously, her eyes widening when she realizes what it is. She gulps and looks up at me. "Are you serious?"

I nod. "Yes, of course. I always told you the shares I was acquiring are yours. I have no need for them. We still don't own a majority shareholding, so you can't use these to boot your father and brother from the company just yet. I'll need another two months or so to make that happen. But once I have the rest, they're yours too. Do with them what you will."

"Why would you give this to me?" she asks, sounding shocked.

I move my chair closer to hers and wrap my arm around

her. "Because I promised you I'd give you back everything you lost, Elena. I never said I wanted anything for myself."

"But what about Matthew? Didn't you want to take revenge? What about Jennifer? Alec, these shares are worth *millions*."

I smile at her and lean in to kiss her, my lips lingering on her. "It's punishment enough that he's marrying her. I can't, in good conscience, make the man suffer even further. Besides, you're my wife. Whatever is yours, is mine. *You* are mine."

Elena smiles, but her smile is uncertain. "I saw the way you smiled at her when we walked in. I was standing right next to you, but she was all you could see. I don't need you to lie to me, Alexander."

She looks away, but I see the way she forces a smile onto her face. The insecurity she tries so hard to hide. I worry that I'm the one that put it there, and that the damage I've already done is permanent.

CHAPTER 42

lena

"Are you ready?" Sofia says.

I nod at her and stare at myself in the mirror. The long pale pink gown I'm wearing is absolutely stunning, and it's probably the most beautiful thing I've ever worn.

I've gotten quite used to Sofia asking me to accompany her for charity events and lunches, but tonight is the first night she's taking me to a gala. I kind of wish Alec didn't have to work late tonight, so we could go together. I know he'll likely end up making an appearance, since this event is hosted by the Kennedys, but it isn't the same as arriving there on his arm.

"Let's go," Sofia says, taking my hand.

I follow her down, where the limousine is waiting for us. I'm oddly nervous. It's been so long since I've been at an event this big. There'll be so many people I know, people I haven't spoken to in years, people that won't know anything about me, except for the rumors Elise has been spreading, and whatever they may have heard about me in the press lately.

I'm trembling by the time we arrive at the Kennedy Hotel. Sofia notices, but thankfully, she doesn't say anything.

The room falls silent when we enter, as it always does when I go anywhere with Sofia. The elegance she emits, the authority —it's unmatched.

My eyes widen in surprise when Alec's grandfather walks toward us. He rarely makes an appearance at these types of events, and I've only seen him once since I married Alec.

He smiles at his daughter and brushes her hair behind her ear gently. "You look beautiful, sweetheart," he says.

Sofia smiles at him. "Thank you, Dad," she says, her voice losing its usual edge when she speaks to him. It's only when she's with her father that Sofia looks like a regular person, just someone's beloved daughter.

He turns toward me and smiles. "So do you, Elena," he says.

I smile at him politely, trying my best to hide how nervous he makes me. Even Alec is careful around him, and I can't risk giving away that our relationship isn't real.

"I'll need to steal my daughter away for a minute, but don't think I've forgotten about the lunch you promised me," he says, smiling, and I grin.

Sofia looks at me apologetically before walking away, and I'm left standing here by myself. I hear the whispers surrounding me, some wonder who I am, some recognize me but don't understand why I'd be here with Sofia. It makes me uncomfortable, and I grab a glass of champagne from one of the waiters, even if it's just to have something to do.

"Well, well, well," I hear someone say.

I turn in surprise, coming eye to eye with Sebastian, my first and last boyfriend.

"Elena Rousseau, back from the dead, and prettier than ever. You lost quite a bit of weight, huh? Lost the glasses and braces too." He grins, his eyes roaming over my body. "I just got back from abroad, and I heard you've fallen on hard times. Rumor has it you've been going around, begging for money. I'd be quite willing to help you, for a price."

I shudder, revulsion washing over me. I can't help but look away. Had he offered me a solution before Alec did, would I have ended up at his mercy? Either way, both men offered a price for my body, and that seems to be all that's valuable about me.

I take a step away, but Sebastian stops me, his hand on my wrist, his grip tight.

Before I know it, his hand is wrenched away, and Alec is standing in front of me. "How about you get your damn hands off my girl?" he says, his tone harsh. "Who the fuck are you even?"

Sebastian's eyes widen, and he looks at me, the expression in his eyes making me shudder.

He straightens himself out and turns to Alec, a calculative expression on his face. "Alexander," he says, nodding politely. "It's great to finally meet you in person."

Alec frowns at him and looks him up and down. "Who the fuck are you?"

I see the indignation in Sebastian's eyes, but he pushes it down and forces a smile onto his face. "You recently invested in my start-up. Fi Solutions?"

Alec frowns and grabs his phone, pushing the buttons angrily as his arm wraps around me tightly. "Do I own any shares in some company called Fi Solutions?" he asks.

His impatience increases with every second that he's left waiting for a reply.

"Sell them," he barks out, before ending the call angrily.

"No!" Sebastian says, his voice raised. "I... why would you? We're starting to become so profitable. We'll give you a great return, Alexander. I can guarantee it. If you sell your shares right now, you'll sink our share price. Please, reconsider."

Sebastian glances at me and grabs my hand, clenching tightly. "Elena, please, tell him."

"And that's where you went wrong," he says, yanking Sebastian's hand off mine, his anger overflowing. "Don't fucking touch my woman. Don't look at her. Don't speak to her. Don't even fucking think about her. If you ever come near her again, I'll do worse than sink your fucking share price."

Alec pulls me along angrily. "Why the fuck do you look so fucking beautiful today anyway?" he says through gritted teeth. "You weren't even sure I was going to be here. For all you know, my grandfather would've done tonight's speech and I never would've even showed up. Who do you look this beautiful for, huh?"

I bite back a smile when he walks me to the dance floor, his arms wrapping around me. He seems restless, and his hands keep roaming over my body. The way he looks at me both amuses me and thrills me.

"Jealousy looks cute on you," I tell him.

"Me? Jealous?" he says, huffing.

"You're not? Hmm... I guess you won't mind if I go dance with Sebastian, then?"

He tightens his grip on me and pulls me closer until my body is flush against his. "Don't even fucking dream about it, Elena. I've read your background check. I know you used to date him. It's enough that you once used to be his. He isn't getting anything more than the memory of you, and even that is too much."

I smile up at him and wrap my arms around his neck. "Okay, husband," I tell him.

Alec twirls me around before pulling me back, and I crash into his arms. "Say that again." I raise my brows, and Alec brushes my hair out of my face. "I love it when you call me husband like that."

"Do you now... husband dearest?"

Alec pauses in the middle of the dance floor and nods. "Yes," he says. "In fact, I want to hear you being referred to as my wife in public everywhere we go. I want people addressing you as Mrs. Kennedy. I want the whole world to know that you're mine."

He drops down on one knee in the middle of the dance floor, and several gasps sound around me. The music stops, and a spotlight illuminates us.

"Elena Diana Rousseau," he says, pulling a ring box from his pocket. My heart skips a beat and I stare at him with wide eyes. He's always told me before we put on an act, so why didn't he this time?

"You've had me enthralled from the moment I ran into you again, all those months ago. I've fought my feelings for you for as long as I could, but it's a losing battle."

He opens the ring box, and I gasp. It isn't the ring I picked— but it's the ring I secretly wanted. He noticed?

"I can't even imagine the rest of my life without you," he says. "Please, will you do me the honor of becoming my wife?"

I blink in disbelief and nod. "Yes. *Yes*, Alec. A thousand times, yes."

He looks into my eyes, and even though we're surrounded by hundreds of people, it's like it's just me and him right in this moment.

Alec slides the ring onto my finger and rises. He threads his hand through my hair and kisses me roughly, with no regard for the people surrounding us, and I kiss him back just as passionately.

I'm breathless by the time I pull away, and both of us are smiling widely. "Alec," I whisper. "The ring?"

He pushes my hair behind my ear and cups my cheek. "Baby, you deserve every single thing you set your eyes on. I'm going to make it my job to give you *everything*, even the things you don't dare ask for."

"Alec," I whisper. "All I want is you."

He smiles, his fingers brushing aside my hair. "You have me, Elena. Forever."

We're so lost in each other that we're both startled when Alec's grandfather puts his hand on his shoulder.

"Congratulations, kiddo," he says, looking as happy as we do. He glances at me and cups my cheek in an uncharacteristic yet totally grandfatherly way. "You picked a keeper. I couldn't be more proud."

He takes a step back and then looks at the two of us. "Marry her before the first of July," he says, his eyes on Alec. "And my position as chairman is yours."

I grab Alec's hand and look up at him excitedly. He grins at me and leans in, pressing a gentle kiss to my forehead.

"We did it," I whisper, and he nods.

Dozens of people surround us, each of them wanting to congratulate us. Amongst the crowd, I spot my family, Jennifer by their side. The hatred on Jade and Elise's faces doesn't surprise me in the slightest—but the devastation in Jennifer's eyes *does*. The way she looks at Alec makes me tighten my grip on him.

He looks at me, a questioning look in his eyes, and I shake my head. I rise to my tiptoes and kiss him with all I've got, cheers erupting around us.

I've never been happier than I am today, yet this happiness feels fleeting, and I'm terrified I won't be able to hold on to it.

CHAPTER 43

lexander

Elena can't stop staring at her engagement ring, and I can't stop staring at her. The wind rustles her hair beautifully, and I'm glad we opted to have dinner on our terrace today. I can't remember any woman ever cooking for me—it's always a chef. Yet Elena, a woman that grew up in the same environment I did, cooks for me all the time. She takes the time to find out what my favorite dishes are and buys exotic ingredients to surprise me with. I'm not used to being taken care of this way.

"It's stunning," she says, her eyes twinkling. "I wish I could show my mom."

Elena never ceases to amaze me. She refuses to give up on her mother, no matter how slim the odds are.

"Do you think she'd like it?" I ask.

Elena nods. "Yeah, it's simple but so luxurious at the same time. Mom would definitely love this."

I smile at her. She lights up when she speaks of her mother, of her memories with her. "Tell me about your happiest child-hood memory," I say, my voice soft.

Elena looks at me and takes a minute to think about it. "I guess my happiest childhood memory would be from when things were still simple. When you were still part of my everyday life. I remember once my parents were so busy arguing with each other that they forgot about my birthday, but Luce and you didn't. I came over to your house, and the two of you had baked me a cake, which was barely edible by the way, and you'd put up all those fairy lights for me. To date, that's still my best birthday ever."

I smile. "Hmm, I remember that. It was the last birthday you spent with us. Lucian called me in a panic when he real-ized everyone forgot about your birthday, and he made me come home from college to prepare you a little party." Throughout the years, most of my memories of my childhood got lost, forgotten. I have more memories with Elena than I realized.

Elena laughs, lost in the memory. "The two of you made my childhood bearable. My home wasn't a place I liked to be at, no matter how hard my mother tried, and you allowed me to escape from it. I always felt loved at the Kennedys."

"You are loved, Buttercup. All of us adore you. I wouldn't have married you otherwise."

"Tell me about *your* favorite childhood memory," she says.

I sigh. "My childhood wasn't very good. I was forced to grow up quickly, but I had to watch my brother enjoy his childhood with you. The two of you always had so much fun with each other, and it made me feel a little lonely. It sounds really dumb, considering I'm so much older than you two, but that's what it was like. My most precious memories are with Lucian and you, and I wasn't really a child anymore then."

Elena presses a quick kiss to my lips. "You've also always had me, you just never realized it," she says.

"Hmm, I'm not sure. Even now that you're my wife, it's still Lucian you're closer to." I sound petty and I know it, but I can't help myself. I empty my glass to take my mind of the sudden loneliness I feel.

Elena holds out her fork for me, feeding me a bite of her fish. "Soon enough we'll be besties too," she says, winking at me.

I laugh, and I suddenly realize that I want nothing more than that. "I'd like that, Buttercup," I say, my voice soft.

Elena feeds me a few more bites and I shuffle my seat closer to hers, so our legs are touching.

"Tell me three good things that happened to you today?" she says, placing her fork down.

I smile at the question. "I should have recognized you the second you asked that question, back at Inferno. It's what you always used to ask me when you were younger. It took me a while to remember why that question sounded so familiar."

Her cheeks redden, and she smiles at me.

"Three things, huh? You made me an amazing dinner, the world now knows that you're mine, and I'm going to fuck you really hard later."

She bursts out laughing. "Alec," she says, her voice teasing. "One of them didn't even happen today, and one is yet to happen."

She shakes her head and takes another bite of her food. "Hey, what do you like best about me?" she asks.

I pause to take her in for a moment. "Your beauty. You're truly beautiful inside and out. I've never known someone who'd sacrifice themselves for their parent on the off chance that it might make a difference. I'm proud to call you my wife. You're good to my mother. I know you hang out with her whenever I'm working late, and she's been happier than I've seen her in years." She blushes and looks away. "What about you?" I ask, half fearing her answer. I haven't given her much to like.

Elena puts her elbow on the table and rests her head against her fist, her face turned toward me. "I like your heart. You didn't hesitate to pull me out of a bad situation, despite us having grown apart. You saved me, in every sense of the word. I like that you're always trying to do the right thing. I like your mind. Seeing you working is such a huge turn on. You're so incredibly driven and smart, it's inspiring to watch you do your thing, even when at times I wish you'd just come to bed instead of working late. I look at you while you work and I cannot believe you're my husband. I'm so proud of you."

I look away, my heart beating quickly.

"I also quite like your face, and your perfect body doesn't hurt either," she says, making me smile.

I lean in to kiss her, and she moans against my lips, her hands finding the lapels of my suit jacket.

"What do you like better? My hands or my tongue?" I whisper against her lips.

Her beautiful face turns crimson and I nip at her lips, a smile on my face. That blush of hers... I can't get enough of it. "Tongue," she murmurs.

If my lips weren't on hers, I wouldn't have heard her, she spoke that softly. "Mm. You do taste delicious. I may need another taste soon."

She bites down on my lips and then leans back to look at me. "I want to taste you too," she says, looking at me through her eyelashes.

I groan and put her hand on my pants, letting her feel my erection. She licks her lips and looks at me. "I've been hard since we sat down. Don't tempt me, woman."

I meant to scare her away, but instead she starts stroking

me. I feel her fumble with my zipper and my eyes widen when she slips her hand into my boxers to palm my cock.

"Elena." I meant to sound stern, but her name sounds like a moan on my lips. She pulls me close with her free hand and kisses me, her tongue driving me insane. "Buttercup," I whisper.

Elena grabs my knees and spreads my legs before sinking to her knees in front of me.

She looks up at me and grabs my cock, slowly lowering her lips, driving me fucking insane. She kisses the tip before sinking her lips down on me, her mouth wet and hot.

I groan and bury my hand in her hair. She drives me insane. That mouth of hers... unreal.

She looks up at me, my cock in her mouth, and that image... *fuck*. "Baby," I groan. "If you look at me like that, I won't last."

She sucks down on me even harder, taking me in even deeper. She moans, and it's like the sound reverberates against my dick, making everything feel even more intense.

"Why the fuck are you so perfect?"

I watch her, my pleasure climbing higher and higher. I grab her hair and pull her away a split second before I come, and Elena gasps.

She looks down at her ruined dress and smiles before looking back up at me, a sultry expression on her face.

"I would've swallowed, you know."

I stare at her open-mouthed. "You'll drive me crazy, Elena. Completely crazy."

She smiles at me. "That's fine," she says. "So long as you're crazy about *me*."

Fuck me. I think I am.

CHAPTER 44

lena

Alec and I wake up to incessant knocking, and before we realize someone's at the door, Lucian and Sofia walk in. Alec sits up, startled, the sheets falling to his waist. He nudges me gently and wraps me in the blankets as I sit up, covering as much of myself as I can.

"I'm sorry, my darlings," Sofia says. "We wouldn't have walked in, but we had no other choice. Neither one of you picked up the phone, and you were so fast asleep the knocking didn't wake you either."

"What is it, Mother?" Alec asks, his arm wrapped around me.

"Elena... it's your mother," she says carefully. My heart drops and Alec tightens his grip on me, both of us bracing for the worst.

"I—the doctor asked us to come to the hospital. He was unclear about what's wrong. He didn't say. We need to go."

I nod and move to get out of bed mindlessly, but Alec grabs me and wraps me in his arms, sheets and all.

"Clothes, Buttercup?"

I nod and glance at Lucian, panic rendering me useless. He walks into our wardrobe and returns a minute later with outfits for both Alec and me. Then he presses a kiss on top of my head and turns to leave. "I'll wait for you downstairs," he says, and I nod.

Alec and I get ready in record time and by the time we're down, everyone is ready to go.

We're all tense as we make our way to the facility my mother is in.

I walk toward her room with dread, my heart beating out of my chest. Alec holds my hand and Lucian is right behind me, but not even their presence sets me at ease. I'm scared of what I'll find when I walk through my mother's door.

Dr. Taylor jumps up anxiously when I enter. "Elena," he says, sounding breathless.

He points to my mother's bed, and to my surprise, my mother is staring back at me, her lips turned up at the corners in a small smile. I rush up to her and grab her hand, surprised to find her finger moving slightly against mine. I stare at her in disbelief, feeling lightheaded from the shock.

"E... E..."

"She's been saying that since she woke up. I didn't want to give you false hope in case she fell back into a coma by the time you got here, but she's been awake for about forty-five minutes now."

He inhales deeply and looks at me with a grave expression. "I put her through weeks' worth of tests, but it was worth it. There were trace amounts of propofol in her blood. We'd been keeping her on the medication her last hospital provided—and they mislabeled the propofol they sent us. I've had all drugs tested. There's no doubt... there was foul play here."

"What is propofol?" I ask, my hand around my mother's.

"It's a drug used to keep someone in an artificial coma. I can't imagine why that would be in her blood. I ran all tests three times, thinking it must be a mistake somehow, but it wasn't. I slowly phased it out of her system until she eventually woke up naturally."

I feel sick at the mere thought of someone doing this to my mother. Alec throws his arms around me while Lucian wipes away the tears I didn't realize had fallen.

"Hi, Sarah," Lucian says, sounding as emotional as I feel.

My mother's eyes move to Lucian's and I could swear I saw a twinkle in them.

"L..." she murmurs, and Alec frowns.

"I think she's trying to say your names," he says, shocked. "She's not just awake, she's aware of her surroundings too."

I start crying in earnest and place my head against my mother's shoulder. "Oh God, Mom. I can't believe it. I knew it. I knew you'd wake up one day."

I sob my heart out, and before long my mother's eyes are filled with tears too, her cheeks wet. Lucian grabs a tissue and carefully wipes her face while Alec wipes mine.

"Your mother doesn't seem to have any muscle contraction. She must have been given regular Botox injections to prevent it, and I suspect she received regular physical therapy to stretch her body too. It doesn't quite add up. You wouldn't do that for a person you're knowingly keeping in a coma."

I nod. "The Botox injections and stretching are two things I insisted on and paid through the roof for," I tell him. I knew she'd need that if she were to walk after her coma. "They did it, because I was paying for it."

Alec gently grabs her hand like I've seen him do before, and presses a kiss to the back of her hand. "I don't think you remember me, but I'm so glad you woke up," he whispers softly.

Her eyes move to his, and another tear rolls down her face. "A…" she croaks, her respirator inhabiting her speech.

His eyes widen, and he looks at me. "She recognizes me, Buttercup."

I tighten my hold on her hand and turn toward the doctor. "Why can't she speak? What will happen now?"

Dr. Taylor smiles at me. "She only just woke up and has been on a respirator for years. We can't just take it off all of a sudden. I did a full checkup, and there's nothing wrong with her vocal cords. She hasn't spoken in years though, so it'll take some time for her to speak the way she used to. She's still drugged too. I suspect she'll be just fine once all the unnecessary drugs are out of her body. I'll have to check her joints in about 24 hours, to see if they've frozen up. If they have, she'll need some surgery, but I don't suspect that that's the case. If all goes well and she can remain conscious for long periods of time, she should be able to go home in about three weeks, provided that she still receives full medical care."

Alec nods and smiles at me gently. "We can get a hospital bed set up in our house. We'll get whatever Dr. Taylor thinks he needs, so in a few weeks we can move her home. We'll keep him on staff to oversee her recovery."

I nod, my mind a mess. I stare at my mother's closed eyes and turn to the doctor in a panic, but he merely shakes his head. "She's tired and overstimulated. I suggest we let her rest. Most patients aren't able to stay conscious for more than a few minutes after they first wake up. Give it time, Elena."

I nod, and though it kills me to do it, I let Alec take me back home so my mother can rest. "You'll take me back tomorrow morning?" I ask. Alec nods. "Of course, but we have to let the doctor do his job tonight."

My mind is a mess the entire ride home, fury coursing through my veins. "I'll murder whoever did this to my mother. We need to look into how this could have happened. Do you think my father had anything to do with it?" I shake my head, my thoughts whirling. "It must've been my stepmother. She must have isolated me on purpose. She knew I'd never find out about what she did because I didn't have enough resources at my disposal." Alec nods and wraps me into his arms. "I'll murder her. I'll wring her ugly fat neck."

He sighs and tightens his hold on me, his hand stroking my arm. "I'd never let you get your hands dirty, baby," he says, sounding as upset as I feel.

"Tell me you'll find out for me, Alec. Promise me."

Alec lifts me onto his lap and looks into my eyes. "My love, I'm way ahead of you. Aiden is looking into this as we speak. It might take a few days or even a few weeks, but we'll get to the bottom of this."

I nod, wiping away the tears that just won't stop falling.

"You promise?"

Alec nods, his eyes blazing with sincerity. "I promise."

With him by my side, there's no way the truth will remain hidden.

CHAPTER 45

lena

I'm restless in the morning, eager to see my mother. Lucian, Sofia, and Alec all look as tired as I do, as though none of us managed to get any sleep.

"Mom is going to want to see Dad, isn't she? How do I explain he isn't here?"

It would devastate her to find out he not only left her, but that he has married someone else already. "Oh God, how do I explain to her that I can't even take her home?"

My heart races, devastation and helplessness constricting my breathing. Alec walks up to me and cups my cheeks, keeping my eyes on his.

"Baby, breathe," he says. "You're fine. She's awake now, and that's all that matters. The rest we can deal with, one step at a time."

Lucian rubs my back gently, his expression as torn as Alec's. None of us know what the right thing to do is.

"She needs to be informed," Sofia says. "But not now, honey."

I nod at her, my heart aching for my mother. I've been wanting her to wake up for so long now, but I haven't given much thought to *what* she'd be waking up to. Everything she had when she got into her car accident is gone now. Her husband, the home she built, and in so many ways, even her son.

"I need to call my brother," I say, my phone in hand. I'm feeling conflicted. He's worked so hard to get me to let her go. I don't even know how he'll respond to this news.

"Elena, *no*," Lucian says, his voice sharp.

I turn to look at him, my brows raised. He looks anguished as he grabs my shoulders. The way he struggles to meet my eyes makes my heart sink.

"There's something I've been keeping from you," he says, his voice soft. "Elliot... he was able to trace the digital footprint of your mother's car. He managed to find the hacker who caused your mother to lose control over her car, and, well, he was able to trace the payments, too. From what he told me, it seems like it was Jade who contacted the hacker, but the payments... the payments came from Matthew. He tried his best to route them through as many countries as possible, but Elliot put his all into tracing them, and it was him, Elena. It was Matthew."

I feel sick. I close my eyes in an effort to remain in control of my emotions, but my body won't stop trembling. "Matthew?" I whisper. "That can't be right. He's an asshole, but he's not... he's not a murderer. He wouldn't do that to his own mother."

Alec wraps his arm around my waist and pulls me closer. I lean against him, my face buried against his chest.

"How long have you known?" Alec asks, his fingers stroking my hair.

Lucian hesitates before answering. "A couple of weeks," he says carefully. "You two were so happy together. I just hadn't seen either of you look this happy in so long, and I wanted that for you. I knew that this news would devastate Elena, and in turn, you."

Hot tears stream down my cheeks, soaking Alec's shirt. I inhale shakily, and Alec tightens his grip on me, enveloping me in a tight hug.

Sofia places her hand on my shoulder, and I pull away from Alec a little. "Elena," she says. "We'll deal with this in due time, all right? For now, dry your tears, and put on a good act for your mother. What she needs right now is love and attention. Everything else," she says, glancing at Alec and Lucian, "everything else can and will be taken care of."

I nod, and Alec brushes my tears away with his thumbs. I try my best to pull myself together, but all I can think about is Matthew. Why would he do this? Was my father in on this?

For years I just thought that the way my life played out was unfortunate, that in part, I must have been to blame for losing all my friends, my connections—for falling out with everyone I cared about, my father included. Now I wonder if it was orchestrated.

I'm still thinking about it when I walk into my mother's room, Alec by my side. He grabs my hand and squeezes, and I smile up at him. Where would I be without him? If not for him, I would have lost my mother by now.

"Hi, Mom," I say, still shocked to find her eyes open. For so long she's looked like she was fast asleep.

I walk up to her, and her eyes follow me. The edges of her lips turn up, and when I squeeze her hand, her fingers move.

Emotions overwhelm me, and I burst into tears involuntarily. I drop my forehead to her shoulder, trying my best not to cry, and failing.

I feel a hand on my back, and I try my best to pull myself together. "I'm sorry," I murmur. "I just missed you so much, Mom. To see you here, to have you look at me... you have no idea how much this means to me."

I sit up and wipe my tears away, my heart breaking when I notice a tear dropping down my mother's cheek.

"Thank you, Mom. Thank you for waking up."

She smiles, her lips opening. "E..." she says, her voice raspy.

I grab her hand and place it against my cheek, cradling her hand in mine.

Mom glances at Alec, and I can't help but blush. "I... do you remember Alexander?" I ask.

Mom nods, and I almost burst into tears again. I can't believe she's actually having a conversation with me.

"Ma'am," he says, grabbing her hand. He raises it to his lips and presses a sweet kiss to the back of her hand, and my heart skips a beat.

"I... um, Alec is my... he's my fiancé," I end up saying. Alec looks at me, his eyes twinkling.

Mom's eyes move between the two of us, and it warms my heart to find so much expression in them.

"E... El... Elena," she says, her voice rough. My eyes widen and I look at her, shocked. "I... l—love... you."

"She's been practicing to say that to you for hours," Dr. Taylor says to me from behind.

I break down all over again, and Alec smiles as he pats my back. "Oh, Mom," I say, choking back sobs. "I love you, too. So much, Mom."

I stare at my mother through the tears, my heart heavy. I'm going to do whatever it takes to protect her.

CHAPTER 46

lena

I pace in the living room, feeling restless. "What can we do?"
I ask.

Sofia, Lucian, and Alec are as lost in thought as I am.

"What do you want the end result to be, Buttercup?" Alec
asks. "Do you want your family to land in jail? Do you want
them to disappear? Tell me what you want, and we'll find a way
to make it happen."

I nod, trying my best to decide what needs to be done, to set
aside the love I've held onto for so long—love neither my
brother nor my father deserves.

"I need to know if my father was involved. I want Jade and
Matthew to go down. I want them, the way they've made me
feel—helpless, cut off from everything and everyone they've
ever known. I want their assets, every single thing they own,
every single thing they care about. I want it all. But above all, I
want everything my mother has ever worked for. When she was

declared brain dead, my father inherited her entire estate. I want that rectified."

Alec starts to pace like I am, restless. "We need to attack them from behind, Buttercup. If they see us coming, they'll safeguard everything. If they even find out your mother is awake, they'll start protecting themselves. For now, I'm going after everyone that's ever treated your mother. If I can get a confession, then that will help tremendously. We have the best lawyers in the country on retainer, so legally regaining your mother's assets shouldn't be hard, but like I said, we need to hit them all at once. We need to get the paperwork in place and have our men show up with eviction notices. I have a feeling they'll need a bit of help leaving the premises."

I nod. "There's one more thing I want," I say.

Alec looks at me, brows raised.

"I want my childhood home. The house my mother called home for so many years. I want it."

Lucian smiles and holds up his tablet. "I asked Elliot to find out as much as he can about the Rousseau assets," he says, a slight blush on his face. He can't even say Elliot's name without blushing, and despite everything going on, that brings a smile to my face.

"The house... it's owned by the company. It's not privately owned. If Alec can manage to gain a majority shareholding, then that'll fall into your hands."

Alec looks at me, his head tilted. "Babe," he says. "We don't even need to. We have your mother. She's alive and well. The shares you inherited, the ones your brother took from you? They revert back to your mother. Her shares and the ones I bought you combined, make up a majority shareholding."

I smile, a vicious type of delight coursing through me. "I want to be there. I want to be there when we evict them."

Sofia smiles at me. "You will," she says, nodding in approval. "You're Elena *Kennedy*," she adds. "You're my daughter-in-law and Alexander's wife. It's time you show the world what that means."

CHAPTER 47

lexander

I push Sarah's wheelchair through the garden, stopping to admire different flowers. She loves the feeling of the sun on her face and the fresh air. I can't blame her, she's been cooped up in a room for years.

We've converted one of the guest rooms on the ground floor into a fully equipped medical room for her, so at least we can keep her at home now. We got her an electric wheelchair too, and she's enjoying being able to move around the house a little.

It took almost two months before we could take her home from our private clinic, and even now she requires round-the-clock care. She's had to learn how to breathe by herself again, how to speak again, and even how to eat. Watching Elena's heart break every time her mother struggles to relearn something is tearing me apart.

"I heard her, you know," Sarah says, and I pause.

She still struggles to move her limbs. In a way, she's like a baby. Her body is mostly fine now, but she needs to relearn how to do basic tasks and how to get her body to listen to her. Thankfully, the neuromuscular electrical stimulation Elena paid so much for prevented muscle atrophy. There's no damage to her joints either, thanks to the stretching her nurses did for her twice a day, so she should be able to walk again within a few months.

I sit down on the grass beside her and look up at her.

"I heard Elena when I was in my coma. I had no concept of time, but I heard her cries and her undying belief in my recovery."

My eyes widen. Sarah surprises me every day. Not only is she recovering far quicker than her doctors expected, but she's also sharp as hell. I thought her mind would for sure be affected by her coma, but it isn't.

"I know Elena isn't at work right now. I know Alaric and Matthew aren't on a business trip, and I know you're married to my daughter—*not* engaged. I know why you married her, and I understand Elena doesn't want me to find out. In turn, I don't want her to know that I could hear most of what she told me throughout the years."

She's just like Elena, always startling me. I tense, unsure what to say. Elena has been handling the lawyers herself, and she's the one that's been coordinating with Elliot and our security team. She's asked us to ensure that either Lucian, Mom, or I accompany her mother at least once a day, when she is unable to be here herself.

I don't know what to say to Sarah. I don't know what Elena would want me to say.

She smiles at me and shakes her head gently. "I need your help to prepare the required documents to turn all my accounts and assets into joint assets between my daughter and me. I won't have Elena depend on anyone ever again—not even you, Alec."

I nod at her even as a shiver of fear runs down my spine. She's ensuring Elena can gain independence from me. If Elena no longer needs me, will she stay? Our wedding ceremony hasn't taken place yet, and my grandfather hasn't been informed of our marriage either. If she wanted a divorce now, I have no way of denying her one.

I breathe a sigh of relief when Elena walks up to us, and rise to my feet. She presses a kiss to her mother's cheek, and I narrow my eyes at her. It takes her a good minute to even notice me, and my mood drops even further. Sarah looks at me and laughs, and I cross my arms over each other. When Elena finally turns to look at me, I'm full-on sulking. Elena grins at me and rises to her tiptoes to kiss me, and I glare at her involuntarily.

"So you did see me standing here, then?"

Elena laughs and pulls me closer, kissing me properly. She wraps her arms around my neck, her lips brushing past my ear.

"You're always the first one I see, no matter where I am, no matter how many people there are. Always, Alec."

I smile reluctantly, and Elena's eyes twinkle in amusement. "You're crazy, you know that, right?" she murmurs.

I grin at her and lean in to kiss her again, properly this time. "You did tell me I should be crazy about you, didn't you? Careful what you wish for, baby."

Ever since her mother woke up, I've discovered a new side to my wife. She's assertive, hardworking, and as ruthless as I am. She's perfect. The way she's orchestrating the Rousseau takedown is going to become legendary, I just know it. I'm pretty sure even my grandfather will be impressed once this all goes down.

Sarah grabs Elena's hand and smiles at her. "Honey," she says. "I need to talk to you."

Elena nods and kneels down in front of her mother, a serene expression on her face.

"Where is your father?"

Elena freezes, and I tense too.

"Is he with Jade?"

Elena stares at her mother, a confused expression on her face. "How... I mean..."

"What about your brother?"

She looks at me, a lost expression on her face, but I don't know what to say either. I kneel down and wrap my arm around her.

Sarah sighs and squeezes Elena's hand. "I think it's time I tell you a story, sweetheart."

Sarah inhales deeply and looks away. "Your father and I were childhood sweethearts. We fell in love young, and I... I was naive. Your father was of the same social standing as I was, but his family was on the brink of bankruptcy. Because of that, my father wouldn't allow me to marry Alaric."

Sarah looks at Elena and cups her cheek. "Until I was told I'd never have children." She tenses, as though the memory still hurts. "All of a sudden, I wasn't deemed a good potential bride for the men my father wanted me to marry. It wasn't until then that I was allowed to marry your father."

She smiles, her smile bittersweet. Elena stares at her mother in shock, a thousand questions flashing through her eyes.

"For a few years, everything seemed perfect. My dowry helped save your father's family, his legacy. I helped him start his own company, and we thrived. I was happy."

Sarah pauses, her mind seemingly somewhere else, as though she's gathering all her courage before continuing her story, and I wrap my arm around my wife, knowing that whatever is about to come will hurt her.

"Then one day, your father brought home a little boy—Matthew. He was only two years old, and he was the most adorable little boy I'd ever seen. Your father told me he'd messed up. That he wanted children so badly that it's all he could think about. He told me he'd never stray again, and he begged me to give him one more chance.

I had many questions, of course. But your father had an answer for all of them. I was torn, Elena. I was mad, but I also always wanted children. And Matthew? He hadn't done anything wrong. So I asked to meet Matthew's mother. That's when I first met her... *Jade*."

Elena gasps, her entire body trembling. I hold her as tightly as I can, wanting to offer her all my support, yet unsure how to. "What?" she whispers, her voice breaking.

"Jade knew that she could never offer Matthew the life that I could, so she told me she'd stay away. That she'd never see her child again, that he'd be mine. She vowed to stay away from my family—from your father."

"Mom," Elena says, her tone anguished. "Please, tell me, am I—"

Sarah smiles and nods. "Yes, you're mine. Of course you are. You're my little miracle, Elena."

Elena nods and rests her head in her mother's lap, trying her best to hold back her tears. Sarah strokes her hair gently, and it amazes me how sweet and caring she looks around Elena, when she's so cunning around everyone else. I guess that's where Elena gets it from—she's exactly the same.

"For a while, everything went back to normal. Your father and I... we managed to work things out, though it was never the same. I was fine, though, because I had Matthew. And not too long after, I had you. Both of you were my entire world, and that was enough for me. At the time, I didn't realize that your father was still seeing Jade. I didn't know that he'd been taking

Matthew to see her every month. I didn't know that Matthew was aware that I'm not his real mother. I had no idea that not only did he stay with Jade, they had a daughter together too. I didn't find out until a few days before my car accident."

I look at Sarah in disbelief. Elise is Elena's half-sister? Elena raises her head to look at her mother, her eyes red. She looks so heartbroken, so hurt.

Sarah smiles and cups Elena's cheek. "So tell me," she says. "Tell me what you've been up to. Tell me what you're planning. Tell me what you need from me, Elena. I've given your father and brother everything... and now I want it back."

CHAPTER 48

lexander

Elena twists and turns in bed, unable to fall asleep. I roll over and wrap my arm around her waist, pressing my lips against her neck.

"Can't sleep?"

She sighs and turns to face me, her nose brushing past mine. She shakes her head, looking lost. "I can't stop thinking about Matthew, about my father... about everything my mother told me. How could Matthew have done this? My mother raised him. Growing up, she always treated us the same. If anything, she'd treat Matthew better. She gave him everything he ever wanted, and this is how he repays her?"

I bury my hand in her hair and sigh, not knowing what to say. I don't think Elena needs me to say anything anyway—she just needs me to listen, so I do.

"And my father? My mother saved his company, and thereby his family, from ruins. He'd be *nothing* without her. He should've been devoted to her, but instead he had an entire second family behind our backs. What kind of person does that?"

Elena grits her teeth, her eyes flashing with fury. I stroke her hair gently, wanting to make her feel better, but unsure how. "It's beyond anything I expected, too, baby. I never liked your brother, but this isn't something I thought he was capable of. We can't reverse time, Elena, but what we can do is make up for lost time. We can move forward. I see how hard you're working, and within just a few weeks, you'll be able to give your mother back every single thing she's lost, and more."

She looks into my eyes and nods. There's hatred flashing through her eyes, and I hope she won't let it consume her. I hope this won't change her beautiful heart. If I could, I'd take the Rousseaus down myself. If it were up to me, I'd never let her dirty her dainty hands. But I can tell that she needs to be the one to do this, and I can't take this from her. I can't take away her control the way so many others in her life have. So I'll stand back. I'll let her handle her business, and if she needs me, I'll be right behind her.

"Alec, all I ever wanted was a family of my own, a husband that would love me. I wanted a home filled with love and laughter—I wanted what I've never had before. But if this is what love is, I want no part of it."

I stroke her hair, my heart breaking for her. Elena has always been naive, and the innocence she views life with is what makes her so unique. It keeps her heart pure in this fucked-up world. I hate seeing her lose it.

"Love... it corrupts," she says. "Looking at your mother and mine makes me see it for what it is. It's selfishness. It reminds me of religion, you know? I lost faith in God, when no matter what I did or how much I prayed, my mother wouldn't wake up. Love is the same way. Blind faith, when logically you know better."

"Baby," I murmur. "That's not—"

I don't even know what to say, because I agree with every single word she just said. Yet when it's Elena uttering these words, it makes me feel horrible. It makes me want to protect her from every bit of pain she's had to experience, every single thing she's had to witness, everything that made her lose faith.

She pushes against me, and I fall onto my back. Elena smiles as she climbs on top of me, and I place my hand around her waist. Her long dark hair covers her shoulder and arm, and I grab the ends of it, twisting it around my fingers.

"You and I won't be like that, Elena," I promise her. "We won't let waning emotions consume us. You and I... we won't let our judgment be clouded."

Elena and I aren't like our parents. Our marriage isn't built on flimsy and changing emotions. Our foundation is far stronger than that.

She nods as I thread my hand through her hair, pulling her closer. I need her in a way I never have before. I need her body close, her lips against mine. I need her locked into my arms. I want to take away the sorrow in her eyes.

Elena smiles as she leans in to kiss me. I raise my hips and turn her over. She falls back onto the bed, and before she can protest, I cover her body with mine.

I fist her hair and kiss her roughly, deeply. A moan escapes her lips as her tongue tangles with mine, but it isn't enough. I want her panting my name. I move down, kissing her neck, marking her as mine.

"Alec," she whispers, and I smile against her skin, satisfied.

I take my time with her, kissing as much of her body as I can reach, driving her insane. My wife isn't very patient, but I love teasing her.

I tug on her clothes, and Elena lifts her hips, helping me get her nightgown off. She's squirming by the time my hands wrap around the fabric of her panties, and her hands roam over my body.

"Alec, stop teasing me," she says, and I grin. I shrug out of my boxers and settle in between her legs.

"Tell me what you want."

Elena looks at me through lust-filled eyes. "You know what I want."

I lean in to kiss her, capturing her full bottom lip between my teeth. "Beg for it."

Elena laughs and pushes against me, making me roll onto my back. Before I realize what she's doing, she's on top of me, my cock sinking deep inside her.

I moan loudly, feeling entirely out of control, and Elena smiles. I wrap my hand right below her chest as she rides me, her breasts swaying. My thumbs brush over her nipples and her eyes fall shut.

"Alec," she moans, and I let the edges of my fingers trail over her dark, hard buds. I twist them slightly, and her muscles contract around me.

"Fuck, Elena," I groan.

I grab her by her hips and thrust up, moving with her, loving the way she looks, the way her body is on display for me. "What a fucking view," I tell her.

The way she looks at me exhilarates me. When we're in bed together, I'm all she can see. When I'm deep inside her, every single one of her worries escapes those beautiful eyes of hers. I fuck her harder, rotating my hips, eliciting a moan from her every time I do.

Watching her face as she gets closer and closer... fuck. I could come just by looking at her.

Elena gasps, and her muscles contract around me, fucking milking me. I groan as she comes, taking me right along with her.

She smiles in satisfaction and collapses on top of me. I wrap my arms around her and press a kiss to her temple. Elena sighs and repositions herself, her head on my chest, both of us still panting. I hold her tightly with one arm, stroking her back with the other.

Amazing sex and mutual trust... it's enough. It has to be.

CHAPTER 49

lena

I look into the mirror, admiring my outfit. I opted for a maroon-colored pantsuit, and even I have to admit that it makes me look... *powerful.*

"You look stunning," Alec says, his eyes roaming over my body. I smile and walk up to him, fixing his matching maroon tie.

I place my palms against his chest, my heart filled with gratefulness. "None of this would be possible without you."

He smiles and brushes my hair behind my ear. "Are you ready?" he asks.

I nod. Three months. It's been three months since we took my mother home. It took me that long to get all legal aspects in place.

Alec holds my hand as we walk down the stairs. The entire ground floor is filled with men dressed in black suits, guns strapped to their waists. My mother stands in the middle, leaning on her cane, Sofia by her side. She still can't walk well, and she can't walk for long, but she's getting there, slowly.

She looks beautiful today, and every time she smiles at me, I'm still struck with disbelief. I almost lost my mother, and what for?

Lucian nods at me from the sofa, Elliot by his side. I smile at him, and nod at Elliot in thanks. He's gone above and beyond for me.

Alec places his hand on my lower back, and I take a deep breath to calm my nerves.

"Tonight, we're taking the Rousseaus down," I say, my heart at ease. It should sound strange to me to say that. Not too long ago, I was a Rousseau myself. Yet I feel nothing but excitement.

"Team Beta will be on standby at their estate, awaiting my orders. Team Alpha will be with Alec and me. We'll be hitting the board room."

I glance at my mother and smile. "I've called for an emergency shareholders' meeting, so they'll be on high alert. At this point, my father should be aware that someone has been buying up his shares, but he's unable to find out who, thanks to Elliot," I say, nodding at him.

Alec purchased all the shares under a privately held company that he gifted me, which would already make it hard to unveil who the buyer is, but Elliot has managed to hide all remaining traces of ownership. From what I understand, my father has already tried to follow the money, only to come up against a brick wall every single time.

"My father won't be too worried yet, because he thinks he still owns a majority shareholding between Matthew and himself. The paperwork proving that we've undone that is right here," I say, lifting a stack of papers for my mother to see. Alec's lawyers have gone above and beyond to assist me with my plans, and it wasn't easy, but they've made it happen.

"All other teams will be stationed at every other property owned by the Rousseau Corporation. We'll be taking over all of them. I want every single lock changed." I glance at Elliot and smile. "And every single access code, too."

He nods at me, looking excited. Elliot is on standby to disable all security systems at every property today, and while it's a momentous task, he's assured me it's a walk in the park for him. Lucian puts his hand on Elliot's knee, betraying his nerves, but Elliot merely smiles at him reassuringly.

"Let's go."

Our teams get into their vehicles while Alec offers my mother his arm.

"Wait," Elliot says, handing me an earpiece. "I'll coordinate with you," he adds, and I smile, squeezing his hand.

Alec, Sofia, my mother, and I head toward the limousine, and it isn't until we're on our way to Rousseau Corporation that the nerves set in.

"You'll do amazing, honey," my mother says, and I nod. Rage fills my every vein at the thought of what they did to my mother. They're going down, if it's the last thing I do.

I smile as I step out of the limousine, and I feel truly fearless as I walk into the building. For years, *years*, I've felt helpless. Not anymore.

I walk toward the board room with just two of our men by my side. Alec, Sofia, and my mother not too far behind me, their pace adjusted to Mom's.

I smile as I push the door to the board room open with force, enjoying the way it loudly slams into the wall.

The members of the board sit up in surprise, and my father looks at me in shock. "Elena?" he says, his voice laced with dismay. "What are you doing here? This is no place for you."

The contempt in his voice irritates me and I grit my teeth as

I walk up to him. I stand beside him, my eyes roaming over the board members sitting here today.

Matthew looks at me, his jaws clenched. "You called the meeting?"

My father laughs and shakes his head. "That's impossible," he says. "I gave her shares to *you*."

I grin at Matthew. "You're not half as dumb as you look," I tell him. "But then again, you've proven yourself to be quite the mastermind, huh? Looks are deceiving after all."

He blinks, a calculative glint in his eyes. Out of everyone, I'm going to enjoy taking him down most.

"I have gathered you all here today to vote on the position of CEO," I say.

My brother smiles in amusement and shakes his head, leaning back in his seat, unworried. "You've managed to buy what? Ten percent of our shares? I'll entertain you today, but let this be a lesson. The next time you waste my time, I'll make you pay."

I merely nod at him. It's not his turn just yet.

"I'm calling to a vote the matter of terminating Alaric Rousseau's position as CEO," I say.

Matthew sighs and shakes his head. "Those voting in favor of having him remain in his position, please raise your hand," he says, slowly raising his own, his tone mocking. He turns to look around the table, his eyes flashing with satisfaction when he finds every single hand raised. He looks at me in amusement, and I smile.

My earpiece crackles, Elliot's voice coming through. "Your mother should be walking in any second now," he says. "You're good to go."

"All those voting in favor of *removing* him from his position, please raise your hand," I say, raising my own.

Matthew laughs, his arms spread. "Can't you count, Elena?"

he asks. "The vote is done. You got your ten seconds of attention, now get out."

"It's not quite done yet," a soft voice says behind me.

I turn to find my mother walking in on Alec's arm. Her eyes find Matthew's, and the pain I see in them kills me.

I grab a stack of papers from my bag and throw them onto the table, papers scattering everywhere. I glance at my mother, and she smiles at me as she raises her hand.

"Can't you count?" I ask Matthew. "Between my mother and I, we own sixty percent of the shares."

He blanches, his eyes on my mother. He looks like he's seeing a ghost, and it angers me even further. I grit my teeth and turn to my father, who is looking at my mother the exact same way.

"You're done," I tell him. I nod at the security team we brought with us, and they help my father out of his seat. He barely even notices, his eyes on my mother.

"This is impossible," Matthew says, looking panicked.

I smile at him. "*Now* the vote is done," I tell him. I nod at my men, and they walk up to him. "Restrain him," I tell them.

Matthew struggles. "You can't remove *me*," he yells. "I'm still a shareholder."

I frown at him. "You mean the shares you *inherited* from a woman who *isn't* dead? Yeah, it doesn't work that way."

He kicks at his chair as my men restrain him, and I shake my head. "Let *this* be a reminder. What goes around comes around, Matthew. Not just your words—your every action. I *will* make you pay. This company, your shares, they should be the least of your worries."

I nod at Aiden, and he hands me a hard drive. I clench my jaw as I look at it, my eyes finding my mother's. She smiles, her smile bittersweet. I walk up to her and wrap my arm around her just as the police walk in.

Matthew freezes when he sees them, his face draining of color. They stop in front of him.

"Matthew Rousseau," they say. "You're under arrest for the attempted murder of Sarah Rousseau. Anything you say can and will be used in a court of law. You have the right to an attorney. If you cannot afford an attorney, one will be provided for you."

I shake my head at him. "Attempted murder is but one of your crimes, Matthew. The doctors and nurses that were on the Rousseau payroll? The ones that knowingly kept my mother in an induced coma? The police have certified confessions from them. They'll be testifying against you."

A tear drops down my mother's cheek as they slap the cuffs around his wrist, his head hanging low. I tighten my grip on my mother as they lead him past us, my heart heavy. I've gone through years of us growing apart, but to my mother, it must feel like she's losing her son all of a sudden.

I inhale deeply before addressing the shocked board members. None of them have said a single word. They're probably scandalized, and it won't take long for rumors about today's events to start spreading—exactly what I wanted. Even if somehow, Matthew gets away with what he did to my mother, his reputation will forever be tarnished.

"I think that's quite enough theatrics for today. I apologize for involving you all. I hereby call this meeting closed. You're dismissed."

Most of them rise from their seats, and many of them head toward my mother. How could I have forgotten? Most of these people are old friends of hers, people that have been here from the very start. Many of them were here when she grew the company into what it is.

Our security team stops them from getting too close to her and she shakes her head, raising her palm. "Soon," she says.

"We'll all be able to catch up soon. I'm not going anywhere, ever again. But today... today my daughter and I have some business to take care of."

She turns and walks away, and I can't help but smile. I was worried today would be incredibly hard on her, but she seems to be coping well.

I follow her, impatient for what's about to come.

CHAPTER 50

lexander

Elena stares up at her family home, a sad expression on her face.

"Don't worry, baby," I say, wrapping my arm around her. "We'll get you your home back."

Elena shakes her head and rises to her tiptoes, pressing a lingering kiss to my cheek. "No," she says. "My home is with you. Today, we're regaining my mother's home."

My heart stirs and I smile down at her. She considers her home to be with me?

"Honey."

Elena turns to look at her mother, her brows raised.

"Let me," Sarah says, her eyes on the property in front of us. "Let me do this."

Elena nods, her hand brushing down my arm until she's got her hand nestled in mine. I entwine our fingers, the two of us following behind Sarah, a dozen men surrounding us.

Elena touches her earpiece and then nods at her mother.

"Systems are down."

Sarah inhales deeply and pushes the gates open. She walks slowly, heavily leaning on her cane, but she's walking. After all these years, she's walking.

I glance at my wife, my amazing wife. Never once did she give up on her mother. She fought for a scholarship and worked three jobs in an effort to afford the exceptional care Sarah received. She did that—a woman that grew up filthy rich. All for her mother.

Sarah walks into the house, and Elena and I follow right behind her. She walks into the living room to find Jade and Elise sitting on the sofa—her sofa. Jade sits up in shock, her hand going over her mouth. She looks like she saw a ghost, the same guilt that Matthew portrayed reflected in her eyes too.

"Jade," Sarah says, her voice tinged with mock surprise. "What are you doing in my house?"

Jade rises from the sofa and walks around it, her face white. She stands behind the sofa, as though she's trying to use it as a barrier.

"You... you were dead."

Sarah looks down at her hands. "No," she says. "I don't think so."

She takes a step forward, and Jade takes a step away from her. Meanwhile, Elise is on the sofa, her eyes wide. Elena nods at our men, and they move toward Elise, restraining her.

"You stay away from my daughter," Jade says, her voice trembling. She glances around the room, realizing that she's outnumbered.

Sarah ignores her and sits down on the sofa, one leg crossed over the other. "Can't say I love what you did to the place," she says, frowning.

She nods at the seat opposite her. "Take a seat."

One of our men grabs Jade and forces her into the seat

Sarah just pointed out, and I smile. I lean into Elena, my lips brushing past her ear. "Your mom is quite badass."

She grins, and I wrap my arms around her. Elena rests her back against my chest, and I put my chin on top of her head. The two of us standing here as though we're watching our favorite show.

"I thought we agreed that you'd stay away from my family," Sarah says, spreading her arms out on the sofa. "So why are you in my house?"

Jade trembles and reaches for her phone, which just makes Sarah laugh. "Don't bother," she says. "Alaric is being detained by the Kennedys, and Matthew has been arrested for attempted murder. But worry not, Jade, soon you'll be joining your darling son."

"You... you—this isn't your house. Not anymore. It's mine. You need to get out," Jade says. "I'm calling the police. You're trespassing."

I press a kiss to Elena's neck. "Good move on Jade's part," I murmur, and Elena huffs.

Elise watches us, looking more panicked by the second, and I narrow my eyes at her. I haven't forgotten that Elise is the reason my wife ended up at Vaughn's—the very same place she'll end up at, eventually. I'll make sure of it.

Elena shakes her head. "It would be, if she actually owned this place. She doesn't."

Jade glares at Sarah, her cheeks slowly regaining color. "Everything that used to be yours is mine now. Matter of fact, it always was. Alaric was always mine, and you're well aware that Matthew is too. It doesn't matter that you raised him for years —he's my blood. Alaric only married you for the money. It's me he always loved."

Sarah freezes—it's subtle, but it doesn't escape me. Elena's grip on my hand tightens, and she takes a step forward, but I pull her back. "Your mom has got this," I tell her. "Let her have this moment. It's been years in the making."

She nods, but she's tense. I tighten my grip on her, hugging her close to me.

"That might well be true," Sarah says. "But it doesn't explain why you're in my house. Alaric and Matthew... you can have them. They're yours. But everything I've ever worked for? Everything I've ever invested in? You can't have that, Jade."

Jade glances at the two police officers that walk in and smiles. Foolish woman.

Sarah nods at Aiden, and he walks up to her with a stack of papers in hand. He places them down in front of Jade before handing Sarah a hard drive identical to the one he gave Elena earlier.

"An eviction notice?" Jade says, her hands trembling.

Sarah rises from her seat and looks around. "I'll have your personal belongings packed, though I doubt you'll need them where you're going," she says, nodding at the police officers. They arrest Jade for attempted murder, and just like Matthew did, she tries to fight it.

"Get her out of here," Elena says, her head tipped toward Elise.

That girl has always had such a big mouth around my wife, but not a single word has escaped her lips today. All I see on her face is the fear and pain she's made Elena feel for years.

The door closes behind them, and Sarah falls to the floor. Elena gasps and runs up to her mother, taking Sarah into her arms.

My heart breaks when Sarah bursts into tears. She hasn't cried once since she woke up. Not when she struggled to speak, not when her limbs wouldn't do what she wanted them to, not even when she was told she'd be in a wheelchair for months.

None of that broke her. But this did. *Love* did.

CHAPTER 51

lena

I sit with my mother as we go through company records, Alec by our side. He wraps his arm around my waist and sighs. "Look, Buttercup," he says. "This all doesn't add up. Overhauling this company is going to be difficult."

I drop my head against his shoulder, and he presses a kiss on top of my hair.

"I'm not surprised," Mom says. "Alaric was never that good of a businessman. Even when you were little, it was me running both our companies. I did it then, and I'll do it now. Between you and I, there's nothing we can't accomplish, sweetie."

I nod, but the task seems daunting. "We need to set up meetings with every single department head," I say, scrolling through the data.

My phone rings, and I frown when I don't recognize the phone number. I haven't given this number out to anyone.

Alec glances at my phone, looking surprised. "Take the call. That phone number, it's my grandfather's."

I look at him with raised brows as I accept the call, confused as to why he'd be calling me.

"Hello?"

"Elena, darling. I heard you're the proud new owner of Rousseau Corporation. From what I've heard, you went in with guns blazing. I couldn't be more proud."

I blush, I can't help it. "Grandpa... it was nothing. It just needed to be done."

"How about that lunch you promised me? I have some time right about now. I can be there in ten minutes or so. I'd love to hear the full story. Besides, I'd love to see your mother again. I haven't seen her in years."

"Of course, Grandpa."

I glance at my mom and smile as I end the call. "Alec's grandfather is coming over for lunch. He said he'd like to see you, since it's been so many years. He sounded quite interested in hearing our full story."

Mom smiles and shakes her head. "Sofia's dad warned me against marrying your father. She and I were very good friends when we were younger, and her father always looked out for me."

I put my hand on my mother's shoulder, my heart breaking for her. Mom has lost so much, yet she still smiles.

I walk toward Sofia's kitchen, startling the staff. Even though Alec and I have our own kitchen, Sofia's is far larger, and it's the one we always use for family meals. Grandpa walks in shortly after I do, a large basket full of vegetables in his hand.

"Hello, sweetheart," he says, grinning.

He holds up a melon for me excitedly, and I stare at it with wide eyes. "Oh, my gosh! I wonder what it'll taste like. Do you think it'll be sweet?"

Grandpa shrugs. "We won't know until we try it. How did you put it? They're *moody*."

I laugh, and Sofia pops her head into the kitchen, a smile on her face. "Thought I heard you, Dad."

She stares at the vegetables on the counter through narrowed eyes and crosses her arms. "Dad... I thought you said I was the only one that ever gets to have your vegetables?"

Grandpa looks at her sheepishly, and I laugh. I love the way Sofia acts around her dad, and the way he treats her. This imposing man is nothing more than a loving father whenever Sofia is around.

"But Elena is going to cook them for *you*," he says, throwing all his charm at her.

Sofia shakes her head. "You didn't even know if I'd be here, and you didn't call me either." She turns to look at me. "Did he call you, Elena?"

Grandpa looks at me with wide eyes and shakes his head ever so slightly, and I just about manage to bite back a smile. "Uh, no," I say, my tone unconvincing.

"I knew it!" Sofia says, glaring at her father.

"Don't blame Grandpa," Alec says, entering the kitchen with my mother right behind him. "He can't help it. The old man never stood a chance. Elena just has a knack for stealing people's hearts."

Sofia nods, as though in agreement, and wraps her arm around my shoulder. "Yes, that's true. My daughter-in-law is so loveable."

Mom clears her throat. "Sofia, you do realize she's *my* daughter, right?"

Sofia narrows her eyes and tightens her grip on me. "Not anymore, she's not."

Mom glares right back at her. "Alec and Elena's wedding ceremony is still three months away!"

I watch the two of them in amusement. Sofia has loved having me around and I've gotten used to spending time with

263

her, while Mom is trying her hardest to make up for lost time. The two have been butting heads over who gets to spend time with me constantly. It's like they're two divorced parents fighting over custody of me, and it amuses me endlessly. It makes me feel loved, and I haven't felt that way in years. I know the playfulness they portray is an attempt to lighten the mood after a couple of tough months, but that they'd even consider doing that for me at all, astounds me. For someone to care enough, to want to cheer me up, it surprises me.

I glance around the room, my heart overflowing with love. For years, loneliness ate at me, and desperation was all that kept me going. Now I'm standing here in a room filled with people that actually want me around, people that care about me.

My eyes find Alec's, and I can't help but wonder if he has any feelings for me. Sometimes it feels like he does, and other times I can't even read him. I'm not sure if love is still something I want. My heart craves it, but logically I can now see where Alec is coming from. Love... it's too much risk. What Alec and I have right now is indestructible. If we fell in love, would it break us the way it did my mother?

He smiles at me, and my heart starts to race. Alec walks up to me, but loud sirens start to sound throughout the house before he reaches me, making us both jump in surprise.

He grabs his phone, frowning. His face drains of color, and my heart sinks. "Paparazzi have surrounded our house. They've breached the perimeter. Our men are working on pushing them back, but there are too many. Aiden tells me there are a few dozen out there."

His eyes find mine and fear runs down my spine. Did they find out? Did they find out about our marriage? Did they somehow find out our relationship isn't real?

I glance at Grandpa. Alec could lose everything.

CHAPTER 52

lexander

"What happened?" Mom asks.

I shake my head. "I don't know."

She grabs her phone at the same time as everyone else, all of us googling our own names and the Kennedy name.

Dread fills me when I find my father all over the news. The headlines have my stomach twisting violently. I click on one of the articles, resignation making my fingers heavy.

A sex tape. My father is in the news because of a fucking sex tape.

I feel sick, but it probably doesn't compare to how my mother must be feeling.

I inhale deeply and start to scroll through my contacts to find Elliot's number. How could he have let this happen? He's got intricate filters set up in order to block this type of stuff from ever reaching the mainstream media, so why didn't he catch this?

"Elliot?" I say as soon as he picks up. "What happened?"

He yawns loudly. "What are you talking about?" he says, sounding sleepy. "*Fuck. My systems are down.*"

"Stop," my mother says. "Stop it, Alec."

She grabs my phone from my hands and ends the call. "Enough now. *Enough.*"

She runs a hand through her hair shakily. When she looks at me, her eyes are filled with heartbreak, but there's determination in her gaze too.

"I know you've been trying to protect me, Alec. I know you've been blocking this type of news for years. But it's enough now. I can't live like this anymore. I can't."

She turns toward my grandfather and tenses, as though she's bracing herself. "Dad... I've tried. I swear, I've given it my all. For years, I've held onto hope, I've held onto the happy memories. But I can't anymore. All I've ever wanted was a marriage like Mom and yours, and for the longest time, I thought that if I endured for long enough, if I proved that my love would always remain strong, then maybe... maybe Anthony would change. You've always told me that marriage is forever, that you work things out together, you don't walk away. But, Dad, marriage takes two. And this marriage? I've been in this on my own for years now."

A tear rolls down her face, and Grandpa walks up to her. He swipes at her tears and a sob escapes Mom's lips. Grandpa takes her into his arms, hugging her tightly.

"Dad... I want a divorce. I know Kennedys don't do divorce, but look at me," she says, her voice breaking. "The whole world knows that my husband cheats on me—I'm a laughing stock. And what for?"

She buries her face in Grandpa's chest, and he closes his eyes, looking as pained as Mom does. "Please, Dad. Let me have a divorce. If you feel you need to disown me because of it, then do what you must. I just ask that you don't let it affect my children."

It kills me to see her like this. Her request shocks me—I never even thought divorce was an option. It wasn't something I thought Mom would ever dare ask for. But she's right. This... this is no life.

"Honey," Grandpa says, his hand brushing over her hair, soothing her. "You're my little girl, Sofia. All I've ever wanted for you was happiness, nothing less."

He glances at me, a complicated look in his eyes. "Had I known about this... had my grandson not hidden this quite so well, then sweetie, there's no way I would've ever *let* you stay. I didn't know, honey. I assumed you two had your problems, but I never imagined it'd be to this extent."

He rubs her back, but Mom can't control her tears. It's like years' worth of heartache is finally finding its way out.

He pulls away to look at her, and the look on his face... I've never seen my grandfather look this hurt before. Mom sniffs, but she's unable to hold back her sobs.

"Get a divorce," he says, shocking us all. "You're my daughter, Sofia. You will always be my little girl. There's no way I'd disown you for choosing happiness. I won't be the reason you remain trapped in a loveless marriage."

I stare at my grandfather in disbelief. I didn't think he'd ever allow that. I didn't think he'd let Mom walk away from her marriage without repercussions.

I tried so hard to protect my mother, but if I hadn't, she might have been able to get a divorce much sooner.

My love for her is what prolonged her pain.

CHAPTER 53

lexander

I knock on my mother's bedroom door. We usually have dinner together as a family at least every few days, but she hasn't been coming down to eat with us. According to the staff, she hasn't been eating much at all.

"Mom?"

She opens her door, and I stare at her in shock. Her eyes are swollen and red, her hair is messy, and she's wearing a house robe. I've never seen her so... undone.

She sniffs and tries her best to smile at me. "I'm sorry, Alec. I just... I don't feel well."

I nod at her. "But you need to eat something. Please?"

She looks at me and sighs as she walks out of her room and down the stairs, not even bothering to change or comb her hair. Her movements are mechanical, as if she's merely doing me a favor. I barely even recognize her. Just a few weeks ago, she'd never have dreamt of walking around like this—not even around the house.

I follow her down, worried sick. Elena, Lucian, and Sarah are already seated. They smile, but Mom doesn't smile back.

"How are you feeling?" Sarah asks.

Mom looks up, and the two of them exchange a look, one of understanding. "Anthony told me to courier him the divorce papers. He won't even come down to speak to me, to fight for me."

I stare at her with wide eyes. I didn't know any of this. I haven't spoken to my father in months. Neither Lucian nor I ever speak to him anymore, and he doesn't reach out either.

Sarah grabs Mom's hand and nods. "Probably for the best. A clean break is what you need."

Mom inhales shakily. "Thankfully, there isn't much he can take. Most of our assets are owned by the company, which in turn is owned by my father. I'll lose some of my property and a decent amount of money, but he won't be able to get his hands on much more than that."

I breathe a sigh of relief. Thank God, Grandpa is alive and well. If Mom had inherited his shares, we'd be in so much trouble—she'd have to give my father half.

Mom barely touches her food, and I see the anxiety in Elena's eyes. She keeps adding small amounts of my mother's favorite foods to her plate, but Mom won't touch any of it.

Throughout dinner, Elena offers to take her on a spa day, and Lucian offers to take her shopping, but she isn't interested at all.

I'm terrified she'll fall back into the same depression she'd only just about staved off when I married Elena. She kept herself going by keeping up a facade, but now the whole world has seen her fall. She hasn't left the house ever since my father made the news, and at this rate, she won't.

I don't know what to do. I'm used to almost everything

being within my control, but this... there's nothing I can do about this.

Mom rises as soon as everyone's done eating and disappears before I can even stop her. Every once in a while, we'll play card games together, and I was hoping to convince her to do that today, but she slipped away before I even had a chance.

I'm restless as I walk back up the stairs, Elena right behind me. She follows me into our sitting room and takes a seat on her favorite chair, as worried and absentminded as I am.

I pour myself a glass of whiskey and tip it back before refilling my glass. "Do you want a drink?"

Elena shakes her head. She pulls her feet up on the chair, her arms wrapped around herself.

I sit down opposite her, the two of us facing each other the way we did when I proposed to her. I drink her in, her long hair falling down her waist, her beautiful face, those stunning eyes of hers. What would have happened if I hadn't run into her that day? The thought of what she almost did tears me apart, but I can't help but wonder whether I made the right choice by chaining her to me. Will she end up like my mother, eventually? She and my mother have the same heart. She's a hopeless romantic. She tries to deny it, both to herself and me, but she can't help herself. She isn't like me. Elena cares about the little things, the way my mother does. She likes having dinner together, falling asleep together. If I'm not home for a couple of days, she gets restless. Elena *cares*. She cares about everything, about everyone around us.

I adore that about her, but it's also something that'll hurt her in the end. Our marriage... it'll never be enough for her. She'll always want more. I see it in her eyes. She wants things I can't give her. She sees things that aren't there.

Elena looks up at me and smiles. "She'll be okay, you know? It'll be difficult, but we're here for her. In the end, she'll be better off without your father. She'll have a chance to live her life the way she wants to, without pretenses."

I nod. "Without pretenses... yeah, I guess—except I'm not sure my mother even knows who she is anymore."

Just like my mother, Elena is losing sight of who she is. I see her light dim every day. It's not just everything that went down with her father. It's more than that. It's me. The way she looks at me... I see her heart break every time I kiss her.

Seeing my mother fall apart kills me. It kills me, and it terrifies me. I'm scared I'm pushing Elena down the same path my mother was on. I'm scared she'll one day find her life empty, that she'll realize she gave up too much for me. She'll find herself unloved, alone, the way my mother did. The things she wants from me, I can never give her. I have no love left to give in this lifetime. And even if I did... I know love doesn't last. It doesn't, yet Elena won't stop longing for it.

CHAPTER 54

lena

I glance at Alec lying next to me. He's fast asleep, his lashes fluttering ever so slightly. I lean in closer, wrapping my arm around him. He sighs and turns away, pushing against me in his sleep.

He's been different lately. He hasn't been himself since his mother asked for a divorce. There's so much distance between us now, and I don't know how to fix it.

I've never seen Alec in this much anguish—seeing his mother fall apart, seeing her hounded by the press... he's hurting right along with her, and it's made him pull away from me more and more.

I run a finger over his arm, eliciting a slight shiver from him. I miss him. He's right here, but I miss him. He doesn't look at me the same anymore. When he smiles at me, it's like I'm just another girl. He hasn't even touched me in weeks now.

I move closer to him, pressing myself against him. I need his skin against mine. I swore to myself that I wouldn't be like my mother, like Sofia, but I want to be all he sees. Even against my better judgement, he's all I want. I'm fighting my feelings so hard, but I'm at my heart's mercy. He'll kiss me, and all reason escapes me.

Alec sighs, his lashes fluttering. He blinks slowly, his eyes finding mine.

"What are you doing?" he asks, his voice raspy.

I tighten my grip on him and press a kiss to his forehead. Alec throws his arms around me and pulls me closer, my head on his chest. He buries his hand in my hair, gripping tightly.

"What's wrong?" he whispers, and I shake my head.

"It's nothing. Just can't sleep."

Alec pulls away to look at me, his gaze searching. "Worried about your mom? She's been recovering just fine. The way she's handling Rousseau Corporation is astounding."

I nod. I am partially worried about my mother, but it's more than that. "Yes, I'm worried about my mom, but also yours. The media has been all over her divorce. It's been so hard on her, and we can't protect her. I'm worried."

Alec nods. "I know, but she's got us. She isn't alone. Your mother has proven to be a pillar of strength, too. Just having her around has made it so much easier on Mom. Those two... they've both been hurt in many of the same ways."

I sigh. "I'm just tired, Alec. I'm tired of all the pain that surrounds us, all the heartache."

"I know, Buttercup." He cups my cheek and presses a gentle kiss to my lips. "But that's just life. Both our mothers chose love, and they paid the price. That's the risk of giving someone your heart—you have to trust that they won't break it, that they won't break *you*. And this world that we live in... it's shallow, it's opportunistic, and it's vain." He brushes my hair behind my ear and sighs. "The past cannot be undone, but we can learn from it."

I nod. He's right. I know he is. But can I harden my heart the way he has? Despite everything that's happened to my mother, to Sofia, my heart still craves what I know I can't have. A small part of me still longs for the things I've never known—a loving family of my own. It's foolish, and I know it, but I can't control my heart.

"Do you really think it's possible to live without love?"

Alec nods as he plays with my hair. "We've been doing it just fine, haven't we?"

His words hurt, yet I smile through the pain. He has no idea that I fall a little further every day.

"Do you love me, Alec? Even just a little?"

He stares at me wide-eyed and sits up; the sheets bunching up around his waist. Alec runs a hand through his hair and inhales deeply.

"Elena, why are you asking me this?"

I sit up on my knees and look into his eyes. "Alec... I just... you and I... we're not like our parents. You know I'd never betray you, and I don't think you'd ever cheat on me either. We're not like them."

He nods, his expression wary. "We aren't, because we have agreements in place. Because our marriage is transactional. You and I don't need to rely on *love* to keep us together. We have so much more than that."

"I understand," I tell him. "I do, Alec. But why does that need to be all we have?"

Alec sighs and looks at me, his expression irritated. "Elena, why are we even talking about this? I gave you an out when I proposed. I told you that if you married me, you'd be agreeing to a life without love. So why do you suddenly want more?" He leans back against his pillow, a dismayed expression on his face. "After everything you just witnessed, you still want love?

You watched multiple lives get destroyed over it, yet you still want it? Why?"

I look away, unsure how to explain myself. "Alec... you and I both grew up in households without love. Is that what you want for our children?"

He looks at me, and the coldness in his eyes has a shiver running down my spine. "All of this... what is this, Elena?" His eyes are flashing with an emotion I can't quite decipher. Is it anger? Irritation? He's making me feel like merely asking whether he loves me is inconveniencing him. "You got what you wanted—you managed to save your mother's life. And I married you so I'll get the job I want. That's all this marriage is, Elena. It's just a mutual beneficial arrangement."

I clasp my hands, trying my hardest to keep from trembling. "That's it?" I ask, my voice breaking. "That's all I am to you?"

Alec looks down at his hands and shakes his head. "I care about you, Elena. Of course, I do. You know I do."

Alec shakes his head and turns his back to me. I hear the words he doesn't say. He cares about me—but he doesn't love me, and he probably never will.

CHAPTER 55

lexander

"You wanted to see me, Grandpa?"

I enter his office—the office that I've always considered to be the ultimate goal. Every time I walk in here, I'm filled with renewed determination. One day soon, I'll succeed him.

"Take a seat."

I sit down opposite him, confused as to why he called me in. I stare at him, struggling to reconcile the person he is in front of Elena and my mother, with the person sitting in front of me.

"How is your mother?"

I look away. "She's fine," I say instinctively, but she isn't. She's been crying a lot, and she's barely left the house, scared of the way the paparazzi hounds her. It's painful to watch, but there's no other way.

"She'll get through this," Grandpa says, and I nod. She will. She must.

My grandfather pushes a stack of documents toward me, a resigned look in his eyes. "I'm old, Alec. Stuck in my ways. I think I know better, simply because I'm older, because I've seen so much, lived through so much. It's because of my stubbornness that your mother stayed in a marriage she should have gotten out of years ago. It's because of me she wasted away years of her life—years she'll never get back. I won't make the same mistake with you."

I take the papers from him, my eyes widening when I realize what they are. "My position as chairman is yours. I'll lift the marriage requirement. You're well aware that I adore Elena, but don't marry her in pursuit of your own goals. If you marry her, marry her because it's *her* you want, because you can't imagine your life without her, because you *love* her. I want for you what your mother didn't get to have—a happy and fulfilling marriage. Don't end up like your mother. Don't do that to Elena."

He hands me a pen and I don't hesitate to sign the contract, my heart pounding. This is everything I've ever wanted, so why doesn't signing this feel as good as I expected it to?

"The board will certify your appointment in the next couple of days. You and I both know that Dylan isn't qualified to take my role, yet my stubbornness almost allowed him to."

Grandpa sighs and leans back in his seat. "It's because of your grandmother. It's because I want all of my children and grandchildren to have what I had with her. Your grandma... she kept me grounded, she was my partner in every way that mattered, my best friend. She made life worth living, and I still miss her every single day. But what I had with your grandmother is exceptionally rare. Just being married doesn't guarantee a bond like that. I should have known better."

I nod, speechless. Never in a million years did I think he'd change his mind, or that he'd admit the flaws in his logic.

"Go on," he says. "Go celebrate. Your mother will be so proud, and Elena will be too. Go celebrate with them."

I rise to my feet and smile at my grandfather. "Thank you, Grandpa. I won't let you down."

He nods. "You never have, Alec. I've never said this to you, but I'm very proud of you. Not just of the way you run our business, but of your heart. The way you take care of your mother makes me so proud. I'm grateful to have a grandson like you."

I smile at him, surprised. He's never once said anything like that to me before, and I never even realized those were words I wanted to hear from him.

I'm still grinning by the time I get home. Not even the paparazzi stationed around our property can dent my mood.

I walk straight up to my apartment, in search of Elena. She and I haven't been the same for a while now... there's a distance between us of my own making. Seeing my mother fall apart the way she did has made me pull away from her involuntarily. I'm terrified that I'll make Elena end up the same way—broken and unloved. The things Elena wants so badly are the very same things that'll tear us apart. I don't understand why she can't see how strong our relationship is, precisely because we *aren't* in love—because love was never the foundation of our marriage. She's seen so many lives ruined under the guise of love, yet she still asks it of me. All I can hope is that it'll pass, that she'll realize sooner or later how destructive love would be to our relationship.

I pause in the kitchen doorway, my eyes on her. Despite every doubt and every fear, she's the first one I want to share this good news with. I glance at her and smile.

She's standing in front of the counter, glaring at some burned cookies, as though they've personally wronged her. "Buttercup."

She looks at me and my heart stirs. There's flour on her cheeks and in her hair, yet she looks stunning. My heart twists painfully. I've missed her.

I walk up to her and wrap her in my arms, hugging her tightly. I haven't held her like this in days. Elena hesitates before she hugs me back, her arms wrapping around my neck.

"What brought this on?"

I pull away a little to look at her and smile. "You're looking at the new chairman of our company."

Elena gasps, holding on to my shoulders tightly. "Are you serious?"

"Yes. I just signed the contract."

Elena smiles, her eyes sparkling with the same happiness I feel. "Congratulations, Alec," she says, throwing herself back into my arms. I hold her tightly, enjoying the way she fits into me perfectly.

"Exactly the type of good news we needed after the tough couple of months we've just had," she says, even though her smile melts off her face.

"Hey, what's wrong?"

"It's nothing, Alec." She cups my cheek, a forced smile on her face. She's trying to portray happiness, yet all I see in her eyes is sadness. "I'm so happy for you."

"Elena, talk to me. Something is clearly wrong."

She sighs and buries her hand in my hair. "I just... I thought you wouldn't get the position until after our wedding."

I stare at her, realization dawning.

She's right.

She married me to save her mother's life, but her mother has woken up now, and I... I married her to guarantee I'd get my grandfather's role. The role I was just given.

She swallows hard and pulls away from me, her arms wrapping around herself. "When you proposed, you said Kennedys don't ever divorce. But they *do* now. Your mother has set a new precedent. Not that that would even matter all that much, since no one knows we're married."

I tighten my grip on her waist, my heart sinking. "What are you saying, Elena? Are you saying you want a divorce?"

She shakes her head. "No. I don't know."

"You don't know?" I repeat slowly.

Elena looks away and sighs. "I don't know what I want anymore, Alec. I don't know."

I pull away from her, my heart uneasy. I take a step away from her, letting her go. "Look, I just need some fresh air," I tell her, walking away.

Elena grabs my sleeve. "Alec, no. Please don't go. I'm sorry," she says, her voice breaking.

I shake my head and brush her off. My head spins as I walk out of the house. I feel sick. The thought of her leaving me tears me apart—but if I were to hold on to her, would I be tearing her apart?

CHAPTER 56

lena

"What's wrong, sweetie?" Mom asks, looking up from her laptop. She's in bed and I'm lying down next to her, just wanting to be close to her. I hate letting her out of my sight. I'm scared of losing her again. I look up at her and shake my head, struggling to snap out of my thoughts.

"You've been acting strange all week. What's going on? Alec has barely been home either. Are you two fighting?"

I grimace, and Mom squeezes my hand. "Sweetie, you're worrying me. What's going on?"

I shake my head and sniff. "It's nothing, Mom."

I don't want to burden her with my relationship issues. I don't want her to worry about me. I wish I could hide how I'm feeling so she'd never have noticed in the first place.

Alec and I have barely spoken in days. It's like we just co-exist. Ever since the topic of divorce came up, our relationship deteriorated beyond repair. He's making me feel like he has no further use for me now that he's become chairman. The way he's treating me... it's what I expected all along. He told me he wanted a wife he could use, someone he wouldn't have to woo, someone that'd stay out of his way.

I would've been able to cope with that if he hadn't first showed me what he can be like. If he hadn't given me a glimpse of what it might feel like to be loved by him.

"Mom, do you regret marrying Dad?"

Her smile is bittersweet, and she sighs. "No. I don't regret marrying your father, Elena. After all, he gave me you. The only thing I regret is staying as long as I did. I should've walked out the second I realized he cheated—the second I realized he no longer loved me, if he ever did at all. There's no shame in loving someone with all your heart, Elena, but that love must be mutual. If you end up giving more of yourself than you get back, you'll end up a shell of yourself, depleted, like I was. Had I walked out sooner, I might have had a different life. Who knows? I might have actually found true love."

I stare at her, my thoughts whirling. "Even after everything that happened, you still seem to believe in love."

Mom nods. "It's not love that did this to me, honey. It's the *absence* of love."

I blink in surprise, and she smiles.

"Honey, the issue both Sofia and I had was that we loved with all our hearts and never received that same love back. Living like that, loving like that, it's not sustainable."

The absence of love... I never thought of it that way. "Wouldn't it be so much easier not to love at all?"

Mom bursts out laughing and squeezes my hand. "Honey, a life without love isn't a life worth living. Besides, you don't get to choose whether or not you love someone. If only. How much easier would life be if we could just make that choice? Love... it doesn't listen to reason."

I think over her words. I've been trying to fight my feelings, but I ended up falling for Alec against my wishes. I want to be the person he's asking me to be—a convenient wife, a partner that minds their own business. But I can't. I can't *not* love him.

The way he takes care of me, the way he defends Luce, and the way he's always protected his mother... He makes it so easy to love him. I never stood a chance.

There isn't much he asked of me in return for everything he's given me. Just three things: to be a good daughter-in-law and his trophy wife in public, and to never expect love. He's given me everything. Without him, my mother might not be lying beside me right now. Yet I can't help but selfishly want more. I can't help but dare hope for more.

I'm still thinking about my mother's words hours later. I glance at the clock as I cook dinner, unsure whether Alec will even join me tonight. Lately he's been working late in his office, and I can't help but wonder if it's because he's avoiding me.

I look up when I hear one of the doors slam and follow the sound to find Alec walking straight into his home office. He used to at least greet me and ask about my day, even on days that he was incredibly busy. I pause in front of his closed office door and hesitate before pushing it open.

"Alec?"

He looks up in surprise, his expression guarded. "Elena. What are you doing here?"

I blink, unsure how to even reply to that. "I heard you walk in."

He nods and tugs on his tie. I walk up to him and place my hand over his, helping him loosen his tie. He freezes as though my touch makes him uncomfortable, and I can't help but frown.

"Alec, what's going on? You and I have barely spoken. You're avoiding me."

He looks at me with raised brows and takes a step away. "I'm not avoiding you, Elena. I'm just busy. Didn't we agree that you'd stay out of my way? It seems like you've gotten too comfortable in this marriage. You and I had an agreement, remember? You're not to bother me unnecessarily. Looks like the sex has made you think you can overstep the boundaries *you* agreed to."

I wrap my arms around myself, trying my hardest to mask how much his words pain me. "You're pushing me away. Why?"

Alec ignores me and sits down behind his desk. He turns his computer on, silently dismissing me.

"Tell me, Alexander. Why are you behaving like this? Is this because of everything that happened with your mother? Is that why you're distancing yourself from me?"

He sighs and leans back in his seat, looking up at me, an irritated expression on his face. "Fucking hell, Elena. There's no reason. What is it you want? Why are you being so fucking needy?"

I stare at him in disbelief and move my hands behind my back in an effort to hide how badly I'm trembling, how badly he's hurting me.

"Needy? Are you kidding me right now? You're the one that told me to talk to you when you hurt me. You're *hurting* me right now, Alec."

He rises from his seat, his palms flat on his desk. "What do you want? Every single thing you've ever asked for, I've given you. I helped you with your mother's care, I helped you take down your father, I helped you regain everything you've lost, and I'm *still* housing your mother and providing her with round-the-clock care. What more do you want, Elena?" he asks, sounding defeated, frustrated.

He sighs and runs a hand through his hair.

"I've given you *everything*, Elena, and I didn't ask you for much in return. All I wanted was a wife that would let me live my own life, Elena. It's all I asked for."

I swallow hard and nod even as my heart shatters. I take a step back and inhale shakily, pasting a smile on my face.

"Understood," I tell him.

Alec hesitates, and for a second, I hope he'll take back his words, but then he sits back down, his eyes on his computer.

I blink back the tears that have gathered in my eyes and paste a bright smile onto my face.

"There's dinner for you in the kitchen, should you want it. I'll stay out of your way."

I turn and walk away, every fiber of my being longing for him to stop me.

He doesn't.

CHAPTER 57

lexander

I glance around my new office, feeling oddly uneasy. This office is all I've ever wanted, so why does attaining it feel so bleak?

I sit up in surprise when my office door opens. No one but my grandfather ever walks in without me being notified first.

My grandfather... and *Elena*, it seems.

My eyes roam over her body, my heart stirring involuntarily. She looks beautiful—she always does. It feels like I haven't seen her in weeks, and I guess I haven't, not really. We barely speak. I asked her for space and she's giving it to me, whether I like it or not.

Just a few months ago, I'd have gotten up to kiss her. She'd have smiled at me as she walked over to me, sitting down in my lap. Now she looks at me expressionlessly.

"I wasn't expecting you. What are you doing here?" I glance at my watch and frown. "I have a meeting in ten minutes."

She nods and sits down in front of me. "I apologize for

intruding," she says, placing her bag in her lap. She glances around, a small smile on her face. "Nice office."

I smile and look around the way she just did. Sometimes I can barely believe I made it either. "Thank you. I've waited years for this. It's all I've ever wanted."

She leans back in her seat, a bittersweet smile on her face. "I'm happy for you," she says, her tone sincere. "I'm happy you've achieved everything you wanted."

She looks down, hesitating, before reaching into her purse. When she looks back at me, her eyes are filled with resignation. Elena hands me a piece of paper and I glance at it in surprise.

"A blank cheque?"

She stares at it and then lets her eyes fall closed for a couple of seconds, almost like she's bracing herself. "You got everything you wanted and you never needed my help at all. I, on the other hand, relied on you heavily." She points at the cheque and smiles. "Now that I've regained my assets, I'd like to pay you back—for everything. My mother's medical bills, the shares you purchased for me, everything."

My heart starts to race, dread filling me, and I grit my teeth. "Why?"

"Our agreement was supposed to be mutually beneficial, but it wasn't. I'd like to remedy that. Besides, since you have no further need for me, we might as well dissolve our arrangement."

I look at her with raised brows as she takes a stack of papers out of her bag. She stares at them before placing them on my desk. My stomach twists violently when she slides them my way.

I smile humorlessly as I pick up the divorce papers. "You want to divorce me?"

She nods, and I start laughing, the sound chilling even to my own ears. Elena's calm expression infuriates me even further, and when she takes off her engagement ring and places it on my desk, I lose it.

I rise from my seat, rage unlike anything I've ever felt before coursing through my body. I walk around my desk and pull her out of her chair. Elena crashes into me, her eyes wide. My hands thread through her hair and I tip her head back, making her face me. I pull her body flush against mine and stare her down.

"There isn't a single thing I'm not giving you. There isn't anything I've ever denied you. I've even given you everything you didn't *dare* ask for. Anything you wanted, Elena, I've given you. There's nothing you're missing. If you're leaving me, it can only be for one reason. Who is it?"

She blinks, trying her best to portray innocence, the same way Jennifer did every single time I had doubts about Matthew and her.

"Alec, there's no one else."

I lift her onto my desk and push her legs apart, holding her the same way I held her at Vaughn's.

I grab her chin and look into her eyes. Her gaze is unwavering, but I'll break her silence. "Remember, Elena. You signed your life away to me."

Her arms wrap around my neck, not a hint of fear in her eyes. "I did," she says. "And now I'm buying it back."

She places her palms against my chest and tightens her legs around me, pulling me closer.

I tighten my grip on her hair, desperation filling my every vein. "Didn't you promise me forever? This is forever to you? Leaving me a mere few months before our wedding? I guess you got everything you wanted, huh? You used me and now you're discarding me."

She looks into my eyes, looking so damn heartbroken. "I love you, Alec."

I freeze and she smiles mirthlessly.

"I love you. I didn't mean for it to happen, but I'm irrevocably in love with you."

I pull away from her, staring at her in disbelief. She laughs, but there's no humor in her eyes.

"You find that harder to believe than me cheating on you?"

I run a hand through my hair, unsure of what to say or think.

"Tell me you love me, Alec. Tell me you love me, too, and I'll rip these divorce papers up right now. Hell, tell me you feel *anything* for me, that you think you *might* love me someday, and I'll stay."

After everything she and I have been through, after everything we've seen... how could she even believe in love? How could she ask it of me?

"Alexander," she says, her voice trembling. She slips off my desk and straightens out her clothes, her head hanging low. "I've spent my entire life loving people that didn't love me back. I won't do it again. I won't. Not even for you."

She looks back at me before she walks away, her eyes dropping to the divorce papers on my desk before the door closes behind her.

CHAPTER 58

lena

I stand at the entrance of the house I grew up in, everything feeling unfamiliar. I walk up the stairs to what used to be my childhood bedroom and pause in the doorway, shocked. My entire room has been converted into a walk-in closet, not a single one of my belongings remaining.

I walk into the room, my fingers tracing over the brand-new dressers that replaced all my furniture. There are over a dozen rooms in this house—there was no need whatsoever to wipe away every memory of my childhood.

I sink down to my knees in the middle of my room, tears filling my eyes. My head drops down to the thick carpet, and I let myself fall apart for the first time in years, hot tears streaming down my face. A sob tears through my throat and I try my hardest to keep it in, but I fail. All I accomplish is choking on my tears, my lungs burning. All the while, my heart feels like it's in physical pain. I've never felt this *broken*.

I curl into a ball, my heart shattered beyond repair. I've lost so much in the last couple of years, and every time my heart broke, I lost a little part of it, leaving my heart forever incomplete. It wasn't until Alec that I dared to hope.

"Honey?"

My mother strokes my arm, and I look up. I sniff, and she holds her arms out for me. I hug her, and she holds me tightly.

"Mom... it just hurts so much."

She nods and holds me closer, my head against her chest, both of us seated on the floor.

"I know, honey. I know it does. You've been so strong, so brave, for so long. Elena, my darling, I'm so proud of you."

Her words just make me cry harder. I almost lost my mother too. What would I have done if I did? I'd have been all alone, without a single person who truly loved me. Without anything to live for.

"Honey, you're breaking my heart. What happened, Elena? Why did you suddenly want to move out of the Kennedy's residence? What's going on with Alec and you?"

I sit up and wipe at my tears furiously, unable to stop them from falling. "I... he doesn't love me, Mom. Maybe I'm foolish for leaving, but it's all I want. I just want to come first to someone. For once, I just want to be the center of someone's universe. I want to be all someone can see. And maybe it isn't possible, maybe that doesn't exist, but being with Alec, knowing that he used to love someone that way, and perhaps still does, knowing he can't give me even a fraction of what he used to feel for her? It killed me slowly, Mom."

Mom leans in and brushes away my tears, a smile on her face. "I see," she says, her voice soft. "And does Alec still love this girl?"

I shake my head. "I don't know, Mom. I don't think so. I don't know. All I know is that he doesn't love me the way he loved her, and he never will."

She rises and holds her hand out to me. I take it from her, inhaling shakily, trying my best to stop my tears from falling.

"Come on, sweetie. Crying on the floor of your old bedroom isn't going to help you. Let's go."

"Where are we going?"

Mom smiles. "To Jade's room."

She pulls me along and walks to the room that used to be hers. My heart twists painfully. I've been so absorbed in my own pain that I didn't even stop to think about how hard this must be for Mom. Being confronted with the evidence of my father's affair, with all the years she's lost, it can't be easy. Yet she smiles as she enters her old bedroom.

She looks around and laughs. "God, so tacky," she says, her eyes roaming over the room. I grin, my tears forgotten. She isn't wrong. The frilly bed sheets are so gaudy.

Mom picks up some of Jade's cosmetics and stares at them. Then she smiles and pulls her arm back, throwing it all against the wall with as much force as she can muster.

"Come on," she tells me, smiling. I stare at her with wide eyes but follow her lead. Before long we're both throwing Jade's belongings against the wall, wide smiles on our faces.

Mom picks up a small jewelry tray that smashes into hundreds of pieces, and we both burst out laughing.

"Mom, there are a couple of things I've always wanted to smash," I tell her, my lips tipping up in a smile.

Mom looks at me with raised brows, and I grin. "Come on."

I lead her down the stairs to the hallway. My heart twists painfully when I see the photo frames that used to house photos of us, every trace of Mom and me removed.

I hand her one and then pick up another. We grin at each other before throwing both frames against the wall, enjoying the way they shatter.

Mom sighs, looking like a weight was just lifted off her

shoulder. "That felt so good," she says, wrapping her arms around me. "Feel better?"

I nod and drop my head to her shoulder. "So much better."

"Good," mom says. "Now that you've got that out of your system, you might finally be able to think clearly." She grabs my shoulders and looks into my eyes. "There's no way that boy doesn't love you, Elena. He looks at you like you hung the moon. Every time you were in pain because watching me relearn how to walk was difficult, he was hurting right along with you. And don't get me started on the way he helped you regain everything we lost. Alec took every one of your pains personal, every grudge you had, he settled. Every step of the way, he's been trying to mend your heart." She smiles and brushes my hair behind my ear. "Now, don't get me wrong. The boy is stupid. Too stupid to see just how much he loves you. I can't even blame him, because he's been burned so badly, and it can't be easy for him to admit to himself that despite his best efforts, he fell for you. But he did, Elena. Alec is so in love with you, and he doesn't even realize it. Nor do you, for that matter."

I stare at my mother, my heart hopeful. "Mom, no... if he loved me, he'd never have let me go."

She cups my cheek and smiles at me. "Give it time. Give him time. The best things in life are worth waiting for."

Mom presses a kiss to my forehead, and my eyes flutter closed. Time... I don't think time can solve our problems.

CHAPTER 59

lexander

I walk into my bedroom and pause. I've always loved solitude, so why does this room suddenly feel so... empty?

I tug on my tie and walk into my closet, my eyes pausing on the empty shelves. There are traces of her everywhere, even the faint scent of her perfume lingers. I sigh and walk toward my bed, but that just makes things worse.

When I look at my bed all I can see is the way her hair spreads out on our pillows, the way she rolls toward me in her sleep, clinging onto me. I'll never have her in my arms again.

I sit down on my bed and run a hand through my hair. I grab my phone against better judgment, a photo of Elena and me staring back at me. I'm pressing a kiss to her cheek and she's smiling, her eyes twinkling with happiness.

I can't do this. I sigh as I walk back out of my bedroom and down the stairs, needing a fucking drink. I can't get her out of my damn mind. Everything reminds me of her. No matter where I look, there are traces of her everywhere. I see her kissing me in the lobby of my office, laughing with my family in the kitchen, smiling at me from our bed. She's tainted every single space, continuously torturing me with the memory of her.

I pause in surprise when I find my grandfather standing by the entrance, keys in his hand. My mother and Lucian are both grinning excitedly as they put their coats on.

Their smiles melt off their faces as they see me approach, and I frown. "Where are the three of you going?"

Mom tenses, and Lucian looks away. Only my grandfather smiles leisurely. "Oh, nowhere," he says. "We're just going out for dinner. I'm retired now, after all. Plenty of time to kill."

I frown at him. "Is there a specific reason you guys are going on a family outing without inviting me?"

The guilt on Lucian's face tells me everything I need to know. They're meeting Elena. I laugh mockingly. "She leaves me and takes my family with her. Fucking ridiculous."

I walk past them, my shoulder slamming into Lucian's angrily.

"Alexander," my grandfather says.

I pause and turn to look at him.

"I told you, didn't I? You let her go, you'll regret it."

Lucian nods. He hasn't spoken a word to me since Elena left, and even my mother seems to be disappointed in me. I don't know why the fuck they blame me when it's Elena that walked out on me. On *us*.

I shake my head and walk out. I'm still seething by the time I pull up at Inferno. Another fucking place that's tainted with the memory of her. My mood just sinks further as I walk up to the rooftop. My favorite spot is hers too.

I sigh as I sit back in the same spot I was in when Elena walked back into my life. I stare at the sky, remembering the way she looked at the stars, a smile on her face.

"Alexander."

I look up in surprise, tensing.

"Jennifer."

She smiles and sits down next to me, looking just as miserable as I probably do. I haven't even thought of her in months. I haven't wondered what losing Matthew would be like for her, how she's been affected by everything Elena did. When did I stop caring about her? When did I start to put Elena's needs before hers?

"Rumor has it that Elena left you."

I frown. It's only been a week. Has she been telling people? Is she going around telling people she's single again?

I grit my teeth and Jennifer smiles. "You never used to get that upset about me, you know?" She shakes her head, her eyes on the skyline. "I'd spend hours with Matthew and all you ever did was ask me if something was going on. But Elena? I saw you two on the day you proposed to her. She was talking to some guy and even though it was clear that she wasn't remotely interested in him, you lost it. You lost your composure."

I look at her and smile mirthlessly. "I don't like sharing my possessions. That's all it was."

"You're in love with her," she says, her smile bittersweet. "I always knew that what we had wasn't real love, you know? I always knew you didn't truly love me—you just convinced yourself that you did."

She leans back in her seat, a sad smile on her face. "There's no excuse for the way I cheated on you, Alexander. But knowing that you didn't love me made it easier. It made it easier to give Matthew a chance."

"What are you talking about? Of course, I loved you. Fuck, Jen. I gave you my heart on a silver platter and you fucking trampled on it."

She shakes her head. "Alec, you loved the idea of me. You

loved the idea of a woman that didn't know who you were, that wasn't familiar with your world. You enjoyed seeing the world through my eyes. It was new to you, and you thrived on it. But you never loved *me*."

I laugh despite the anger I feel. "That's bullshit."

Jennifer smiles. "Is it? What's Elena's favorite color?"

"It's red."

"Favorite food?"

"Chocolate chip cookies."

She smiles, her expression sad. "What about mine?"

I blink, drawing a blank.

She shakes her head. "You loved the idea of me, but you never even truly knew me. Nor did Matthew, for that matter—maybe that'll make you feel a little better. He was just using me as a pawn against you. He was playing some sort of fucked up game that you aren't even aware of."

I frown, and she looks away.

"From what I gathered, he's held a grudge against you for years. Ever since his first girlfriend left him for you. Ever since then he's been fixated on taking away everything you have—business deals, your girlfriends, assets. If you set your eyes on it, he wanted it. I didn't realize that until it was too late. I was just another conquest, another victory in the silent war he waged against you."

"What the fuck?"

Jennifer laughs, her face tipped up at the sky. "*What the fuck*, indeed. What Elena did to him... it was a blessing in disguise. He was unhinged, and had she not done what she did, I'd have become that madman's wife."

Jennifer rises from her seat and smiles at me. "I know you have your reasons to stay away from love. I know what your family has been through—what your mother has been through. I know I played a role in making your trust issues

297

worse yet. I know how hard it is for you to love. I know, Alexander, because throughout our entire relationship I did all I could to pierce the armor that surrounds your heart, and I failed. But Elena? She did it without even trying."

She cups my cheek, her smile bittersweet. "I came here because one of my friends told me you were here. I want you back, Alexander. I realize how badly I fucked up, how well you treated me. I know what I lost."

She leans into me, and I look into her eyes. She looks fragile, insecure. "I love you, Alexander. Despite everything I've done, everything I've put you through, I do truly love you," she says, letting her hand drop to the side, tears gathering in her eyes. "So, I'll do the right thing, despite what my heart desires. I want you to be happy, Alexander. Truly happy. The way you smiled when you were with Elena? I want that for you, and I know I can never give you that."

She takes a step away from me, a single tear dropping down her cheek. "I haven't been the best version of myself, Alec. This world... the world you operate in? It's not for girls like me. I hate who I've become. I hate how Matthew changed me. But Elena? Elena belongs with you. She's your equal in every way that matters, in every way that I couldn't be. Alexander, you deserve to be happy, more so than anyone else I know. So please, go after that happiness before it's too late. I lost my chance. Don't lose yours."

She smiles at me and walks away, her words reverberating in my mind long after she's gone.

CHAPTER 60

lexander

I'm certain I'm fucking hallucinating when I hear Elena's laughter as I walk into the house. I stop in my tracks, my eyes closing as my stomach drops. My heart clenches painfully and I take a steadying breath.

I'm almost at the stairs when I hear it again. Laughter. But this time, it's my mother's. I tense and turn to follow the sound toward the kitchen. My heart races with every step I take. She can't be here. She left.

My entire body is rigid as I lean against the kitchen doorway, my eyes finding her instantly. Fucking beautiful.

She's got flour in her hair and a smear of chocolate on her cheek, but she's the most beautiful thing I've ever seen.

Her smile drops when she notices me, and she looks startled, her cheeks turning rosy. The room falls silent, and it isn't until then that I realize my entire family is here.

Lucian and my mother are standing opposite Elena, while my grandfather is standing next to her. They look guilty when they see me standing here, and my mother and brother both look away, not bothering to hide their dismay.

"What a warm welcome," I say, my voice dripping with sarcasm.

Grandpa clears his throat and glances at his watch, before smiling at me stiffly. "Alec, my boy. What are you doing here? Slacking already?"

Elena wraps her arms around herself, smearing even more chocolate on herself. She looks away, but I want her eyes on mine.

I drag my gaze away from her and shake my head. "Just needed a sick day, that's all. Not feeling great."

Elena's eyes shoot up to mine, concern reflected in them. She scans my body, a frown marring her beautiful face. She looks fucking stunning. Looks like she isn't struggling to sleep, like I am. I bet she isn't spending every waking hour thinking of me, memories replaying in her mind.

I glance around the room and shake my head as I walk away, leaving my heart behind. She's got my family spellbound. She left, but it looks like she only left *me*—not my family. I can't believe they're inviting her over behind my fucking back. Even my damn grandfather is in on this shit.

I walk into my bedroom and lean my forearm against the wall, my eyes falling closed. Just seeing her wrecks me, but she looked perfectly unaffected. Uncomfortable at most.

I take a steadying breath, willing my body to listen to me even as every fiber of my being demands that I go to her. I've only just about got my raging heart under control when my bedroom door opens.

Elena walks in, freezing when she finds me standing by the door. I straighten, and her eyes roam over me.

"What are you doing here?" I ask, my voice coming out harsher than I intended.

She bites down on her lip and takes a step closer to me. The way she clasps her hands in front of her tells me she's nervous.

"You're not feeling well?"

I stare at her, unable to figure her out. "Since when do you care? You fucking left, didn't you? Why are you here now?"

I take a step closer to her and she takes a step back, crashing into the door. I lean over her, caging her in with my forearms, my face inches from hers. "I don't need your fucking fake concern, Elena," I snap, my jaws clenching involuntarily.

I look into her eyes and the anger and hurt I see in them throws me off. "That's right," she says. "Why would you need me, when you've got Jennifer?"

She pushes against my chest, hard, but she fails to move me. "Let go of me, Alexander," she says, her tone harsh.

"Jennifer? What the fuck are you talking about?"

Elena laughs, the sound shrill and humorless. "You don't need to pretend anymore, Alexander. You've probably been seeing her all along, haven't you? Forget it. You and I are no longer together. You can do whatever you want. Forget I came here at all."

She ducks underneath my arm, and I grab her hand, pulling her back to me before she can rush off.

"Seriously, Elena. What the actual fuck are you talking about?" I ask, confused.

She turns around to look at me, her eyes filled with accusation. She pulls her hand out of mine and jabs my chest with her finger. "You... you... asshole!" she yells. "It's been two weeks and you're already back with her, photos of the two of you getting intimate all over the tabloids. *Two weeks*, Alexander. I know you don't care about me, but did you need to rub it in that way? Did you need to publicly humiliate me?"

She shoves me, putting her weight into it, and I stumble

back. Her cheeks are flushed, her eyes shimmering with unshed tears. I can barely make sense of what she's saying.

"Elena..."

I grab her and push her back against the wall, pinning her wrists above her head to keep her from shoving me, jabbing me. There's no way there are any photos of me anywhere, so I have no idea what she's talking about. After Mom's divorce, Elliot has taken extra care to keep us out of the news as best as he can. There isn't much that doesn't go through him first. Unless... unless he screwed me over. I wouldn't put it past Lucian to ask it of him. My brother would pick Elena over me any day, and if he thinks I was unfaithful, there's no way he'd let Elliot brush it under the carpet. God damn it.

"I don't know what you're talking about, baby. Seriously. I have no idea," I say, my voice soft, pleading.

Elena is breathing hard, her lips slightly parted, her chest rising and falling rapidly. She's so fucking beautiful, and even more so now that her eyes are flashing with anger. I bridge the remaining distance between us, pressing my body against hers.

"So you weren't with her at Inferno? I saw the photos, Alexander. Cut the crap. I saw the way she was holding your cheek like she was about to kiss you, and you let her. You let her touch you. What else did you let her do? It couldn't have been a more perfect reminder that it's only my body you were after. It's no surprise you replaced me so easily, and with the woman you *actually* wanted too. That worked out perfectly for you, huh?"

She glares at me, but I see the pain in her eyes, the heart-break. She's hurt over some dumb misunderstanding.

"You should know better than to trust a paparazzi photo, Elena. Besides, you *left me*. Why would you care if I'm fucking someone else? So what if I Jen and I get back together? Don't pretend to care."

She wrestles her wrists loose and pushes against my chest,

pure anguish overshadowing her anger. "That's not a denial, Alexander. You know what? You're right. I *don't* care. I hope you're happy with her."

I stare at her, trying to figure her out. Throughout our marriage, she's mostly kept her emotions to herself, as best as she could. But now? Now her pain is on display for me. She isn't holding back the way she used to. Her anger, her jealousy, her pain. I want it all.

I wrap my hand around the back of her neck, my thumb resting on her throat so I can feel her heart racing for me. She swallows hard, and I smile as I lean in, my lips brushing against hers, startling her. Elena freezes for just a second, and then she pulls me closer, rising to her tiptoes. I kiss her, and she opens up for me, her tongue tangling with mine desperately.

"Alec," she moans, and I smirk against her lips. I tug at her clothes, pushing her dress up, and Elena yanks on my pants, sending the button flying. I lift her into my arms and against the wall just as her hand wraps around my cock. She doesn't even bother with the rest of my clothes.

"I hate you," she says, and I suck down on her neck, punishing her for her words, marking her roughly.

"No, you don't," I tell her as I pull back, admiring my work.

Elena groans as her legs wrap around me. The way she pushes up against me drives me wild. She lines my cock up against her perfectly, and I slip into her in one deep stroke.

"Fuck," I groan, my forehead dropping against hers. "You're so fucking wet, baby. How are you this wet?"

Elena tightens her grip on my hair, her eyes still flashing with anger. "Just shut up and fuck me, Alexander."

I pull back almost all the way, teasing her. "What did you call me?"

She glares at me, rotating her hips, wanting me deeper, but

I hold onto her hips, denying her demands. "*Alec*," she says, my name a plea on her lips.

A burst of satisfaction courses through me, and I smile in delight as I push back into her, *hard*.

"Good girl," I tell her, taking her lips, losing myself in her. I've fucking missed her. Her body, the way she feels, the way she moans my name. I've missed feeling this close to her.

I lift her up higher against the wall, driving into her at an angle I know she loves. The way she moans is unreal.

"Oh God, Alec," she says, panting. She looks into my eyes, and I watch as desire overcomes her. Her muscles tighten around me, and she fucking milks me.

I shudder as I come deep inside her, my head dropping to her shoulder. We're both panting, and Elena pushes against me. I lower her to the floor gently, and she shoves me away, creating distance between us, the moment broken.

She fixes her clothes, her cheeks bright crimson. When she looks back at me, there's no passion left in her eyes, there's only anger. "Forget that happened," she snaps. "Sign the goddamn papers and let's be done with this."

She walks to the door and opens it forcefully.

"Elena."

She pauses and turns back to look at me.

"Nothing happened with Jennifer. I ran into her and spoke to her for a couple of minutes. I shouldn't have let her touch me at all, but I swear to you... all she did was touch my face. That is all."

Elena shakes her head, her expression sorrowful. "Just sign the papers, Alexander. I don't want to do this anymore. I'm sick of being reminded of the way you used to love her, and probably still do. I'm tired. I'm done. I'm done coming second to the memory of her."

I cross my arms over each other and shake my head. "Never," I tell her. "I'll never sign. If you won't be with me, I'll make it impossible for you to ever marry someone else. I'll never let you go."

She looks sorrowful as she tears her gaze away. "You already have," she says, her voice breaking.

Elena walks out, the door slamming closed behind her.

CHAPTER 61

lexander

I stare up at Elena's house and lean back against my car, my eyes on her window.

"Are you ever going to talk to her?"

I jump in surprise, my eyes widening when Sarah walks up behind me.

"You've been coming here every night for two weeks now. This is getting creepy, Alec."

I smile nervously. "I'm sorry. I didn't realize you were aware of my presence. I didn't mean to disturb you."

I don't even know what I'm doing here. I keep telling myself that I'll do what's best for her, that I'll let her go. When she married me, she never had a choice. I want her to find her own happiness, I don't want to hold her back and chain her to me. Yet I can't get myself to sign the papers.

Sarah smiles and leans back against my car, standing next to me. She looks up into Elena's window the way I just did and shakes her head.

"So instead of calling her, you just stand here for hours in hopes of catching a glimpse of her?"

I look away and shake my head. "No... I... I don't mean to come here, yet somehow this is where I end up every night. It isn't intentional, it's just... I don't know."

She laughs. "Alexander Kennedy, flustered. Never thought I'd see the day."

I look down at my shoes, unable to even force a smile.

"She's going on a date tomorrow, you know? She's moving on. It's about time. It's been a month since you two separated."

I freeze, my eyes finding Sarah's. I feel sick, the feelings coursing through me are ones I can't even describe. Violent anger, intense fear... and regret. Intense fucking regret.

Sarah pats my arm. "It's for the best," she says. "Elena has had a tough life so far. She deserves to be loved, to be spoiled. She deserves to be swept off her feet. And you... you can't give her what she needs, can you?"

She smiles as she walks away, and I stare after her. Elena... on a date. My mind spirals out of control, showing me images of her with someone that isn't me. If she goes on that date, will she kiss him the way she kissed me? Will she smile at him? Will she ask him about three good things that might have happened to him that day? All those things that she used to reserve for me, will she give it all to someone else?

CHAPTER 62

lena

I wake up to the sound of my window rattling and sit up in alarm, fear gripping me. I glance at the window and freeze, my eyes widening in shock when I realize it's being pushed open by someone. I rise to my feet, ready to scream for help, when I recognize him. I'd recognize him anywhere.

"Alexander?"

He closes the window behind him, his movements uncertain as he walks up to me, and I meet him halfway.

"What are you doing here?"

He cups my cheek, tenderly, and I place my own hand over his, concerned.

"Alec, your hand is freezing. What's going on?"

He shakes his head and wraps me into his embrace, holding me tightly. "Elena," he whispers, my name a plea on his lips.

I pull away from him, worried. I've never seen him look so vulnerable before, so hurt.

"Alec, why are you here? Did you... did you seriously just climb through my window?"

I haven't seen him since that time in his bedroom. I'd just about given up hope. I was certain that walking away was the right choice, yet here he is, standing in front of me in the middle of the night.

"I-yes. I did. You have so much security, this was the easiest way to get to you."

I stare at him in disbelief as he grabs a strand of my hair and pushes it behind my ear. "I promised myself I wouldn't approach you. I was going to let you go, Elena. I wanted you to have everything I knew I could never give you."

He drops to his knees, trembling. Alec wraps his arms around me, his head pressed against my hip.

"Alec, you're worrying me."

I sink down to my knees the way he has, and he grabs my shoulders.

"Elena," he says. "I can't do it. I know you deserve better, but I can't stay away. I can't."

My heart starts to race as I look into his eyes. Alec wraps his hand around the back of my neck the way he likes doing, his thumb resting against my throat.

"I know it's fucking selfish. I fucking know. But fuck. I can't live without you. I can't let you walk into someone else's arms." He drops his forehead to mine and inhales shakily. "You always ask me about three good things that happened during my day, but baby, everything good in my life is you. The three best things to have happened in my entire life were meeting you, marrying you... and falling in love with you."

My heart skips a beat, and I look at him with wide eyes.

Alec looks anguished, desperate. He raises his hand to my face and gently strokes my cheek with the back of his hand.

"When I met you, I thought love was a fucking sham. I wanted no part of it. I didn't think love could last."

He threads his fingers through my hair, his hand trembling. "Elena, I don't know if I'm ever going to be good enough for you. I don't know if I'll ever be what you need. All I know is that I love you. I would rather spend a year with you than a lifetime without you. I'm willing to give you everything, Elena. I'm willing to give you my heart, and trust that you won't break it. But even if you do, baby, even if you tear my heart apart, you're worth it. You're worth everything."

Alec tightens his grip on me, his eyes filled with desperation. "Give me a chance to show you I can be what you need. Let me show you I can be a real husband. Give me just one single chance. Just one, Elena."

He pulls away to look at me, his gaze searching. I've never once seen him look so vulnerable, so disarmed. I stare at him, part of me certain this must all be a dream, yet it isn't.

"Alec, I don't want to play games. This is the rest of our lives that we're talking about. I need you to be sure. I need you to promise me forever. I need you to tell me you'll be mine, heart and soul, that you'll love me until we're gray and old. If you can't do that, then please, just walk away. Walk away before you shatter what remains of my heart."

He cups my cheeks, his eyes on mine. "I swear to you, Elena. I'll love you till the day I die, and I'll spend the rest of my life proving that to you. I promise you all of me, forever."

I lean in, and Alec freezes, his body tense. My lips brush against his, and he groans. He pulls me closer, his lips crashing against mine hungrily. Alec kisses me with blatant desperation, and I tremble against him. When he pulls away, I'm panting, eager for more. The way he looks at me... it's like I'm all he can see.

"I've missed you, Alec."

He rises to his feet and lifts me into his arms, placing me down on my bed. "I've missed you too, baby. So fucking much. I can't even sleep without you. Everywhere I go, I'm reminded of you." Alec joins me in bed, his body hovering over mine. "I can't eat without missing the food you make me, I can't walk into my office building without thinking of the way you walked away. You're everywhere."

He lowers his body on top of mine, and I bury my hands in his hair. He looks heartbroken, regretful.

"Elena, tell me you'll give me another chance."

I nod, and the relief in Alec's eyes is palpable. He smiles at me, his anguish making way for happiness.

"I want to hear you say it. Tell me you'll be mine."

I smile at him. "Alec, I've always been yours. I always will be."

He leans in and kisses me, slow and deep. I lose myself in him, my hands roaming over his body. His touch is as frantic as mine, both of us tugging at each other's clothes. Before long, I'm lying underneath him, my bare skin against his.

"I want you, Elena. I want you for the rest of my life."

His hand trails over my body, and I gasp when his fingers find their way between my legs. "I fucking knew you'd be wet for me, baby. Tell me, have you missed me? Have you fantasized about me?"

"Yes," I admit. "Yes, to all of it."

He chuckles, the sound low and sexy. "I dream of you, Elena. I dream of the way you moan my name, the way you look at me when you come for me. I'm tired of living off the memory of you. So show me," he says, his thumb stroking over my clit. "Come for me."

He looks into my eyes as he pushes me closer and closer until I can't take it anymore. "Alec," I moan, my muscles tightening around his fingers.

He smiles in satisfaction. "Good girl," he says, leaning in for a kiss.

I kiss him the way I know drives him insane until I've got him panting, desperate for me. "Elena," he says, his tone pleading. "I need you."

I nod, and he pushes into me slightly, taking his time.

"You want this cock, baby? Tell me you're mine."

I whimper, and he grins.

"I'm yours, Alexander Kennedy. All yours. All of me."

Alec slams into me the way he knows I like, his forehead dropping to mine. "Fuck," he says. "I can barely take it. Your pussy is so fucking good."

I wrap my arms around him, my lips finding his. Alec fucks me slowly, his strokes deep, driving me insane. I can already feel the pressure building inside me, all over again.

"You want to come for me again, don't you?" he asks, his voice husky.

I nod at him, my nails scraping over his scalp.

"Tell me you'll marry me. I want it all. The whole wedding ceremony, everything. I don't care how long you make me wait, so long as I get to see you walking down the aisle toward me."

My heart warms, and I nod. "I'll marry you, Alec, for the whole world to see."

Alec gives me what I want, and I come again, but this time I take him right over the edge with me. He groans and drops his forehead to mine, both of us trying to catch our breath.

He turns us over and holds me in his arms, my head on his chest. His hands caress every part of my body, as though he thinks I might disappear if he lets go of me.

"You won't go on that date, will you?"

I blink, startled, and sit up to look at him. "What date?"

Alec stares at me in confusion. "Your mother told me you're moving on. She said you're going on a date with someone, and I want that for you, Elena. I do. I want you to be happy. But I... I think I can be the one to make you happy."

I tense, my stomach recoiling while my heart constricts, sudden devastation overcoming me. I look at Alec, feeling more alone than ever, even though he's right beside me.

I'm quiet as I get out of bed, my movements slow.

"Hey, what's wrong?" Alec asks, his brows raised. I see the confusion in his eyes, and it gives my pain an angry edge.

I slip my nightgown on and cross my arms over my chest, my eyes roaming over his face. I take in his messy dark hair, those eyes that I love beyond reason, the way my sheets bunch around his hips.

I love this man with all I am. I've given him all of me, my entire heart and soul, when all he asked for was my body. And that's where I went wrong.

"You need to go, Alec," I say, picking up his scattered clothes from the floor. My heart twists, the feeling foreign and painful beyond measure. I smile through it and throw his clothes on the bed, turning my back to him.

I hear him rise just as I open my bedroom door. "Security!" I shout, my voice breaking.

"Elena, what the fuck?" Alec wraps his arms around me from behind, enveloping me in a tight hug. "What's gotten into you so suddenly?"

I lean back against his chest, my eyes squeezed closed. I'm holding on by a thread. The feel of him, these arms... they feel like home to me. But just like my childhood home, Alexander is toxic.

I turn to face him, my palms against his bare chest. All he's wearing is his boxer shorts and I glance at the rest of his clothes, still on my bed. I take a moment to collect myself, to gather to courage to say what I need to.

"Alexander," I say, my voice soft. "You were going to let me go. You didn't want me until you thought someone else did. You don't want me, Alec, but you don't want anyone else to have me either. That's not *love*. It just isn't."

Two of my security guards enter my bedroom, both of them clearly shocked to find Alec in my bedroom.

I take a step away from him, my hands dropping to my side. "Give him a chance to get dressed, and then escort him out," I say, nodding at my security team.

"Elena, are you insane?" Alec says, his voice raised. "How could you even for a single second think that I don't love you? You're my entire goddamn world, baby. You're everything to me. My life hasn't been the same since you walked back into it. Fuck, I don't *want* it to be. I want you. I can't live without you anymore—I need you, baby. I need your smiles, your hugs, your wit. I need you."

I look back at him, taking in the desperation in his eyes. He's being held back by two men, but his entire focus is on me.

"But you did. For weeks, you lived just fine without me. You were ready to let me go. You didn't change your mind until you thought someone else might have what you consider to be yours, Alexander. I'm not something to be owned, I'm not an object you can label as yours."

I look down at my feet, trying my hardest to pull myself together, to keep my tears at bay long enough to finish saying what I need to. "I deserve more, Alec. I deserve everything I've given *you*. I'm done settling for less, and I'm done telling myself that I need to be happy with the few scraps of affection people throw my way. I'm done with you."

A tear rolls down my cheek and I let my eyes fall closed. "Escort him out," I say, turning my back to Alec, my bedroom door falling closed behind me as I walk out on him, on *us*.

CHAPTER 63

lena

I walk into my house after an incredibly long day at work and pause in the doorway, my eyes roaming over the hundreds of peonies filling the room. Mom smiles up at me, a beautiful bouquet in her hands.

"Honey, if you don't speak to him, he'll just keep sending you flowers."

"Donate them."

We've been donating flowers to a different charity every day, for weeks now. Alec knows I don't ever keep them, yet somehow new flowers appear in my house every single day. Mom denies it, but I know she's colluding with him.

I shake my head and walk towards the staircase, ignoring the flowers. How does he even know that peonies are my favorite? Was that part of his background check too?

"I had the staff put the bouquets with notes on them in your bedroom," Mom says, and I pause on the stairs. The notes... it's the notes that always get to me.

"You should've thrown them out."

My heart is racing as I walk into my bedroom, dozens of bouquets covering every horizontal surface in my room. I hate myself for looking forward to these, but I can't help it. I sink to my knees and grab the bouquet closest to me, lifting the card from the flowers carefully. Just seeing his handwriting sends a pang of longing through my heart.

The three best things that happened today were the following:

1. Catching you sneak a glimpse at me from your bedroom window this morning

2. Writing you this note. It makes me feel like I still get to talk to you, even though you blocked me everywhere. Seriously, baby, unblock me. I miss you.

3. Loving you. Spending my days loving you makes every day great by default

I raise the note to my chest and clutch it tightly. It's been weeks. He's been sending me flowers for weeks, without relenting. I was certain that he'd get bored with this, with the chase. I can't tell if I've just become another conquest to him, a challenge. Is any of this real? Is this just a game to him? I wonder if he's just seeing how long it'll take to wear me down. I reach for the next bouquet, my hand trembling just slightly.

All I want to do is take you on a date. Just one. You think I didn't want you until I thought I'd lose you to someone else, but that isn't true. The only reason I ever even remotely considered letting you go was because you deserve the world, Elena. You deserve more than I can give you. I will never be good enough for you, baby. A better man would have walked away by now, but I never claimed to be a good man. All I claim to be is yours.

I pull my knees to my chest and wrap my arms around myself. Every fiber of my being is begging me to go to him. I reach for the third and last card. Every single day, there are three cards, and today is no exception.

When I proposed, I told you that divorce wasn't an option. It still isn't. I'll never sign the divorce papers. I won't let you go, Elena. I made that mistake once and I'll never make it again. I'll be waiting for you to come back to me for the rest of our lives.

I bite down on my lip as hard as I can in an effort to keep my tears at bay, but a lone tear drops down my cheek nonetheless. I'm shaking as I walk up to my window, knowing what I'll find. Every morning and every evening, he's here.

I lean against the wall, just out of view, my eyes on him. He looks thinner, his clothes looser. Even from this distance I can tell that he's tired. Despite that, he's got his laptop on the hood of his car, trying to get some work done. Every few seconds he glances up at my window, his expression portraying despair.

This can't go on like this. This needs to stop.

I brace myself as I walk down the stairs. Mom smiles as I walk out, and I shake my head. I don't understand why she's siding with Alec, why she wants us to get back together.

Alexander straightens when I walk through the gate, his body rigid. I walk up to him, and his eyes widen.

"Elena," he says, his voice tinged with disbelief. The way his eyes roam over my body, the desperation in his eyes... it guts me.

"Alexander, you need to stop coming here."

He leans back against his car and crosses his arms. "No."

I raise my brows and mirror his stance, my arms crossed over my chest. "I'm not giving you a choice."

"Baby, you're underestimating how far I'll go to catch a single glimpse of you," he says, his voice soft, pained. "I can't sleep if I don't see you before bed, and my days don't start right if I don't get to see you before work."

I run a hand through my hair, my face tipped up toward the sky. "What will it take to get you to stop?"

Alexander smiles, and my traitorous heart skips a beat. "One date. Let me take you on a date."

"One date?" I repeat. "If I let you take me on a date, you'll stop coming here?"

"Yes, I promise. If you let me take you on one date, I won't show up here uninvited anymore," Alexander says, looking sincere, yet somehow, I don't trust his words.

I look into his eyes, taking in the need and the desperation that he's got on display for me. I've never seen him look so vulnerable before.

"Fine," I say, the words leaving my mouth before I even have a chance to think it through properly. I walk around his car and Alec runs after me, rushing to open the door for me. "I didn't realize you meant right now," he says, helping me into the car.

I look up at him, brows raised. "Why, is now not a good time?"

Alec shakes his head. "No, not at all. This is perfect." He leans over me, buckling me in, his hands lingering on my skin. His scent washes over me and my heart constricts painfully. I've missed him, and it's hitting me even harder now. I look up, and my lips brush against Alec's cheek. He inhales sharply, his eyes dropping down to my lips before he swallows hard and pulls away, tugging on his tie nervously.

I watch him as he walks back around the car and gets in. This is the closest we've been to each other in weeks—since that night he climbed through my window.

Alec places his hand on my thigh as he starts the car, and I look at him through narrowed eyes, eliciting a smile from him.

"Hey, you said it was a date, didn't you?"

I purse my lips and nod. I hope I can get through this date safely. I hope that by the end of the night, what's left of my heart will still be intact.

CHAPTER 64

lexander

Just having her sitting next to me has my heart racing. It's been weeks since I last touched her, and part of me thought I never would again. I didn't think she'd ever speak to me again. For weeks, she's been ignoring my presence at her house and every gift I've sent... she's been ignoring *me*.

"Don't take me anywhere public."

I tighten my grip on the steering wheel and glance at her. "Why not?"

She looks at me, her expression unreadable. "I don't want people to think we got back together. I saw the speculations in the tabloids, the rumors. I want no part of it."

My heart wrenches and a sense of loss washes over me. I park the car by the side of the road and glance out my window, unsure what to do, what to say.

"Are you seeing someone?" I ask, the words leaving my lips involuntarily.

Elena looks at me, her eyes flashing with something I can't

quite decipher. She's never been hard to read, but tonight she's shutting me out.

Elena turns away and opens her door, stepping out of the car. I follow her lead and walk up to her just as her door slams closed.

She leans back against my car, and I lean into her, my arms on either side of her, caging her in. I want to take a step closer and feel her body against mine, but I resist. Instead, I take in her beautiful face and those eyes that haunt my dreams. I see her every time I close my eyes, but she... she's moving on.

"Why don't you want to be seen with me, Elena? What does it matter if we end up in a tabloid or two?"

I try my best to keep my raging thoughts in check, but I fail. Is she dating someone? Her security team is as good as mine, and no matter how hard I try, I've been unable to find out what she gets up to, where she goes, who she spends time with.

"Does it matter?" she asks, her gaze unwavering.

I raise my hand to her face, pushing her hair behind her ear gently. "It does," I say, trying my hardest to act like my heart isn't fucking breaking. "You're still my wife, Elena."

Her eyes flash with anger and she grits her teeth. "Not by choice. We're separated, Alexander. I'm only your wife on paper, and if I have it my way, I won't be for much longer. You might not want to sign, but that won't stop me from obtaining a divorce. My lawyers are working on it as we speak."

I take a step back, my stomach recoiling. "You want to leave me that badly, huh?"

Elena looks away, her entire body tense. It's clear that she doesn't want to be here. She doesn't want to be with me, and I can't help but wonder who she wishes were with her right now, in my place.

When she looks back at me, there's a forced smile on her

face. "Well, I promised you a date, didn't I?" she says. "I'll give you tonight, Alexander, and in return, you'll let me go."

One night. That's all the time I have left with her. For weeks I was certain that she was hurt and that she needed me to prove to her that I love her, that I won't give up on her or walk away, no matter how hard things get.

Now I realize I was wrong. It's not me she needs at all. She doesn't need my love, she doesn't need me to prove anything to her. What she needs is for me to let her go, so she can truly move on and live the life she deserves. A life without me.

I move to stand next to Elena, both of us leaning back against my car, her shoulder brushing against mine. Her face is tipped up toward the stars in the sky, and I stare at her, taking in her beauty. The idea of her being with someone else makes me violently angry, it makes me want to chain her to me. But I can't be selfish with her. Not ever again.

This beautiful woman has given up her entire life to save her mother's, her every hope and dream. There's no one that deserves happiness more than Elena does, and if it isn't me that she'll be happy with, then I need to walk away. I need to do it, even if it kills me.

"Tell me three good things that happened to you today," I ask her.

Elena looks at me, her eyes widening just slightly in surprise. The question broke through her cold demeanor, and she smiles. "Hmm, three things? My mother and I went out for breakfast together, and just having her sit opposite me is still surreal. I also managed to cut costs in Rousseau Corporation's marketing department by ten percent, and, well... I went on a first date today with someone."

I freeze, my heart twisting painfully. I can't even describe the pain I feel at those words. My heart feels like it's in physical pain, and my stomach turns in a way it never has before. Heartbreak... that must be what this is.

"I wondered why you were home late today," I say, staring up at the sky to keep my jealousy from showing. "Must have been a good date, considering how late you got back. It's no wonder you finally bothered to come speak to me—to ask me to stay away." I turn to look at her, my eyes dropping to her lips. By the time she came home tonight I'd been standing in front of her gate for hours. She didn't come home until after ten, but she came home alone. I lift my hand to her face, my thumb stroking her lip. "Did he kiss you goodnight before walking you to your car?"

I swallow hard and drag my eyes away. Did he make her laugh? Did he get to hold her hand? Did she give him what used to be mine?

"Alexander," she says, her voice soft. "Don't."

I run a hand through my hair and let my eyes fall closed. She's been all I've been able to think about for weeks. I've been in such a bad state that my grandfather has had to step back in at work. Everything I thought I ever wanted feels meaningless without Elena, but she... she's been going on dates, she been getting over me.

I look at her, and it hits me. I lost her. I lost the one good thing in my life, and I only have myself to blame. Tonight is all she'll give me, and she isn't even doing it willingly. I coerced her, the way I did when I made her marry me. I was always her last resort—whoever she's with now is who she chose. I might not like it, but Elena deserves to have a choice. She deserves the world.

I hold my hand out for her and force a smile to my face. "Will you dance with me?" I ask, my voice soft. If tonight is the last time I get to hold her, then I have to make the most of it.

Elena turns to look at me, startled. "Here?"

"You and I danced in that cramped little space at Inferno, so why not?"

I grab my phone and put on the exact same song that was playing that night, and Elena takes my hand. I pull her closer, my arms wrapping around her waist while hers wrap around my neck. Having her this close, *fuck*.

Elena and I sway to the music, and she laughs when I twirl her around. "We still can't dance for shit," she says, leaning back in my arms. I look at her, and she takes my goddamn breath away. She's so beautiful, and the way she smiles, fucking hell.

She leans into me, her chest pressed against mine, and she still fits into my arms so perfectly. How could this woman not be made for me?

My eyes drop to her lips and I swallow hard. Her grip on me tightens, and I tilt my head slightly, moving just a little closer. I want just one last kiss. I want her lips pressed against mine, just one more time. Elena's breathing quickens, and she rises to her tiptoes.

Her lips brush against mine and I can almost taste her. Her eyes fall closed, and I kiss the edge of her lips. She inhales sharply and threads her fingers through my hair, pulling me closer. "Alexander," she whispers.

I pause at the sound of my name, pulling away reluctantly. I cup her cheek gently, my thumb brushing over her lips. She looks at me as though she can't figure me out, and I force a smile onto my face. She wouldn't even be here with me if she had a choice, if I didn't ask for a date in return for staying away. What she wants is for me leave her alone, yet here I am, wanting far more than she's willing to give.

A kiss... I have no fucking right.

"Come on, Buttercup," I whisper. "I'll take you home."

CHAPTER 65

lena

The way he looks at me... I've never seen such raw pain in his eyes. "You're taking me home?"

Alec nods and holds the door open for me. He leans in when I sit down, as though he's about to buckle me in the way he always does, but then he pulls away. He swallows hard and takes a step back before closing the door.

He's silent as he steps into the car and leans back in his seat, covering his face with his arm, inhaling deeply.

"Hey, are you okay?" I ask, suddenly worried.

He pulls his arm away and nods at me, a bittersweet smile on his face. "Yes, of course."

Alec raises his hand to my face and brushes my hair aside gently. "Thank you for tonight, Elena, even though I didn't give you much of a choice. When it comes to me, you've never had much of a choice—you didn't even have a choice when you married me. I'll respect your choices this time, Elena. I'll do as you asked. I'll let you go."

Fear grips me at his words. "Why? Why so suddenly?"

I was convinced he was only going after me because he doesn't want me to be with anyone else, so why is he letting me go now?

He doesn't respond. He just drives in silence.

"I guess you lost interest now that someone else has had me, huh?"

Alec grips his steering wheel, his knuckles turning white, yet he doesn't respond. His silence only increases my anger.

"Don't like tainted goods? Can't stand the thought of someone touching what's yours, so now you don't want it at all?"

Alexander stops the car suddenly, the wheels skidding. He turns to look at me, his eyes coated in anger.

"Elena, what do you want me to say? I'm at a loss here. I love you. I love you with my entire fucked up heart. I love you, okay? Does it hurt to know you've been with someone else when you're the only thing I can think of? Yes. It fucking does. You cheated on me by going on that date and whatever the fuck else you've done, because whether you like it or not, you're still my goddamn wife. Despite that, I'd take you back in a fucking second, because I fucking love you!"

He looks out the window, visibly trying to compose himself, and I stare at him in shock. Cheating is the one thing Alec would never condone, yet he would, for me? He's spent weeks standing in front of my house, sending me flowers with notes, my favorite foods, and even some random things that briefly came up in conversation, like the beautiful fountain pen I told him about months ago.

I was convinced it was all a competition to him, that he didn't want me, but couldn't stand the thought of me being with someone else either. But maybe, just maybe, I was wrong.

Alec inhales shakily and drives me home in silence, his

body tense the entire time. The gates swing open and he parks in front of my house.

He opens the door for me and I step out of the car, expecting him to offer me his hand the way he always does, but he doesn't. Instead, he takes a step back and walks me to my front door, keeping some distance between us.

I turn to look at him and he sighs as he cups my cheek, his eyes roaming over my face.

"I love you, Elena. I don't even know when it happened. I wanted you to be mine from the second I laid my eyes on you at Inferno. It started off as mere possessiveness, and before I knew it, you had me enthralled. You stole my heart day by day, and I didn't even realize it. I didn't realize that you fucking *own* me, until you left."

His hand drops to his side, and he smiles, his smile bittersweet. "Above all, I want you to be happy. I won't be selfish with you, no matter how badly I want to. I won't chain you to me when you chose to leave. You're not one of my belongings. I can't decide your fate. I can't tell you what to do, who to be with. You've made your choice, and it wasn't me. I'll respect that, Elena. I don't want to, but I will. You deserve true happiness, you deserve everything you've ever wanted. I was never good enough for you, and I never will be. I'll do as you asked, Elena. I'll let you go. It'll kill me to do it, but I'll sign the papers. I'll set you free."

He takes a step away, his expression anguished. I grab his hand, and he pauses, his eyes filling with hesitant hope.

"Thank you," I say, my voice soft. The way his expression falls tells me everything I need to know. He thinks I went out with someone else, and despite his past, despite his trust issues, he wants me back. I pull on his hand, and he takes a step closer to me. "For this first date."

I wrap my arms around his neck and rise to my tiptoes, my

lips crashing against his. Alec groans when I kiss him and buries his hands in my hair. He pushes me against the front door, deepening our kiss. The desperation in his touch sets me ablaze, and I moan when he lifts me into his arms. My legs wrap around his hips instinctively, and feeling him pressing against me, knowing he wants me just as badly, it's got me losing my mind.

Alec and I are both panting by the time he pulls away, and his forehead drops to mine. "Baby, the date you were talking about..."

I laugh, I can't help it. "I'm sorry, Alec. It wasn't a lie. This is the first real date you've ever taken me on. It wasn't staged for the press, it was just you and me. You've taken me home and kissed me goodnight... it was perfect. And yeah, part of me did think you were only chasing me because you thought there was competition."

"And now?" he asks, his tone hesitant. "What do you think now?"

Alec lowers me to the floor gently, his hands on my waist.

"Now I think that you should take me on another date."

Alec laughs and leans in for a kiss. "Really?" he says, pulling away. "You'll date me?"

I nod and reach up, my hands threading through his hair. "I will. Let's date, Alec. Let's spend some time together. Let's see if in a year we still want to be together, when all that we've got is *love*."

Alec presses a lingering kiss to my forehead. "Very well, wife. Let's date. We'll date for as long as you want us to, but in the end, I still want to see you walk down the aisle toward me. I want to marry you for the world to see."

I smile at him, my heart racing. "Maybe. If you're lucky."

CHAPTER 66

lexander

Elena walks into the kitchen and looks at me with raised brows when she sees me standing behind the stove.

"What are you doing?" she asks, her tone careful and curious.

I laugh at her expression, but I can't even blame her. On one of our dates we tried baking a pie together, and I almost burned down our entire kitchen. She's right to be cautious.

"Don't worry," I tell her. "I got instructions from Grandpa. You go get ready for dinner."

She glances at me suspiciously and looks back at me as she walks away to get ready for tonight's date.

Fifty-six dates. Elena and I have gone on fifty-six dates since we got back together exactly a year ago, and I don't think I'll ever get enough of her.

It took me four months to convince her to move back in with me, and in those four months, every single time that I had to take her home after a date was pure torture.

I'm excited as I set the table. I've managed to transform our terrace into a floral sanctuary. It's filled with white peonies, Elena's favorite, and there are candles and fairy lights everywhere. She probably doesn't even remember telling me this, but she once told me that one of her favorite childhood memories was when Luce and I threw her a birthday party. I'd hung fairy lights everywhere, and she loved them.

I hear Elena gasp behind me, and I turn to watch her walk toward me, her eyes roaming over everything I've prepared. I stare at her in awe. Her beauty takes my breath away, and it still astounds me that she's mine, that it's me she chose.

"Alec," she says, her voice trembling. She walks up to me and I wrap her into my arms. She rises to her tiptoes and kisses me. Her lips still make me lose all reason, and they always will.

"I guess the decorations kind of gave it away, huh?"

She smiles at me and nods. "Yes. *Yes*."

I shake my head at her and brush her hair behind her ear. "I haven't asked you yet."

She pouts, and my heart squeezes in this strange way it's only ever done for her. "But dinner will get cold, baby. I slaved away for you, you know?"

She pouts even further, sending me those puppy eyes she knows I can't resist. Why does she have to be so cute?

"Ask me," she orders, and I laugh as I do as I'm told. I drop down to one knee in front of her, my hand reaching into my pocket.

I hold her engagement ring up, the very same one I proposed with the first time. While we never got divorced, Elena made it clear that the papers don't matter to her. In her opinion, we aren't married until we hold our ceremony. I've been holding onto her ring all this time, waiting for the right moment, giving her the time she asked for—one year.

"Elena, you drive me insane in all the best ways. You light

up my days, and you've shown me what true happiness looks like. When you walked back into my life, I was half a man. I was incomplete, my heart jaded and shattered. But then there was you. You came crashing into my life, making me question every belief I held onto for so long. Day by day, you stitched my soul back together, and you never even realized you were doing it. You complete me, Elena. You made me believe in things I never thought I'd have. You made me believe in Forever, after all. That's what I want with you, baby. I want forever, with you. I want to wake up next to you for the rest of our lives. I want you to be the last thing I see before I fall asleep, my arms wrapped around you. I want to grow old with you and raise a family with you. I want it all. I want the arguments, the ups and downs life will throw our way. I want it all, and I want it forever."

I inhale deeply and look up into her eyes. She's fighting her tears, but it's a losing battle. "Will you marry me?"

"Yes," she says, and I slide the ring onto her finger, my heart racing. A tear drops down Elena's cheek as I rise to my feet, and I swipe it away with my thumb.

"I love you so much," Elena says, her voice trembling.

I kiss her, my lips lingering on hers. "I love you more."

Her hands roam over my body, and I see the need in her eyes. A low chuckle escapes my lips and I smile when she tugs on my tie impatiently. I love everything about her, but this might well be one of the things I love most. The way she wants me so unapologetically.

I lift her into my arms, one hand behind her back, the other underneath her knees, and she smiles as I carry her to our bedroom.

I place her down on our bed carefully and she rises to her knees, her fingers finding their way to the buttons on my shirt.

"You know what this reminds me of, baby?"

She looks up at me, and I smirk.

"Our wedding night. You were just as eager. Just as hungry for my cock. And you still want it, don't you? Even after all this time, you still want me stretching out your pussy, filling you. I bet you're wet already."

Elena looks at me as she tugs my suit jacket and shirt off my shoulder in one go. "You know I am, but just to be sure, you should probably touch me and find out."

I laugh. This woman...

I join her in bed, both of us tugging at each other's clothes, until at last, we're naked, her skin against mine. She gasps when my fingers find their way between her legs.

"So wet and I've barely even touched you."

My fingers slip into her, and I tease her, keeping her right at the edge. The way she looks lying in our bed, her hair spread out on our pillows, her lips slightly ajar. Fuck. She's everything. I could come just looking at her. She gasps as I touch her, getting her closer and closer.

"Come for me," I tell her, swiping my thumb over her clit.

She looks at me as her muscles contract around my fingers, my name on her lips.

"Good girl," I whisper, leaning over her. "Now you're going to take my cock, aren't you?"

"Please," she moans, and I push into her.

I hold myself up on one arm and wrap my other hand around her neck, my thumb resting against her throat. "I'm going to fuck you like this for the rest of our lives, Elena. You will always be mine, you hear me?"

"Yes, Alec. I'm yours. All yours."

She gasps when I pull back and then thrust back into her. The way she feels around me, the way she whispers my name. I can't imagine ever getting enough of her.

Elena's nails mark my back, and her lips find mine. "I love you, Alec," she murmurs against my lips, her voice husky.

That's all it takes for me to lose it. I come deep inside her, my forehead dropping to hers. She's panting as hard as I am, and I smile.

This... this is what real love feels like. Lying here with her is true happiness.

CHAPTER 67

lena

"You look beautiful, honey," Mom says, tears in her eyes. She touches my veil, straightening it for the third time. I grab her shoulders and smile at her, my heart overflowing with happiness.

"So do you, Mom," I tell her honestly. She looks amazing. It took her almost two years, but she's walking without a cane now, and she radiates happiness. I was terrified that she'd feel like there was nothing left for her to live for, considering what she woke up to, but that hasn't been the case at all. She's thriving, and it's been amazing to see her rebuild her life.

"Are you ready?" she asks.

I nod at her, my smile so wide that it hurts my face. "More than ever."

This time, Alec and I tried to do things right. We decided to go with a far more low-key wedding than we initially planned. We're now having a small outdoors ceremony, with only our loved ones present. No press, no big spectacle, just us.

Alec and I chose to remain engaged for a year, so I could plan our entire wedding and involve my mother. Going dress shopping with her, visiting multiple wedding locations; those are all memories I never thought I'd get to have, but now I do. I've loved every part of it, even the endless arguments between my mother and Sofia about the flavor of our cake, and Grandpa's continuous and totally unhelpful involvement.

Mom takes my arm, and together, we head out of the little cottage we rented. We walk towards the aisle slowly, pausing at the start of it. Everything is just as I wanted it. There are flowers everywhere, and the sun is shining down on us. But most importantly, Alec is at the end of the aisle, looking as impatient and nervous as I expected him to be.

My eyes find his instantly, and my heart starts to race. He smiles at me, looking more emotional than I've ever seen him before. Lucian slaps his arm and laughs, but Alec doesn't take his eyes off me for a second.

I can't believe this is really happening. I've waited so long for this day—though Alec may very well have been even more impatient. He's been counting down the days for the last six months, driving me completely insane with his daily countdown reminders.

I'm trembling with nerves as Mom and I walk toward him, the train of my dress and my long veil trailing behind me. Alec looks enthralled, and when Mom places my hand in his, he raises it to his lips, kissing my knuckles. "You look beyond beautiful, Elena. Stunning."

I smile at him, and together we turn toward the priest, my mind drifting back to our first, legal, wedding ceremony. It was swift and impersonal, hardly memorable. Today isn't anything like that. Today is everything I could've ever wished for.

Alec turns to me and smiles, my hands in his. "Elena, every day you help me see the good in life. You brighten my days, you uplift me, and you do it all without even trying. I didn't know what happiness was until you walked into my life, forcing emotions out of me I thought were long lost. You've shown me what true love is, and I vow to return that love tenfold every day, for as long as I shall live. I promise you forever, Buttercup. I promise you all of me, forever."

I smile up at him, my eyes filling with tears. It still feels surreal to hear him promising me forever, when for so long, he was adamant that it didn't exist.

"Alec, I was lost before you found me. You were light in a world that was filled with darkness, and you will always be my saving grace. You're so easy to love, and you don't even know it. Every single day I look at you, and I count my blessings. When we ran into each other after so many years, I asked you what you'd wish for if you had one single wish. I can honestly tell you I have no wishes left, because you've made them all come true. I'm going to spend the rest of my life making sure you have nothing to wish for either. I will love you forever, Alec."

He blinks, and I'm surprised to find his eyes shimmering with tears. Alec looks away and bites down on his lip, a smile on his face. When he looks back at me, his eyes are filled with wonder, as though he, too, is counting his blessings.

The priest smiles at us, and Lucian hands us our wedding rings, his hands trembling. He's just as emotional as we are.

"Alexander, do you take Elena to be your wedded wife? Do you promise to love her, comfort her, honor and keep her for better or worse, for richer or poorer, in sickness and health, and forsaking all others, be faithful only to her, for as long as you both shall live?"

He smiles at me and nods. "I do."

The priest nods at him, and he slides my wedding ring onto my finger, grinning all the while.

"Elena, do you take Alexander to be your wedded husband? Do you promise to love him, comfort him, honor and keep him for better or worse, for richer or poorer, in sickness and health and forsaking all others, be faithful only to him so long as you both shall live?"

"I do," I say, my voice loud and clear.

My heart races as I slide Alec's ring onto his finger, and the priest smiles at us.

"I now solemnly declare you husband and wife. You may kiss the bride."

Alec pulls me closer and sweeps me off my feet as he kisses me, loud cheers erupting around us. He drops his forehead to mine and grins. "Finally," he says, and I giggle, my happiness overflowing.

Our family walks up to us, and Grandpa is the first to reach us. "Congratulations, kids," he says, wrapping his arms around the both of us. Both our moms have tears streaming down their faces, and even Grandpa looks suspiciously emotional. He clears his throat and pulls back, straightening his clothes. "Come on," he says. "I'm excited for this feast we're having."

I laugh, and Alec shakes his head. "I'm pretty sure most of our family is really only here to get a taste of your vegetables, Grandpa," he says.

I glance around at everyone that's surrounding us, still partially in disbelief. I can't believe how lucky I am, how happy I am. My mother is smiling at me, and Alec's hand is wrapped around my waist.

I've got everything I've ever wanted, my mother by my side, a husband that truly loves me, and a family of my own choosing.

Alec leans into me, his lips brushing against my ear. "I love you, Mrs. Kennedy," he whispers, making my heart skip a beat.

I rise to my tiptoes and wrap my arms around him, pulling him in for a kiss. "I love you, too," I say, breathlessly.

Alec grins at me. "Forever?" he asks, and I nod.

"Forever."

EPILOGUE

lena

My heart squeezes painfully as I stare at my brother on the stand, the judge passing a life sentence, his punishment the same as Jade's and my father's.

Their trial took almost four whole years, and they nearly got away with what they did—until Alec revealed the last judge's corruption, and a new judge was assigned, putting us back at square one. My mother's case was practically unheard of, and that delayed their judgment even longer than I would've liked, but it didn't prevent it.

I glance at my husband, my heart overflowing with gratitude. Without him, my family would have gone unpunished. My mother would have died.

And I? I'd have lost my reason to live.

He looks at me as though he can read my mind and wraps his arm around my shoulder, offering me silent support. I drop my head to his shoulder, a bittersweet smile on my face.

Mom grabs my hand and squeezes tightly, her eyes on Matthew. He's led away, and I don't see an ounce of remorse in his eyes. There wasn't any in my father's eyes either.

Part of me was hoping that maybe, just maybe, my father was innocent in this. Maybe he just didn't realize what Matthew and Jade were up to.

Naive till the end, I guess.

My mother's old doctor testified that my father was the one that instructed him to keep her in a coma. Since the payments were all traced back to Rousseau corporate accounts, I assumed it was all Matthew, but it wasn't. Matthew and Jade might have caused the accident, but it was my father that left her in the state she was in for so many years.

"Come on," I tell Mom. These trials have done more damage to my mother than her coma did. She's heartbroken. Every testimony she heard tore her apart, over and over again. I hold her hand as we walk out, and the way she trembles pains me to no end. "It's over now, Mom."

She nods, forcing a smile onto her face. Alec glances at her, the concern I'm feeling reflected in his eyes. He holds the car door open for her, and Mom smiles at him.

"Shall I take you home?" he asks.

"No," she says, shaking her head. "Your mother is expecting me to join for lunch. You know what she's like. She'll just worry if I don't show up. Besides, she'll make me feel better."

Alec nods and opens the passenger door for me. He buckles me in, his touch lingering, like it always does. The way he looks at me brings a smile to my face. It's been almost a year since our wedding ceremony, but he still makes me feel giddy.

Alec holds my hand as we walk into the restaurant, and Sofia and Lucian rise from their seats, their eyes on my mother. Mom smiles, and the relief in their eyes is instant.

All eyes are on Mom as we sit down, and she's visibly uncomfortable.

Alec wraps his arm around the back of my chair and clears his throat. "So, I think Elena and I won't make it for our family trip," he says, instantly agitating both women. "I want to go on a second honeymoon."

They glare at him, both of them crossing their arms over their chest. "You went on a honeymoon last year! You promised us that we'd do a family trip together."

Alec nods and glances at the two of them. "Yeah, but you two can't even decide where to go, so Elena and I aren't going at all."

Our moms look at each other and immediately start to bicker about the location of our family trip.

Alec winks at me and leans in to kiss me, his lips lingering on mine. "Thank you," I whisper against his lips, grateful he managed to draw attention away from my mother.

"You can thank me in bed," he says, and I laugh.

"Come to think of it," Sofia says, straightening. "It's about time that we add to our family, just in time for our family holiday."

She reaches for her bag, her eyes on Lucian. Alec's grip on me tightens when she takes out a manila folder, and Luce blanches, pure devastation filling his eyes. I raise my brows, confused.

Sofia pushes the folder toward Lucian, and he takes it with shaking hands. "It's about time you get married too. Your brother is so happily married," she says, glancing at us. "I want that for you too. I want you to have everything that I never had."

Lucian closes his eyes, and the despair he emits goes straight to my heart. I place my hand on Alec's thigh, indicating for him to do something, and he straightens.

"Mom," Alec says. "I don't think that's a good idea. Lucian is still quite young. There's no need to rush into it. Besides, Grandpa abolished his marriage requirement, so Luce doesn't need to marry if he doesn't want to."

She smiles at him and shakes her head before looking at Lucian pointedly. "Open it."

"Mom," Lucian says, his voice breaking. "I—"

He shakes his head, swallowing down his words, and instead, he opens the folder.

Lucian glances at the contents and then buries his face in his hands, visibly emotional, but Sofia smiles.

I glance over at the folder, shocked to find only one single thing in it. A photo of Elliot.

Lucian inhales deeply, trembling, and then he smiles. He looks at his mother with such gratefulness that it brings tears to my eyes.

"Lucian, I can't think of a better son-in-law than Elliot. Don't you think it's about time that you formally introduce him to me? I promise I won't scare him off with marriage talks just yet, but for now he's the only candidate in my folder."

Lucian smiles even as he blinks back tears. I can't imagine how much of a relief this must be to him. He's been wanting to tell her for over a year but just didn't know how.

"I love you, Mom."

She smiles at him and grabs his hand over the table. "I love you too, sweetheart."

Alec gently brushes my hair behind my ear and Lucian grins at me. "Elena," Luce says. "I'm so happy right now... I think now would be the perfect time to make Mom just as happy. Both our moms, actually."

Alec kisses my shoulder and nods, a pleased smile on his face. I grin nervously as I reach into my bag, taking out two identical envelopes. I've been carrying them everywhere with me, waiting for the perfect time. So far, we've only told Lucian, and only because he was ready to call an ambulance last week when I spent an entire morning throwing up.

"Today does seem to be a day of new beginnings," I say, smiling at Alec. I push both envelopes toward our mothers, and they both pick them up at the same time. They open their presents, and Mom starts to cry, while Sofia tries her best to blink back her tears.

"Is this real?" Sofia asks, her eyes shimmering with unshed tears.

Alec nods and wraps his arm around me protectively. "Yes," he says, smiling at the sonograms in their hands. "You're both going to be grandmothers."

Alec presses a kiss to my temple, and I look around the table filled with my loved ones. A few short years ago, I was desperate and all alone. I was on the verge of losing my mother.

And now she sits in front of me, smiling at a sonogram of her grandchild. I've got my husband's arm wrapped around me, his eyes filled with love.

"I love you," he says, and I smile.

"I love you too, Alec."

He's not just made my every dream come true. Every single day, he makes it so that I don't even want to fall asleep, because my dreams are no longer as good as my life with him is.

Alec smiles and brushes my hair behind my ear. "Tell me you'll always love me."

I nod, grinning. "Always."

Alec leans in and presses a kiss to my forehead, and I can't help but tease him. "Though... I thought you didn't believe in forever?"

He chuckles and shakes his head. "I do, if it's with you. You've got me believing in forever, after all."

Forever with Alec isn't nearly enough, but it'll have to do.

Download an exclusive extra scene of Alec and Elena with their kids a few years from now

Want to catch a glimpse of Elliot and Luce? They make a small appearance in Until You: a Brother's Best Friend Romance

ALSO BY CATHARINA MAURA

Until You: A Brother's Best Friend Romance

Left without a job and evicted from the house she so carefully turned into a home, Aria is offered two choices: move back in with her brother... or take the job her brother's best friend offers her.

Their lives weren't meant to collide — but everything changes when Grayson realizes that Aria is the mysterious woman behind a wildly popular vigilante platform.

She's the woman he's been falling for online, the one whose coding skills outdo his, the one he's been trying to track down.

It's her. And she's off-limits.

ACKNOWLEDGMENTS

It takes an entire team to publish a book, and I'm incredibly grateful for the amazing individuals on mine. Specifically Lidón and Ashley, both of whom dropped everything to help me turn this story into what I knew it could be.

Ladies, I adore you, and I'm so grateful to have met you. My life is forever changed because you are in it.

63327244R00212